VOICES FROM THE TITANIC

VOICES FROM THE TITANIC

JIM WALKER

Nashville, Tennessee

Printed in the United States of America

0-8054-1771-0

Published by Broadman & Holman Publishers, Nashville, Tennessee
Editorial Team: Vicki Crumpton, Janis Whipple, Kim Overcash
Typesetting: TF Designs, Mt. Juliet, TN

Dewey Decimal Classification: F
Subject Heading: MYSTERIES—FICTION / TITANIC—FICTION
Library of Congress Card Catalog Number: 98-43017

Published in association with the literary agency of Alive Communications, Inc.,
1465 Kelly Johnson Blvd., Suite 320, Colorado Springs, CO 80902

Library of Congress Cataloging-in-Publication Data

Walker, James, 1948–
Voices from the Titanic : a novel / Jim Walker.
p. cm. — (Mysteries in time series)
ISBN 0-8054-1771-0
1. Titanic (Steamship)—Fiction. I. Title. II. Series:
Walker, James, 1948– Mysteries in time series.
PS3573.A425334V65 1999
813'.54—dc21

98-43017
CIP

1 2 3 4 5 03 02 01 00 99

THE MAIN CHARACTERS

M*organ Fairfield*. Morgan is a survivor of the *Titanic* disaster. Newly arrived in New York, he assumes his new position as a reporter for the *New York Herald*. Even though he is the recipient of a generous trust fund from his parents, Morgan wants very much to prove his worth as a crime reporter.

Margaret Hastings. Margaret is a *Titanic* survivor. She lost her fiancé when the ship sank, but Morgan has always been the love of her life.

Clarence "Call" McCall. Call is the ace reporter of the *New York Herald*'s crime division. He is cynical and hardened by a life on the streets of New York and resents the fact that he has been assigned to tutor the cub reporter Morgan Fairfield.

Harry Dixon. Harry is the city editor for the *Herald*. He rules the paper like a despot and is said to be old enough to have reported Noah's flood.

Hunter Kennedy. Hunter is an actor currently appearing in a play. But the Hunter that Morgan and Margaret knew was murdered on the *Titanic*.

Patricia Bennett. Patricia is the niece of the *Herald*'s publisher. She is a hardheaded, no-nonsense newspaperwoman who is driven to prove herself in a world where men seem to call the shots.

Ed Leslie. Ed is the manager of the theater. He takes an unusual interest in Margaret and in Hunter Kennedy.

Captain Casey Connor. Connor is the captain of homicide detectives.

F. H. Lardner. Lardner is the captain of the *Mackay-Bennett*. It is the vessel assigned to recover the bodies of the victims of the *Titanic* disaster. Lardner is an actual historical figure.

Miss Irene Saunders. Miss Saunders is the elderly "Witch of Wall Street." The woman has long-term bitterness and uses her wealth to gain revenge on her enemies.

Mrs. Gloria Thompson. Gloria is a survivor of the *Titanic* and a friend of Margaret and Morgan. She is a young widow of wealth and has great wisdom, which she uses to advise Margaret.

Miss Kitty Webb. Kitty is a *Titanic* survivor and was the mistress of Benjamin Guggenheim. She has deviously managed to lay her hands on part of the man's wealth and is using it to back the play Hunter Kennedy is appearing in.

Jake O'Leary. Jake is a reporter on the *New York Herald*. Like Call, he has many underworld contacts and a great deal of ambition.

Fredo Giavanni. Fredo is a sergeant with the New York police. He is also a friend and reliable source of information to Call.

Sergeant Jimmy Ryan. Ryan is a police sergeant and a plainclothes detective. He takes a special interest in the story Morgan and Call are working to solve.

Geraldine Farier. Gerry is an older cleaning woman who once worked for the *Herald*. She is hardened by life on the streets and her abuse of alcohol but has a soft spot in her heart for Call.

PART I
RUSH TO JUDGMENT

CHAPTER 1

The weather in Halifax was calm and overcast; fog curled out over the harbor like a blanket gently laid on a newborn baby. Only hours after the *Titanic* had gone down, the papers all over Canada had carried the news of the total eclipse of the sun. The eclipse had been called the greatest celestial event the country had seen in over fifty-three years. Special editions soon followed, however, reporting the *Titanic* disaster. Since then, the news of frozen corpses floating in the North Atlantic had overshadowed the erasure of the sun.

Many, of course, thought the two events were connected, the heavenly announcement of tragedy followed by the floundering of the unsinkable *Titanic*. Calmer heads in Halifax, however, made no attempt to link the judgment of God to the grand pride of the White Star Line.

Captain F. H. Lardner stood on the bridge of cable ship *Mackay-Bennett* and watched the men wheel block after block of ice up the ramp.

He stuck his hands deep into his coat pockets. The gold braid on his sleeves peeked out and showed his rank in spite of the plain blue jacket he wore. He watched as a group of pasty-faced men in black stood on the dock. More than forty members of the Maritime Provinces Funeral Directors Association would be on board to see to the dead. The crew were all volunteers, in spite of the double pay that was being promised to each man.

Ships at sea were keeping a wide berth from the scene of the disaster. The captains wanted to avoid their passengers being subjected to the sight of hundreds of bodies floating in the distance. They also wanted to make certain that they kept south of the ice field that was streaming out of the North Atlantic.

Even then, the warnings had been too late for some. The German liner *Rhein* reported bodies and wreckage at latitude 42.01N, longitude 49.13W.

The *Bremen* sent word that she had passed more than one hundred bodies at latitude 42.00N, longitude 49.20W. The crew reported watching as one woman, clad only in a nightgown, floated by with a baby clutched closely to her breast. They saw another woman clinging to a shaggy dog. They saw dozens of men frozen together in their final, desperate struggle for life.

Lardner pushed open a side window to the bridge and poked his head out. "Let's step lively, mates. I want to make the tide."

Several men were carrying coffins and following behind the men with the large blocks of ice. They picked up their pace, and one raised a hand in the captain's direction to acknowledge that they'd heard the captain.

"Captain," one of the men in black attire shouted. He looked at the other men gathered around him and then took several steps toward the ramp. "I am still expecting ten more of our morticians."

"And who are you, sir?"

"Snow, John Snow. I have been asked by the White Star Line to oversee the funeral arrangements. We need these other men with us and the instruments they are bringing. We're going to have our hands full as it is."

Lardner nodded. "I'm sure you will, sir. I'm sure you will."

Lardner leaned his head back into the wheelhouse and slid the window shut. He rubbed his hands together to give him some warmth. The engines had been going for hours now, but Lardner's blood always seemed to run cold at the wrong time. A smile crossed his face as the first officer, Charles Hitchens, stepped onto the bridge. The man held in his hands a polished white cup, the kind Lardner liked. The thick mug held heat well and warmed a man's hands while its contents warmed his belly. "I thought you might like a cup of tea, sir."

Hitchens was a young man, not yet thirty. He'd served in the navy for a short time, and he wanted most of all to command. But the chances for command in the small Canadian Navy were quite limited. His clean-shaved face was spotless, and his pointed chin showed a nick from his quest to present himself well.

Lardner grinned. "You thought right." He reached out and took the cup with both hands, wrapping his thin, white fingers around the still hot mug. He liked the feel of the scalding red liquid. Holding it up to his mouth, he sipped, savoring the aroma of the tea. "Do you have the cots laid out?"

"Aye, sir. Fifty extra in the dining room. They won't be comfortable and they may not sleep, but they can all lie down and suffer together."

Lardner slowly sipped the tea. "This is about as far from a pleasure cruise as I can imagine, Charles."

"Aye, sir. That it is. We do have enough food and provisions to last us a little over two weeks."

"Let's hope and pray it won't take that long."

"You never can tell what the seas will do out there, sir. We've never seen anything like this before."

"No one has, Charles." He sipped the tea, looking over the rim of the cup at the mate's grim look. "No one has."

"We will have one hundred coffins and a large number of canvas bags stored below deck. I rather doubt they'll be enough to take care of what we find, however. From what I hear, the first-class passengers will get the coffins."

"They paid for them, didn't they?"

Hitchens shook his head. "One would think class distinctions would end with a man's death."

"And just how many cemeteries have you been through lately, Charles?"

"Not many, I'm afraid."

"A man's money follows him all the way to the grave but, thank God, no farther."

"I suppose we're all alike at the feet of God."

Lardner stepped over to the window and looked out on the harbor. He held the cup to his lips. "That is one of the remarkable things about this whole matter, Charles."

"What's that?"

"On that ship were some of the wealthiest people in the world along with many of the poorest. But in the final analysis, the Atlantic showed no favoritism." Lardner continued to stare out to sea, as if haunted by the ghosts of those floating on the water. "God's judgment comes to all, rich or poor. A man's soul is just that, and it has no pockets."

Hitchens patted his pocket, his eyebrows lifting. "That reminds me, sir. I have something odd here." He pulled out a folded sheet of paper and opened it up to read. "Our wireless operator picked this up last night over the wire. He thought it odd enough to write down. It reads, 'Disaster inevitable—stop. You can forget about the old girl now—stop. Good thing J. P. took up sick—stop. Make certain ships are in position—stop.'"

Hitchens lifted his head from the paper. "What do you make of that?"

"Someone talking about the disaster, I shouldn't wonder."

"That couldn't be, sir. It was sent almost an hour before the *Titanic* hit the berg."

Lardner set the cup down. It was the first time he'd allowed the thing to be out of his hands. He stuck his hands in his pockets and rocked back and forth on the balls of his feet. "It's probably totally unrelated. Some man lost his wife and was saying good riddance about her to a friend."

"I should doubt that, sir." Once again Hitchens looked down at the paper. "It was being sent to William James Pirrie."

Lardner's face twisted. He put a hand on his chin and seemed to be pulling on it. "Not the William James Pirrie we know of, the Canadian who runs Harland and Wolff?"

Pirrie had been in all the papers along with Harland and Wolff, the firm that had constructed the *Titanic*. All of Belfast was in mourning now, supposedly along with Pirrie.

"I'm afraid so, sir. The wire was being sent to Belfast."

"Who sent it?" As Hitchens held up the paper to read it, Lardner jerked it from his hands. His eyes followed the page to the bottom. When they fell on the name the wireless operator had written, they widened.

THURSDAY

APRIL 18

9:05 P.M.

CHAPTER 2

People had seldom seen a lightning storm like the one that unfolded over New York harbor that night. Long slender fingers of fire struck the belly of the dark clouds, causing a steady rumble of thunder. The *Carpathia* swung around the overbearing statue of the great lady with her torch as the light from the sky lit up her face and outstretched arm. Since midmorning of April 15, Captain Rostron, plowing through deep fog and thunderstorms, had made no delay in taking the survivors on to New York.

With a look of horror spreading across his face, Morgan Fairfield stood at the fantail of the ship and watched the boat pursuing them. Reporters were screaming at the top of their lungs, bouncing up and down at the bow of the chase boat like comical pop-up heads on a musical calliope. "Jump, jump. We'll pick you up and pay you three hundred dollars."

He watched as a reporter quickly scrambled to the front of the pack, elbowing his way forcefully to the vanguard of the mob. The man's long brown coat blew open, and his bowler was pulled down past the place where it should have stopped on top of his ears. His ears were angled out and looked like the doors of a taxicab waiting for a fare. The man waved his arms, pushing aside several men standing next to him. "The *Times* will pay five hundred." He pointed directly at Morgan. "Come on boy, jump. You're a healthy lad. We'll pluck you out."

Morgan caught sight of a lone figure standing tall and lean behind the pack of reporters. The man had steely black eyes and a hungry look. His eyes sparkled even at a distance, looking like two black bullets set in a stark, craggy face. Lightning flashes illuminated his unruly shoulder-length silver hair and craggy features. He seemed oblivious to the gusting, frigid air. He stared up at the *Carpathia*, seemingly straight at Morgan. Just then Margaret Hastings thrust her hand under his arm. Morgan smiled distractedly at her. When he looked back at the boat, the strange man was gone. Morgan shivered.

Margaret studied Morgan's look. "They're not all like that."

"Oh, really? Is that who I have become?" Morgan had a new job with the *New York Herald*. They would be expecting him at his desk once they found out that he'd actually survived.

"No, of course not."

"That or a sniveling prude who writes about garden parties in the Hamptons."

"You can be anything you want to be. You'll be the best reporter there is. Just because they hired you for a society column doesn't mean that's where you'll end up, especially after what you've been through."

Morgan continued to watch the scene as the boat chased them. It was plain to see that those men were willing to pay any price or endure any amount of disgrace just to be the leader on the street with a firsthand account of the *Titanic*'s sinking. He shook his head. "If I'm not on the back pages with personal accounts of teas among the social elite, I'll be one of them, an ambulance chaser with little regard for human feelings. They're like a snarling bunch of wild jackals picking over the bones of the fallen. They may not be responsible, but they're certainly not going to leave anything on the ground."

"You could never do that."

Morgan dropped his head and shook it slowly. "Maybe not, but they'll have me writing about the *Titanic* from now to kingdom come."

Margaret pulled herself closer. "You have lived it. A reporter should write about what he knows, shouldn't he?"

The deep horn that sounded from the *Carpathia* cut them short. It also told everyone aboard that they would soon be pulling up to the dock. Both Morgan and Margaret could feel the ship shift its speed into a slower, almost gliding chug.

The small boat filled with reporters swung around, and the ruckus of the yelling men began anew with the *Titanic* survivors on the starboard side. The passengers there were now being subjected to the temptations offered by the journalists.

Suddenly, Morgan and Margaret heard the sound of someone hitting the water, and they stepped over to the side to see the spectacle. One of the crew from the *Titanic* had given into the temptation.

The reporters on the boat extended a white crooked pole in the man's direction. He reached out from the water and grabbed hold. They heaved him up the side of the boat and within minutes covered him with blankets, gathering around him like hungry chickens at the sight of a lone worm.

"That ought to satisfy them," Margaret said.

"I doubt it very much. They'll only want to hear how everyone else's story sizes up with his." He pointed to the crowd beside the dock, now swelling in number to the thousands. "They'll take some poor woman in her grief and ask silly questions while they watch her cry, and then they will grab some bewildered orphan child and begin to pump him for what it's like to be all alone in the world."

Margaret looked up at him, a note of sadness in her eyes. "Darling, we should be thankful that we're here to answer any questions at all. I feel bad for you, though. Seeing you like this makes me think that while you may have survived, some of your dreams didn't."

Morgan nodded and pulled her close. "Yes, you're right, darling. I know I'm only feeling sorry for myself."

"Why should you?"

"I'm a man and I'm here with you, the woman I love. So many others will never be with those they love." His voice trailed off. "So many women and children." He gulped and looked her in the eye. "I'm here and Peter is not."

She could see the tears forming in his eyes, and she began to cry herself. Only days ago Peter had been the man she was supposed to marry and Morgan the one she was supposed to forget. Now she and Morgan were here together, and Peter was gone. Reaching into her purse, she took out a lace handkerchief and pushed it into her now flowing tears. "I know. He was a fine man, a wonderful man." She dabbed her eyes. "You know, Peter's uncle and aunt will be here to meet us."

"Would you like me to talk to them?"

She shook her head, fighting off the idea. "No, that wouldn't be right. I'll tell them myself. I just have to make certain that I get to them before Mother does. There's no telling what she might say."

Morgan wrapped her in his arms and held her close. "I'll be here for you if you need me."

Suddenly, they both heard a commotion on the port side of the ship. Morgan took Margaret's hand, and they both went to watch. What they saw sent shivers down their backs. A reporter from one of the chase boats had managed to catapult himself onto the deck of the *Carpathia*. He got to his feet, just as two of the crew grabbed him. The man wrestled with them until one of the officers stepped up to the man and landed a stiff punch to his jaw. The punch dropped him to the deck like a suit of empty clothes.

The officer shouted, "Put this man in restraints and take him below."

Two of the crew grabbed the man and dragged him off to the stairs that led below deck.

"Amazing," Margaret said.

It was only minutes later when the ship eased into her moorings next to the White Star Line's berth. The massive crowd on the dock surged forward.

"Here, here, come along you two." The voice was the shrill screeching voice of a sailor. "We've got to get you to shore. Your relatives will be waiting for you." The thin string-bean man stepped forward and, putting his hand on Morgan's back, gently gave him a shove toward the gangway.

The dock was a mass of humanity, and yet even there, the class distinctions were notable. A private train had been sent to ferry away the most wealthy of the grieving widows. Their menservants pushed people aside and, with bags in hand, steered the ladies through the mob.

Morgan noted with some comfort that John Jacob Astor's oldest son was there to greet his father's young bride. Evidently, the scandal of his parents' divorce and his father's subsequent marriage to the young Madeleine hadn't kept him away. It was just the kind of breeding that Morgan knew would have made the father proud. The young man extended his hand and arm in warm greeting to the young widow.

Morgan and Margaret soon caught up with Margaret's mother. April Hastings was wringing her hands. Her dress looked rumpled, but all in all, she was still her stately self. She held her hourglass figure erect and her chin high. Her high cheekbones had a touch of rouge still on them, even though the color was slightly smeared. "There you are. I was worried about you. We have to send a wire to your father, you know. He'll be worried sick."

Morgan noticed Margaret looking over the crowd. He knew she was looking for Peter's aunt and uncle. She was ignoring her mother, however. He leaned down close to Margaret. "Will you know how to recognize them?"

"Who?" April asked. "Recognize who?"

"Peter's aunt and uncle," Margaret snapped. "They'll be here to meet us."

"Oh, dear, yes," April responded.

Morgan dropped Margaret's hand. Even though April had expressed her gratitude at Morgan's having saved her daughter, he knew that he wasn't her first choice for a son-in-law. He might not have even made the list at all when it came to someone suitable for her daughter. "I'll be happy to call your husband for you, Mrs. Hastings. The two of you must be very tired. I'll send a wire tonight, and you can send another tomorrow morning after you've had your rest."

"Why, thank you." The woman seemed relieved. Her voice was low. "We'll be staying at the Waldorf Astoria."

She took Margaret's arm and started off, and then she suddenly turned back in Morgan's direction. "Tell him not to come. Margaret and I will be booking a passage home just as soon as one becomes available."

"I'll be sure to tell him," Morgan replied. It was just like April Hastings to make certain Margaret wouldn't be in Morgan's company for very long. Margaret looked back plaintively at Morgan. Neither one of them was quite ready to tell April that Margaret had agreed to become his wife. But their caution about bringing the matter up in the wake of Peter's death might mean that it would be months before he saw Margaret again. That wouldn't do, and both of them knew it.

The two women started to walk away, Margaret's eyes still riveted on Morgan. A woman suddenly rushed up to them out of the crowd. "Just a moment, Margaret, not so fast," the woman called out. It was Gloria Thompson, the attractive young widow who had attached herself to Margaret and Morgan during the voyage.

She took Margaret's hand away from her mother and pulled her back toward Morgan. "I was hoping to speak to both of you before you left. I know this may seem like the worst of times, but I just wanted to give you a warning."

Gloria looked at the both of them, taking turns fixing each with a gaze into their eyes. "This may sound strange, but I know what I'm speaking of. I am a widow myself, a young woman left alone before my time. For the first year I was haunted with guilt because I was here and he was gone. I was practically paralyzed by it. Don't let that happen to you. You are both here because God has willed it so for a reason. Find that reason."

She reached out and grabbed the lapel of Morgan's coat. "And you, Morgan Fairfield, you're a reporter, a writer. You find out just why this all happened. Find out who is responsible." She shook him gently. "Do you understand?"

Morgan nodded. "Yes, I understand."

Releasing his coat, she smoothed it with her hand, although an army of washerwomen with irons couldn't have put it right. "Fine. Now I expect the best from you two, and I expect an invitation to your wedding as well."

Margaret smiled. "Don't worry. You'll get that."

"Good. Now the both of you go along and live. *Live*."

Margaret smiled and nodded. Turning around, she hurried back to her mother. Morgan stroked the side of his face, feeling the effect of being without his razor. "Thank you for that, Mrs. Thompson."

"Don't you thank me, Morgan Fairfield. You're the hero."

Morgan stuck his hands in his pockets and sheepishly took his place in a line being formed for the homeless survivors. He may have been a first-class passenger, but he was now down to the twenty-pound note in his pocket.

It was then that he spotted Lilly, his childhood nurse. She was looking over the crowd, straining to find him. Morgan knew deep down that she would have come from Newport to find him. He wasn't sure, however, if Lilly even knew that he was still alive. The woman was as beautiful as he'd always remembered. Her black hair had turned somewhat gray, but she carried herself with dignity, her trim figure and high cheekbones showing a hint of good breeding and status. No one would have guessed her to be an employee. Morgan had certainly never treated her that way.

He tried to relax, and he walked in her direction, keeping his eyes on her and hoping she wouldn't become lost in the crowd. When he got closer, he smiled. "Lilly."

The woman turned, caught his eye, and broke into tears. Morgan reached out and pulled her close to him. "I knew you'd be here."

She continued to sob on his shoulder. "How could I not be here? I've been praying for days. You've had me so worried."

He held her close, patting her back. "Well, I'm here now. We'll find you a room here in town so we can talk tomorrow. I have so much to tell you, but there's so little time now."

"Morgan Fairfield! Morgan Fairfield!" The sound of Morgan's name being shouted above the cacophony of noisy voices brought his head up. A man in a rumpled brown suit, his head wet from rain and his red hair falling down over his face, was milling through the crowd shouting Morgan's name.

Morgan waved. "Over here. Over here. I'm Morgan Fairfield."

The man grinned and picked up his pace, plowing through the crowd. He extended his hand. "The saints be praised. You don't know how glad we are to see you."

"And who are you?"

"Oh, yes, I'm sorry." The man grinned and stuck his thumbs through the straps in his suspenders. "I'm Jake O'Leary of the *New York Herald*." He grabbed Morgan's hand and pumped it. "Normally I wouldn't have come out to greet you this way. We'd have waited and let you find us."

Morgan introduced Lilly to the man.

"Pleased to meet you, Madam." He turned and looked over the crowd of people wandering around the dock and looking equally bewildered. "Frankly, we didn't even know if you were still alive, although we held out some hope."

He then slapped Morgan on both shoulders with the open palms of his hands. "You're going to be quite the popular man at the paper. The chief has you a room at the Waldorf tonight and expects to see you first thing in the morning."

"The Waldorf? The Waldorf Astoria?"

"There ain't no other. Right now, you're about the most popular property we got. I think he'd a put you up in a king's palace if we had one of them."

Morgan watched as Margaret and April made their way through the crowd. He caught sight of Margaret crying with and hugging an older couple. Evidently they were Peter's relatives. Arm in arm, the four of them disappeared. At least he wouldn't be far from her.

CHAPTER 3

Jeremy Fetters was nearing forty. He'd been an engineer on the *Olympic* and now represented the only surviving engineer from the *Titanic*. Most of the crowd had long since gone their way, and he'd stayed to watch the last of the *Titanic*'s lifeboats lowered from the *Carpathia* and into the water beside the dock. They were all that remained. The plaque on each one said *Titanic*, chilling reminders that there had been all too few of them.

The rain continued to fall, and he wiped his face and put his black cap back into place. The white top of the cap was streaked with grease, but the bill still had some shine on it. He supposed he was glad to have survived, but still the idea that many he knew hadn't dropped a cloud of gloom into his mind. He could see their faces and almost hear their voices.

He stuck his hands into his peacoat pocket and looked down at his brogans. They were in poor shape with deep cuts across the tops and gouges where he had kicked at the sharp steel of the door to the watertight compartment. The same door that closed before his friend Harry had been able to get out. Now Harry was at the bottom of the Atlantic and, from the way Jeremy felt, he knew he should be with him.

The light was dim. Only the distant beams from streetlamps and the lights still blazing on the *Carpathia* lit the area. The lights from the ship reflected out over the harbor, leaving a trail of cat's-paws across the black water.

He swung his head around and watched the three men walking in his direction. The man in the middle was staring directly at him, while the other two seemed to be looking from side to side. It was as if they were being careful not to be seen, although they would be hard to miss. Two hours ago the dock had been brimming with people waiting for the *Carpathia*. He'd overheard someone say that there were over ten thousand people waiting. Now there was just him, him and the men sent to find him.

He raised himself to his full height of five feet seven inches. It was all he had to carry his 200 pounds, and with the deep blue peacoat he had on, he looked something like an unshaven bowling ball.

The small group stopped in front of him, the man nearest the street still letting his eyes wander. "Name's Bain, Alister Bain. You Fetters?" the man in the middle asked.

Jeremy looked the men over. Bain, who seemed to be the leader, was bulky and had dark hair and eyes. His full beard was wet with ringlets of black hair still dripping water from the rain.

"Yes, Wilde's gone though. Went down with the ship."

Bain smiled, a deep smirk that showed a perfect set of white teeth gleaming behind his beard. "Yeah, that's too bad." He looked at the man to his left. "Ain't it?"

The thin man nodded, his hands stuck deep in his overcoat pockets.

"You got ma money?" Jeremy asked. "Five hundred dollars?"

"We're here to pay you," Bain responded. "Pay you in full."

"Good. I wanna be out of here and find a berth going back to Southampton just as quick as I can."

"Well, we'll do all we can to send you on your way."

"Good. That's just the way I bleedin' want it. I don't want to be nowhere around when they start in to asking questions."

The taller man standing to Bain's right nudged him and bobbed his head back in the direction they had come from. Jeremy could see the policeman, and now Bain turned and spotted him too. The sight of the beat cop brought the conversation to a halt.

They watched the cop, spinning his nightstick on the end of a short length of rawhide, walk toward them. He threw it out, twirling it, and caught it as it spun back into his grasp. The sound of the rhythmic movement echoed over the empty dock with a series of slaps. The heels of the man's boots blended into the smacks of the nightstick against his bare hand.

As he got closer, Bain turned around and forced a smile. "Evening, officer. Bad night for a walk."

The pudgy policeman came to a halt, rocking back on his heels and toes like a punching bag one would find at a carnival. He stopped the twirling of the baton and, using his left hand, raked a sheet of rain off the bill of his cap. "I'd say it's a bad night for anyone to be out and about. What are you gents doing out here?"

Bain flashed a broader smile. "We're just here to meet an old friend of ours. Came in tonight on the *Carpathia*."

The policeman's eyes lit up, and he glared at Jeremy. "And would that be you?"

"Yes, sir."

"You on the *Titanic*?"

Jeremy bowed his head and mumbled. "I was. It ain't something I care to talk about though."

"Well, if you were part of the crew on that death ship, I can understand why. What a horrible thing. I wouldn't want anything to do with it myself."

Bain put his hands in his pockets and held his head high. "We're just here to take him out for a couple a pints of forgetfulness."

The policeman turned around and pointed toward the street with his nightstick. "The Brass Rail's a likely spot over there. They cater to seamen, and they'll be plenty of folks who'll buy you all you can down, coming in on the *Carpathia* like you did."

"Thanks, officer," Bain said. "I know the place."

The policeman reached into his jacket pocket, and Jeremy could see that his action caused all three men to stiffen. He pulled out a cigarette. "You gents have a light?"

The taller man to Bain's right quickly fumbled in his pocket with his left hand and drew out a box of matches. He opened it and, striking a flame, held it up to the policeman's dangling cigarette. The flame on the end of the match lit up the man's face, and Jeremy could see the policeman studying it as he puffed his cigarette to life. A long scar meandered down the man's left cheek and came to a halt just below his chin.

The cop drew a deep puff and let it escape in a cloud of gray smoke. "You get that in a knife fight?"

The match burned the man's finger, and he dropped it to the wet dock. "Yeah, with my brother when I was fourteen."

The cop grinned. "Not much for family life, are you?"

"No, I reckon not."

"But he's behaving himself now, officer," Bain added. "Can't say the same for his brother though."

"Well, you boys best all be behaving yourselves. You go on to the Brass Rail then, and tell 'em O'Toole sent you."

"We'll do that, officer," Bain said. "You needn't worry none about us."

"Good." The policeman drew another deep puff. "That's just the way I like it 'round here."

The policeman ambled off in the direction of the *Carpathia*. His walk was easy and he once again started the swinging of his shiny black stick.

Bain turned to the man with the matches. "You should have just handed him the matches. He saw your face."

The tall man dropped his chin and stuck the box back into his pocket. They watched as the policeman took a sharp right turn at the edge of the dock and then paraded past the anchored ship. The man's steps were precise, as if he had walked the same route before over and over. He finished his walk alongside the well-lit ship and then swaggered off into the darkness.

"You got ma money?" Jeremy asked.

Bain, stepping over to the side of the dock, peered out at the boats from the *Titanic*. He seemed to be paying little or no attention to Jeremy as he walked along behind him; he seemed only to be counting the assembly of white bouncing boats. Each of the lifeboats took turns bobbing the harbor, and rising in sequence with the swell and then dropping back down into the black water.

"I just want ma money. Then I'll be off. You'll never see hide ner hair of me again."

Bain turned around and stared at him. "You know, you didn't actually do what you were paid to do, neither you nor Wilde."

Jeremy raised his hands and brought them down in frustration. "We never had the chance. We hit that bloody berg before we were in position. The upshot was the same, just like you people wanted. That ship's down, and that's that."

Bain frowned. "Ah, but that's the rub, ain't it. She's down all right, but nobody knows we put her there. Now what's the point in that when a body's trying to get the world's attention?" He pointed to the boats. "Now all they're going to be talking about is the lack of boats. Not one word on the cause or what we had to do to pull it off."

"So we should have kept her afloat just so we could sink her later?"

"That's right, my man."

"Bloody stupid, I'd say. What difference does it make?"

"Makes a lot of difference to my boss. I mean, what good is it if when you go to kill a man he gets himself struck by lightning? It ain't no good, no good at all. I mean, you want people to know you killed him and not some freak act of nature."

Jeremy heaved a sigh, putting his hands on his hips. "Then you best give me my five hundred dollars for something else then."

"And what would that be?"

"For keepin' ma yapper shut, that's what. With what I know, you people want to keep me happy and on the next boat back to England. Given the stir all this is going to cause in America, you don't want people breathing down yer necks, now do you?"

Bain scratched his beard. "You got a point there, my man." He leaned over in Jeremy's direction. "And you ain't told nobody, has you?"

Jeremy shook his head. "No, I been quiet as a tomb. You think I'd want people to know I was a party to this? I'd never get papers to sign on again. Not with nobody to haul nothing. That money may seem like a lot to you. But it ain't gonna last me for the rest of my life, and it would have to if I told what I knew."

Bain looked back at the other two men. "Looks like we're going to have to pay him to shut him up, don't it, boys?"

The man with the scar shrugged his shoulders. "Don't make no difference to me. We might as well pay him right here and now." He looked off at the lifeboats. "Seems kinda seemly too, I suppose, given all these here boats from the *Titanic*."

Bain laughed, "I guess it does at that." He signaled to Jeremy and pointed down the dock to a spot where the lights from the street didn't reach. The place was still far enough away from the *Carpathia* to prevent them from being easily seen. "We'll go over there and pay you off."

"Good." Jeremy stepped out in front of them and made his way over to the shadows. "The sooner we get this over with, the better I'll like it."

The three men looked at one another, and Bain smiled at them. "After you, gentlemen."

To a casual observer, it might have looked like a group of men in a huddle. That is, until the short stocky man tried to bolt away from the group. The three men grabbed him. Moments later he fell into their arms. They lowered his body over the side of the dock, and he fell into the water with a splash.

CHAPTER 4

The offices of the *New York Herald* were a blur of white shirts and baggy pants, all furiously hurrying about. Morgan wound his way around the desks, drawing scarcely more notice than a stray dog wandering around. He stopped at a desk where a man was stretching the night's kinks out of his shoulders. "Where might I find the city editor?"

Just then both of their heads turned at the sound of bellowing, a series of roars mixed with curses. The glass door to an office was flung open, the blinds rattling against it. A short man in a natty gray suit backed out of it, slowly, one step at a time. The roars and curses continued to pour out of the office and were followed by a billowing cloud of paper. "Take this bilge and bring me back something I can print!" the voice roared. "We don't just report the news at the *Herald*, we make it. Now go make me some!"

The man at the desk smiled up at Morgan. "The old lion is in his lair, but I wouldn't bother to close the door behind you."

Morgan guessed at once that he was being directed to the site of the encounter. He gulped. "What's his name?"

"Dixon, Harry Dixon, and he's been here since Adam got thrown out of the garden. Some say he reported it. Others say he got thrown out first, and once you meet him you'll know why."

Morgan stepped cautiously around several other desks and quietly approached the open door. He stopped and knocked.

The man at his desk had white hair over his ears that showed off his polished bald head. His tie was crooked and his shirt unbuttoned at the top. His round shoulders were slumped over the desk as he read. He looked up at Morgan, a pair of small round glasses perched at the base of his tiny button nose. Morgan could see a hint of blue in his eyes from behind the thick glasses. A red beard mixed with gray and white covered his face. Not long, but not well kept either. "What do you want?" he growled.

"I'm Morgan Fairfield."

The man's heavy, bushy salt-and-pepper eyebrows raised. "Morgan Fairfield, our society reporter? The one who came in on the *Titanic*?"

"Yes, sir."

The man jumped to his feet, his large mitts fastened in clenched fists on his desk. He then stood upright, hitching up his pants and planting his ample belly over the top of his belt. He walked around his desk and held out his hand. "I'm Harry Dixon, city editor."

"Pleased to meet you, Mr. Dixon." Morgan shook his hand.

"You won't be," Dixon said. "Not when you get to know me. And you can drop that Mr. Dixon stuff. Most call me 'the old man' until my back is turned. Then what they call me can't be repeated in any Sunday school. You can call me Harry, or you can call me Chief."

"Yes sir, Chief."

Dixon rounded Morgan and closed the door. "Drop the sir stuff too. I don't want your respect. I want your fear." He motioned toward a shabby red leather wingback chair. "Sit yerself down, Fairfield. We got special plans for you."

"I did have a matter I'd like to take up with you, er, Chief."

Dixon rounded his desk and took his seat as Morgan squashed himself down into the shabby chair. He waved his hand at Morgan. "If it's about where you're staying, you can forget about it. We got more important things for you to do right now than have you look for a place to drop your carcass. The room and the meals are on the *Herald*'s tab. Senator Smith from Michigan is due to begin hearings on the *Titanic* in the ballroom of the Waldorf, and we want you right there."

"No, sir, it's not about that."

"Well, what is it then?" Dixon looked at his watch. "It's 7:20 already, and I want you working at 7:00."

"I am sorry about that. I had an early breakfast with an old friend of the family this morning, a woman who up until last night didn't know if I was alive or dead. Then I had to put her on the early train for Newport. But it's about my assignment with the paper—the society pages."

Dixon waved his hand as if he were brushing off a pesky horsefly. "You can forget about that, Fairfield, at least for now. We want you writing down all you can about the *Titanic:* what it was like, the crash into the iceberg, and who in the blazes was responsible."

Morgan nodded. "I understand." He wanted to say *sir*, if for no other reason than out of respect for the man's age, but he thought better of it. There were a number of things he would have to forget about his breeding if he was going to work at the *Herald*, and this was no doubt the most minor of them. "But it's something else."

"What boy?" Dixon glanced at his pocket watch again. "Time's a wasting."

"I don't want to work on the society pages, not now, not ever."

Dixon drew himself closer in the well of his desk. He folded his hands and pumped his fingers up and down, blinking his eyes repeatedly as a sickly smile creased his lips. "And what, pray tell, dear boy, do you want to do for us?"

"I want to work the crime section of the paper."

"The crime section?" Dixon laughed. "And what does a mere strapling from Oxford know about crime on the streets of New York?"

"I know about a murder on the *Titanic*. A series of murders."

Dixon's mouth dropped open. "You can't be serious."

"Oh, but I am. I was there. I saw it."

Dixon leaned back in his swivel chair. The sound of the squeak was almost deafening. He studied Morgan carefully. "And you think I'm going to put you on one of our most guarded group of writers just because you give me some fanciful tale?"

Morgan gulped. If there was a time for bravery, this was it and he knew it. "It may seem fanciful to you, but it's all true. I can write about the *Titanic* and being a survivor and then work my way into the murders on board if you put me on the crime reporter's roster. If not, I'm certain the *New York Times* can and will."

"Are you blackmailing me, boy?"

"You can call it what you will. I'm a good writer. Too good to spend my days writing about garden parties. I'll give you what you want on the *Titanic* and then some. Then I'll turn my attention to the more important areas of news reporting."

Dixon opened an ornate wooden box on his desk with a carving of a lion on it. He pushed it over in Morgan's direction. "Want a cigar, boy? If you got guts enough to threaten the old man here, you got guts enough for a Havana."

"No, thank you. I don't smoke."

"Well, I will." Dixon reached into the box and pulled out a long, thick cigar. He bit the end off of the thing and then ran it through his mouth to moisten the paper. Reaching into a silver cup, he pulled out a match, ran it over his battered desk, and ignited a flame. With two fingers, he held the cigar over the bright flame to singe the edges of the end he was going to light. He then put the cigar into his mouth and held the flame to the crisply cut end, puffing it to life.

"Being a good writer is the least of your problems, boy. It might even get in your way around here. You have to think and, more important, think fast. But most of all, you have to know what a good story is and how to make it a better one. You have to smell out a story before it bites you in the breeches in the form of a headline from one of our competitors."

Dixon leaned back on his chair and puffed on the cigar, sending plumes of gray smoke into the room. "So far, you ain't shown me nothing except that you know how to be late and that you know how to swim."

Morgan got to his feet. "I'm sorry to have wasted your time. I'll have my bags out of my room this morning."

Dixon dropped forward on his chair. "Now, hold on. Who told you to go? It ain't many men who quit before they're hired."

"Does that mean I'm on the crime page?"

"That's exactly what it means. Maybe I'm getting soft or just feeling especially charitable this morning. You can have the job. It won't mean a raise in pay, though, not until you've shown me you've earned it."

He took the cigar out of his mouth and pointed the ash-covered end at Morgan. "You just better show me something boy, and quick. I want a story on the *Titanic* on my desk by 2:00 this afternoon, and it better be good reading."

"Yes. I can do that."

"You will do that. I don't want no poppycock about the color of the carpets, either. I want a riveting story on the *Titanic*, as told by a survivor, in every edition of the *Herald*." He stuck the cigar back into his mouth and grinned. "You're going to have to work with Call too."

"Call?"

"Yes, a real sweetheart he is. He works New York crime, and he ain't going to be terribly happy about being a nursemaid to you either. It might mean a serious increase in his drinking problem."

Dixon got to his feet. "Do you drink?"

"Nothing in the way of spirits, sir."

Morgan could tell his lapse into politeness had been noticed and that it wasn't appreciated.

"Well, then one of you two will be sober. You'll be an oddity to Call. The people he's around who don't smoke or drink are the stiffs he meets in the morgue. Don't you wind up there, though, unless Call puts you there." He smiled. "Of course most men who work with Call start drinking. The man doesn't just stick to writing about crimes; he wants to know all the answers. He has this craving for the whys of a matter."

Morgan stepped to the door. "How do I find this Call?"

Dixon walked around his desk. "I better take you there myself. He won't believe it unless it comes from me." He stopped short of the door and pushed his glasses back up the short bridge of his nose. "You understand that you won't get a second chance here. I expect serious stuff right off the bat. You disappoint me, and I'll do more than fire you. I'll throw you out on your behind—personally."

Morgan nodded. "I understand."

Dixon opened the door. "Follow me, boy."

Morgan worked at keeping up with the man as he wound his way around the desks to an area in the corner of the room. Everywhere he went, Morgan could see people working hard at appearing to work hard. They were also trying to avoid looking at Dixon and were staring straight into the papers they were shuffling or trying to write on. Typewriters banged noisily.

When they got to the corner, Dixon yelled, "Where's Call?"

One of the reporters pushed back his green eyeshade and pointed across the room. "Just coming out of the biffy."

Both Morgan and Dixon watched as the tall angular man stepped across the room. He was pulling a comb through his silver hair. Morgan was stunned. It was the man he had seen studying him on the chase boat the night before.

As the man stuck his comb back in his pocket, a frown formed across his face. "To what do I owe the curse of this visit from you?"

"You can save your curses until after I've told you what I've got on my mind," Dixon replied. "This is our *Titanic* survivor, Morgan Fairfield. He's going to do a series of stories on the sinking, and he'll be working with you. I want his story on my desk by 2:00, and it better be good."

Call shook his head. "Now you've got me mollycoddling some cub reporter."

Dixon laughed. "Yeah, ain't it a crime?"

Morgan felt more than a bit sheepish. He was obviously unwanted by all he surveyed and would have to do his best just to keep them from throwing him out. Right then, all he could do was bite his tongue. "You were on that boatload of reporters last night, weren't you?" he asked.

"That I was."

"What makes a crime reporter come out to meet a group of *Titanic* survivors?"

Call smiled. "Most killings I report on only have one murder victim. When it comes to a corporate disaster like the *Titanic* though, it looks as if the big boys annihilate them by the thousands."

"What if I told you I saw some people murdered one at a time on the *Titanic* before we even hit the iceberg?"

Call gave him a blank stare, but Morgan could tell that he'd piqued the man's interest. That was a small victory in itself.

Just then a copyboy with a pencil behind his ear, who looked to be no more than twelve, came running up. He handed Call a piece of paper, which the reporter read. "It seems we have another *Titanic* murder," Call smiled. He reached and grabbed his coat and hat off an oak coat tree.

"And what would that be?" Dixon asked.

Call turned, "They just fished the body of a *Titanic* engineer out of the harbor. Somebody stabbed him last night."

He started to leave, but Dixon called out after him. "Take Fairfield with you, Call. You two are going to be joined at the hip."

CHAPTER 5

Both Margaret and April Hastings had found their room at the Waldorf posh and accommodating with two four-poster beds, a sitting area, and a dressing room off the water closet. Margaret turned the pages of the morning edition of the *Times* and stirred her eggs while waiting for her mother's return from the front desk. April had gone downstairs to send a telegram to inform Margaret's father of their safety and of her plans to travel home by way of the next ship. Margaret was certain that April would already be asking about a return passage. She didn't know how she was going to break the news to her, that she had no intention of returning to England, at least not now.

She leafed through page after page of news reports on the *Titanic*, some of which contained parts of the story that she could barely recognize. It sent chills up her spine to read the stories of the survivors. She knew that so many others were learning about it for the first time, but for her, reading about it seemed like reliving it.

Suddenly there was a knock at the door. Margaret got up from her place and walked across the deep-pile carpet to turn the lock and open the door. It was Gloria Thompson.

"I'm so glad to see you." Margaret practically pulled the woman into the room. "Are you staying here as well?"

Gloria laughed, "Of course I am. I'm just down the hall. It wouldn't do for an oil widow to be in any place but the Waldorf Astoria, now would it?"

"No, I suppose not." She motioned to the settee. "Please have a seat. I need to talk to you."

Gloria walked over to the pink, overstuffed sofa and, spreading her dress, sat down. "I see you're having breakfast in your room. I did too. Somehow I couldn't face a public restaurant just yet. Reporters are everywhere."

"I know. I hate being a prisoner. Maybe it will die down soon."

"That's not likely, dear. Heaven only knows when we'll be able to live a normal life again."

Margaret pulled up a chair in front of Gloria and sat down, wringing her hands.

"What seems to be the problem?" Gloria asked.

"How long will you be staying here in New York?"

Gloria shook her head slightly and raised her eyebrows. "I'm not exactly sure. I've lost much of my clothing. I guess the fish are dressing well." She forced a laugh. "I need to do some serious shopping before I go home. I'd also like to see the sights."

Raising her head and looking at the ceiling, Gloria sighed a deep sigh. "I live in Oklahoma, you know." She dropped and locked her gaze on Margaret. "Can you imagine what it will be like to be in a small town as the only resident survivor of the *Titanic*? I'll have to repeat myself a hundred times, and still they won't be satisfied. You'll be all right, though. You can go back to England and blend in."

"That's what I wanted to talk to you about."

"Going to England? You're not afraid of ship travel are you?"

"Well, yes, I am. I can't bear the thought of boarding another ship so soon, and my mother wants us on the next ship to England."

"You shouldn't be afraid, my dear. These things are so very rare."

Gloria scooted forward and took Margaret's hand. "That's not all there is, I'll bet."

Margaret shook her head silently.

"You don't want to leave Morgan, do you?"

Margaret nodded. "You see me very clearly. I only hope my mother doesn't. I don't think she could bear the thought of my staying here so close to Morgan. This thing with Morgan is going to take quite some time for her to get used to."

"Does she know about your feelings for him?"

Slowly, Margaret shook her head. "I haven't said a word. It's hard for me to get used to it myself. That's one of the reasons I wanted to stay in New York for a while. I want to spend some time with him, but Mother wants us on the next boat."

"I see."

"She would never permit me to stay without a chaperone."

"And you want me to be your chaperone?"

"Could you?"

Gloria laughed. "My dear, you have no idea of what a hard taskmaster I can be. I like your company, and I would insist on it."

Margaret gripped her hands tighter. "That would be wonderful. I would love that, as long as I'm not going to harm any timetable you might have."

"Have no fear of that. I may be here a month or better. Would that give you enough time?"

"That would be wonderful."

"Fine." Gloria got to her feet. "Then count me in as your accomplice." She grabbed Margaret and hugged her. "We'll have a roaring good time."

"I would love it. Of course, I can pay my own way."

"Don't worry about that, dear. You'll be my companion as long as you're not on the arm of Mr. Fairfield."

"He may be much too busy for me with this new job of his."

Gloria smiled. "Honey, a man in love is never too busy for the woman he puts his affection on, and if I've ever seen a man in love, it's Morgan Fairfield."

Just as Margaret was walking Gloria to the door, the key turned and April, with both hands clutching brochures, stepped into the room. "I've found us a wonderful ship," she said, shaking the photographs. "It sails for Liverpool the day after tomorrow." She opened one of the brochures and held out the picture of a stateroom for Margaret's inspection. She then smiled at Gloria. "So nice to see you again, Mrs. Thompson."

"Likewise," Gloria responded. She gave Margaret a knowing look. "I can see that you two ladies have things to discuss. I won't keep you from them."

She opened the door and, stepping out into the hallway, pointed. "I'm in 415, just down the hall. In case you need me."

She nodded at April. "You have a fine daughter, Mrs. Hastings. I'll take very good care of her."

When Margaret closed the door, her mother was staring at her. "What did she mean by that?"

Margaret hung her head and walked across the room, putting as much distance as possible between her and April. She pushed back the curtains and stared outside. "Mother, I simply can't get on another ship, not right now."

"Nonsense. We have to go back, Margaret. We have to go back at once. Your father is a distraught man without us. You know how helpless the dear is."

Margaret whirled around. "I simply can't, Mother. I need to be on dry ground for a time. I think I'd die if I set foot on another ship."

April stepped closer to her. "That is ridiculous, dear. You'll think better of it in the morning."

She would have moved closer, but Margaret put up her hand to ward her off. "No, Mother, I can't. Tomorrow or the next day will make no difference."

April put the brochures on the table and folded her hands. She always folded her hands before giving a mother-daughter lecture. "This is absurd, darling. Fear must be faced. It can't be avoided. You have nothing to worry about. This ship is perfectly safe."

"The *Titanic* was unsinkable, Mother."

"And do you think this captain will take any chances whatsoever after what's happened? I think not." She drew her fingers across the air in front of her face, dismissing Margaret's reasoning. "I won't hear any more of this foolishness. How can I leave you in New York? You've no place to stay and no chaperone. It's simply out of the question."

"That is what Mrs. Thompson was referring to, Mother. She needs a companion and will be here a month or more. I have agreed to be that companion."

"You what?" April asked the question in a shrill voice, almost in a tone of anger.

"I have agreed to stay on as her companion. Given my fears, it seemed the most sensible thing to do."

"It is not sensible. You are a single woman living with your parents. You will do as I say."

"Not this time, Mother, not now. You don't seem to understand. I lost Peter on that ship out there. I'm absolutely petrified to take another trip so soon. And then there's the matter of Peter's relatives. What kind of person would I be to simply go back home and forget to see them. They had planned on such a nice affair. It wouldn't be right." Margaret shook her head. "No, I owe Peter that much."

"And what makes you think you'll be any more courageous a month from now?"

"I don't know that for sure. All I do know is that I'm terrified by the idea of getting on another ship just now."

"And are you equally frightened to take another man?"

Margaret clinched her fists and dropped them to her side. "What do you mean?"

April stepped closer. "You know exactly what I mean. Morgan Fairfield. Are you staying here to be near him?"

Clasping her arms around her chest, Margaret did her best to give the impression that the thought had never occurred to her, and what was more, that she was offended that her mother would even think such a thing. She turned away. "I'm surprised at you, Mother. Morgan will be much too busy with his new job to give me so much as the time of day. I will be here as Gloria Thompson's companion. Nothing more and nothing less."

"Somehow, I find myself filled with doubt as to that."

Margaret turned back around quickly. "Think what you want. I am not getting on that boat. You can stay with me here if you like, or you can go and I will come as soon as I can."

"You know that I can't do that. What will the ladies' literary society do without me for a month? What will your father do? Who will see that he dresses properly?"

Margaret on any other occasion might have resorted to tears, but this time she knew that would never work. It wasn't sympathy she sought. It was the chance to be a woman and make her own decisions. "Father is your duty, Mother. I'm quite sure he needs you. I simply must stay here right now, stay here until I have my courage back. I'll be perfectly safe with Mrs. Thompson. You needn't worry. You have your duties to do at home, and right now I have my grieving to do here."

April sat down quietly on the couch and looked up at Margaret. "And is part of that grieving Morgan Fairfield?"

"My grief is my own concern, Mother. Besides, Peter has family here in New York. I must see them. I plan to honor Peter and honor his last request."

"And just what was that?"

"That is my own concern now. Peter is gone and I am here."

It was less than an hour later when April gasped. She had been reading the paper's society and arts section. She pointed to an ad dealing with the theater. "Look at this," she said. "Hunter Kennedy is due to perform at the Grande today. The paper says he's opening with Gilbert and Sullivan's *HMS Pinafore*."

Margaret put down a book she was reading. "That can't be our Hunter Kennedy."

"It most certainly can. The paper here calls him a survivor of the *Titanic*. It's right here in bold print."

Margaret dropped her book and got to her feet. She walked quickly over to her mother and took the paper from her hand. There she read:

HUNTER KENNEDY—*TITANIC* SURVIVOR

Opens today in Gilbert and Sullivan's
HMS Pinafore, a bawdy romp of the deep at the

Grande Theater. Not to be missed.
Matinee at 2 P.M. Evening performance at 8 P.M.

Margaret slowly put down the paper. “Amazing,” she said, “Simply amazing.” She shook her head. “I just can’t believe it.”

Margaret knew the last time she had seen Hunter Kennedy was in the swimming pool on the *Titanic*. He was dead, and both Morgan and she knew he had been murdered. She looked up at April. “Mother, would you care to join me for the matinee? This is one performance I simply can’t miss.”

CHAPTER 6

Morgan and Call had taken more that twenty minutes to walk through the crowds in Central Park. The rain from the night before had scrubbed everything clean, from the chalk drawings on the sidewalks to the flowers themselves. Ladies pushed their carriages through the park, and several men were enjoying a ride on horses.

Call was a tall man. Morgan guessed him at over six feet four inches, and he walked with a long stride. Even though Morgan was over six feet tall, keeping up with Call through the park was a matter of some difficulty. It was only after they'd been walking some that the age difference began to show and Morgan caught up with him. "You keep a good pace," Morgan said, panting slightly.

Call ignored him. He continued his walk as if Morgan wasn't even there. The way the man was bent on pushing him aside made Morgan more than a little angry. He reached out and grabbed his sleeve, pulling him to a halt.

Call swung around, a sharp sneer on his face.

"Look," Morgan said, "I know you don't want me along. I asked for the job of crime reporter, but I didn't ask for you. Why don't we both just make the best of it?"

"Are you through?"

"What do you mean?"

Call pulled out his pocket watch and snapped open the lid, giving the time a quick glance. "We're burning daylight. If you're through with this schoolboy quest for professional courtesy, then we can go do our job."

"I just thought we could both be pleasant."

Call closed the watch and dropped it back in his vest pocket. "You can be pleasant for the both of us. The first thing you'd better learn is that where the newspaper business is concerned, there is no professional courtesy."

He jabbed his finger into Morgan's chest. "If I can take credit for your story, I will. I'll put my name on it and not lose a wink of sleep. That's courtesy in my book. A reporter from another paper would take your story and run you over with his cab on the way to file it."

He pulled his sleeve out of Morgan's grasp and, turning on his heels, once more set out at a gallop.

Morgan ran to catch up. "Where are we going?"

"I know where I'm going. You just have to watch me."

"Don't you think you could tell me how you think on this?"

The question brought Call to a halt. He turned and looked him in the eye. "I'm going to the morgue. You better get to know that place well. By the time you find out about a murder, the victim is more than likely there." He squinted his eyes at Morgan. "On second thought, by the time *you* find out about it, he'll more than likely be in the cemetery."

When they got to the edge of the street, Call hailed a cab with a shrill, earsplitting whistle. They got in the cab and within minutes were getting out in front of the city morgue. Morgan followed as Call stopped at a street vendor and bought a fresh bouquet of spring flowers. Without saying a word he took to the stairs after Call, two at a time.

Call sauntered up to the receptionist's desk. The woman seated behind it appeared to be in her late thirties. She had mousy hair and a face covered with pockmarks. She'd obviously taken a great deal of time to cover them with heavy pancake makeup. He took off his hat. "Good morning, Mimi. You're looking especially beautiful this fine day." He held out the flowers. "I know these bright offerings can't compare with you, but I thought I'd bring them anyway. You just might make them blush even more."

The woman's face had had a frown on it when Morgan first spotted her, but now her expression blossomed into a wide smile. She reached out and took the flowers. "My, how you do go on, Call. I bet you say that to all the girls."

Call leaned over the counter and pinched her cheek. "Just to you, my fine lass. Just to you."

She beamed, fluffing the bouquet. "Somehow I had a feeling I'd be seeing you this morning. And what sort of favor would you be looking for today?" Grinning, she slumped forward in her chair looking directly up at him. "You know I always enjoy doing you a favor."

Call returned the smile. "I'm certain that's so, Mimi, dear. I just have a minor one this morning, though, and one that won't require any work on your part at all."

She giggled the type of laugh one would associate with a schoolgirl. "Oh, Call, you're never any work, none at all."

Call cast a quick glance from side to side, giving the impression that what he was saying was for her ears alone. He lowered his head in her direction, and his voice as well. "That husband of yours is a mighty lucky man, my dear. Don't tell him I brought you flowers." He grinned. "On second thought, maybe you should tell him. Might make the old boy toe the line more."

They both laughed. Call went on. "This morning, though, I'd just like to see the stiff brought in from the docks. You know the one. The seaman from the *Titanic*."

She smiled, pushing her swivel chair back from the desk. "Somehow I thought you'd be in for him." She got to her feet. "Let me check to see if the coroner is still in there. He won't let you in, but one of the examiners might be persuaded."

Call watched her go down the hall. "Tell him I'll make it worth his while."

Morgan was amazed at just how quickly Call could change his total disposition. The man could go from a demon to a darling in the twinkling of an eye. Of course, Morgan realized that Call was really after only one thing, and that was what was best for Call. Everything else was negotiable.

Call turned around, eyeballing Morgan. Call was handsome in a rugged sort of way, with sharp features and deep brown eyes. His mustache was neatly trimmed and waxed at the ends. But the man's eyes were the most striking. They were like a book. You could almost read his thoughts by simply looking into his eyes. Right then, all Morgan saw was disrespect, that and a sense that Call was a man who lived his life alone. Morgan doubted that anyone had ever been close to him, at least not for long. Morgan swallowed. "That kind of thing must be hard on your wife."

Call blew a laugh past his mustache, almost dismissing the observation. "I'm not married. Fact is, I don't know any decent reporter who is." He crossed his arms and, leaning back, continued to study Morgan with a sick smile. "If you want a wife and the kiddies, go back to the society page."

Moments later Call spotted Mimi down the hall. She was holding a door open and waving them forward. Morgan followed.

"Clifford will give you ten minutes," Mimi said. She rubbed the tips of her fingers together. "Ten minutes for five dollars."

"Sounds more than fair, darling." He leaned over and gave her a peck on the cheek. "You've been the breath of spring, sweetie. I won't forget it."

Call and Morgan stepped into the autopsy room. Metal tables were scattered throughout the room, many of them holding sheet-draped corpses. At a far table under a bright light was a man in a dirty white smock. He stood in front of the only corpse with the sheet pulled back.

They wound their way around the tables, and Morgan could see Call pulling a five-dollar bill out of his pocket. When they got to the table prepared for viewing, he slipped the bill into the palm of the man's hand. "We appreciate your time, Clifford. What do we have here?"

The examiner was a short, stocky man. One of his ruddy cheeks was streaked with what appeared to be blood. His blond hair was unkempt and tufted on top like a stack of hay that had fallen during the night. "Who is this?" he asked, looking at Morgan.

Call looked back in Morgan's direction. "Oh, him. That's Fairfield. He's a cub I'm showing the ropes to."

The man looked Morgan over, stroking his chin. "I guess it'll be all right. I ain't used to no group tours, though."

"Just pretend he's not here. That's what I'm doing."

The examiner looked down at the body. The sheet had been pulled back, revealing the torso and exposing the knife wound. "What we have here is a man in his thirties, I'd say. He wasn't in the water that long, so I'd put the time of death at around midnight." Looking up at Call, he grinned. "Give or take an hour."

"Do we know who he is?"

Reaching for a bag at the foot of the table, the examiner pulled out a smeared card. "Here's his seaman's card. This here is Jeremy Fetters, or Festers." He handed the card to Call. "You see if you can make it out."

Call cast a quick glance in Morgan's direction, and Morgan was at once glad that he had his notebook out and was busily jotting down notes. Call dropped his gaze, peering carefully at the card. "*Fetters*, I'd say. Engineer, second class." He handed the card back.

Reaching back down into the dirty bag, the examiner pulled out a seaman's jacket. "The insignia on it bears the name *Titanic*. He must have come in last night on the *Carpathia*." He dropped the tunic to the floor.

Call shook his head. "Shame, shame. Man gets himself spared and rescued from one disaster only to find his own personal one. Any money on him?"

"Nope, picked clean."

"Have you done anything to him?" Call asked.

"No, just cleaned him up a little. The coroner will do the autopsy before lunch."

Morgan moved closer to the examining table and leaned over the corpse. The man's skin was a milky white, and the angry wound extended from his right shoulder to a point close to his left hip. A portion of his intestines poured out from the lower part of the wound.

"I can tell you one thing," the examiner said. "Whoever did this used a sharp knife. They had to cut through a wool tunic, and it appears to be a pretty clean cut."

"The man was left-handed too," Morgan said.

Both Call and the examiner looked at Morgan, studying him like he was a man from another planet.

"Who was?" the examiner asked. "Fetters here?"

"No, Fetters was right-handed. The murderer was left-handed."

Call stepped back and put his hands on his hips. "Now, just how do you know that, from a Ouija board?"

Morgan reached down and lifted up the man's right hand. "He has more calluses on his right hand, much more than on his left. Given the fact that he was an engineer, I take it he used his hands a lot, his right hand especially."

The examiner scratched his head, then cocked it to one side. "And the murderer? How do you know he was left-handed?"

"I think I can do better than that." Morgan laid the man's hand back at his side. "The man who killed Fetters came at him from behind." Morgan raised his left hand, simulating a knife blade pointing downward. "He reached over Fetters's back and gashed him, pulling the blade downward."

"Now how do you know that?" Call asked.

"I was on the fencing team in school. I've seen plenty of cuts—though, thank God, none this deep." He pointed to the wound, tracing his finger along the smooth line. "You can see here the path of the blade. It enters him from the shoulder area and drags down to the stomach and below, exiting here. That's why you have a portion of his intestines ripped and outside the body cavity. For a wound to run this direction, a right-handed man attacking him from behind would have entered him below and dragged the knife upwards, not the other way around."

"What if he came at him from the front?" the examiner asked. "He could have pushed the blade in and then raked it down."

Morgan shook his head. "Not likely." He pointed out the area near the top of the wound near the man's right shoulder. "You see here. There are no bruises. If the murderer had been right-handed and had struck the initial blow from the front, this would be the deepest cut and it would have grown more shallow as it was extended. There also would be a bruise."

"Well, I'll be darned," the examiner exclaimed.

"If you examine the man's tunic, I think you'll find that the rip extends outward at the bottom with a slicing cut at the top of the shoulder. And if it is a clean slice, it shows that the murderer reached around him with the sharp edge of the blade up." Morgan surveyed the length of the corpse. "I'd say it's a safe bet the murderer was a taller man too."

The examiner once again picked up the tunic and held it up. It was plain to see that the cut near the shoulder had been a slice, followed by a ripping of the material downward. The examiner peeked around the outstretched garment. "Amazing. You're right."

Using both hands, Morgan gently separated the skin above the wound. "You see, up here the wound is shallow." He moved his hands along the wound showing that it gradually deepened. "He was sliced into with a raking motion downward."

Call crossed his arms. "You seem mighty cocksure for a rookie."

"I can use my eyes." Morgan stood away from the table, folded his arms, and stroked his chin. He looked over at Call and smiled. "Of course, they could have hung him upside down and then killed him, but I wouldn't count on that."

The examiner was nodding at all of Morgan's thoughts. He looked up and ran the back of his hand across his cheek. "Makes sense to me. I'll pass that on to the coroner."

"Don't tell him where you got it," Call shot back. "You just get suddenly brilliant yourself."

Morgan had stepped over to the sink and was lathering up his hands. Clifford reached over to Morgan with his outstretched hand. "What did you say your name is?"

Morgan rinsed his hands. "Morgan Fairfield."

The man pumped Morgan's hand. "I'm pleased to meet you, Fairfield. You ever get tired of turning out newspapers, I think we've got a spot for you."

"Right now he's working for us," Call said. "He came in on the *Carpathia* with Fetters here. He was on the *Titanic*."

Clifford walked them back to the door and opened it.

"Like I say, Fairfield, we've always got a spot for you here. Pay's pretty good too."

"Now don't you turn his head with money. The man's got ink in his veins, or so he says."

A short time later they were both on the top landing of the marble stairs in front of the city morgue. Call looked at Morgan. "You said you're good with a sword?"

"A foil, actually."

"That's good to know." Call grinned. It was the first time Morgan had seen the man smile at him. "When it comes time for me to kill you, I'll make sure I don't try to use a sword."

CHAPTER 7

Morgan and Call paraded onto the dock area. Morgan was swinging his arms and was a little more at ease with himself. He knew Call had been impressed with his observations at the morgue, even if he hadn't said so.

Call once again opened his watch and looked at it. "We can't take long here. Smith has the hearings scheduled to start in a little over an hour. It wouldn't do for you to be late. And I have to have your first *Titanic* story by 1:30 at the latest."

"Why are you reminding me?" Morgan asked. "I can tell time."

Call dropped the watch back in his pocket and raised his chin. "Just thought you might need some prompting."

"Thanks, but I'll make out just fine. I'll just need a typewriter and a desk."

"You'll have one in the hotel lobby."

"Good, then I'll do all right." He started to walk on but stopped in his tracks and looked at Call. "So, do I get to be an adult now?"

"What do you mean?"

Morgan motioned with his head back where they had come from. "Did I show you that I have a brain?"

Call's expression was impassive. "Kid, you showed me things I've never seen before, and if you stick with me, I'll show you what the world really looks like."

"And do I get treated as an adult?"

"You almost get treated as an adult. I still haven't seen your writing, and I'm not much interested in your school papers on Shakespeare. You show me you can write like an adult reporter, and you might have a chance to stay on with the paper. But if you can't write worth a hoot, then you're going to be gone anyway. I tell you, I've only got so much capacity for companionship, and I'm not about to waste any on some youngster just passing through that ain't got enough time left for a cup of coffee."

"Fine, but you don't have to like me and, frankly, I don't think I'll ever like you. Just treat me civilly. That's all I ask."

"We'll see how your writing goes. That's when I'll have to worry about treating you any way at all."

They soon spotted the sergeant in charge of the investigation. Call pointed at him, "That's Sergeant Rorke. He'll be the one in charge here." The man was something like an oversize bear with hands as big as catcher's mitts.

"Are all the cops in this city Irish?" Morgan asked.

"You're catching on, boy. Just don't aggrandize England, and you'll get along just fine here."

With Morgan in tow, he stepped up to the big man. "Got it all unraveled, Rorke?"

The sergeant clasped his hands behind his back and rocked on the balls of his feet. Morgan could tell his smile was anything but sincere. "Well, now, I've been expecting you. The boys from the *Times* have been here and gone. You're a little late."

Call grinned. "We were somewhat busy solving this case for you. Thought we'd drop by and get your angle, though."

Rorke cast his eyes on Morgan. "Who have you got tagging along?"

Call stepped back. "This here's Fairfield. He's a new man. Came in on the *Carpathia* last night."

Morgan could see the big policeman's eyes widen. But the fact that Call even said that he was a man was what stuck in his brain.

"*Titanic* survivor?" the cop asked.

"Yes, sir."

Rorke smiled at Call. "I like him. He's polite. Not like others I could name." He looked back at Morgan. "You gonna be at the hearings today?"

"He's helping to cover them," Call answered the question for him. "Being as he was out there, he's going to be able to tell the truth from horse pucky when he hears it."

Rorke kept up the rocking motion. "That'll be news itself, coming from a paper like the *Herald*."

"Hey, now," Call said. "It just depends on who you read." He looked around the dock. "You bring last night's beat cop in?"

Rorke pointed to a pudgy cop who was talking to a few reporters. "That would be O'Toole over there. He's had a long night. We had to keep him 'round after his shift, so I wouldn't talk long to the man."

"I'll keep that in mind." Call tipped his hat and walked over to the rear of the group. He and Morgan waited patiently until the group had finalized their questions on everything from what the body looked like to what O'Toole had for breakfast that morning. When the last of them had closed their notebooks, they rushed off to file their stories.

Call, with Morgan behind him, stepped forward. "Sorry we missed all that," he snickered. "Sounds like they asked you everything there was to know."

Morgan noticed that O'Toole looked a little fidgety. The man reached into his jacket and pulled out a bent cigarette. He straightened it and positioned it on the end of his lower lip. "You got a match?" he asked, the cigarette bobbing on the end of his lip. "Forgot to carry mine last night."

"Sure." Call fished in his pocket and came up with a small box of matches with the name of a local watering hole on it. He tossed them to the man. "Keep 'em. I got plenty."

"Thanks." O'Toole took out a match, shakily struck it, and held it to the end of his smoke. He puffed the thing to life and sat back, sucking it in deeply.

"You find the body?"

"About 6:00 this morning."

"Where?"

O'Toole got to his feet and pointed over the edge of the pier to a spot near the floating *Titanic* lifeboats. "Right about there. He was a floater."

"You ever see the man before?"

Morgan continued to scribble notes, making sure he got Call's questions as well as the answers. He was also careful to note any type of body movement or anything unusual in the way the man reacted.

"Nah, I ain't never seen him. They say he came in with all the people on the *Carpathia* last night, so he ain't from around here at all."

"They pulled in around 9:30," Call said. "Most of the dock was empty by 11:00. If he was killed close to midnight, he must have been easy to spot. How often do you come by this area on your beat?"

"About once every hour or so."

"And did you see anyone around the dock area here, anyone at all?"

Morgan watched the man as he nervously sucked a couple of times on his cigarette. He noticed that O'Toole looked over to where Rorke was standing. The big sergeant was watching them from a distance, but his eyes were trained on O'Toole.

O'Toole dropped his eyes to the ground and took another puff. "No, I didn't see nothing. It was raining last night, and folks didn't stay around. I would have seen anyone close by here, but I didn't see nobody."

"OK, thanks for your time. You best be getting home and getting some sleep."

Call nodded in Morgan's direction, and the two of them crossed the dock to a place that looked to be full of fish markets and pubs. "You get all that?" Call asked.

"Yes, I did, what little there was."

"What do you think?"

Morgan closed his notebook and dropped it and his pencil into his pocket. "To be honest with you, I don't know what to think. It seemed to me the man was lying, but I wouldn't know why he should."

"Some cops make a habit of lying to the press, but usually they're the ones in business suits and offices."

They walked across the street and pushed their way into the Brass Rail. Call stepped up and pushed a one-dollar bill across the polished bar. The bartender was gingerly waxing the bar with a soft yellow cloth.

"What'll it be, mate?"

"Just a few questions, that's all."

The bartender picked up the bill and shoved it into his pocket. He leaned down over the bar in Call's direction. "You a cop?"

"No, we're reporters, but anything you tell us won't be repeated."

"Fair enough."

"You have any seedy-looking customers come in after midnight last night?"

The man laughed. "Most all my customers look like that."

"You must have had a busy night, what with all that crowd waiting on the *Carpathia*."

"I did at that. The place was full, but after 11:00 or so it was quiet as a tomb. I own the place, and I was almost tempted to shut her down."

Morgan sauntered to the rear of the bar. The lights were dim. Many lamps were broken, their shattered sides allowing more illumination to escape from the chimneys. A slick green paint covered the weathered walls. In spots the paint was dabbed quite heavily to conceal the cracks, but it couldn't quite do the job.

He then noted the pictures hanging on the wall. Many of them were ships with one thing in common—they had all gone down in the Atlantic. He was sure the owner would find a spot for the *Titanic*. Other pictures were of lost and heroic seaman. It was plain to see that the Brass Rail humored seamen. It was equally obvious that the place was practically empty just now. It was just too early to drink, even for a drinking man.

He looked back and spotted the bartender now pouring a glass for Call. Maybe what they said about Call was right. Any man drinking at this hour undoubtedly had a serious drinking problem. For that type of man, liquor was more than recreation; it was mother's milk.

A large, yellow tabby, with a mouse in his teeth, crept out from behind a cracked open door. A man was growling. The cat catching his prey had obviously awakened the man. The big cat dropped the mouse to the floor between his paws and batted it, keeping his eyes riveted on the poor creature for any signs of life.

Morgan maneuvered around the cat and its helpless victim and stepped to the door, pushing it open. There on a cot was an unshaven man in an undershirt and a pair of brown corduroy trousers. His feet, stockinged in dirty white, hung over the end of the bed. "I'm sorry to disturb you."

The man groggily sat up, blinking his watery eyes in Morgan's direction.

"You work here?" Morgan asked.

"Yep. I'm the swamper. I clean up mostly at night for dis here bed and some supper. What da ya want?"

"I wanted to ask you a couple of questions. I hear that the place was empty after 11:00 last night."

The man swung his feet off the bed and bowed his head, sinking it into his open fingers. He rubbed his face vigorously. "Pretty much. We had some fellers come in past midnight, but that was all. It sure was a mess, though, from the earlier crowd, the folks waiting up fer them people off the *Titanic*."

"How many?"

The man stretched. "Hundreds."

"No, I mean the men who came in after midnight."

"Oh, three I seem to recollect."

"You know any of them?"

The man laughed, "Funny thing, that. One of them said O'Toole, the cop, sent them. But one of them, goes by the name of Bain, I've seen here aplenty."

Morgan scribbled notes furiously. "You see a knife on them?"

The man laughed. "Mister, everybody in the Brass Rail carries a knife."

"They stay long?"

The man shook his head. "Not long. They had a couple of drinks, laughing and such, then took on off. Left me and just Bud out there. He locked up and went upstairs to bed, and me, I jest finished my mopping and come on back here to sleep."

Morgan closed his notebook. "Thanks, you've been most helpful."

The man got to his feet. "You a cop?"

"No, just a reporter is all."

"Well, ain't ya gonna leave me nothing for my trouble?"

"Of course," Morgan said. "I'll leave it with Bud."

The man swatted lazily at the air. "I jest bet you will."

Morgan stepped out the door and made his way over to where Call was finishing his drink and laughing with the bartender.

"You solve that rat problem back there?" Call asked. The bartender sniggered.

"You might say that. You got a fifty-cent piece on you?"

Call's eyes widened. "Now you're borrowing money from me? If it's a beer you want, I'll buy you that."

"No, all I've got is a twenty-pound note."

"OK. But get yourself some money. This is the last from me."

Call reached into his pocket and slapped down the fifty-cent piece on the bar. Morgan pushed it over to the bartender. "Here, Bud, this is for the man in the back. I woke him up, I'm afraid."

The bartender looked puzzled, but he reached over and pulled the coin in his direction.

Morgan and Call walked out onto the dock.

"We better catch a taxicab," Call said, "or, on second thought, a streetcar for the Waldorf. I'd like to be there earlier so we can interview some of the survivors."

They started walking down the street. "You learn anything back there?"

"Oh, now you're asking me?"

"Yes, now I'm asking you. You satisfied?"

"Reporter to reporter?"

"I still haven't seen anything you've written, but yes, reporter to reporter."

"I learned that O'Toole was lying through his teeth. Bud the bartender too. The swamper back there said three men came in after midnight, and one of them said O'Toole sent them."

Call nodded.

"I learned something else too."

Call stopped and stared at him.

"The swamper knew one of the men, a regular, he said. He said the man's name was Bain."

CHAPTER 8

Morgan and Call stepped off the streetcar in front of the Waldorf and hurried through the crowd. Many of the people were rushing up the stairs, hoping to take their places before the hearings began in earnest. Women wore their best hats, feathers dancing on the tops of their heads as they walked, their dresses showing every movement of their bodies. It was a milling throng, and Call pulled out his press pass to stick in the brim of his hat. He pulled a second one out of his pocket and handed it to Morgan. "Hang on to this, boy. You'll have to show it a hundred times, which is why I keep mine where they can always see it."

Morgan smiled and handed it back. "You better keep it in case you lose yours." He reached into his pocket and produced a pass with his name on it. He'd already taken the trouble to thread a safety pin through the thing, and carefully he pinned it to the lapel of his gray day coat. "I picked this up before I reported to the office this morning."

"Good for you. You can think ahead."

Morgan smiled. "I've been thinking ahead since I put my first train set together." He pointed up the stairs to the glass doors. "Shall we get on with it?"

This time he was determined that Call would follow him. He took the big set of marble stairs two at a time, stopping at the top to open the door before the doorman could get in place. He smiled broadly and held the door open for Call, bowing low and sweeping his hand to the side with a big smile on his face.

"You're feeling your oats, aren't you, boy?"

"You bet I am." Morgan followed Call in the door. "I'm working at solving a murder, and I'm just about to write my first story, a story that will be on the front page with my name under it."

"Now what makes you so sure of that?"

"I'm the one who survived the sinking, aren't I? What good would it do for the *Herald* to feature a story written by a guy who stood on a chase boat?"

Call gave him a smug look, his lower lip pouting. "Just make sure it's readable, boy."

Morgan spotted Bruce Ismay surrounded by a group of lawyers and what appeared to be bodyguards. Ismay was fast becoming the heavy of the entire episode. The papers were roasting him. Being the highest ranking survivor of the White Star Line had its distinct disadvantages. Not only had he survived, but on the trip to New York, Ismay had taken the private quarters of the *Carpathia*'s doctor while others slept on deck. This didn't exactly make him the most popular figure among the survivors. Morgan stepped up to him, elbowing his way past two hardcases. "Mr. Ismay. It's me, Morgan Fairfield."

The man looked at Morgan, a sleepy distant look that showed his mind was preoccupied. He nodded at Morgan and turned to follow his lawyers into the hotel's crystal-chandeliered East Room.

Call reached out and grabbed a second man by the coattails. "Hey, Franklin." The man stopped. "Reporter for the *New York Herald*." Call dropped the man's jacket and pulled out his notebook, making ready with his pencil. "So, Mr. Franklin, can we expect the rest of the *Titanic* survivors shortly? Or maybe you've made repairs, and we'll soon see the ship itself pull into harbor."

Franklin squinted at Call. The small glasses perched on the end of his nose were held to his neck by a silver cord. The frown on his face dropped them to a spot alongside the middle of his vest. "You disgust me," he said. He then spun on his heels and followed Ismay and the cohort from the International Mercantile Marine Company into the hearing room.

Call turned his head and smirked at Morgan. "That was Philip Franklin, vice president of the White Star Line. We had many reports on your ship, and Franklin took it upon himself to constantly remind us that the *Titanic* was unsinkable. He told us all that damage was minor."

Call looked around at the stream of reporters. "Amazing to think of how many of these reporters actually believed him. Simply amazing. Never believe anything from the man with the most to lose."

Morgan and Call followed the mob and took their places in the packed, standing-room-only chamber. The room was jammed, and getting in wasn't an easy matter. Being at the Waldorf Astoria on that day had become a matter of public conscientiousness. Because so many of the city's elite had been lost or widowed, one didn't dare not to show up if one wanted the best of invitations.

Many of the spectators were members of New York's upper crust. They were all anxious to hear about the fate of many of their country club cronies. Those who didn't have relatives among the lost had friends or business associates. Even if they didn't have a direct association with someone listed among the dead, it would have been unseemly not to be there. What would people have thought? So they packed the place, with fans wagging to keep the small amount of air stirring in front of their faces.

Morgan took out his notebook and made his pencil ready to write. He knew he already had his story; still, he would sprinkle it with quotes from the morning's hearings.

The conference table in front held Senator William Alden Smith, a populist Republican senator from the landlocked state of Michigan. His long ringlets of brown hair were slickly curled behind his ears, and his blue eyes cast a steady gaze at the illustrious members of society gathering in front of his sudden sweep of power. It had been his impassioned speech in front of the senate the day after the sinking that had propelled him into this sudden prominence. The rest of the committee fanned out along the table on either side of him, the members from the two parties fairly even with the Republicans enjoying a slight advantage.

Smith banged his gavel on the table several times. "Order! Order! I'm calling this hearing to order."

There was a murmuring hush to the crowd. Obviously, everyone was enjoying the show.

Across from the committee was the table of initial witnesses. Bruce Ismay, the head of the White Star Line, was also the president of International Mercantile Marine Company, the White Star's American parent. J. P. Morgan had financed IMM, and Morgan knew full well that his great uncle's name would never come up at any time during the hearing, even though he was the owner—lock, stock, and barrel. Ismay had not only made certain that he wasn't on the *Titanic* at the time of its sailing, but he had made certain that he was removed from any noticeable responsibility for it.

How like Uncle J. P., Morgan thought. *He wants his hand in the till with his face out of the papers*.

Seated with Ismay was Franklin and the senior surviving officer from the *Titanic*, Second Officer Charles Lightoller. Lawyers from IMMC were spread out beside them, with the company's burly bodyguards forming bookends at the witness table. Ismay had received so much vilification from the American press that he no doubt thought them vital for his safety.

Senator Smith cleared his throat and, lifting a glass of water, took a drink. The massive, wall-length windows surrounded the politicians in front with a halo-like glow. It was like the bar of eternal judgment, with the man Ismay, nervously twirling his mustache, the sinner at question. "Will you kindly tell the committee the circumstances surrounding your voyage?" Smith asked.

Ismay remained seated but hunched forward in his chair. "First, I would like to express my sincere grief at this deplorable catastrophe."

Morgan edged his way through the crowd as Ismay droned on. He really had no desire to stay to listen to all of the testimony, especially to the whitewash that Ismay no doubt intended to speak. He was far more interested in the witnesses to follow, men who even now might be swapping stories in order to get them right. Being actually aboard the ship when it went down, he knew he could recognize fact from fiction.

He edged his way out the two huge doors. It felt good to be free from the crowd. Looking across the lobby, he saw someone he knew at once. It was Boxhall, the *Titanic*'s fourth officer. The man was talking to another member of the *Titanic*'s crew.

He started across and was halfway there before Boxhall recognized him. "Here, here, it's Fairfield," Boxhall said. He left the crewman he was talking to and rushed to meet Morgan. "I wasn't sure if I'd ever see you again."

Morgan hugged the man, both of them slapping each other on the back. He pushed him back. "You look fine in your new uniform."

Boxhall laughed. "Well, I can't say the same for you. That's the same outfit I saw you wearing on the *Carpathia*."

Morgan looked down. "Yes, I know. Shabby business, isn't it? I haven't had time to look for more. I'm going to wire my uncle for some of my trust money so I can do a little shopping." Morgan held out his feet. "The shoes are even a little bit too big for me. Feel more like slippers, they do."

"I had to get dressed up for the charade in here today," Boxhall said.

Morgan bobbed his head in the direction he'd come from. "I was just in there. Made me sick to listen to the start of the thing. What are you going to say?"

"Anything they ask me."

Morgan smiled. "Who's *they*?"

"The White Star Line, of course." Boxhall smiled. "You don't think I was speaking of those American politicians, do you?"

"No, I suppose not. I am going to need your help, though."

"My help? Why my help?"

"Hunter's murder, of course. I'll fill you in on what more I know of it, but I'm a crime reporter now. I may need you to come to the police with me just to prove there was a murder."

"You do have Margaret, don't you, old man?"

"Her mother seems determined to take her back to England as soon as possible."

"I'll do what I can for you. But right now I'm White Star property, and I can't begin to tell you the extent of how far that goes. The American press have been butchering us. You'd think we sank our own ship deliberately. By the by, did you manage to get away with that attaché case you were given?"

Morgan knew Boxhall could only be referring to the satchel the dying man had given him in England just before the *Titanic* sailed. Boxhall knew about it but had little idea of its contents. Only Hunter Kennedy had seen that. The contents were important, however, and should have gone to the American War Department. "No, I'm afraid not. It went down with the *Titanic*. Why do you ask?"

"Some bloke from the American Secret Service was asking me questions about it. He'd heard that somehow I was involved in security matters aboard ship and came to me. I did give him your name, so you ought to be hearing from him."

"Oh, fine, I suppose I'll have to get involved now." Morgan shook his head. "As if I didn't have enough on my hands. They'll probably ship me off to Washington. Let me ask you, Boxhall, do you know an engineer for the *Titanic* by the name of Fetters, Jeremy Fetters?"

"Yes, I know Fetters, sturdy man that one. I'm surprised I haven't seen him here."

"And you won't either. He's a dead man now. They found his body floating near the *Titanic* lifeboats this morning."

"Suicide?"

"Hardly. Somebody stabbed him last night."

Boxhall shook his head. "Bloody shame. He came from the *Olympic* with Wilde. The two of them seemed to be close, which was a mite unusual."

"Why is that?"

"There's a long way between a ship's chief officer and an engineer, old man. I wouldn't expect you to understand, but take it from me, it was unusual."

"Can you think of anyone who might want to see him dead?"

"A robber, I suppose."

"I doubt that. You forget, like the rest of us who came in on the *Carpathia*, the man was broke as a tinker's purse." The reminder of how broke he was caused Morgan to look down at his wrinkled coat. It hung on him as an overcoat would on a scarecrow. Many of the men who, like Morgan, had been in the water were forced to acquire clothing on the *Carpathia* that were either hand-me-downs from the crew or from the passengers. Morgan didn't know where his coat had come from, but it was plain that it had seen better days.

He ran his hands down the lapels of his coat. "I think I'd better do some shopping. Then maybe we can have lunch."

Boxhall pointed to a stairway that led to the floor below. "I hear there are shops down there. I'm sure they have one with men's clothing."

"OK. I'll do it. I mean"—he looked down at his baggy trousers and, grabbing the sides of the legs, gave them a sharp tug—"this is pathetic."

"Where shall we meet?"

Morgan pointed across the lobby to where a bank of typewriters had been set up for the press under the stairs. "Why don't you come get me there? I've got a story to do, and it has to be good."

"Oh, I'm sure it will be. You better get off with you, old man. I'll mix a bit and get back to you in an hour or so."

Morgan started toward the stairs, waving his hand over his head. "Just pray they let me in. I might be far too shabby to be seen in their store."

A little over an hour later, the hearing broke for lunch and Morgan had completed his shopping. He was overjoyed at having on a pair of shoes that actually fit along with a new blue suit and white shirt. They felt good. Without giving the first thought to the whereabouts of Call, he found a typewriter and busily pounded out the first of his articles on the *Titanic*. He knew full well that most people would want to hear about the ship's collision with the berg, and that was just what he was writing. With heavy strokes he hit the keys. He knew his story had to be right and be right the first time. It not only had to make sense, but it had to sound American. That would be the hardest part.

Morgan fully expected that the next words he would hear would be Call's sarcastic voice asking him why he hadn't finished the article. Instead, he heard the sound of Boxhall's voice before he ever saw him. He continued to tap out the last of his article until Boxhall put his hand on his shoulder and shook him.

"Fetters, the engineer," Boxhall said.

Morgan stopped his typing and looked back at the man. Boxhall had a curious look on his face, as if someone had just ice-skated over his foot on dry ground. It was a painful expression mixed with curiosity. "Yes," Morgan said, "Fetters."

Boxhall shook his head. "I've been thinking about him ever since you told me he'd been killed."

Morgan turned around in his chair.

Boxhall shook his finger in Morgan's direction. "You know, the last time I saw Wilde he said something about Fetters and something very curious."

"What was that?"

"He asked me if I'd seen Fetters, and I told him no. He had a ghostly look on his face." Morgan noticed that Boxhall was getting more animated as he told the story. "Of course, this was after the order had been given to lower the lifeboats. You have to remember, people say and do muddled things during a scare." Boxhall went on. "It was something I pushed out of my mind until now. I just counted it as panic."

"What was it?"

Boxhall put both hands on Morgan's shoulders. "Wilde shook me and told me to tell Fetters that the *Olympic* was going down."

Morgan pushed his pencil behind his ear and forced Boxhall's arms away. "What did he mean by that?"

"I don't know, but now Fetters is dead and so is Wilde. Both of them served on the *Olympic*. We never knew why they were transferred at the last moment, and Wilde's being aboard bumped all the officers down a notch. Instead of being the third officer, I became the fourth." Boxhall shook his head. "Strange what people say when they know they're dying, isn't it?"

Morgan gulped. "Yes, strange."

CHAPTER 9

Call, one of the last people to leave, came sauntering out of the hearing room. The lobby was a buzz of activity and noise; conversations were lost in the din of raised male voices. Women huddled arm in arm, talking quietly about what they had observed and craning their necks to see whether certain people had bothered to come. Call, along with several other reporters, quizzed Lightoller. It was plain to see, however, that he didn't like the answers he was getting. He closed his notebook and frowned. Looking around, he caught sight of Morgan and went hurrying over. "You got that story yet?" he asked.

"Finishing it up now." Morgan picked up the first page of copy and handed it over for Call to read. "By the way, this is the *Titanic*'s fourth officer, Joseph Boxhall."

Call gave the man a glance, took the page, and began to read.

"We were just planning to go to lunch," Morgan went on.

Call looked up. "That'll have to wait. You and I have another call to pay during the lunch hour."

"Where would that be?"

Call pointed to the typewriter. "Just finish your story, and let me worry about that."

Morgan turned back to the typewriter. "Boxhall here knows all about the murders on the *Titanic*," Morgan said over his shoulder. "He can verify what I have to say."

That caught Call's attention. He put down the first page of Morgan's story and turned his attention to Boxhall.

"You know about murders on the *Titanic*?"

Boxhall gulped. "Yes, I do. I don't really know what I'm allowed to say about them, though."

"What do you mean, 'what you're allowed to say'?"

"I haven't cleared anything with the White Star offices."

"Just tell me the truth. Has the truth been cleared by your office?"

Boxhall smiled. "Some of it has."

"Which part? You're not saying anything to the gentlemen in the room over there. Why can't you tell us? Was Morgan here right about there being murders aboard before you hit the iceberg?"

Boxhall looked at Morgan as Morgan continued to type. "Yes, you could say so."

"And what would you say?"

"It hasn't been investigated yet."

"That's what we're doing—investigating it."

"Yes, but you're the press." Boxhall leaned down over Morgan's shoulder. "It looks like you've got plans for lunch. I best be shoving off. I'll see you around this afternoon, I hope."

Before Morgan could respond, Boxhall rushed off across the lobby and toward the main doors. Morgan pulled the last page out of the typewriter and turned around, handing it to Call. "There, satisfied?"

Call picked up the pages and put the last one in place. He glanced at Morgan. "Your friend isn't talking."

Morgan glanced over to where Boxhall was scurrying out the door. "He will. You'll see."

"I hope so. Few people will take the word of just a reporter. You'll find that out soon enough."

It took Call a short time to finish reading Morgan's first installment in the series intended for the *Herald*'s front page. Both of them knew it had to be not only strikingly effective but well done. Morgan watched him read, watched every gesture and every grimace. Finally, Call lowered the pages and looked Morgan in the eye.

"Well?" Morgan asked.

"It'll read."

"Is it good?"

Call signaled to a copyboy standing nearby; he picked up a brown envelope; and, scribbling Dixon's name on it, handed it over to the youngster. "Get this to the city editor right now!" he barked. The boy turned on his heels and ran for the door.

"You didn't answer me. Is it good?"

Call got to his feet and slung his overcoat over his shoulders. "I said it will read. You may not win any award over that one, but you show promise. What more do you want to hear?"

Morgan got to his feet and buttoned his new jacket. "Nothing. If it suits you, it suits me."

It was a little less than a half hour and a taxi ride later when they walked up the steps to police headquarters. Morgan followed Call through the halls as policemen greeted Call by name. Some smiled while others frowned. It was obvious that he was no stranger to the New York men in blue. He stopped and asked several questions about the case of Jeremy Fetters. The last man pointed down the hall, and Call took off like a shot. Morgan was at his heels.

Call knocked on the door with the words CAPTAIN CASEY CONNOR blazed across the smoky glass that used to be a window. Without waiting for an answer, he pushed it open. "Captain Connor, I understand you're heading up the investigation into the *Titanic* seaman found this morning."

The captain was a big man with broad shoulders and neatly slicked black hair. A part that looked like the man had used a knife was cut in the top. It left a white streak of bald head down the middle with two shiny cascades of jet black hair plastered to his scalp. Two uniformed officers were standing by his side, obviously engaging him in conversation.

Waving a pudgy hand in Call's direction, he tried to shoo him away. "Can't you see I'm too busy to talk with the likes of you?"

Call held up both hands. "Fine, fine, have it your way." He started to back away. "It just so happens, though, that we have something that might interest you."

"There's nothing you could have that would interest me unless you want to bring the killer in."

"We just might be able to do that in another day or so."

Morgan watched the man's expression change. He cocked his head slightly and squinted in Call's direction. "Is this more of your blarney?"

"It's no joke, my man. We may have some good leads. And we were hoping to get some from you."

Connor looked up at the two policemen. "You can belay all this business till I finish with these reporters here."

The two cops stared at Call and Morgan and reluctantly brushed them aside as they stepped out the door.

Connor waved his hands in a forward motion. "Come on in, then. I ain't got all day, but I'll hear you out. Come on in and have a seat."

Call stepped in and took a chair beside the man's desk while Morgan sat farther away on an old leather couch. The couch was so saggy that Morgan thought how it might take extra effort just to get out.

"This is a new reporter of ours, Connor—Morgan Fairfield. He was a survivor on the *Titanic*. Came in last night on the *Carpathia*."

"You boys never give a man any rest, do you?" Connor asked.

"Not when they have a good story we don't. Fairfield here claims to know of murders that took place on the *Titanic* before they hit the berg."

"Oh, is that so?" Connor smiled. It was a type of smile that one would use to keep a child entertained. His smooth shaved face and lantern jaw showed a perfect set of white teeth, except for one gold tooth in the middle. "And who, pray tell, met their fate before God said it was time for all the rest?"

"There were several," Morgan said. "We found out the IRA was involved. They tried to blow up the ship."

Connor chuckled. "The IRA, is it? They seem to be guilty of everything. I shouldn't be surprised if someone came in here and told me they killed Cock Robin, too, and were responsible for pushing Humpty Dumpty off his wall."

"I'm afraid this time they found a prime target," Morgan said, "all those rich Englishmen bobbing about in the Atlantic. And think about what it might do to English shipping interests."

Connor pointed his finger at Morgan. "You might have a point there, son." He pulled out a sheet of paper and began taking notes. Looking up, he smiled at Call. "You might have a bright boy working for you now, Call. I always felt you could use some help in the thinking department. What did you say this boy's name is?"

"Morgan Fairfield, but that's another murder, another time," Call said. "We'd like to find out just what you know about this Fetters business."

"Not much I'm afraid." Connor sat back. "The man was killed around midnight, and from what we can see it appeared to be a robbery."

"The crew were flat broke when they left Southampton," Morgan said. "They were due to be paid when they got to New York."

Connor grinned, his gold tooth sparkling. "Well, now, maybe we have some local hoodlums hereabouts who don't know much about the man's pay schedule." He shrugged his shoulders. "They see a sailor and take him for an easy mark. Most are just looking for drink money." He looked down and wrote more notes on his paper. "I'll keep that in mind, though." Glancing back up at Call, he smiled. "Like I say, maybe you got a thinker here, Call."

"What can you tell us about the beat cop who found the body, this O'Toole?" Call asked.

"Nothing much. Good man. Been on the force four years. He does his job. Walks his beat. Makes a good number of pinches and goes home to a wife and three kids."

"How long has he been in America?" Call asked.

Connor seemed startled by the question. He blinked his brown eyes and scooted forward in the chair. "Why would you ask a silly question like that?"

"Just curious, that's all. We can find out from the immigration people if we have to."

Connor gave off a grunt that rippled his lower lip. "I'm not rightly sure about that. It may be six years or better."

"And he's a member in good standing of New York's finest already."

"We take good men wherever we can find them. Now tell me, what's your interest in this thing?"

"I am a crime reporter, and this most definitely is a crime. Morgan was on the *Titanic*, and anything having to do with that piques our interest considerably."

"And what might you know about it?"

Call looked back at Morgan. "I can tell you one thing, our young protégé here discovered that the man who killed Fetters was left-handed."

"Is that so? And what makes you so sure of that?"

Call smiled. "Let's just call it good police work."

Connor stared at Morgan. "It would seem we do have a lot to learn from you, young man. I am interested in what you have to say about the *Titanic* too. It seems to be quite the hot subject these days."

Morgan started to speak, but Call cut him off. "That will have to wait for another day, Captain. We've got a killer on the loose here."

Call got to his feet and Morgan, with a great deal more difficulty, got to his.

"And where might we find you two if we come across more information?" Connor asked.

Call pulled out a card and dropped it on his desk. "Morgan's staying at the Waldorf."

"The Waldorf? They must be paying you boys pretty well for you to come up with digs like that."

Connor followed Call and Morgan to the door. He put his hand on Morgan's shoulder. "So you're the new guy," he said.

"Yes, I am."

Connor laughed. "And Call here is showing you the ropes, I gather."

Morgan forced a smile. "Yes, he is."

"Well, some of my men just might take you with them and show you what really happens on the streets of New York. Give you something that won't have to be spoon-fed to you."

"I'd like that," Morgan said.

"Good." Connor slapped him on the back. "I'll see to it. Always pays to do you boys a favor. We scratch your backs and maybe you'll scratch ours, eh?"

Morgan nodded.

They walked down the hall, and Call pulled Morgan aside. "O'Toole's an Irish immigrant."

Morgan looked puzzled.

"There's a waiting list for men to get on the New York City police force. It might be interesting to find out just how long Mr. O'Toole had to wait."

CHAPTER 10

Margaret waited patiently for her mother for a short time and then began to pace the floor. She lifted the small, heart-shaped watch that hung around her neck and looked at it. Then she began to wear a path in the carpet, retracing her steps over and over.

April called out to her from behind the dressing room door. "Dear, if you're hungry, you can eat one of those sandwiches we had sent up. It's going to be a long day, you know."

Margaret stepped over to the table and lifted the top to the silver tray. She picked up a small, chicken-salad sandwich that had the edges of the crust cut off and held it to her mouth. "I'm worried about the time, Mother. I'd like to get there early." With that, she took a bite out of the sandwich and patted the corners of her mouth with the napkin.

April strutted into the room, busily fastening the last of her pearl ear-bobs. The dress she had just bought for the occasion was a pale green one that wound up her waist and then blossomed up to her neck in lacy covered tumbles. "Ladies don't arrive at the theater early, my dear. It just isn't done. I wouldn't think of standing around and trying to make conversation with total strangers or ushers. Haven't I taught you better than that?"

Margaret set down the sandwich, only one bite missing from the smooth, buttery bread. "I need to talk to this man calling himself Hunter Kennedy."

April fastened the earbob and shook her head slightly to see if it held in place. "Why, my dear? If the man chooses to appear in the theater, what concern is that to you?"

"Because Hunter Kennedy, the Hunter Kennedy we both knew on the boat, is dead. If this man claims to be Hunter Kennedy, then that is a bold lie."

"Perhaps he survived, just as the advertisement claims."

"Mother, the last time I saw him he was dead, very dead. There is simply no way this man and the man we knew are the same."

"And what do you propose to do about it?"

"I don't know. But I do think the theater company should be made aware of this hoax."

April walked over to the sofa and picked up the small, lacy parasol she had purchased to go with her outfit. She opened and closed it several times to once again make sure it was in proper working order. "I don't see how you can do anything of the sort, my dear. We'll simply sit there and watch the performance like ladies. You'll have your curiosity satisfied, and then we will come back and enjoy the evening in the restaurant. I'm tired of living in here like a trapped animal."

"And what about the reporters?"

Placing the parasol back on the couch, April once again returned to the mirror. "We will have the waiter shoo the despicable beasts away so that we can enjoy our dinner."

"I did ask Gloria Thompson to accompany us. She'll be able to recognize a fraud the same as we would."

April smiled, but Margaret knew she wasn't happy about the company. Any reminder that Margaret was going to remain behind was something she'd rather do without.

"Wonderful," April said. "Then I can leave her instructions on what to do with you."

"You mean on who to keep me away from."

April stood in front of the full-length mirror and busied herself with positioning the sweeping brim of her new white hat. She made minor adjustments to make certain it stayed in just the right spot before pushing the long hat pins into position. "I only want to make certain that you are well occupied, my dear."

"And that my heart is unoccupied."

April turned around suddenly and shook her gloved finger. "You have just lost a fiancé. To be seen with another man would be unseemly."

"Especially Morgan Fairfield."

April put her hands on her hips. "You can take that any way you want."

"You forget, Mother, that if it hadn't been for Morgan I wouldn't be here at all."

April nodded. "I'm well aware of that, and I'm very grateful, but that doesn't mean that he's capable of caring for you for the rest of your life. What kind of life would it be for you to be married to some grimy, newspaper reporter?"

Margaret was glad a knock at the door stopped her from saying what was on her mind. The days of her life being managed by another were over, and she knew it even if her mother didn't. She marched across the room and opened the door. "There you are. Please come in."

Gloria stepped into the room. It took her only one look at Margaret to know that she was upset. "I hope I'm not interrupting anything."

"Why, of course not," April said. "Margaret was just all unhinged over not getting to the theater early. Please come in. I'm just fixing my hat." With that, she shoved in the final hat pin. "There, now we can go."

The three women made their way down to the lobby. The place was a flurry of people waiting turns to gain admittance into the hearing room for the afternoon session. It was as if the world had stopped in its tracks awaiting a final word on the *Titanic*. Heads bobbed trying to see the front of the crowd, and outside the line grew ever more intense.

"Goodness me, this is a disaster," April said.

"I think we've made it through the real disaster," Gloria said. "I should think we'd take anything compared to the North Atlantic."

April put her hands to her ears. "But it's so noisy."

Gloria looked at Margaret. "Will you ever be able to forget the sound of all those people in the water? I know I can't. It was the most ghastly sound on earth, like the cry of all of history for salvation."

Margaret shook her head. "And women sat in the boats, each woman pretending the sound was somebody else's husband."

"Must we talk about this now?" April asked.

Spotting a doorman, Margaret asked him to hail them a taxi. It was a matter of minutes before it pulled up and then but a short time later when it deposited them on the curb outside the Grand Theater. The three women got out, smoothing their dresses from the ride.

"Here, I'll buy the tickets," Margaret said.

The two women watched her take her place in line.

"I understand my daughter is to become your companion."

"For a short while. Unlike the two of us, she lost someone on that ship. I think the experience has been devastating for her."

"Not quite devastating enough, perhaps."

"What do you mean?"

"She still has this childhood fancy for one of the survivors."

"You mean Morgan Fairfield?"

"Yes. It's always been a rather frivolous thing. You know how a young girl's head can be turned against her own best interests."

"Or her greatest happiness at times."

April's eyes narrowed. "This is not the case with Margaret. I would appreciate it if you kept her occupied while she is here. Her father and I have never approved of this infatuation of hers. The truth is, she should have been married years ago to a man with a future rather than pining away for this childhood chum. And she almost was, had it not been for . . ."

"The *Titanic?*"

"Yes, that ghastly ship *Titanic*."

Gloria smiled. "Mrs. Hastings, I'm afraid that disaster took the lives of over fifteen hundred people. It would seem that far more has been lost than the plans for your daughter."

Margaret returned with the tickets in hand, for the moment sparing her mother further embarrassment. "I got good seats for us in the orchestra section."

April put her hands to her ears. "Mercy, no, how will I ever hear again?"

"I hear the music is fun," Gloria said.

The three women took their programs and filed into the theater, walking across red and yellow Oriental carpet. Curtains hung from the ceiling to the floor and spread out along the walls. The doors and walls seemed to be held up with golden angels, their wings holding the papered wood in place. Overhead was a series of crystal chandeliers, each one seemingly as large as the taxicab they had taken to get there. Margaret presented their tickets to the uniformed usher, a man in tight, off-white breeches, a red velvet tunic, and a pillbox cap jauntily cocked on his head.

He quickly led them to their seats, which were prominently situated in the second row. It would give them a good view of the man purporting to be Hunter Kennedy. Margaret could hardly wait.

Margaret read the program and the cast of characters, her eyes falling on the name of Hunter Kennedy. From everything she read, it would seem that the man she would watch perform the role of the captain of the *Pinafore* would be the same man she and Morgan had come to know and love. The program made a special point of noting that this Hunter Kennedy was recently arrived from England, having survived the sinking of the *Titanic*.

The crowd filled in around the women, and in a few short minutes the orchestra struck up a collection of the bombastic tunes that would make this such a special performance. The lights dimmed and the curtain rose, revealing what was to look like an English warship. The women sat in silence as the band played and the chorus sang.

It was some time later that Margaret first spotted the actor in his captain's garb. At first Margaret blinked. The man looked remarkably like Hunter. His red hair and dashing blue eyes were the spitting image of the man. The beard gave him away, however. It was close-cropped, hugging the sharp, chiseled features of his face, and neatly trimmed. Even at a distance, anyone could tell that the Hunter Kennedy she had known would never have been able to grow such a beard in only a few short days.

When the man took center stage and began to sing, Gloria looked over at Margaret. "Quite a likeness, isn't he?"

Margaret nodded silently.

"I am the Captain of the *Pinafore* and a right good captain too," the man sang, his voice carrying into the rafters. "And be it understood I command a very good, a very, very, very, good crew."

The chorus joined in, much to the delight of the audience—all of the audience, that is, except the three ladies.

When the final curtain rang down, Margaret was on her feet, heading to go behind the stage area. She was making her way out the door when the actors came on stage for their final bows. Had April been seated next to her, instead of Gloria, she knew without doubt that April would have tried to stop her. As it was, Margaret rushed past the usher and out the door before either April or Gloria knew she had gone.

"Where do I go to get behind the stage?" She asked the question to a man wearing a black bowler. The man was sitting on a stool next to the cashier's window. He had a build that filled out his shirt in the right proportions, a dapper mustache, and shining dark eyes. She could almost read his thoughts as he smiled.

"You a relative?" he asked.

"Yes. I know Hunter Kennedy. I wanted to offer him my congratulations."

"I'm the manager here, and normally we don't let the audience in to see the actors. They are a bunch of rogues, you know."

Margaret nodded. "Yes, I suspect so."

"But in your case I'll make an exception." The man pointed to a black door behind one of the hanging curtains in the lobby. "Go through that door and turn right when you can't go any farther."

Margaret thanked the man and opened the door, hurrying along the dark corridor. Several caged lights with pink bulbs cast an eerie glow along the black walls. When she got to the back wall, the hall made an abrupt turn to the right. She followed it to the area behind the curtains where it finally opened behind the stage.

Actors and actresses were laughing and running seemingly everywhere. There were smiles all around, and Margaret thought they were obviously pleased. She grabbed one of the stagehands, a young man with his shirtsleeves rolled up. "Where might I find Mr. Kennedy's dressing room?"

"Come on. I'll show you." The man took her by the arm and led her behind another set of curtains. He pointed to a number of doors. "His is the third one down." Smiling at her, he said, "Good luck."

Margaret hurried past several actors who were loudly talking. Stopping by the door the stagehand had indicated, she gave it several loud knocks.

"Come on in," the voice behind the door shouted. "I'm still dressed."

Margaret turned the knob and, stepping in, closed it behind her. She stood for a moment with her back to the door, watching the man as he stared at a mirror and scrubbed his face.

"Can I help you?" The man turned around and saw her. "Well, well, I hope I can help you." He got up from his stool. "You're a lovely thing, you are."

Margaret took a hard swallow. "Thank you. I enjoyed your performance very much."

"Here, here, let's not stand on ceremony." He motioned to the couch. "Please have a seat."

Timidly, Margaret slunk over to the couch and sat down. Much to her amazement the man swooped in right next to her, extending his arm over the couch and onto her shoulder, fingering her dress. "I say, have we met before? Are you a fan?"

"Yes, I enjoy the theater, but no, we've never met."

He smiled, his blue eyes dancing. "Well, there are many women drawn to actors. Must be something about the smell of the greasepaint, I should wonder."

"I thought you performed well." Margaret edged herself away from him. "And after such a harrowing experience, it must have been difficult."

"Yes, the *Titanic*. That was quite the ride, eh what?"

Margaret noticed a number of newspapers stacked on top of a table beside the couch. No doubt the man had been reading about the disaster. "I should think that will give you quite the publicity, given the fact that you're playing in the *Pinafore*."

"I certainly hope so. What with all the hubbub, we can use all the press we can get."

Margaret was staring hard at him. He did have a remarkable likeness to the Hunter Kennedy she had known. "And how ever did you survive?"

"Ah, there's the rub. There's times a man gets himself into a pickle and doesn't know which end is up. But a body has to have his wits about him at all times."

"I have a friend who's a newspaper reporter. I'm certain he'd love to do a story on you."

"Really, now?"

Margaret was certain that his initial glee at the idea of being a *Titanic* survivor might fill him with a sense of dread at the notion of being discovered to be a fraud. What might seem like good publicity just as easily might backfire.

"That would be wonderful."

His response shocked her.

"How could we set that up?"

The door to the dressing room opened. The manager from whom Margaret had gotten directions poked his head in the door. "I see you found him."

"Yes, thank you."

Kennedy motioned for the man to step into the room. "Do you know this beautiful creature?"

The manager walked in, his hand flicking some lint from one of his lapels. "I just met her in the lobby. She said she was looking for you."

"The young lady has a friend in the press. She says he might want to do a story on me and the play."

"Splendid. That does sound marvelous. Did you tell her about the party for the cast tonight? Maybe that would be a good time for it."

Kennedy picked up a scrap of paper and scribbled an address on it. He handed it to Margaret. "Here you are, my dear. It's the Big Top, and it's right around the corner from the theater here. The party's at 10:30. Do you think you can make it?"

Margaret eyed the paper and wadded it up in her hand. She looked up at him and smiled. "Nothing could keep me away."

"That's capital!" Kennedy exclaimed.

"I should be going now, though," she said. "My mother's waiting for me in the lobby."

"Will you be bringing your mother?" Kennedy asked.

"I should say not."

He put his hand to her shoulder. "That's probably best. We'll keep late hours, probably too late for her."

"What about your reporter friend?" the manager asked.

Margaret smiled. "Oh, he'll be there. You can count on that."

CHAPTER 11

Having endured the afternoon's testimony alongside Call, Morgan lay on his bed. It had been a long day following a night with very little sleep. He doubted if he'd had more than a few hours sleep while on the *Carpathia*. Lying on a blanket on the cold, rolling deck was something that didn't provide for a great deal of rest, and while Ismay may have made out superbly in the ship's doctor's stateroom, it was doubtful that any of the other *Titanic* survivors had rested quite so well. He pitched on the bed, furiously fighting to find some rest in the late afternoon. The sound of loud knocking on his door finally roused him. He sat up slowly and rubbed his eyes. "Who is it?"

He heard the sound of laughter behind the door. "It's the police."

Morgan eased his legs from the bed. They felt like iron. "All right. Hang on. I'll be right there."

He slowly got to his feet and tramped across the room to the locked door. Turning the lock, he opened it.

A man in a wrinkled brown suit stood at the door alongside a uniformed officer. The man in the suit tipped his beaten hat. "I'm Sergeant Ryan, and this is Officer Walsh. The captain sent us to fetch you."

Morgan backed into the room, followed by the two officers. "Whatever for? Have I done something wrong?"

Ryan laughed. "No, nothing wrong. The captain said you were a new crime reporter. He said if we got on to something to come and fetch you."

"Captain Connor?"

"One and the same. He said you were staying here." Ryan shot a glance at Walsh and smiled. "We didn't quite believe it. I mean, a reporter in the Waldorf Astoria. But we checked at the desk, and here you were. Oh, by the way, they had a message left for you there. I'm to deliver it."

He handed the folded note, which was written on Waldorf stationery, to Morgan. When he opened it, he recognized Margaret's handwriting right away. It read:

> Dear Morgan, I must see you tonight. Very important. Meet me at the front desk at 10:30 tonight and I will take you to see Hunter Kennedy.
>
> Margaret

Morgan stuck the note deep in his pants pocket. "What time is it?"

Officer Walsh opened his silver pocket watch. "It's just after 6:00."

"In the morning?"

The men both laughed.

"No," Walsh said. "In the evening."

Morgan walked over to the drapes and pulled them aside. Dusk was settling over the city, and streetlights were casting faint, pale yellow glows. For a moment he thought he had slept through the night. He probably should have. As it was, he had been asleep for only an hour and a half. He leaned against the window. "Good. I'm so tired, I thought I'd been sleeping all night."

"The night is young," Ryan said. "Hasn't even started yet, actually."

"Just give me a minute, then," Morgan said. He walked over to where his coat was hanging on the back of a chair and quickly put it on and straightened his tie. Stepping over to the vanity, he looked in the mirror. He dipped both hands in the basin and splashed water on his face.

"You won't be needing to look too good for where we're going," Ryan said.

"Nah, you sure won't," Walsh agreed.

Morgan stretched. He noticed Ryan looking at his watch, perhaps trying to make certain it agreed with his partner's.

"We'd better get moving along," Ryan said. "It doesn't pay to be late for these things."

Ryan had the look of a hardened cop dressed up in a suit. To any casual onlooker, he would have still been a cop, either that or a thug. The man, his suit tugging at the seams, was of sturdy build. His brown hair crept down from under the sides of his hat, and his sharp brown eyes were given to boring into a man. He was clean shaved except for a pencil-thin mustache that was barely noticeable at a distance.

Walsh was taller, rather lanky, Morgan thought. His uniform looked freshly pressed and his shoes shined. The badge on his chest was radiant with the glow of fresh silver polish. Dark muttonchop whiskers curled down almost to his chin.

"Where are we going?" Morgan asked.

"You want crime, don't you?" Ryan asked. "Don't you have to see crime in order to report it?"

"Yes, of course."

"Then we better be off," Ryan said. He opened the door and held it open for Morgan.

Morgan walked out, closing the door after him.

"Aren't you going to lock it?" Walsh asked.

Morgan shrugged. "Why? Anything of value that I have right now is on me."

The three of them headed down the stairs, Ryan explaining what they were doing on their way to the lobby. "We got a tip that a group of bank robbers are making a split tonight. It's our chance to catch them all, and with the money too." He turned and pressed his finger in Morgan's chest. "And it's your chance to report the story—as it happens. Sound good to you?"

"Almost too good to be true."

"Well, it's true all right," Walsh added.

The three men crossed the lobby and spun their way out of the heavy glass revolving door. Within moments they were on the street, with Morgan doing his best to keep pace with the two policemen. Their pace was fast, and in the twenty minutes or so that followed the start of their walk, Morgan could feel the blood once again returning to his legs. He was just getting his second wind when the men turned down a dark side street.

It was plain to see that they were no longer in the fashionable district that made up the Waldorf's neighborhood. The street was dark, and the wooden houses that were on either side of it were terribly in need of paint. They approached a brownstone building, and Ryan brought them to a halt. "This is it. They're on the third floor."

"How did you find out about this?" Morgan asked.

Ryan brought his face close to Morgan's. "We got ourselves a right good snitch. He does us a favor from time to time, and we do our best to keep him outa prison. He thinks it's a fair exchange, and, in times like this, we tend to agree."

"Will he be there?" Morgan asked.

"I rather doubt it. More than likely the man will keep himself as far away as possible, given what we're about to do tonight."

"Shouldn't you have more men?"

Ryan pulled out a revolver. "Why? We're both armed. They no doubt don't have more on them than a couple of sharp knives and a skeleton key. It'll be fine. You're perfectly safe."

He looked at Walsh. "You go 'round to the fire ladder, Walsh. Mr. Fairfield and I will take the front door."

Walsh gave a tip of his cap and ran around to the alley. Morgan could hear his shoes on the polished cobblestones as he was getting into position.

"Are you up to this, Fairfield?"

Morgan could feel his heart beating faster. It was something he couldn't say no to, however. Not if he wanted to remain on the job as a crime reporter. "I'm ready."

"Good man." Ryan swatted him on the back. "You just follow me."

As Morgan headed up the first flight of stairs, he could imagine what Call would say the following morning when he handed him his story.

The very fact that he was going to be a part of the capture of desperate men was far removed from just coming along after the fact and making sure all the names were spelled correctly.

He followed Ryan quietly up the stairs, although he didn't know why. The walls seemed to be paper thin, and he could have sworn that he was hearing three different conversations all at once, one of them punctuated by yells and a woman's screams. He slid his hand over the wallpaper to keep his balance on the rickety stairs. The walls were rough and peeling. One section on the stairs above had broken through the floor. The wooden stays that held up the stairs were drooping almost head high to where he was standing. He ducked under them.

He followed Ryan around the corner of the second-story hall and onto the stairs above. The man had his gun out. It gave Morgan a start. If this was as safe as he said, what was the need for a firearm?

Ryan looked back in his direction. "You with me?"

Morgan nodded.

They made their way up the stairs, pausing partway to step around the section that had broken through. Morgan slunk next to the wall where Ryan had stepped. If the stairs held him up, Morgan was sure that he could make it. He stepped lightly past the break in the floor and then onto the section that Ryan had passed over. If the robbers weren't dangerous, the stairs could just as easily kill a man.

They got to the landing on the third floor, and Ryan paused. "Their room is at the end of the hall. We'll go up to it and tell them they're under arrest. That ought to give you plenty to write about. We've been after these people for weeks now. They hold up stores. You all right?"

"I'm fine. Let's get on with it."

"Attaboy. Let's do it."

Morgan moved behind Ryan past several noisy rooms. When they got to the end of the hall, Ryan once again called a halt in front of the door. The door was a bleached orange around the panels and had a crack in it the width of a quarter. "That ought to be no problem to break down, ya think?"

"I shouldn't think so," Morgan whispered.

"Good man." Ryan shook his shoulder. "You'll do all right." He looked to his left at a peeling green door. "Let me check this side door. It leads to the back of the end apartment in these places."

Stepping over to the door, Ryan twisted the knob. Surprisingly, it opened. He skulked inside and into the darkness.

Morgan stood at the door and listened to the men inside. They were laughing, and one of them asked for the time. Morgan knew full well that desperate men like this were often filled with as much bravado as they were filled with liquor. He only hoped they were also filled with enough common sense to come quietly.

When Ryan stepped back into the hall, Morgan signaled him over. "There seems to be three or four men in there. Shouldn't we have help?"

"Nah, no need for that. We're going to hit them from both sides. They'll give up the ghost pretty quick that way."

"Two sides?"

"Yeah. I'm going in there, through the back door."

"What am I going to do?"

"No doubt the door is locked here. We're going to let you be the main force. They don't know how many men we have out here. They'll believe the worst."

"The main force? How am I going to do that?"

Ryan pointed to the open door that he had said was the back entrance to the apartment. "When I go in there, you give me a minute to get in position."

Morgan nodded silently.

"Then I want you to yell in your loudest voice, 'Everybody come out with your hands up. It's the police.' You think you can do that?"

"I think so."

"Good." Ryan shook his arm.

"What do I do then?"

"You count to three, then rare back and kick in the door. When I hear your kick, I'm going to jump in the back of them with my gun drawn. They won't be expecting it. They'll all be watching this front door. We'll have them dead to rights."

Morgan took a hard swallow. "What if they shoot at the door?"

"They won't do that. Trust me. I'll be in there so quick they won't have time to think. They sure won't have time to rush you with a knife."

"I don't know about this."

"Look, boy, you said you wanted to find out about the crime beat. We're counting on you now. By the time we go back and get some more men, they could all be gone. You wouldn't want that on your conscience, now would you?"

"No, I suppose not."

"Good, then you just wait for me to get around to the back. When I hear you yell, I'll get ready. When I hear you kicking that door down, I'll jump out."

Morgan's heart was beating faster as he watched Ryan disappear through the open door and into the darkness. Now he was all alone. He wasn't really alone, but it felt like it. This was certainly something he had no intention of ever telling Margaret about. It would keep her up nights for years to come.

Morgan braced himself and crept up next to the door. He took a deep breath. Then in his loudest and most menacing voice he yelled out, "This is the police! Everybody come out with your hands up!"

He could hear movement and loud voices inside the room. He began to count one, two, three. Then with all his might, he raised his foot and kicked in the door panel.

Morgan's foot was far too strong for the weak door. It shattered the panel, and before he knew what was happening his foot was through the door. Off balance, he fell violently to the floor.

The next instant was a mass of explosions. He heard several blasts of what could only have been shotguns. Large chunks of the door, along with several pieces of the wall, flew right over him. Had he still been standing, he would have been cut down like ripe wheat.

He rolled over in the direction of the open back door. Crawling in, he closed it behind him. He lay there for what seemed like the longest time, panting and trying to catch his breath. He heard the sound of men running down the hall, and then he laid his head back on the floor and closed his eyes, thanking God.

Moments later, the door opened. Morgan jerked his eyes open. It was Ryan, standing there with the revolver in his hand. "Are you all right?"

"I am now."

"They got away out that door you kicked in."

"Where were you?"

"I had a little trouble getting through that back door. If you'd been there, though—"

Morgan cut him off. "If I'd been there, I'd be dead."

CHAPTER 12

Morgan lay flat on his bed for what seemed like hours. He tossed and turned, fitful and unable to rest. He could never tell Margaret what had happened, but something told him he should tell Call. The man was streetwise, and he knew New York City and the police. If what had happened to him was just something of a usual nature that got out of hand, Call would know it. If it was something that should never have happened, he wanted to hear it from Call.

He rolled out of bed, his sock feet hitting the floor. Picking up his watch from the table beside his bed, he saw that it was 10:10. It was almost time to meet Margaret, and that alone brought his senses into full focus. If she was leaving, it might be one of the last times for him to see her. She no doubt had planned the rendezvous for when her mother was sound asleep, but why the mention of Hunter Kennedy? Had she found out something else about his murder?

He reached over and picked up his only shirt. There was a smudge on it, and he would try to wash it off. It would have to last him until tomorrow, until his uncle could wire him the money for a new wardrobe. He stepped into the bathroom and filled the sink. He lathered the corner of a washcloth with a small dab of soap. With his finger in the corner, he rubbed at the spot on the shirt. There. It wasn't as good as new, but it could at least go out in public. If only a man's soul could be this easy to clean. He knew full well, however, that most men just wanted to be able to go out in public. Becoming presentable without becoming clean was the thing that motivated many.

He put the shirt on, buttoning it and examining the spot. It would do. Tucking his shirt in, he grabbed his only tie and wrapped it around his neck. A double knot would work, and Morgan tied it as if it were second nature to him. Picking up his jacket, he put it on and straightened his tie in the mirror. Now he could see Margaret.

He hurried down the stairs, hoping that Margaret would be early. It had been a day since he had seen her and, even though he'd been busy, he felt every second of it. Just the sight of her brought every good thing that he carried in his mind and body to the surface.

How foolish he'd been to have thought he could live without her while he tried to make a name for himself and earn his way in the world. That would have been like going blindfolded into a fight with a blade.

He hurried down the three flights of stairs, pushed the bottom door open, and stepped into the lobby. There she was, seated on a round, leather couch and tapping her foot. She was obviously just as anxious to see him as he was her. He tried to walk calmly toward her, smiling like a man out on a stroll. When she looked up at him, however, he knew his game was up. He broke into a big smile. There was no use pretending anymore.

He walked up to her and, putting his hands on her arms, pulled her ever so slightly to her feet. "There you are. I'm so glad to see you, darling." He knew that kissing her at the moment would be out of the question. Such displays of affection were best done out of sight, and yet with everything within him he wanted to, and he wanted to do it badly.

She threw her arms around him and kissed him. It shocked Morgan, but he didn't hold back, and he wasn't about to correct her. "And I've been dying to see you all day," she said. "I have so much news for you." She sat down and reached into her purse.

Morgan looked around the lobby. It was much less crowded than it had been all day, but people were still coming and going. "Couldn't we go somewhere else to talk?"

"There's no time." She pulled out a scrap of newspaper. "We have to go to a party."

"A party?" The very idea of spending one of Margaret's last nights with him in the presence of total strangers made him a little sick at his stomach. He wondered if perhaps he'd overestimated her feelings for him. That would have been natural. He had been in love with her all of his life, and she'd just lost a fiancé. "Margaret, I don't really want to go to a party, not tonight of all nights."

"Well, you have to. There's someone you simply have to meet."

"Who could be that important?"

She handed him the scrap of newspaper, the one advertising the play *HMS Pinafore*. "See for yourself."

Morgan took the paper and began to read. His face turned pale and then began to burn. "This is an outrage."

"I saw the play this afternoon with Mother and Gloria Thompson. I also went to his dressing room afterward and met this Hunter Kennedy. He does look a lot like ours, remarkably so."

"But he isn't." Morgan handed the paper back to her. "The man is an impostor."

"But aren't you the least bit curious?"

"Why should I be? It's obvious they want to capitalize on all the publicity surrounding the *Titanic*. They are no more than vultures."

"Well, I for one am curious." She put the paper back into her purse. "I'd like to see how a man could think he knew Hunter well enough to become him should anyone ask."

"Did you tell this man that you were actually on the *Titanic*?"

"No, I didn't. I didn't want to frighten him away, not until after you had seen and talked with him. That's what we're doing tonight. I told him and the theater manager that I had a friend who wrote for the newspapers who might want to do a story on him, and he seemed eager for it."

"I'll just bet."

"So they invited me to a party for the cast tonight and asked if I would bring you."

Morgan's gaze went to his shoe tops. He knew Margaret couldn't miss the disappointment he felt. "There are few people in this world as self-serving as an actor."

"Unless it's a reporter."

That cut Morgan to the quick, perhaps because he knew it was true. Here she was, intensely curious about this man and wanting him to come along and help. Of course, all he could think about was spending a few hours with Margaret, without being in a crowd and without having to talk to someone who disgusted him even at a distance.

"But, Margaret, this may be one of our last nights together. I really don't want to spend it at an actors' party."

She reached up and put her hand on his, getting his attention. "I'm staying Morgan. I'm not going home with Mother."

He could hardly believe his ears. "How are you doing that?" He gulped. "Why are you doing that?"

"Mrs. Thompson has asked me to stay on for a while as her companion."

"Really? That's wonderful. And your mother agreed?"

Margaret dropped her head a bit. "Well, I wouldn't say she was overjoyed, and I wouldn't say she even agreed. Let's just say she recognized that it was something that I could do, with or without her blessing. As to the why of my doing such a thing, I told her that it was my duty to see Peter's relatives, and it is. I also told her I was more than a little afraid of boarding a ship so soon."

"Somehow, my dear, your timid streak never seems to come out too convincingly."

However, much to his dismay, Margaret began to shake and tremble. Morgan once again picked her up and held her close. "I'm sorry. You have every right to be frightened."

"It was a horror. I'll never forget the sound of those people in the water. I still hear them at night. It's almost as if they're calling out for me, for me personally."

"There was nothing you could have done, except live."

She pushed him away slightly and looked into his eyes. Tears filled hers. "What I didn't tell her was that I couldn't bear to be apart from you, not now. I need you as I've never needed anyone before."

He brushed her hair back, savoring the feel of his finger on the edge of her face. "And I need you, darling. Just the thought of you close by fills me with great joy." He smiled. Things were getting far too personal for the lobby of the Waldorf Astoria. "Now, what would you like for me to do at this party tonight?"

"Just talk to this Hunter Kennedy. Find out who he really is."

"All right, I will."

The taxi ride to the Big Top restaurant took no more than fifteen minutes, but Morgan was afraid it would break him. He'd converted his twenty-pound note into American currency earlier in the day and still had hopes it would last until his money wire arrived. He peeled off several bills from the small wad in his pocket, paid the man, and then stood back with Margaret to see just what they were getting into. Even at this late hour the place was a blaze of light. It was plain to see that the Big Top catered to the theater community. From the street they could hear a small band on the second floor playing ragtime tunes. Morgan held the door open for Margaret.

A balding man with a wide smile and a wider middle waddled toward them, his apron swaying on his hips. "Table for two?" he asked.

"No, thanks," Morgan said. "We're here for the cast party."

The man began to laugh and slap his knee. "Oh, the musical. I just love that show. I saw it tonight." He signaled for them to follow him.

The place was fixed up like the inside of a circus tent, with straw on the oak floor and paintings of elephants and tigers adorning the walls. One wall had a collection of grinning circus clowns staring at the customers who walked by. Overhead, a tentlike awning, looped over the hanging lights, hung in billowing colors.

Morgan eyeballed it. "That looks like a fire hazard to me."

Margaret tried to hush him as they followed the man to the stairs.

"The party is going on up there," the man said. "They'll be here for hours. We'll probably have to carry some of them home." He laughed.

"Sounds like quite the party," Morgan said.

"Oh, yes; yes, indeed."

Morgan and Margaret climbed the stairs and soon walked out on what would otherwise have been a large dance floor. Waiters carried plates of food, and the band in the corner blared out the lively tune.

"There you are." A man rushed at them from across the room. "I'm so glad you could come."

Margaret recognized the theater manager. He was dressed well for the occasion in a black tuxedo and crisp white shirt, which made his black eyes dance and his teeth sparkle.

Margaret backed away slightly, allowing Morgan to shake the man's hand. "This is the manager of the theater," she said. "He gave me directions today."

The man laughed. "Always happy to accommodate a desiring fan of one of our actors." He continued to shake Morgan's hand. "The name is Ed Leslie."

"I'm Morgan Fairfield." Morgan shook the man's hand. He noticed Leslie's look suddenly change, and he wondered if somehow the man recognized his name. "Do I know you?" Morgan asked.

"No, indeed, but I know you."

"From where?"

"Wasn't it you who wrote that outstanding article on the *Titanic* sinking, the one that appeared today in the *Herald*'s special edition?"

Morgan smiled. "Yes, that was me."

"It was splendid. Almost made me feel that I was right there with you. Of course, I wouldn't have wanted to be."

"Of course," Morgan agreed.

"You had an article appear today?" Margaret asked.

"Yes, he did," Leslie said, "And a fine one too. I shall look forward to the rest of your series."

Morgan nodded at Margaret. "Yes, I got it out this afternoon."

"Young lady, when you said you had a friend in the newspaper business, I had no idea it was a man whose writing appears on the front page."

"Well, I'm sure that will last only as long as the *Titanic* stays in the headlines."

"You're too modest. You do fine work. I'm sure you have a bright future. Have you met our hero of the *Titanic*?"

"You mean Mr. Kennedy?" Morgan asked.

"Yes, let me introduce you. You two can talk while I entertain the lovely lady."

Morgan and Margaret followed Leslie as he crossed the large room, taking care to avoid the waiters with their trays balanced high over their heads. Morgan could see from a distance the man Leslie was leading them to. Except for the beard, he did look remarkably like Hunter. He was also caught up in the company of several women, each giggling and trying her very best to maintain his attention. Morgan almost smiled. Hunter would have been proud to be mistaken for the man. It was so like him.

"Hunter," Leslie said, "you do remember the young lady who called on you this afternoon?"

Kennedy turned and smiled, momentarily diverting his attention from the other women at his side. "Why, yes, of course. How could any red-blooded man possibly forget such a beautiful drop-in?"

"And this is her reporter friend, Morgan Fairfield."

Kennedy bowed slightly. "Pleased to make your acquaintance, Fairfield."

"I've been looking forward to it," Morgan said.

Leslie continued with his introduction. "Mr. Fairfield here was also a survivor of the *Titanic*. In fact, the first of his stories about the disaster appeared this very evening on the front page of the *Herald*."

"Indeed, the front page?"

"It does seem to be the story with the greatest value these days."

Kennedy crossed his arms, intent on studying Morgan. "And I suppose you have questions for me. I am sorry I don't remember you."

Morgan smiled. "That's funny, because I remember you very well."

"You do?"

"Oh, yes, in such a short time I came to consider you my best friend."

"Is that so?" Kennedy's smile suddenly disappeared. He took Morgan by the arm and led him away from the group. Morgan cast a quick glance back in Margaret's direction. She was being well occupied by Ed Leslie, and he, at least, seemed to be enjoying it.

Kennedy spoke matter-of-factly. "Well, it's not every day that a man finds a best friend that he's never known."

"No, I should say not. But if you are Hunter Kennedy of Cork County, Ireland, whose father is a beleaguered Protestant minister and who appeared on the London stage of late, then you are my best friend."

"I am all of those things, but I'm having great difficulty in placing you, sir."

"You were in *Charley's Aunt* in London. I laughed my head off afterward, but I wasn't laughing at you."

"But I was. I was in that play."

"Well then, Hunter, you look much better than the last time I laid eyes on you. The last time I saw you, you were murdered in the saltwater pool of the *Titanic*."

Kennedy's eyes widened. "You must be mistaken."

"No, but you are, sir. Deception is slippery."

Kennedy's eyes darted around the room. Finally he spotted the person he'd been looking for.

A strikingly attractive and well-dressed brunette had just entered the room. "Ah, there she is. I have someone who can vouch for my identity. In fact, she is the financial backer of our play. You should know her if you were on the *Titanic*." Kennedy extended his arm and pointed the lady out. "Kitty Webb. You must come and meet her."

Now it was Morgan's turn to panic. He knew full well that Kitty Webb was the one who had murdered the real Hunter Kennedy. It was just as obvious that the impostor did not. If Morgan so much as let his face be seen, the sense of panic might be too great to control.

He grabbed the man and stopped him in midstep. "Now, look here. Both you and I know that you're not Hunter Kennedy. Hunter Kennedy was murdered. I was there and I saw it. He didn't go down with the ship as the rest of the people did that night. He was already dead. I have others, some who are appearing at the hearings, who can swear to that." He pointed across the room to Margaret. "That woman over there. She saw him floating in the pool. She is a witness. Don't deceive yourself by thinking she came to see you in that play today just because she's a fan of Gilbert and Sullivan. She came to see you, to see the man masquerading as the man she had come to know, the man she knew was already dead."

"Look." Kennedy grabbed Morgan on both arms. An angry scowl formed across his lips. "You don't know what you're talking about. I don't know who you met on that ship and who might have called himself

Hunter Kennedy, but what you're saying is dangerous. If you breathe one word about what you think you know, I'm a dead man."

"That seems to be your problem."

"It may be my problem, but if you keep spreading these lies of yours, it will be your problem."

CHAPTER 13

While Morgan was at the party in the glittering theater district, Call was on the other end of town standing in near darkness. He pulled up the collar on his overcoat and patted his pocket. It wasn't often that he carried his .32 Colt revolver, but tonight he felt much safer with it. He didn't want trouble, especially with his gun back in his bureau. He walked along the dock to the place being used by the White Star Line. Bobbing in the water were the thirteen lifeboats, the only things left from the mighty *Titanic*, the only things that remained of man's monumental climb to the brink of self-dependence.

He listened to the lifeboats banging together, the clatter of wood dull and hollow, empty. The choppy water was giving them a last ride. He shrugged his shoulders. Call had never been one given to superlatives. Most patriotic speeches made him want to regurgitate, and the ballyhoo following the launching of the *Titanic* had made him positively ill. There was a smug sense of justice about the picture, however. Man was simply never made to exist on his own wits alone. Call knew that he had been more of a believer in fate than in God, but still the irony of the matter struck him. "The ship that not even God could sink." Maybe there was a personal God after all—perhaps some divine being who could see the folly of man and set out to teach serious object lessons when nothing else seemed to work.

A pair of drunks stumbled out of the Brass Rail, singing a bawdy song. Call watched them weave down the darkened street, leaning on each other as they tried to blend their voices. It struck him that perhaps this was the best picture of humanity after all. People out of their minds with their own doings, clinging to others and trying to make some sound that would go beyond themselves. They couldn't, however, and perhaps neither could he. He would try to come to the truth, though, and let the devil take the hindmost.

He started down the dark side of the dock, toward the light. The lights inside the Brass Rail were filtered through glass painted a mix of red and green. The colors almost seemed like a celebration of Christmas, though he knew that most likely red and green were the cheapest paints possible.

He stepped up on the boardwalk and pushed open the bat-wing doors. Cigar smoke reeking of cheap tobacco flooded past him and out into the street.

Several chairs had been overturned at the table nearest the door, and Call moved around them. The last man to be seated in one of them was sprawled on the floor, arms outstretched where he had landed. Call sat on a stool near the bar and watched Bud, the owner, pour drinks at the other end.

It wasn't long before a smooth hand slid over his shoulder. He turned around, and his eyes met the painted smile and the dull, doelike eyes of a woman who was of obvious easy virtue. Her heavy and puffed lids were painted a soft blue and caked with heavy mascara. Nevertheless, her eyes were like silent pleas from the deepest part of her wounded soul. The woman was easily in her late thirties, but life on the street had turned her into a woman of forty-five pretending to be a seventeen-year-old debutante. She smiled, and a crease formed from the corners of her mouth and wrinkled a mole on the brim of her cheek, one that she had painted a deeper black.

She pursed her lips and opened her mouth to speak. Call smelled her rancid breath even before he heard the words. "Evening, sugar." She ran her hand up his face, pushing his hat back slightly as her fingernails caressed his cowlick. "You sure are a handsome gentleman." She grinned. "So very good-looking." Dropping her hands to his shoulders, she squeezed them gently. "And so strong too."

"I'm sorry, honey, but I'm really not interested."

She leaned toward him in her low-cut blouse, wiggling her shoulders and displaying plenty of what was left of her femininity. "Are you sure you're not interested?" Her voice peaked at a higher range.

Bud turned around and shot him a look. It wasn't a friendly look. The man moved closer. "You here to ask more of your questions?"

"No, I'm here for a boilermaker." Call turned back to the woman. "Why don't you tell him what you're drinking?"

She looked up and spoke in a husky voice. "Whiskey."

Bud flicked his bar towel. "That I can do." He grabbed a bottle, poured a shot glass full of the amber liquid, and set it before her.

Reaching under the bar, he pulled out a semiclean beer mug and held it under the tap, filling it almost to the brim. He took a shot glass from a rack in front of the mirror and poured in two fingers of what appeared to be bourbon. Holding the small glass of liquor over the beer, he dropped the bourbon into the still foaming yellow substance, turning it into a milky brown. He sat it down in front of Call. "That'll be twenty-five cents."

Call reached into his vest pocket and, producing a quarter, slammed it down on the bar.

"I don't appreciate you boys coming around here making trouble for me."

"What trouble?" Call took a heavy sip of the substance.

"You know what trouble, all those questions your man asked my swamper."

The woman downed her drink with one quick sling of her wrist. She then clung to Call, almost cooing. "He can't be no trouble, Bud. He'd be no trouble for me."

Call ignored her, which was hard. "We always like to be sure we get the story straight."

"Well, you ain't got no story."

Call smiled and took another deep swallow. "Oh, we've got a story, all right. We just have to make sure we get your name spelled correctly."

The woman, almost lost in her own conversation, kept hold of Call's arm. She leaned toward him and asked in a rasping voice, "Are you a reporter?"

Bud put both hands on the bar and leaned toward him. "You put my name in that paper of yours, and it'll be the last time anybody hears of your name."

Call patted the woman's hand gently, almost to keep reminding himself that she was there still clinging to him. But he answered Bud, not her. "Is that a threat?"

"What if it is?"

Once again the woman broke into their conversation. She was in her own world, a world where everything turned out the way she wanted, where she never had to wake up from the dreamlike state she was in. "I like reporters," she said. "I like all smart men. They can write and tell stories. Could you tell me a story?"

Call concentrated on Bud. "I ain't no wet-nose kid you can put a scare into. I have the most powerful weapon known to mortal man." Call reached into his pocket and pulled out a pencil. He waved it in front of the man's face.

"Do you see this thing? This simple pencil can put you clean out of business. I could close you down tomorrow if I wanted to."

Bud backed away. "What do you want from me? I ain't done nothing. I'm just a simple businessman looking to make a living."

The woman pointed at the pencil. "See, he's got a pencil to write with." She leaned over on him batting her eyes. "Could you write me a story?"

Call took another drink, draining the glass by a third. He wiped his mouth with the back of his hand. He then looked at the woman. Call tried to imagine her as a little girl, an innocent little girl sitting on her father's lap and listening to a bedtime story. She was far from that now. He felt pity for her, wondering just what her father would say. Once again he patted her hand. "Hang on, sweetheart. I'll take care of you in a little bit."

He turned back to Bud. "You call covering up another man's dying making a living?"

"I jest help my friends and customers, that's all."

"I'm your customer tonight."

"But you ain't my friend."

The woman wound her arm around Call's even tighter. "I'll be your friend, sugar."

Call kept his attention on Bud. "And I suppose the Irish Tommy-knockers are?"

Bud nodded, "From time to time they are. When I need them they're here, while yer uptown in that newspaper office."

"I can be very friendly," she said in a sultry voice.

Once again, Call picked up the pencil. "Don't think I can't reach you from uptown."

"I ain't scared of you."

"You should be. Very scared."

Call took another drink, draining the glass. "Why don't you just tell me where I can find Bain?"

Bud's eyes lit up. He stepped up closer. "If you want Bain, yer in luck." He pointed toward the rear of the bar. "The man's seated at the very back. He ain't hard to miss. Big chunky feller. I'll tell you one thing, though, he ain't scared of no pencil."

Call slid off his stool. "Just so you are."

The woman was still hanging on to his arm. Her pasty smile had changed very little, a pitiful plea wrapped in face powder and rouge. "You said you was going to take care of me. I can take care of you. Been so long since I had me a handsome gentleman like you are."

Call dug into his pocket and took out two one-dollar bills. He pulled the woman's hand off his arm and pressed the bills into it. Closing his hand around hers he looked into her sad eyes. "You take this and find yourself a room for the night, a room by yourself. Tomorrow you head uptown to the *New York Herald.* Ask for Call. I'll see if I can't find you some work to do to keep you off the streets."

The woman opened the palm of her hand and stared at the bills.

"Will you do that?" Call asked.

She didn't answer, didn't so much as even nod her head. She just looked up at him, her mouth parting slightly.

Call patted her hand. "OK, hon, I'll see you tomorrow then. I've got work to do tonight."

He walked off and left her standing there. He didn't figure he'd ever see her again, certainly not the next day. That type of woman seldom changed, but then that was true for almost anyone. Habits die hard and are much more convenient than thinking a matter through.

He focused on the back of the bar where several tables sat in the shadows. Bain would be where he could see anyone coming. Suddenly, in midstride, someone caught hold of the sleeve of his jacket.

Looking down, he spotted a familiar face. "Gerry, is that you?" Geraldine—Gerry—Farier had lived her life in the city of New York. As a young woman she had disguised herself as a boy and shipped out on a tramp steamer. When she became too mature to pull that off, she lived on the streets. She'd also served her time cleaning for the wealthy and mopping the floors of Macy's department store.

The last time Call had seen her she was mopping the lobby of the *New York Herald*. It was just the kind of job Call had in mind for the woman he'd just walked away from.

She laughed, showing missing and blackened teeth. "Yep, it's me all right. I gots me a job close by now." Her teeth were discolored from her constant habit of chewing on a plug of tobacco. She leaned over and spit a steady stream of brown liquid into a brass spittoon and then wiped her mouth with the back of her hand. "What is you doin' here?" she asked.

She took a moment to fix her pathetic rolled-up hat, the brim of which had curled up during the rainstorms of years gone by. He was sure the hat had once been pink, but it was hard to tell just what the color was now.

"I'm working on a story."

"A story, is it?" She cackled, her eyes dancing. Her eyes were almost a steel gray, but they tended to blend into the surroundings. There were dark circles around them, tumbling down her face in a series of deeper and deeper wrinkles. Her hawklike nose was narrow and just a shade crooked.

Call glanced up to see two other women seated at the table. Their looks could have told the story of this side of town. It seemed he had run into the society of broken-down street women. "Yes, I've got a story to do. I'm just here to check my facts a little."

Gerry sputtered and giggled, ramming her elbow in the ribs of the woman seated next to her and pointing at Call. "Checkin' his facts, he is. This here used to be my feller when I worked downtown for the paper. Ever once't in a while he'd even bring me a flower." She leaned in Call's direction, her eyelids slipping down to half-mast. "That was mighty sweet of you, mighty sweet for old Gerry."

"Everybody needs to be special once in a while, Gerry, and I think you are."

She patted his arm with her wrinkled hand. "You're mighty sweet, you are."

Call put his hand up to the brim of his hat, tugging on it to show respect to the women. "If you'll excuse me now, ladies, I need to go do my job."

"Not so fast." Gerry grabbed him by the arm and pulled him closer. He could smell the stink of her breath now. "I got me a story for you, one you're gonna want to hear about."

Call patted her hand. "I'm sure you do, darling, but your story is going to have to wait a mite."

Gerry shooed him away with her hand. "All right, you go ahead. Don't mind us none. You go do your job, and we'll stay here and do ours." She turned to the other women. "Won't we, girls?"

They all laughed as he walked away. He could hear their giggles. He couldn't help but think of how someday soon they wouldn't even be a memory. They'd be gone with no one to mourn, no one to hold hearings at the Waldorf Astoria on what happened to them. No one left to care. It paid to show that you cared for someone while they were still here.

He walked past a table full of gamblers. The light was brighter there, which allowed them to see their cards as they hunched over and fanned them out. They reminded him of the bluff he was going to have to run when he talked to the man named Bain.

The place was much busier than when he and Morgan had stopped by. There was even a woman waiting tables. Then he spotted Bain. The bulky man, his dark eyes riveted on Call, had his chair leaned against the far wall in a place where he could see everything happening in the room. His half-empty beer glass sat in front of him, along with a bowlful of pretzels. He had a full beard, dark and curly. Much to Call's delight, the man was alone.

Call walked up to the man's table. "You Bain?"

"That I am, Alister Bain. What can I do for you?"

"It's more what I can do for you."

Bain crossed his arms. They were fleshy and covered with dark black hair that showed beneath his rolled-up shirtsleeves. "Now just what could you do for me?"

"Keep you off the gallows."

Bain laughed, but his eyes were dead serious and blazing with fire. Bain looked straight at Call. "You don't see me standing near the gallows, do you?"

"Not yet, but unless you talk you soon will be."

"Now, just how do you suppose that?"

"The sailor that was killed the other night, we have a witness that puts you at the scene of the crime, and right when the thing took place."

Bain dropped his chair to the floor. "That's impossible."

"Is it? You better think again."

Bain shook his head. "Even if it was true, nobody would say nothing."

Call smiled. "Don't you bet on it."

"O'Brien wouldn't let nobody say nothing."

Call recognized the name of O'Brien, Damon O'Brien. The man was a powerful Irish warlord who controlled the shipping industry in New York City and Boston. Anything that went on with the ships that left those places happened because O'Brien said so. Nothing went past the man, and everything went into his pockets.

Call leaned over the table and put his hands on it, locking eyes with Bain. "Do you really think he would jeopardize all that he has for the likes of you?" Call shook his head. "No. With our witness, he's going to toss you to the dogs and never miss a bite off his plate."

Bain leaned back in his chair once again, steadying himself against the wall with his right hand. The motion wasn't lost on Call. The man was right-handed. Call took out a piece of paper and laid his pencil on it. He would run the bluff one better. "We know it wasn't you that used the blade on Fetters, but unless we hear better, you'll hang while he spends the money. Why don't you just write down the man's name. Then maybe you can walk."

Bain sat in silence, but the silence was deafening. Call could see his mind working away, wondering just how much was already known. He once again brought the chair down with a thud. Picking up the pencil he scrawled on the paper and pushed it in Call's direction. "There, but you ain't heard nothing from me. As far as you're concerned I didn't have nothing to do with it."

Call folded the paper and stuck it in his pocket. He turned on his heels and started back toward the door without saying a word. He passed Gerry, tipping his hat.

"Good night, honey," she growled.

When he walked back in the bar area, he spotted the woman who had seemed to attach to him earlier. She was now curled up next to a sailor, pouring the man another drink. Call knew she'd never take his advice. Some people just couldn't change.

Bud gave Call a quick glance and then turned away.

When Call pushed open the bat-wing doors, he stepped out to the dark street. He had taken no more than two quick steps when he heard the sound of footsteps behind him. He didn't see the man, but the next thing he felt was a crushing blow to his head. The heavy object mashed his hat down and sent his head to swimming. He dropped to his knees and fell flat to the cobblestones. The world was spinning around him, and bright lights were going on and off inside his skull. Then all was blackness.

CHAPTER 14

The theater manager, Ed Leslie, made his polite good-byes to a few of the guests who actually came from polite society, people who weren't members of the cast. They'd been invited more for their ties to New York society and for the people they knew. He shook the hand of a young woman he thought he should remember. She was dressed in an immodest, sequined black gown that trailed down to her ankles, and she giggled as she bent low. The woman was leaving with one of the cast members, and he was certain that everything that was to be known about her he would hear tomorrow. He thought they picked a good time to leave, a time when the cast was still relatively sober.

As far as the cast went, he knew he'd never be the last to leave. Many of them were just getting started, and the waiters had stopped bringing trays of food out to the tables. They continued with large mugs of foaming beer and more, much more.

He watched Kennedy leave by the side exit, and even though the man's talk with Fairfield had been short, his disposition had noticeably changed. He'd no longer gone into the midst of the group as the adorable charmer with appeal to women. He'd been tight-lipped with barely a smile crossing his face, and that only when it was forced by someone else.

Fairfield seemed to have quite the effect on Kennedy. Leslie knew he'd have to talk long and hard with the reporter before his job was through. It might make his job a bit more difficult. But that would have to wait until tomorrow. Right now, he had Kennedy on his mind.

Leslie nodded at several of the cast. "You take care that you make rehearsal tomorrow. You'll have to get to bed when the people here shut the place down."

They muttered something and seemed to nod in agreement, but he knew full well they had no intention of quitting until they could no longer stand up. For the sake of tomorrow night's performance, he hoped that wouldn't be too long. Actors were a strange breed. He knew that all too well. They spent a great deal of their lives starving for both food and attention, and when they had both at hand, they tended to grab it with both hands and squeeze.

Leslie grabbed his cloak from the brass stand and swung it around him as a Spanish matador would tease a bull. Taking his top hat, he made for the side door, the same door Kennedy had gone through moments before. Because Kennedy had had a head start, Leslie knew he wouldn't be noticed. The trick now would be to find out just which way he had gone and hope he hadn't caught a cab. There was a chance he would lose the man, and that would be too terrible to consider. But it couldn't be helped, not now.

The stairs groaned, sagging underneath him. It was plain to see they weren't used much. It did give him a sense of relief that he hadn't decided to follow Kennedy closer. He'd have been heard for sure. He clamped down on the brass bar to spring the door open to the street and slowly eased the heavy metal door back into place. He could hear the gentle splatters of a spring shower. The blasted rain couldn't wait, he supposed, but at least he had the cape. He hunched it up over his shoulders and ran toward the end of the block. His shoes splattered in time with the falling rain, making the sound of a duck at play. The lights that hung overhead caught the shine on his shoes, and they flickered slightly as he kept up his pace.

Stopping and peering around the corner, he caught sight of a distant figure walking in the rain. The man had the build of Kennedy, but at that distance he couldn't be sure. He watched as the man walked out into the street, waving his hand at a taxi just turning the corner up ahead of him.

Leslie stepped out into the street, looking back at the now darkened theater district. Just when there seemed to be little hope, he spotted a black car idling with its lights on in front of a small hotel. He crossed the street and broke into a dead run. It wasn't until he crossed the street that he noticed the markings on it. It was a cab.

The driver was seated in the vehicle. Leslie stuck his head in the window. "Are you free?"

"No, sir. I ain't. I'm waiting for a man I just dropped off. He said he'd be right back."

"What's he paying you?"

The cabbie twisted his face into a frown. "A dollar, I suppose."

"I'll pay you two."

With that the man's frown broke into a broad smile. "Jump in, mister. You got yourself a cab."

Leslie cranked the handle on the door and jumped into the backseat. He nudged the cabbie's back. "Get going. Just drive."

The man shoved the gears into position and dropped the clutch, lurching the vehicle out into the street. "Where to, mister?"

Leslie spotted the taillight of the taxicab he hoped was the one Kennedy had taken. It had taken the cab ahead a short while to round the corner and back up to pick up the man Leslie thought might be Kennedy. Luckily it was all the time Leslie had needed. He rested his arm on the cabbie's shoulder, and with his finger pointed straight ahead. "Follow that taxi. Just don't get too close."

The cabbie turned his head and, with a quick glance, caught his eye. "Are you serious?"

"I'm dead serious."

The cabbie stepped on the gas. "Mister, for two bucks I'd follow Peter Pan."

Leslie smiled. Not only had he been lucky enough to find a taxicab but a cab driver who was somewhat knowledgeable of the theater.

They drove for what seemed to be twenty minutes or more, taking care not to get too close to the car ahead of them. "They seem headed to the wharf area," the driver said.

Leslie sat back and tried to relax. It was too difficult. He didn't want to take his eyes off the taxicab in front of them. Sliding to the front of the seat, he hung on and continued to watch. The vehicle took a sharp right turn. "Slow down," Leslie said.

The driver slowed down and eased into a right turn behind the cab in front. Kennedy had gotten out and was paying his driver. The man gave Leslie a start by looking up at them as they drove by.

"Keep driving down the block," Leslie said. He pointed to the next street. "Turn there and pull over."

He jumped out of the cab and handed over his two dollars.

"Do you want me to wait for you?"

Leslie thought it over. "Yes, why don't you. I don't know how long I'll be, but you can keep the meter running."

The man turned the yellow timer all the way over. "Oh, I'll do that." He smiled. "I'll be around."

Leslie walked back to the corner and peeked around the building. He saw the taxicab pulling away. That was one good thing. When Kennedy finished his rendezvous, he'd have to look for a cab.

He patted his hat down firm as the rain continued to fall. The falling rain made a staccato sound on his hat as he walked. It took him no more than a minute to find the place where Kennedy had been dropped off, but he saw no sign of the man. The street was dark, and he knew the docks were quite close. Many of the buildings had large double doors that were padlocked. They were warehouses with apartments squashed down on their tops and stairs that were held up with a series of worn wooden scaffolds.

Leslie backed into the street, craning his neck to try to spot a light from one of the darkened windows in the upstairs apartments. He spotted one near the corner with a light, but the light didn't come from the end apartment. It appeared to come from an apartment several doors down.

He started up the stairs. When he got to the top landing, he opened the door and stepped into the hallway. Leslie froze in his tracks, a wad of spittle rising in his throat. He gulped. There was a man in the hall. He was seated on a chair, balanced so that he was leaning against the wall, his left hand on his lap and his right hand hanging down with his fingers spread. The man appeared to be asleep. At least the sound of the door opening hadn't roused his attention. Leslie wasn't sure if he had dozed off or if he simply thought one of the other tenants had caused the sound and was choosing to ignore it. In any event, it was certain that Leslie couldn't hope to merely stop at the door and try to listen in on the conversation in the room.

Leslie decided that he would try one of the doors, preferably the one that was located beside the apartment he wanted to listen in on.

If the door was locked, he would simply walk past the man and down the hall, as if he belonged there. It was almost a humorous thought, a man in top hat and evening clothes living in a cheap, dockside rooming house.

He took a couple of cautious steps. The shoes he wore had water in them, and even he could hear the soft squeak of the leather on the floor. The shoes gave off a spongy gush as rain left its trail on the threadbare carpet. The man in the chair moved slightly, but only to get himself more comfortable.

Leslie grabbed the knob, and the door sprang open. He stepped inside.

The place was dingy and dirty. Papers were scattered over the floor, and a hunk of cheese, with a knife stuck in it, was on the table in the middle of the room. A cot was near the window. A man was sprawled on it, his arms hanging off the bed and his knuckles scraping the floor. The man's snores were almost buzz-saw quality.

Leslie moved over to the wall that separated the two apartments. Pipes, painted gray, ran down from the ceiling to the floor below. Behind the pipe he could see a place where the wall had been hastily patched. A piece of wood the size of a man's hand covered it, and Leslie worked at pushing it aside. It had some give to it and moved ever so slightly.

Leslie could see a sliver of light. He pressed his eye to the hole. Looking through it he could see a rather large man with balding red hair sitting on a chair. He had sharp blue eyes and puffy cheeks. The man was dressed well with an open white shirt that allowed his chest hair to blossom in a mass of gray and red. His ruddy face was clean-shaved, and his hands were folded under his ample belly as he sat. His hands were large, and his fingers looked like hot dogs.

"You just get close to them. Be their friend on the stage, their Irish friend," the large man said.

Leslie could see his back as Kennedy paced back and forth. "I want out of this. I'm not comfortable with all the pretending. It's too much to ask of a man. I was fine the way things were. I had a supply going. We were shipping."

The big man dropped his gaze to the floor and shook his head. "But who was to know that ship was going down? Taking on Kennedy's name seemed like a good way to get you closer to the people with money, people who could help us, who could help you."

"There's something about it that seems almost sacrilegious to me. I mean, it's almost like stepping on the grave of the dead."

"You're getting soft on me. You need to keep your wits about you. Being where you are and meeting all those people is bound to bring in more dollars. With more money, we can double, even triple, what we ship. Besides, you're an actor. What could be more perfect?"

"Nothing's perfect now, is it?"

"Where's the stuff you already have?"

"Close. I had another buy a few days ago, an officer in the army. I'm going to need more money, though."

"You know what to do about that. You get it from your friends. You buy the weapons, and we ship them. Works out best all around."

"But I take all the risks."

"That's because you're a patriot."

"And what if I run into a problem?"

"Have you had a problem?"

Kennedy stopped pacing, his back to the wall, cutting off Leslie's view. "Nothing I can't handle I suppose."

"Well, if you do run into one you can't handle, you just let me know. What do you have so far?"

"Two hundred rifles, ammunition, and sixty-odd pistols."

"All first-rate?"

"U.S. Government issue."

"You'd better turn them over to me. I'll move them, and then you can have your money."

"I've got another buy in two days, and I'm going to pick up some money tomorrow night from a sympathizer. He wants to see what I already have. If I give them to you, I'll have nothing to show the man."

"I have to have something to show the boys back home. They need those guns." The big man leaned forward. "And I need something to show for all my trouble."

Leslie heard a loud coughing and wheezing from the man on the cot. Leslie was paralyzed, as if handcuffed to the dark wall. The man rolled to his side and put one foot on the floor. The chill of the bare wooden floor seemed to stimulate the man slightly, and he began to smack his lips.

His eyes blinked, roaming the room. The man's sleepy gaze suddenly fell on Leslie. There was no way Leslie could disappear.

"Who in the blazes are you?" the man shouted.

Leslie edged his way to the door. "Sorry, wrong room."

"Yer a thief." The man bounded out of his bed and pulled the knife out of the cheese.

"What could you possibly have that I'd want to steal?"

Flashing the blade, the man bounded at Leslie. "I don't take to thieves."

"And have you ever seen a burglar in evening clothes?"

The thought stopped the man in his tracks. He stopped and stared. "Now that you mention it, I ain't."

Leslie turned the knob on the door and stepped out into the hall. The man in the chair was now on his feet, and Leslie smiled at him and nodded. Turning on his heels he made his way out the door and down the stairs. When he hit the street, he started to run. Rounding the corner, he saw the waiting cab pull up to the curb. "The Hotel Europa," he said.

"For two bucks?"

"I think with what I paid you already your normal fare ought to be more than enough."

With that, they sped off into the night, Leslie suddenly feeling very cheap.

CHAPTER 15

The *Herald*'s newsroom was alive with activity. It had been since the special editions on the *Titanic* and its hearings began hitting the streets. Everywhere men in dirty shirts were flying to their typewriters and copyboys were running frantically between the desks. Morgan was already at a desk in that corner of the room dedicated to the crime writers. He was pounding out the next installment of his firsthand account of the sinking, this time making special reference to the loading of the lifeboats. The *Titanic* carried more lifeboats than was required by law, and already the law was being called an international scandal.

Morgan got a tap on the shoulder from a reporter standing at his desk and drinking a hasty cup of coffee. "Better watch out, boy. She might be coming for one of us."

He looked up to see a young woman dressed in a tight skirt and a white blouse buttoned up to her neck. Her raven black hair was woven behind her head in a bun, and she walked at a quick pace with sensible shoes. He could see even at a distance that she was an attractive woman with a button nose and businesslike brown eyes. She walked up to the man downing the last of his coffee. “Where do I find Morgan Fairfield?”

The man grinned. “You’re standing right in front of him, Miss Bennett.”

Morgan looked up. “I’m Morgan Fairfield.”

“I’m Patricia Bennett, and we’ve got work to do this morning. Whatever you’re working on can wait.”

Morgan tried to protest. “I’m doing my second article on the *Titanic*. It has to be done by noon today.”

“As I said, it can wait. Get your coat and follow me.”

“Better do as she says, boy. She’s the publisher’s niece.”

She glared at the man with a look that could stop a train. “I’m more than that. I’m an editor for the morning copy.” With that she drove her sharp finger into the man’s chest. “And you are a reporter—just a reporter.”

Morgan got to his feet, took his suit coat off the oak coat tree, and put it on. He hadn’t been at the paper long enough to know who was who in the office, but he had been there long enough to follow directions, and this was a woman who most definitely looked like she knew what she was doing. “All right, let’s go,” he said.

He followed her around the desks and out into the hall. They hit the stairs, seemingly running. “Where are we going?”

“To jail.”

“To jail?”

“Yes, that’s where Call is. We have to bail him out.” She stopped and turned on her heels before she completed the final word in her sentence. “Again.”

He trailed her down the second flight of stairs. “Why take me?”

She didn’t even turn around to answer him. “Because you and he are working on a story. Dixon thought he might have something on it. Why, I’ll never know. The man ties one on almost every other night.”

She raced out into the street and, putting two fingers to her mouth, let out a shrill whistle. A nearby taxi stopped, and they got in. “The police station,” she said.

"I still don't understand why this involves me, Miss Bennett," Morgan said.

Her eyes seemed to pop wide open. "Look, *you* can call me Pat. Unless you're with me at some glittering event and people are within earshot, and I sincerely doubt that will ever happen, don't call me Miss Bennett. Am I understood?"

"Yes."

"You're here because Dixon said to take you. You seem to have been appointed Call's guardian angel. Dixon said you were a competent writer, and I've seen your first piece. It'll do. Call trusts no one. The man digs up dirt and doesn't tell anybody. Even if for some misplaced reason he has decided to trust you, even a little bit, Harry Dixon thinks you should be there to find out what he knows, if anything. I, for one, think the man only knows where to find cheap booze and cheaper women."

"He seems to be a good reporter," Morgan added.

"You have no idea, do you? He's more than a good reporter; he's a great one. He's never satisfied with just reporting something that happens. He wants to dig and keep digging until he finds out who or what is responsible. Our motto at the paper has always been 'we don't just report the news, we make the news,' and Call is the best of the best at that. But as a human being he's the worst of the worst. The man has no scruples, none at all."

"Is that a problem for a newspaperman?" Morgan asked. He saw for the first time the merest hint of a smile on her face.

"None at all. Of course, Call has his own set of reasons for exposing corruption. From what I hear, the woman he was going to marry committed suicide. Stupid thing, really. He was young, and so was she. The girl's father was a banker and was going to be arrested as an embezzler. The girl's mother had died years ago, and with her father going to jail and a wedding that couldn't be paid for, it was just too much for her. Of course, knowing Call, none of that would have made any difference to him."

The taxi let them off at the police station. After Pat paid the fare, along with a stingy tip, they made their way up the steep stairs, burst through the glass doors, and strode into the waiting room. Pat walked up to the counter and rang the small bell with authority.

An overweight desk sergeant with unbuttoned tunic waddled up to the counter.

"Can I help you?" Then he recognized her. "Oh, it's you, Miss Bennett."

"Yes, and we've come to bail him out."

The man opened his book and followed his finger down the page. "I got him all right."

"Well, I'm glad to hear he didn't break out."

"Follow me." He signaled them around the counter and through the open door. The man picked up his clipboard and spoke over his shoulder as they passed several desks. "You can pay the fine at the clerk's office."

"I know where it is," she said.

Unlocking the outside of the cell block, the sergeant led them down the corridor of open cells to the one given to Call. He inserted the key to turn the lock. "The man was unconscious and drunk and disorderly down at the dock area last night." He pushed open the door. "But I suspect you know how it goes with him."

"Yes, I know quite well," Pat said.

Call was lying on a cot. The sergeant shook him. "Wake up, Call. You're sprung. These nice people are here to bail you out."

Call let out a moan and then turned over, putting his hand to his head.

"Who was the arresting officer?" Morgan asked.

The sergeant flipped through the clipboard, searching for his record of the arrest. "O'Toole," he said. "The man's gone home for the day, though."

Morgan reached down and shook Call. "Are you awake?"

Call once again moaned and then popped open one eye.

Morgan sat down on the cot and placed his hand on Call's head. "The man has a lump the size of a goose egg. He's been bleeding too."

"His type don't often come quietly," the sergeant responded.

Pat folded her arms, growing increasingly impatient with waiting for Call. "I'll go pay his fine. You see what you can do to get him on his feet. I should think the alcohol has worn off by now."

"Just a second. There are some things we need to ask the sergeant here, and I think it would be best if you stayed."

Morgan's direction took her completely off guard. She didn't seem to know what to do. She bit her lower lip. Morgan looked up at the big policeman. "Sergeant, could you explain to me how a man could be arrested for being drunk and disorderly and unconscious at the same time?"

It was plain to see the question went off in Pat's mind like a flare in the black of night. "Yeah, that's a good point." She pointed to Call. "How's even *he* going to do that?"

The big policeman stroked his chin. "I suspect he was drunk and disorderly before he blacked out."

"Might be hard to do it the other way around," Pat shot back.

"And he was arrested then for being unconscious?" Morgan asked. He smiled. "I've only been in the city a short time, Sergeant, and if that were the case, I've seen plenty of people who need arresting."

"So have I," Pat added. She moved closer to Morgan. "You'd be arresting the entire lower East Side on a Friday night."

"Well, maybe I got that wrong," the man said. He looked down at his clipboard once again. "I guess he was drunk and disorderly, and O'Toole had to use his nightstick on him. We found a .32 caliber pistol in his possession."

"And Call was threatening the officer with it?" Pat asked.

"Well, not exactly."

"So this O'Toole just saw him drunk and decided to club him over the head?" Morgan asked. "Is that standard police procedure? Because if it is, again I've seen lots of New Yorkers who are prime candidates for a beating."

"I'm sure he had his reasons."

"And who issued the complaint?" Morgan asked. "I assume someone called for the officer's help in dealing with this brutal drunk of a reporter."

"Good question," Pat added. She put her hands on her hips. "I'd like to know the answer to that myself."

Once again the sergeant looked at the clipboard containing the arrest record. "No, I'm sorry. There's no complaint here."

"I see," Pat spoke in a low voice. "No one was complaining, Call was drunk, your cop thought he was disorderly, and he just decided to club him over the head."

"Look, Miss Bennett, that's all something that will have to be taken up in court."

"And it will be," she shot back. "You'll be lucky if you don't get sued. In fact, the paper may just want to have a few words with the police commissioner over this."

The sergeant shrugged his shoulders. "Doesn't matter to me." He looked over at Call. "Course Call here don't exactly have the record of a Boy Scout to back him up, now do he?"

A string of guttural curses came from the cot. "Quit talking about me like you're making funeral arrangements for some stranger," Call said. "I'm right here. If you want to know what really happened, why don't you ask me?"

"We would have," Pat said, "if we knew you were sober."

Call swung his feet off the cot and sat with his throbbing head in his hands. "Oh, I'm sober all right. Wish I weren't right now." He looked up at her. "And, Patricia, I'd say a few extra glasses of Kentucky bourbon once in a while would do you a world of good."

Morgan could see Pat's face flush. He wasn't sure if it was because of what Call had said or because he'd dared to call her Patricia. In either event, Morgan wouldn't have wanted to be on the receiving end of the woman's anger. But the way Call was feeling already, it didn't make that much difference.

She turned on her heels and headed for the door. "I'll go pay his bail. You get him up and moving around." She stopped on the other side of the bars and looked through them at Call. "You still have a job to do, Call, no matter how much you drink. I'd suggest you get with it." With that she disappeared down the corridor. The sound of her shoes rippling off the bare brick walls was followed by several whistles from the men in their cells.

"She's something, that one," the sergeant said.

Call looked up. "Tell me about it."

The three men walked slowly out of the cell block, trying their best to help Call keep his feet under him. When they got to the desk, the sergeant emptied a basket and began to itemize the things found in Call's pockets, including his wallet and a few cough drops. The sergeant held up the revolver with his fingers on the trigger guard, as a man would discard a dead rat. He dropped it into Call's hand. "You'll want this, I reckon."

"Yeah, I will." Call stuffed the gun back into his overcoat pocket.

Scooping up a number of bullets that had been removed from the gun, the sergeant counted them out. He laid them one at a time in the palm of Call's hand, "One, two, three, four, and five. We didn't find number six."

"I always leave the hammer on an empty chamber," Call said. "Wouldn't want to shoot myself."

"Well, you did have a sixth round." The man held up a spent cartridge. "It was under the hammer." He bounced it in his hand. "We're gonna hang on to this, though."

"Well, see, it was blank," Call said.

"It's the one smart thing you did last night," the sergeant said. He handed over a sheet of paper for Call to sign. "Here, this says everything you came in with, you went out the door with."

Call opened the wallet. It was empty. "Hey, I'm sure I had more than sixty-five dollars in this wallet last night."

"Well, you didn't when they brought you in. Must have been some drunk you went on."

"I had a boilermaker and paid fifty cents for it, not sixty-five dollars."

The sergeant shrugged. "All I know is what I read, and this here says you were flat broke."

"You protect us from the thieves in this city by hiring them to walk the beat," Call murmured. He leaned over the table and signed.

"There now, you're free to go."

Morgan and Call carefully walked out the door and stopped to wait for Pat. Call shook his head. "That's my first time of being robbed by the police. I've spent a few nights in there before, nights I belonged in there. But I always came out with what I went in with. It disillusions a man. I can tell you another thing. I didn't have an empty cartridge in that gun of mine. I had five live rounds." He stuck his hand in his pocket and his face went white.

"What's wrong?" Morgan asked.

"I'm missing a piece of paper, too, a very important piece of paper."

CHAPTER 16

The second day of the hearings saw a noted change. They were moved to the larger Myrtle Room to accommodate the crowds. No doubt the authorities thought that with the New York society gentlemen, now free from the office on a Saturday, the new room would accommodate them along with their overdressed wives. Since the hearings the day before had involved a large standing-room-only crowd, Morgan and Call were only too happy the hotel had made arrangements for the show. It was going to be a show, too, that was apparent. No doubt it would feature the latest in technology, the Marconi wireless system. Guglielmo Marconi himself had taken a seat along with his one-time fiancée, the beautiful and rabid suffragette Inez Milholland. Call pointed them out to Morgan, along with a number of the surviving luminaries of the society elite.

They watched as Harold Bride, the man who would be the star witness, was wheeled into the room. The entire crowd hushed as a nurse in starched whites pushed the man's wheelchair forward.

"The White Star Line spares no expense when they try to make a statement, do they?" Call whispered.

Bride was only twenty-two years old and looked as if he'd never shaved in his life. His face was drawn and pale and his foot elevated and bandaged. The nurse pushed him into position in front of the committee table and then took a chair that someone in the front row had been nice enough to scoot into place for her.

After the usual niceties, Senator Smith began the questioning. "Were you on duty when the wireless message was received from the *Amerika* regarding the proximity of icebergs in that longitude?"

"No, sir."

"Did Mr. Phillips, the wireless operator, say that such a message had been received?"

"No, sir."

"Did you ever talk with the captain about such a message?"

"There was a message delivered to the captain in the afternoon, sir, late in the afternoon, regarding—"

"On Sunday?"

"Yes, sir."

Call leaned over in Morgan's direction. "You better leave this to me, and go get your article written. You might even see someone you know who can give us better information." He patted Morgan's shoulder. "I really want to know who was responsible for the number of lifeboats. If anything significant breaks here, I'll come and get you."

Morgan excused himself, stepping over several reporters and making his way toward the lobby. The large ballroom hadn't been designed to be stuffy. The walls were an ivory white, and high above them ornate angels were carved into a golden ceiling. It was almost as if the bar of heaven's justice had decided to bring the testimony of the survivors under its roof so that the angelic hosts could observe humanity in all of its folly without ever having to leave their ivory palaces. The towering windows were open, and Morgan could feel the slight breeze as it rippled the silky white curtains and gave off the coolness of the showers from the night before.

He nodded at the doorman, who quietly cracked the door open. Morgan stepped through and, rounding a corner, made his way over to the hotel desk. He had to check to see if his uncle had managed to send the money wire. The man behind the long polished mahogany desk was a cool, middle-aged man who, Morgan was sure, had practiced the art of appearing to be above any dilemma. He had a dapper mustache, and what was left of his hair was slicked back against the sides of a balding and highly polished head. "Excuse me. Do you have a wire for Fairfield, Morgan Fairfield?"

The man nodded. "Let me check, sir." He walked over to the ornate wooden hornet's nest that made up the mail slots for the hotel, probed the section for the third floor, and pulled out an envelope. Gliding back over to where Morgan stood, he pushed the yellow envelope across the counter. It was a wire.

Morgan ripped it open. It contained a money wire for 10,079 pounds, which amounted to almost $49,000 in American currency. It also contained a personal note from his uncle.

Dear Morgan—stop
Enclosed you will find a sum to see you established—stop
It represents 5% of your trust—stop
John Baxter—stop

Morgan put down the wire. *How like Uncle John*, he thought. *Nothing personal, not even a sense of relief that I had survived. That will come later in a letter from Aunt Dottie. The man is brief, especially when it involves money.*

Morgan cleared his throat to draw the man's attention. "Excuse me, I wonder if I might make a deposit into a bank here."

The man stepped over. "You may use our bank, sir. It's right across the street."

"I really have no time right now. I'm a reporter, and I'm covering the *Titanic* hearings."

"We can make the deposit for you." He reached under the counter and produced a deposit slip.

Morgan wrote it out, deducting two hundred dollars in cash. He had no idea of when he could expect his first check from the *Herald*, but the idea of continuing his life as a pauper was something he didn't relish. He also had to buy some new clothes and pay for the ones on his back. He handed the money wire and his deposit slip over to the man. The man's expression changed slightly when he read the amount. A definite sense of warmth came out for the first time. Reporters were generally not thought highly of, but a reporter who actually had money was a different thing.

The man reached into a drawer and took out a stack of bills. He counted out two hundred dollars in twenties, tens, and fives. "I'll see to this right away, sir—personally."

"Thank you." Morgan turned around with a great sense of relief. What he saw next caused the relief to escalate into pure joy. Margaret was walking through the front door with Gloria Thompson. The yellow dress she had on picked up the color of her hair. He straightened himself to his full height and walked proudly in her direction.

Gloria spotted him first. "Why, Mr. Fairfield, how nice to see you this morning."

"Have you ladies been for a walk?"

"No," Margaret said. "We put mother on a boat for England, the Red Star Liner *Lapland*."

Gloria slipped her arm around Margaret. "And now this lady of yours is feeling exceedingly guilty about not going home with her. I'm glad you are here to cheer her up."

Morgan took Margaret's hands in his. "I'll take you ladies out to dinner tonight. I just got some of my money from Uncle John, so I'm feeling in the mood to celebrate."

"I shouldn't have let her go," Margaret said. "When we got there, we discovered that many of the crew from the *Titanic* were going back on the same ship. You know how superstitious mother is. It sent a sense of panic into her."

"I'm certain she'll be all right. Your mother is a very strong woman. She's already survived the world's greatest disaster at sea. What more could happen?"

Margaret's look made it all too obvious that Morgan wasn't being a great deal of comfort. Gloria pulled her closer. "The captain of the ship assured us that they had enough lifeboats for everybody. They had some new ones recently brought on board and are planning to have a boat drill."

Morgan shook his head. "Amazing. If they can do that a week after the disaster, why couldn't they have done it two weeks ago in England?"

Just then their heads were brought around by the noise of a crowd coming from the Myrtle Room, where the hearings were being held. A large phalanx of men, with none other than Senator Smith in the lead, charged around the corner. Morgan spotted Call in one of the wings of the group.

"Marshall!" the senator called out. Across the room Morgan watched as three men in suits sprang to attention. Smith walked up to them, his hands on his hips. "I want you to go to the Brooklyn Naval Yard. Commandeer a boat if you have to. You are to stop the Red Star Liner *Lapland*." He handed over a piece of paper. "Here are the names of five of the *Titanic*'s crew. Serve them with subpoenas, and bring them to me. Is that understood?"

The three men dashed out the door to the street.

Call sidled up to Morgan, a smile on his face. "You can't outrun the long arm of the law. I guess Ismay decided he could send a few fellas home. Tried to sneak them out."

"How did Smith find out about them?"

They watched the senator storm across the lobby and pick up the phone on the desk. "Brooklyn Naval Yard," he said. He waited a few moments. "This is Senator Alden Smith. There is a ship sailing this morning, the *Lapland*. Do you know where it is?"

The senator took out his watch and pried open the lid while waiting for the report on the other end of the line. He knew that whoever was taking his spot in asking questions at the hearings would be concerned. Smith had done most of the interrogating so far. The English press had been depicting Smith as an incompetent backwoods politician. Even many of the American newspapers had been calling him a fool, but he was anything but that. The man was an attorney, a builder and operator of railways, and the publisher of a reasonably sized newspaper. In addition, he was the chairman of the board of a company that operated a fleet of Lake Michigan steamboats. To make matters more interesting, and possibly the hidden reason why he was being pilloried by the American press, he was an avowed enemy of J. P. Morgan and his trusts. Morgan was going to avoid introducing himself to the man. The association he had with his great uncle often cut both ways.

Smith patted his foot on the carpet. "Lower New York Bay, you say? Past the Statue? I have men on board that ship that must be removed.

They are not to leave American waters, is that understood? Have a boat standing by. I'm sending U.S. Marshals, and I expect you to get them on board that vessel."

He banged down the receiver and then caught Call's eye. Smith walked over to where Call was standing with Morgan and the women. He shook his hand. "Nice work, young man. Your country and I are very grateful. If I can ever do anything for you, you have only to ask."

"No problem, Senator," Call said. "I'm only too happy to help."

With that, the senator turned and marched back toward the hearing room. A swarm of men followed—all, of course, except Call.

Morgan stepped around Call, staring him in the eye. "How did you know that? You were in jail last night."

Call grinned. "A good reporter is working all the time, boy. When I'm not, the people who keep their noses to the ground for me are. I just thought I should pass that on to the good senator from Michigan. Figured it would be worth the show as well as my name on a story."

Gloria Thompson cleared her throat. "Aren't you going to introduce us to the nice gentleman, Morgan?"

Morgan stepped back, a pink flush rising in his cheeks. Moments when he felt a great sense of euphoria had always seemed to be the times when he let proper etiquette fall flat. But those were the occasions when humility was called on, so maybe it was for the best. He introduced the two ladies to Call.

Call nodded at Margaret but took Gloria's hand and bowed. "Charmed, madam."

"Equally, Mr. Call."

"It's just plain Call. And what brings you ladies to our fine city?"

"We were together on the *Titanic*," Morgan said.

Call's expression turned serious. "I trust you ladies were not part of the widow brigade."

"My husband died a few years ago," Gloria said, "but Miss Hastings here lost her fiancé."

"I am sorry to hear that, miss. People tell you that you will forget those things, but you never do. You are urged to get on with your life, but the simple fact is that your life often becomes less, and it no doubt should."

"You sound like you have lost someone dear to you," Gloria said.

Morgan watched Call's eyes narrow slightly. A flash of pain surfaced and just as quickly disappeared. Morgan wondered if he'd imagined it. It was as if Call was fighting back a memory, and Morgan knew just what that memory was. He wished he didn't. Right then, he felt like an intruder in the man's life. "Let's just say this: I'm intimately acquainted with grief. Unfortunate part of my job as an investigative reporter, I'm afraid." Call's eyes twinkled at Gloria as if she were the only person in the room.

He's a master at sidestepping personal questions, thought Morgan. In many ways Call was still a complete mystery to Morgan, and the seasoned reporter seemed to like it that way. Morgan didn't even know if Call was his first or last name. He did know that Call was a chameleon, able to move in and out of character at will. One moment a ladies' man, the next a drunken brawler, and the next a brilliant writer. Morgan was more than a little nervous about introducing him to a sweet woman like Gloria.

Gloria stepped closer to Call and picked up his hand. Morgan had never seen the woman looking so radiant. Her white hat, with a hint of netting that covered the tops of her eyes, swooped down over her very pretty face.

"Intimacy is just the word I would have chosen too. Without great injury, men or women simply are not capable of great intimacy. How can one know the joy of gain without the pain of loss?"

Surprisingly, Call seemed enchanted by the woman. His face softened, a look of innocence mixed with wonder. "I've never thought of it that way before."

"Few of us ever do," Gloria said. "We simply get bitter and turn our backs on life." She laughed. "Or we pick up speed, hoping that the more we do, the more quickly time will pass."

"Or we realize that life is shorter than we thought. There'll never be enough time . . . or a next time," Call said.

Morgan coughed nervously. He felt like he was eavesdropping on a private conversation. Besides, he felt more comfortable with the cynical, less personal Call.

Gloria smiled and looked back at Margaret. "Here I am taking your time, dear. I'm certain that you and Morgan have much to talk about. And, of course, we will have to do a little shopping if Morgan is going to take us to dinner. It wouldn't do to be seen in the same dress twice in one day, now would it?"

Morgan knew that Gloria knew how to poke fun at the rich and their attention to fashion. She was from a small town in Oklahoma. Margaret smiled, and that alone lifted Morgan's spirits. He stared at her intently, not noticing the men who had walked up to them. Then he spotted Ryan, the policeman who had almost cost him his life. "Can we help you?" Morgan asked.

Ryan looked sober. "Actually, we're here for you, Call."

"You find my sixty-five dollars?" Call asked.

"No, I'm afraid not. We're here to arrest you for the murder of one Alister Bain."

"You can't be serious."

"I'm afraid we are. The man was shot with a .32, and you and your gun were the last to be seen with him. You better come along with us."

"This is ridiculous."

Morgan and the two women stood aside as the policemen started to lead Call from the hotel. "It's got to be some mistake," Morgan said. "Or something worse."

Call grabbed his arm. "Look, go find Gerry Farier. She's a woman I saw at the bar. She used to work for the paper. She can place me leaving the bar with Bain still sitting there."

PART II
WEARING OF THE GREEN

CHAPTER 17

Morgan, the sweat beads puckering on the smooth skin of his forehead, wound his way around the desks on the *New York Herald*'s fourth floor. He didn't bother to knock on Dixon's door. What the man was doing didn't matter anymore. He twisted the brass knob and stepped into the room.

Dixon was leaning back in his chair trying to do his best to hold his own with Patricia Bennett. He jabbed at the air with his lit cigar in the woman's direction and was spouting off in a growl about the layout of the day's special edition. For her part, Patricia was leaning over the man's desk with both hands on Dixon's blotter. She appeared to have been making her point quite nicely. They both seemed to stop midsentence. Turning their heads, they looked at Morgan.

"What are you doing here?" Dixon asked. "Shouldn't you be at the hearings?"

Morgan lurched to a stop and raised himself to full height. "Call's been arrested."

"Again," Dixon sputtered. He clamped the cigar back into his mouth. "It's a little too early in the day for that, isn't it?"

"He's been arrested for murder."

Dixon dropped the cigar into his lap. He scooted his chair from the desk and with one swift stroke knocked the cigar to the floor. He beat out the live coals that were burning a hole in his breeches. "Murder?" he muttered. "Who is he supposed to have killed?"

"Some man we have reason to believe was involved in the murder of an engineer off the *Titanic*."

"That case. I didn't know you were following that one still."

Morgan nodded. "I take it that's where Call was last night. They say the man was shot with Call's revolver."

"I told him never to carry that thing," Pat said. "I knew it would get him into some predicament."

"He must have been on to something," Morgan responded. "If he hadn't been, this wouldn't have happened. We've got to bail him out of there."

Both Patricia and Dixon exchanged glances. The young woman stood upright and tugged at her sleeves, putting them back into position. She shook her head. "The bail will be high for something like that. I'm not sure the paper will spring for it."

"Can we get him a good lawyer?" Morgan asked.

"Nance is the paper's attorney," Patricia responded, "but he's not a criminal lawyer. He mostly protects our interests against some sort of libel action."

"Well, then, see if Nance can find us a good criminal attorney," Morgan said. "He's going to need one and fast. You've also got to see that Call gets out of that jail. What he was doing was business for the paper."

Dixon reached down and fished the cigar from the worn carpet. He brushed his mustache aside and mashed the cigar between his lips, the edges of gray spindly hair hanging down the sides of what was left of the Cuban stogie. "The man's got a point there." Taking out a fresh match, he raked it over the top of his desk and puffed the bitter weed to life once again.

He blew a plume of smoke in Patricia's direction. "See what you can do with the front office." Wrapping a stubby finger around it, he pulled out the cigar and pointed it at Morgan. "In the meantime, you get over to the jail. Talk to Call. See just what he was onto. You may have to follow up whatever he was onto until we get his sorry can out of that jail."

"What about the hearings?" Patricia asked.

Sticking the cigar back in his mouth, Dixon gave it a soft chew. "Fairfield, you go find Jake O'Leary. He's the man I sent for you when the *Carpathia* came in. Send him over there until you can get back. The man takes shorthand. What he lacks in writing he makes up for by taking good notes."

He shook his head slowly. "You boys got yourselves into a peck of trouble. Most of the time it's where we want you, but now it's the paper's trouble."

Morgan and Patricia left Dixon muttering to himself, and Morgan once again found himself following the woman around the desks of the newsroom. "Do you really see a problem with getting bail for Call?"

She stopped. "The paper has a ceiling on everything. Nobody here wants to tie up money in the courts, especially for someone with Call's reputation. Think about how it's going to look. The *Times* and the *American* will have a heyday over this one."

Morgan looked out over the busy room. "Think about how it's going to look in here. You have a man doing his job who's now being railroaded. Nobody here is going to pursue a story if they know the paper can't, or won't, back them up. They'll be tiptoeing around every lead they get for years to come."

"You've got a point there. I'll do my best. I'm not promising anything, though. We've got a paper to put out, and that takes money."

"At least get a good criminal attorney over there. Maybe there's something that can be done."

She turned to walk away but stopped dead in her tracks. "I almost forgot. You've got a call to make on someone." Swirling around in her pocket, she produced a slip of paper and handed it over to Morgan. "It seems that you've made a fan."

Morgan looked at the paper. It had the name and address of a Miss Irene Saunders. "Who is this? You know I'm engaged or, at least, almost engaged."

Patricia smiled. "No, I didn't know. Well, I wouldn't worry about Miss Irene. The woman's old enough to be your mother, maybe even your grandmother. She's one of the richest women in New York as well." She snickered. "Maybe she can put up the money to spring our Mr. Trouble out of jail. You just go and be charming, and we'll all be grateful. The old woman hasn't seen the light of day since you've been born."

"Oh, fine. I'm to write first-person stories on the *Titanic*, learn to be a good reporter from a man who can't stay out of jail, and be the charmer for some ancient dowager of New York society. You sure you don't want me to sweep up around here when I'm done?"

Patricia's face broadened into a grin, which showed off the dimples in her cheeks and made her eyes dance. "Welcome to the newspaper business, Fairfield. Now get to work."

Morgan watched her march off in the direction of the stairs, her hips swaying and giving off the slightest hint of femininity in spite of the way she tended to bark at the men who got in her way. He could only hope she would do the right thing and become Call's champion to the men on the upper floors.

He made his way to where several reporters were gathered at the coffeepot. They had taken a more relaxed stance when Patricia Bennett had left the room.

One of the men was Jake O'Leary. He was wearing a checkered suit that buttoned all the way up to his bright red necktie. The man's boyish grin was slightly marred by the fact that he obviously hadn't taken the trouble to shave that morning. While the red stubble on his face wasn't showing enough to keep people staring at the moment, it would be highly noticeable by late afternoon. O'Leary spotted Morgan right away. "There you are. How's the room at the Waldorf?"

"It's a bed."

"A bed?" O'Leary grinned. "It's a bed they make up for you every morning. A man might as well bring his mother to work."

"I wouldn't know about that. My mother died when I was just an infant."

That seemed to cast a pall over the men's conversation, but only for a moment.

"Dixon asked me to tell you to go over to the hearings," Morgan said.

"And where will you be?"

"I've got to go to jail."

"Already?" O'Leary grinned. He looked around at the other reporters gathered around. "It takes most of us months to get thrown in the slammer. How do you move so fast?"

"Call's in jail. I need to find out how he's doing and what he knows."

O'Leary's face suddenly grew longer. "I heard about that, but I thought it was just a rumor."

"No rumor. He's in jail for murder."

"Murder? Who's he supposed to have killed?"

"Some informant, I think."

"I've had me a few I'd have liked to have throttled, but none that I've done away with—so far."

"It's probably just a misunderstanding. The man's dead, though, and Call may have been one of the last to see him alive. Do you know a woman named Gerry Farier? She used to work here, and Call said she probably saw him leaving the bar and saw that the man he was supposed to have killed was still sitting there."

"She doesn't sound familiar to me. Bloody shame." O'Leary shook his head. "I suppose we make a living by being in the wrong place at the right time. Sometimes a man can get too eager, though. He can be in the wrong place at the wrong time. I know Call. He's always pushing his nose where it doesn't belong. Something like this was bound to happen sooner or later."

"Isn't that what we're supposed to do—poke our heads into places that make people uncomfortable?"

O'Leary took a black bowler from the coatrack and cocked it on his head. "Yeah, it is. You just have to make sure that when you see that door closing, you jerk it out in time. You've got to report the trouble, not become the trouble."

"I'll tell him you said that."

O'Leary put up both hands, waving them at Morgan like a man signaling a truck to move forward. "Just leave my name out of it. I've got plenty to do without getting Call madder than a wet hen."

Morgan pulled out the small slip of paper Patricia had given him and looked it over. "Do any of you know anything about an Irene Saunders?"

The group all laughed.

"You mean the Witch of Wall Street," O'Leary said.

"I don't know who or what she is."

"Most of us don't either. I doubt anybody does. Nobody's seen the woman for years. She took millions from her parents when they died and has multiplied that sizable nest egg into many millions more. What does she want with you?"

"She wants to see me."

"What for?"

"Maybe she just wants to hear more about the *Titanic*, though for the life of me I don't see why I should take my time to go chat with some woman I've never met just to satisfy her curiosity."

"You better go. That woman could buy and sell this paper and you with it."

"I think I'm past the point of actually letting someone's money make me do anything."

The fact that Morgan's uncle had wired him at least a part of his trust fund had done quite a bit to give him more confidence. In a way, he both hated and liked the feeling. He didn't much care for the smugness of the wealthy and how they seemed to carry themselves above the common worries of life. And he certainly lost no love for the class consciousness he'd grown up with in England, but now he felt like one of the wealthy, at least deep inside where no one could see. It was where he planned to keep those feelings too, deep inside.

"I don't think I'm ever going to get to that point," O'Leary laughed, "at least not on this earth." He turned to walk away, and then gave Morgan a parting thought. "Tell Call hi for me. You can tell him I won't be following him around for stories for a while too. The man goes places I'd rather not be found in."

CHAPTER 18

Morgan, fully expecting to see the lawyer sent by the paper, walked into the police station. He still didn't know if they were going to be able to get Call out on bail, but somehow he had to find a way to tell the man that help was coming. He also wanted desperately to find out just what Call had been able to uncover the night before. Whatever it was had been important enough to frame the man, and Morgan knew he'd have to go about proving that.

From what little Morgan knew about Call, he knew the man wasn't about to say anything about his sources to anyone. He only hoped Call might now trust him enough to tell him what he knew. Morgan knew that as far as Call was concerned, being green and innocent gave Morgan only one advantage—he was too stupid to be double-dealing. He didn't know enough about the business, and he didn't know enough about the city.

The police hadn't proved to be the greatest source of comfort so far as Morgan was concerned. He'd gone with them and had almost gotten killed, and now Call had been thrown in jail on what Morgan assumed were trumped-up charges.

He stepped up to the long counter that separated the lobby from the desks of the police. He rang the silver bell, which attracted a burly sergeant who sat behind his desk on the other side. The man glanced up from the paper he was reading and slowly got to his feet. He ambled over to the counter like a teddy bear left out in the rain for much too long.

"I'm from the *New York Herald*, and I'd like to see Call, if I can."

The man cocked his head, eyeballing Morgan carefully. "I don't see why not."

"Is he all right?"

That idea caused the man to break out into a broad smile. "When have you ever known that man not to be all right? He's like a ray of sunshine in our jail. Even if we didn't have to keep him, we'd want to all the same."

That idea seemed odd to Morgan, as if Call were serving a purpose for the greater good of the city just to be arrested.

"Follow me," the man said. He took out a ring of keys from his pocket and walked with Morgan at his heels around several desks and into a hallway that led to an empty room for the officers. Many of the men's coats were hanging on brass hooks on the wall, and a coffeepot was whistling on the stove.

The officer walked over and took the pot off the burner. He made his way to the first of the locked doors and turned the key in it. Morgan noticed the smile on the man's face. "I'd take you down there," he said, "but you can't miss his cell. It's the one with the gaggle of people in front."

"People?"

The bubbly-jawed man laughed. "Yeah, Call always draws quite a crowd." He pointed down the gray-painted hall. "Go down to the end and turn right. You can't miss it."

Morgan walked quietly down the long hall. It didn't matter how soft his steps were, however. Anybody close by was bound to be attracted by the sound. Each and every man in jail seemed to crave attention, rather to be noticed for being a human being more than just another part of the wall. For the men cooped up in the quiet cells of the city jail, the slightest sound from the hall was always a reason to sit up and take notice.

Every kind of riffraff known to man collected in those small dustbins of society. Some small men sat on the edge of their bunks and dangled their feet over the sides of their cots, the toes of their shoes barely touching the slab beneath them as the men swung their legs back and forth. Other taller men sat stoop shouldered under the upper cots. Zombies from another time and place; Gulliver's lost travelers.

Each man turned to look at Morgan as he walked by, their hollow vacant eyes starving for a kind word, staring through him as he passed by. They'd long since gone beyond the stage of merely gawking at a man.

As Morgan neared the corner of the cellblock, he heard riotous laughter, the sound of the living among the dead.

He rounded the corner and saw a group of policemen at the end of the hall. Some were standing outside the cell, while others had dragged chairs into the hall to form a small amphitheater. They were intent on following the progress of what was happening inside the cell. Morgan could tell at once that Call was turning on his charm, even if it was directed at the men in blue.

He edged his way to the cell and looked inside. Call had his back to the wall. He had removed the top cot and was using the bottom cot as a multipurpose card table. Call shuffled the deck in midair, grinning at the policemen who were surrounding the makeshift table with their chairs.

"You see, gentlemen, a table is totally unnecessary. It just gets in the way, actually, and it makes a terrible noise when I drag a man's money in my direction." He glanced at the man seated across the cot. "Now, George, you don't like to hear the sound of your money being dragged away, do you?"

The policeman shook his head.

"I didn't think so." Call pointed to the man. He threw the cards out in a clockwise direction, making a careful count, almost deliberately dummying down the whole process. "One, two. Does everyone have two cards? I wouldn't want anyone missing a card."

Pointing once again at the man seated across from him, Call grinned. "Especially you, George. I wouldn't want you short of that queen of hearts I just gave you."

The policeman picked up the card Call had just dealt him. He looked at it and slammed it down on the cot. "How'd you know? How'd you know it was the queen?"

Call smiled. "Fact is, George, my friend, I'm going to give you three queens. It doesn't help to have a man fold when you plan on cheating him out of everything he owns, now does it? A man's got to believe, George." He laughed. "At least until I turn over my cards."

Every eye was riveted on Call as he dealt out the next three cards. The policemen picked up their cards, and the man across from Call immediately threw his back down. "Three queens, just as you said. How did you do that?"

He looked at the men seated to either side of him. "Did anybody see what he did?"

The officers all shook their heads.

Call picked up his hand and slowly turned them over. "Nine, six, ace of clubs, ace of spades, ace of hearts." He smiled. "My three aces beat your three queens every time."

The men all laughed.

"You see, the tricky part is not in giving you cards. Nobody looks when a man gives out cards. It's when the dealer takes a card, that's the hard part." Call smirked. "Of course in your case, George, it's easy. You pick up every card dealt when it goes down. All I got to do is make them high enough to get you excited."

That brought another round of laughter, long and hard. "So how come you're working as a poor reporter instead of living uptown?" one of the policemen in the hallway asked.

"That's easy." Call lifted his head and caught sight of Morgan. "A man who knows what I know would wind up in jail."

The men all began to laugh, this time louder. "That's a rich one," one of them said.

"But you gentlemen should excuse me now. I see that my young protégé has arrived." Call's eyes twinkled. "Probably with my ransom money. Now, which of you gentlemen should we pay it to?"

The remark brought another round of laughter as they began getting to their feet and shuffling toward the cell door.

"You don't mind if my friend here comes in the cell with me, do you? You get paid to keep people in, not to keep them out."

"Nah," one sergeant spoke up. "You just make sure he ain't got no file with him. I don't know what we'd do if you finally decided to behave yourself."

The man stood aside as Morgan stepped through the door and then with one abrupt motion slammed the steel cage shut.

"Now don't you men go to using what I've shown you here today." Call leaned up against the bars so the sound of his voice would carry. "I wouldn't want those good boys out on the beat to go around broke till they learned their lessons from you men."

The blue-clad column continued to laugh as the policemen made their way down the cellblock. Their voices drowned out the footsteps.

"You seem to know how to get along wherever you are, don't you, Call?"

The words had barely come out of Morgan's mouth when Call swiveled around and grabbed him by the lapels on his jacket. He threw him against the wall and then rammed his arm into Morgan's throat. Leaning into him, Call's words were quietly menacing. Morgan saw a look of viciousness in the man's eyes. Call was like a tiger in a cage, a cage that Morgan now found himself in as well.

"What are you doing here?"

Before Morgan could answer, Call pushed his arm harder into Morgan's throat. It stopped any words before they had the air to even form. "You don't get it, do you, boy? Those people intend to kill us. They will stop at nothing until both of us are off this story. I don't know why yet, but I intend to find out."

He drove his arm harder into Morgan's Adam's apple. "If you show up here, you let these people know that you're in on it with me. They'll think I'm telling you everything that's in my head. And believe me, if you knew what was in there, your life would be cut so short you'd wish you had died on that ship out there. The less you see of me, the longer you're going to live. Do you understand what I'm telling you?"

Morgan tried to nod, but it was difficult.

"Now, I'm going to let you off this wall and you're going to haul yourself out of this police station. You're going to leave, and you're not ever going to look back. You're going to go back to writing something you know about, the *Titanic* and that iceberg it hit. Am I making myself understood?"

Call let up slightly on Morgan's throat, and Morgan managed to nod. Straightening himself up, Call backed away slightly and smoothed Morgan's coat.

Morgan ran his hand up his neck and swallowed. "I thought we were working together."

"Listen, you gave me a man's name that may have been involved in killing Fetters. I found that man last night. He's connected to the Irish Tommyknockers in this town. Now he's dead, and they say I killed him. To make matters worse, the people who are sworn to protect us want our heads. Do you want to go up against that?"

Morgan gulped and squeezed his neck ever so slightly. "I don't understand. Why all this over a man killed by some Irish thugs on the pier?"

"What's the biggest story in this town, this country, this world right now?"

"The *Titanic*."

"You remember I told you about crime where the murderers are corporate bigwigs?"

"I remember."

"I might have been half joking then, but I'm not now. Fetters came off of that ship. He was carrying no money. The only thing important that man had was what was inside his head. I'd say somebody killed him to make sure it never left that head of his. The man was dangerous. We're looking for whoever killed him, and that makes us dangerous. One of the men who killed him was Bain, and now he's dead and I'm in here for killing him. You figure it out."

Morgan's look was one of shock, but he knew in an instant that it all fit. "And you think whoever is responsible has the police working for them?"

"At least part of the police. We just have to find out the part that still might work for us."

The sound of footsteps in the hall made Call back away farther from Morgan. A broad smile came over Call's face, magically transforming the beast into a thing of innocence and beauty.

When Call saw the man, his expression changed still more. Morgan could see Call relax, and instead of a phony pasty smile, Call almost beamed.

The visitor was a thin man in a police sergeant's uniform. His complexion was dark. He had jet black hair and a thick mustache that not only covered his upper lip but threatened to take over his lower lip and chin as well. He grinned at Call and flashed a broad smile. "They finally got you, I see."

"Yeah, you know what a desperado I am."

The man put the key to Call's cell in the lock and turned it. "I came over just in time. It's not really my job, but they're letting me take you over to the hall of justice. You have a lawyer there."

"It's about time." Call pointed to Morgan. "This is Morgan Fairfield. He's one of our reporters. You won't be seeing much of him, though, 'cause I told him to stay completely away from this." He shot Morgan a glance. "If he knows what's for his own good."

"Pleased to meet you." The man looked at Call and then at Morgan. He motioned with his head in Call's direction. "The man must really like you if he doesn't plan on using you. Call here uses everybody, and he has to hate me a lot because he's always trying to use me."

"This is Fredo Giuseppe," Call announced. "He's a cop, but at least he's not Irish."

Fredo laughed. "My father would be the most surprised man in the world if I was."

"He's not too bright, either," Call added.

"If I was, do you really think I'd be here?"

CHAPTER 19

It had been a busy day for Patricia Bennett, busy and frustrating. She climbed out of the cab near the docks, paid the driver, and then stood there watching it drive away. The light of day made her feel somewhat safe, but the look of some of the sailors standing dockside unraveled whatever starch she had built into her petticoat. She wasn't going to let them stop her, though. She'd never been one to let a man stop her from doing what she knew had to be done.

She walked down the dock, still seething at what her uncle had told her. The paper had just so much money they could provide for bail, and it was doubtful that would be enough to cover Call. She knew she had to find a way to get Call out of jail. He would be his own best defense. She knew that. As long as he was locked up, he wouldn't be able to pursue any leads he'd developed so far. To her knowledge, there was only one man who knew his way around the streets of New York enough to uncover all the holes in the state's case, and that man was Call.

This area, near the bar on the street detailed in the police report, was the only place she knew to start. Call was never one to let anyone sniff out his stories. The man had an independent streak in him that would take up Fifth Avenue. She knew full well that if he ever found out that she was trying to snoop into what he'd already done, he might up and quit the paper. Of course, if she could find a way to save his sorry hide, that might just be enough to placate him.

She stepped over the gutter, which was still filled with the smelly remains of the night before on the dock, and onto the aged boardwalk that fronted the street. The copy of the police report in her hand showed her where Call had been found the night before, and she looked to her left to spot the entrance to the alleyway that marked where he'd been knocked unconscious.

She was standing right in front of the Brass Rail, and her nose turned up at the smell of the place. Cheap liquor and stale beer always had a way of turning her stomach. It certainly wouldn't make her seem more at ease. She'd have to fight it, though, fight the nausea and anything else that got in her way.

She pushed open the swinging doors and heard the clear laughter of the men around the tables. It sent her head to ringing. Doubtless they'd find great fun in watching her, but then most men did. Where she worked, though, they had the brains to keep their amusement to themselves. Here they didn't.

She stepped over to the bar. Behind it a man was wiping the beer mugs with what was plainly a dirty dish towel, very dirty. He lifted his chin and, spotting her, walked to where she was standing.

"Can I help you, Miss?"

She pulled out a business card and slid it over the bar. "I am Patricia Bennett. I'd like to ask you a few questions about one of our reporters."

The man picked up the card and studied it. He turned it over in his hands as if inspecting the paper it was printed on. That made Patricia wonder if he could read. "Do you mean Call?" he asked.

"Yes."

"He was in here a couple of days ago with another one of your reporters. Young feller too. Didn't figure him for a real reporter, though. Thought he might have been just a note taker."

"You mean a secretary?"

"Yep, a secretary."

The man leaned over the bar to get closer to her, and his smell made her pull away.

"Now, how can I help you?"

"I am more interested in the night he was arrested."

"You mean the night he up and killed Bain?"

"I mean the night he was arrested. Can you tell me who he spoke with?"

The man leaned back slightly and stroked his pudgy chin. "Well, let me see. Things like that are mighty hard for a feller to remember."

Patricia reached into her purse and took out three one-dollar bills. She slid them toward the man. "Will this help?"

His eyes brightened and he smacked his lips. "That just might help a whole lot." Picking up the currency, he folded the bills and stuffed them into his pocket. "Yes, I do remember. He spent some time with a certain lady who was trying to give him the old come-on. A lady of—"

"The evening?" Patricia added.

He swallowed and grinned. "Yes, ma'am, a woman of easy virtue. He didn't go with her, though, just was real nice to her. A real gentleman he was." He pointed to the table nearest the door. "She was seated right there."

"Is that her usual place?"

The man nodded. "Yes, I suppose it is."

"And do you know this woman's name?"

He bunched up his lower lip, like a child who had been ordered off to bed, and shook his head. "Nah, I don't see much of her."

"Have you seen her since?"

"Can't say as I have."

"But you know the place she usually sits."

He twisted his eyebrows downward. She could tell that she wasn't getting her three dollars worth, certainly not of the truth.

He leaned on his elbows, his chubby arms bulging out from the rolled-up sleeves of his dirty white shirt. "Them types like to sit close to the door. That ways they can get the men who come in, or maybe have one last pass at them 'afore they leave. You know how it is."

"I can imagine."

"Well, ever'body's got to make a buck, don't they?"

"I suppose so. Where was Bain seated?"

The man leaned over the bar and pointed to the dark area at the rear. "He was at his usual table, all the way in the back."

"You do seem to notice where people sit, don't you?"

He picked up a dirty shot glass and tried to give it the appearance of cleanliness. "That's my job, serving customers. Generally I know where they sit and what they're drinking."

"And what did Call drink that night?"

He laughed. "A boilermaker. Know what that is? You take a mug of beer and drop a shot glass full of whiskey—"

"I know what it is."

"Well, that's what I served him."

"And you think that would be enough to get a man like Call drunk?"

He raked the back of his hand slowly over his cheek. Even from where she stood Patricia could hear the sound of his stubble as it grated against his knuckles.

"Normally I'd say no. But with somebody like that reporter of yours, it may have just been enough to put him over the top. A man gets a job he can't stomach, and he starts drinking his breakfast and works his way through the day."

"Call is a good reporter. He likes his job."

The man grinned. "Yes, ma'am, if you say so."

"I do say so." She paused and took a breath, trying hard not to breathe too steadily through her nose. The stench was oppressive. "So he had his drink and went back to talk to this Bain?"

"That's about the size of it."

"Then he came stumbling back and made it out your door before he collapsed drunk outside."

"I suppose so."

"So he must have shot Bain in the back of your saloon."

"No, ma'am. Bain's body was found in the alley next to my place."

"I see." Patricia smirked. "So my drunken reporter shot him back there and just dragged his body out, without your seeing it, so that it could be found in the alley."

The man's eyes widened.

"The questions get harder," she said, "especially when you're seated on a witness stand and have a lawyer asking them."

"I don't rightly know how he did it. I just know he did."

Patricia smiled. "I can see that you're going to make a fine witness for the prosecution. When did Bain leave?"

"Must have been shortly after Call did."

"And there are other witnesses to back that up?"

He shook his head. "I don't really know that. I just know what I saw."

"You know where people sit. You know what they order. You evidently see only my reporter leaving the bar, and you can't identify anyone else. Is that right?"

He gulped. "I suppose so."

She wrapped her fingers tightly around the strings of her purse. "I hope you know that the penalty for perjury covers supposing."

"I ain't lying."

"Maybe somebody is paying you more than my three dollars. Do we have a bidding war going on here?"

She could see the man's anger rising. A slow crimson began at his collar and colored his cheeks. "Maybe I should take two of those three dollars back?"

"Lookie here, Miss Bennett, or whatever your name is, I done told you what I seen. That ought to be enough for you. It was for the police."

"I'm sure it was. It may not be good enough for our lawyer, though. You'd better put that thinking cap of yours on a little tighter before you get on that witness stand."

"You threatening me?"

Patricia smiled. "Who, me? Do you think a little slip of a woman could bully a big strong man like you? Especially one that looks the other way when people are killed. I should think not. I wouldn't dream of such a thing."

He drew back. "I just know what I know. That's all, and that's all there will ever be."

"Until somebody comes along and offers you a better reason to forget, I'm sure."

Patricia hadn't noticed the two men who had walked up to the bar next to her. Just then, they edged closer. She caught their smell first, the smell of cheap cigars mixed with whatever it was they'd been drinking.

"We got us a pretty little number here today, don't we?"

She turned and gave them a stare, a sort of condescending gaze mixed with disgust. With most men that was all it took. The man closest to her had on a torn cotton vest that was dyed black. The rips in it displayed the dingy yellow shirt he had on underneath. The man's four- or five-day growth of beard on his face underscored his disinterest in what he was wearing or how he looked.

His chest was as big as a barrel, and the trousers that hung from his ample middle were held up with a rope instead of the usual belt. His companion was wiry and thin and wore an apron smeared with what Patricia took to be fish blood.

The larger of the two men, the one next to Patricia, nudged his friend with his elbow. "This one would be a cute trick, wouldn't she?"

"Yeah," the smaller of the men slurred.

Patricia ignored them and turned back to the man at the bar. "Our attorney will be contacting you to get your complete story. I hope that by then your memory will clear up."

The man shrugged his shoulders.

"Now, why don't I just go back and look at the table you say Bain was at. Maybe we'll find the bullet hole there."

"Suit yourself." He leaned over and pointed to the back of the bar. "It's the very back one. Bain sat with his back to the wall."

"Thank you." She started to leave, but the larger of the two men next to her grabbed her by the arm.

"We're talking to you, lady."

She stopped, peeling the man's fingers from her arm. "Find someone else to talk to."

"We want you, missy," the second man said. "You're right pretty."

The larger of the two men grinned. "Yep. Why don't you come to our place for a while?"

"I'm certain that would be most impossible."

"Now why is that?"

"Because I'm sure the rock you crawled out from under wouldn't be large enough to accommodate two people."

The man behind the bar laughed as Patricia walked away. His laughter was cut short by the stares of the two men, but she kept moving toward the back of the room. She didn't expect to stay long. Right then she was looking forward to never seeing the inside of the Brass Rail again.

As she passed a table of older women, one of them reached out and grabbed the sleeve of her dress. "Are you Miss Bennett?"

Patricia stopped and looked down at the woman. "Why, yes, I am."

"You still at the *Herald*?"

"Yes."

"I used to work there. I mopped the halls at night. I seen you leave sometimes, plenty late too. Thought to myself what a grand thing it was to have a woman working in a fine dress in a place like that."

Patricia smiled. "Thank you."

"I seen my friend Call here the other night." She gave off a broad smile that showed missing and blackened teeth. She leaned closer to Patricia, giving off the now all too familiar odor of beer. "He brung me flowers when I was working there once't in a while."

"You saw him here the other night?"

"Yep, sure nuff did." She looked back at the other older women at the table. "You girls remember that reporter I told you about, don't you?"

The other women nodded their heads.

"Did you see him talking to the man seated at the table back there?"

"You mean Bain? We sure did."

"And did you see Call leave?"

The old woman nodded her head. "Yep. Was sorry to see him go too."

Patricia bent down and took the old woman by both arms. At this point the smell coming from her didn't matter anymore. She just wanted to make certain she got the story right. "And how long after that did you see Bain leave?"

The woman cackled. "Bain don't leave till he has to when he's got money for a drink. He stayed here maybe two, three hours more."

"Are you sure of that?"

"Sure as the sun shines, I is."

"Can I speak with you for a moment in private?"

The old woman looked around at her friends. "Hang on a bit, girls. I got to have me some talk here." With that she slowly got to her feet.

Patricia took her by the arm and led her several paces away to an empty spot among the tables. "We may need you."

"Need me? Whatever for?"

"Your friend Call is in big trouble. What you just told me could help him a great deal."

The old woman wiped her mouth with the back of her hand. "Shoot, I'd do anything to help Call. That man's been nice to me."

Patricia thought the matter over. She looked back and could see the bartender watching her, and the thought that he might ask the old woman questions after she left sent shivers up her spine. For some reason she knew that witnesses had a way of turning up missing in this case, missing or dead. "Then you need to get your things and come with me."

"Get my things? Why for?"

"Just trust me on this. What you know is very important to Call, and you need to be someplace where we can get a hold of you."

"I ain't got me much in the way of things." She looked down at her dress and then back at the table where she'd laid her bag. "Just what you see here and a few dresses and fixin's at my place."

"Then I'll buy you all the dresses and . . . fixin's you need. Will you come?"

The old woman shrugged her shoulders. "Sure, why not? I ain't got much to keep me here."

"Fine. We'll change all that. From this point on, you're hired by the *New York Herald.*"

CHAPTER 20

Morgan made his way along Fifth Avenue, stopping at a busy intersection to watch several cars sputter by, followed by a slow ice wagon drawn by a pair of tired-looking horses. He glanced at the slip of paper he'd been given, looked up at the street sign, and turned, starting a slow walk. He would stop from time to time, looking at each house.

The houses were all large. Many had ornate lions standing guard with stone claws raised in defiance. The gates were polished and formidable, closed to the traffic on the street. In any other setting, they would have looked like palaces that needed surrounding gardens and prancing horses. Here they were merely stone monuments to the power of the elite limbs of society. Each inhabitant was a member of the best the city had to offer: the right clubs, the best churches, and the smartest yacht harbor.

He glanced down at the paper and then back up at the gilded numbers on the stone gate in front of him. It was number 369, the one he'd been looking for. He straightened his new necktie. The suit he was wearing was a Brooks Brothers, gray with a hint of muted rose lines running through the material. He looked the part for this section of town. Or he at least looked like a stockbroker. From what he'd heard about the woman, his suit would be the type of attire she'd expect and perhaps even appreciate.

He opened the iron gate and swung it closed behind him. The gate gave off a moan of iron. He made his way up the cobblestone walkway to the flight of steps in front of the house. He looked up at the gray edifice. It was all of six stories, with green shutters closed to the outside world. Gargoyles, perched on the corners and under the roof of the house, stared down at him with malice on their faces and screams on their lips. Their waggling tongues were frozen in terror.

He smiled slightly when he saw the angels, their wings outspread to bear the weight of the stone, holding up the balconies. They seemed to indicate the only safe place a man could go in the house to escape the demons surrounding it, and in order to do that, one would have to step inside.

He climbed the marble stairs, unconsciously counting each one as he went. When he got to the upper landing, he turned and looked down. He counted them again. Thirteen stairs led up to the house. *Odd*, Morgan thought. *Perhaps the woman is superstitious, or rather wants her guests to be intimidated by their own fears*. It was subtle and far less noticeable than the creatures who guarded the house itself.

The doors were bright green, almost bright enough to have had a light shining inside of them. A heavy brass chain hung to their left, and Morgan reached out and gave it a tug.

He listened as the bell played a morose tune, deep and ominous. The tune was out of place. Morgan thought he could recognize the familiar notes of "Bless Be the Tie That Binds." If there was one place on earth that could never bring about the reminder of Christian love, it would be this place.

Moments later the right door cracked open and Morgan stepped over to place himself in full view. The man who had opened the door wore a black tuxedo and a high, starched collar. His head was bald except for the few plumes of white over each ear. His nose was sharp, almost hawklike, and his eyes were a piercing blue. "May I be of assistance to you, sir?"

"I am here to see Miss Saunders."

The man opened the door ever so slightly, and he looked Morgan over more carefully. He seemed to study him, not only looking at his clothing but seemingly even trying to look into his mind, his inner thoughts, his past, his family. "She sent for me. My name is Morgan Fairfield."

That brought the door fully open. Militaristic in movement, almost like a guard at Buckingham Palace, the man took one step backward. "Please come in, sir."

Morgan stepped through the door. The heavy green curtains were drawn, and the lights were low. The foyer had an array of swords fanned out like sunbursts on the walls. They were impressive. *Keeping them shined must be quite the chore*, Morgan thought.

"Right this way, sir. If you will be so kind as to follow me."

With that, the man turned on his heels and marched across the marble floor. Ornate Persian rugs, each one carefully positioned to form a series of barriers, were stretched side to side, not one of them facing the door.

The man came to tall oak double doors off the hall and slid them open. They moved effortlessly on rollers into the walls. He turned to face Morgan. "If you will kindly wait here in the smoking room, I will see if Miss Saunders will see you."

Without so much as a word, Morgan stepped into the room.

The man stared at him as if getting a last minute's approval from some unseen power and then closed both doors.

Morgan took a few steps into the middle of the room. A large crystal chandelier hung directly above him from the dark oak ceiling. What little light crept past the drawn curtains danced on the carved orbs that hung daintily under the chandelier, creating a small grouping of rainbows on the white wallpaper. Morgan realized that the orbs must be prisms of some sort. They were the first, and perhaps the only, hints of bright color in the entire house.

The remainder of the walls looked like what one might find in a stockade. Muskets were arranged in two circles, their muzzles pointing toward the center with the polished stocks fanned out in the same sunburst effect he'd seen with the swords in the foyer. The arrangement almost reached the floor but had space on top for future additions. Morgan had seen many of the castles in England. This was often used by the barons of an estate to intimidate visitors with a man's power. But from what Morgan had learned of the Saunders woman, she might have been better served to have hung stock certificates.

Two large cigar humidors stood in two of the corners of the room with groups of burgundy overstuffed leather furniture surrounding them. The tables were polished mahogany with marble tops and clawed feet.

Morgan stepped over to one group. On the wall in two groupings, one on either side of the muskets, were pictures of babies. Some were children only one or two years of age, but most were infants dressed in crib clothes, asleep or appearing to be asleep.

Morgan glanced at the other side of the room. On either side of the rifles on the wall there was another grouping of photographs. He walked over to them, eager to see just what had captured this woman's fancy. What he saw shocked and horrified him. The photographs were all of men; men lying in death in their coffins. He looked over each one carefully. Some were young, and some were quite old. There were no mourners in the photos, only the men in their last repose.

He backed up to look at the arrangement. On top of the display of guns was a vacant frame, as if the woman was saving a place for someone very special.

The doors slid open, and he almost jumped back to the middle of the room. It was obvious the woman had hung the photographs to be seen, but so far as Morgan was concerned, he didn't much care to give her the satisfaction of knowing that he had looked.

It was the butler, however, who stepped into the room, his hands dangling at his side. Morgan noticed the man's fingers for the first time. They were long, thin, and creamy white without a trace of color. The man had a smudge of color in his cheeks, and Morgan wondered if he hadn't used powder and a dab of blush. "Miss Saunders will see you now."

"Thank you."

"Please follow me, sir."

From what Morgan had just seen, he wondered if the Saunders woman hadn't taken her butler from some well-to-do funeral parlor. He certainly would have fit in such a place, and it was obvious to him that was just the kind of place she would have gone looking for him.

The man stepped across the large hallway and around the sweeping stairs. Two large staircases wound up the belly of the house, one on either side. They formed a sweeping mahogany horseshoe pouring out onto the marble floor. Above, Morgan could see a number of balconies that overlooked the foyer. Large groups of people could have formed a series of private boxes, each one ascending in height to the upper floors, and each one with an excellent view of the people who came into the house.

Morgan followed the man between the stairs and toward a room with two paneled oak doors. The man opened them and stood aside waiting for Morgan to enter. As Morgan stepped inside, the butler announced, "Mr. Morgan Fairfield, ma'am." He then closed the doors without following Morgan inside.

The room was dark, with only a simple glowing candelabra on a lace doily. The six candles had been recently lit. Morgan strained his eyes and stepped forward. He could see the figure of a woman in a large chair behind the candles, but with the glare of the candles, he couldn't quite make her out.

"Come closer, young man."

Morgan took another step.

"Closer, dear boy, so I can see you."

Morgan walked up to the table with the candles. He could see her now, and he had to work at trying not to react. The woman was small, no doubt under five feet tall. Her feet barely touched the floor. Her face was the color of bread ready to enter an oven, a cool, pasty white with soft, powder-filled wrinkles. The woman's nose was almost girl-like, a button of youth arrested in time. Her eyebrows were a snowy white, but her hair was jet black. This was a woman who had obviously taken the constant trouble of dying her hair but who evidently didn't want to get the dye close to her eyes. And very pretty eyes they were too—blue with sparkles of light. But it was the dress she wore that would set her apart from other women. She was wearing a bridal gown, stark white with pearls sewn into the bodice. A large string of pearls hung around her neck. They had a hint of pink in them. A diamond tiara was on her head. It was dazzling.

She pointed to a chair beside the table, motioning like a queen to a subject. "Please have a seat, Mr. Fairfield."

Morgan sat down. Even from the chair he could make out the perfume the woman wore, "Evening in Paris." The odor was heavy, almost oppressive. He'd seen the perfume in stores before in a dark blue bottle with the Eiffel Tower etched on it, and the aroma had always seemed blue to him, like crushed flower petals fermenting in a Chinese sweet and sour sauce.

"Do I know you?" Morgan asked.

She chuckled slightly and waved a lace handkerchief in front of her face. Again, Morgan could pick up the strong odor. No doubt the woman had more than just one Evening in Paris in that hankerchief of hers. It smelled more like a week in Paris. The gloves she wore were lace, with the fingers missing. "Why, no," she said, "but I do know you, Mr. Fairfield." She chuckled. "I like to watch young men I admire."

"You know me?"

Reaching for the table beside her, she picked up a couple of newspaper clippings. "You are the young man writing about the *Titanic*, aren't you?"

"Why, yes, ma'am, I am." Morgan was glad he'd already turned in his story for the day.

She held the clippings up to her eyes as if rereading them. "I find your work very interesting."

"I'm glad you approve, Miss Saunders. It isn't often a reporter has someone who truly admires his work."

"It must have been awful for you." She paused, a gentle smile forming on her lips. "Being so close to death and then being cheated like that."

"Cheated?"

"Well, you didn't die, now did you?"

"No, but many others did."

Her smile grew more pronounced. "Yes, they did, didn't they." She said it in a breathy whisper. "It must be truly difficult for you to forgive yourself for living while so many others died."

"Yes, ma'am. I have had thoughts along those lines."

"Forgiveness can be such a difficult matter. I find blame so much easier."

"I am a Christian, Miss Saunders. I suppose you might say that it's far more effortless for me to forgive someone else than for me to forgive myself."

The woman narrowed her eyes, her smile widening. "Yes, ever the valiant man, the true believer, I see. You are much too high-minded to hold a grudge against anyone but yourself."

"I suppose so," Morgan agreed.

"I think you will find in time, though, young man, that no amount of charity spent on others can erase one blot from your own soul if you are the one who put it there."

"You seem to know a great deal about guilt, ma'am."

"Young man, I know a great deal about everything. I know about guilt, and I know far more about blame and retribution. The wheels of justice turn slowly, but they do turn. I also know about Christians like you. You people seem to think you can put aside all wrong with the mere singing of a hymn."

"I'm afraid the pain of forgiveness is more dear than that, Miss Saunders, much more."

"Yes, but you see, in my world forgiveness still has pain, pain for the offender."

Morgan was beginning to grow impatient. He twisted in his chair. This was something the woman was quick to spot. "You must be wondering why I sent for you."

"Yes, ma'am."

"I knew the woman who called herself your mother."

"My mother?"

"You are of the Fairfields of Newport aren't you?"

Morgan nodded. "Yes, I am."

She inched closer, her feet touching the floor now. "She was a sweet woman, a very sweet woman, and her husband was a brave and noble man."

"They saved my life."

"I am well aware of that, and you strike me as an honorable and honest man. A man who has no fear of people in power."

"Thank you."

She smiled. "You will need all of those qualities and more, I fear."

"I'm afraid I don't understand."

"No, how could you? You are new to this country and to the people who run it. But you are a reporter now, and a very good one, I'd wager."

"I'm working at that."

"Good, then you won't leave any stone unturned, will you?"

"Unturned at what?"

"At finding out the man responsible for the *Titanic* disaster."

"The man responsible? You mean Ismay?"

"Mercy sakes, no." She laughed again, dabbing her mouth with the handkerchief. "That man is an office boy with a pension to protect." She leaned closer. "No, I mean the man who has the most to gain from the disaster."

"And just who would that be?"

She sat back in her chair and began to laugh. "Mercy sakes, Mr. Fairfield. You do have some homework to do, don't you?" She waved the handkerchief in Morgan's direction. "You go do some reading. I think you will find at least one name that you know very well."

"Are you referring to my great uncle?" Morgan knew quite well that she could only be talking about J. P. Morgan, a man he was very familiar with because he was the man he'd been named after. He was also the principal investor in IMM, the parent company that owned the White Star Line.

"You see, you are a bright boy. I can think of no greater exposé than one coming from a nephew of the man. People would have to believe it, now wouldn't they?"

"I write only the truth."

Her raspy voice almost quivered with emotion. She shook her finger at him. "That's exactly what I'm counting on, Mr. Fairfield, your writing the truth."

"And just what is this to you, Miss Saunders?"

"Shall we simply say that in this instance I have stakes in the truth coming out, both personal and financial? As such, I will give you all the help I can."

"What sort of help could you possibly give me?"

Her eyes twinkled. "I am a woman of means in this town. You will get help from me, but you will never know it." She picked up a bell and rang it. "Mortimer will show you to the door now. The next time you come to visit me, I would very much like for you to bring your young lady, your fiancé."

Morgan got to his feet somewhat shakily. He didn't remember telling anyone about his relationship with Margaret, certainly not of his intentions toward her. How this woman had learned of it boggled his mind. Had the butler read his mind? He shook his head as he turned to leave. *Maybe she is the Witch of Wall Street*, he thought.

CHAPTER 21

The courtroom had been jammed with people all day. Call sat in the courthouse holding cell and read the paper, thumbing through each section carefully, as if he hadn't a care in the world. When he heard the clang of the doors at the end of the hall, he looked up in time to see the attorney who represented the paper, Jim Nance, followed by another well-dressed man that Call recognized at once.

The two men waited outside the cell door while the bailiff turned the key in it. "Good to see you, Call," Nance said. "Are you doing well?"

"Under the circumstances."

The bailiff let both men into the cell, clanged the door shut, and walked away.

"Do you know Joel Paget here?" Nance asked.

"Only by reputation. It is good to see you, and I can only suppose that someone is paying you besides the *New York Herald*."

Paget smiled. "You are good. Yes, I'm being paid, and no, it's not by the *New York Herald*."

Joel Paget was all business. But he always seemed to have a pleasant smile on his face, as if he knew the outcome of any trial before it started. Call liked that kind of smug confidence in a man, probably because it was so much like him. Paget had a snappy, double-breasted blue suit on and shined shoes. No detail had been overlooked, right down to his diamond stickpin. His neatly combed black hair covered the growing bald spot that ran down the middle of his head, and his dark brown eyes looked right through a man.

"I thought so," Call said. "Mind telling me who my fairy godmother is?"

"I'm afraid I can't do that. I don't ask the guilt or innocence of any man, and I never divulge my retainers. I can tell you one thing, though, with who you have on your side, we are going to get you out of here."

"Today?"

"Yes, today."

Nance spoke up. "No matter how high it goes, we've got your bail covered, Call."

Jim Nance was a pudgy man who had too many courses on each menu. If he stopped with oysters for the next five years, that would be more than enough. The buttons on his vest were well anchored, and Call thought that was a good thing. With what the paper paid him, he ought to be eating well even if he didn't sleep well.

Call leaned back and laid the paper down. "I am a little disappointed. A man like me does his job by making enemies, not by grooming some bigwig with deep pockets. I guess I haven't been doing my job."

"We're going to work on getting the case dismissed," Paget said. "We hope we won't even need your sponsor's money."

"Patricia Bennett found a witness," Nance said.

"Patricia? What's she doing in my business?" He ground his teeth while he spoke. "Bad enough I have to put up with her orders without having her run around and clean up after me."

"Don't look this gift horse in the mouth, Call," Paget snickered.

"No," Nance added, "This witness is someone who saw you leave the Brass Rail long before Bain. This might be one occasion where your love for the bottle saves you. We have the time of your arrest, and if this woman can testify to what she saw, you'd have been under arrest while Bain was still sitting in that saloon."

"Woman?"

"Yes, a cleaning woman who used to work for the paper."

Call's face turned white. He got to his feet. "Do you have any idea of the danger you put that old woman in?"

Paget smiled. "Don't worry. Patricia has her safely put away. No one can touch her."

"It would seem our Miss Bennett was thinking ahead," Nance added.

Call sat back down, mumbling to himself. "I don't care who gets me out, just so I get out. This is a trumped-up charge, and you both know it."

It was a mere twenty minutes later when the bailiff came and unlocked the holding cell door. He led the small group down the hall and out through a door that led into the chambers of Judge Hiram Winters. They took their places behind a long table, and the judge looked up. "Next case."

The clerk stepped forward. "The people of New York against Mr. Clarence McCall."

The judge looked out to where Call was standing with Nance and Paget. White whiskers barely concealed the man's rolling jaw. His pudgy face was set sharply by two blue eyes. "How do you plead?"

Paget stepped forward. "Your honor, I am representing Mr. McCall."

That brought a broad smile to Winter's face. He folded his hands and leaned forward. "I wouldn't have thought this was in your league, Paget."

Paget glanced back at Call and then turned around, smiling. "I don't think this will take too much of my time, Your Honor, or the time of this court."

"Good. I'm glad to hear that. New York seems to take all of my time. Now how does your client plead?"

"Not guilty, Your Honor."

"Fine, I'm happy to hear that." He looked at the prosecuting attorney, a man who was seriously overmatched. "What do I hear in regards to bail, Mr. Snodgrass?"

"Your Honor, this is a trial for felony murder. The people request that the defendant be held without bail."

Paget stepped closer to the judge. "Your Honor, my client is a respected reporter. His work requires him to be free."

"I know who he is, counselor, and I wouldn't throw that word *respected* around too much in this courtroom."

"There is no threat of flight, Your Honor. We have a witness who can place the victim long after Mr. McCall was arrested for being drunk and disorderly. Frankly, my client would just like to get this matter to court and dispense with it as soon as possible."

Winters looked at the prosecutor. "Is that right, Snodgrass? Do you know about this witness?"

"I know of no such witness."

"Then I suggest you do your homework. If you people would find the facts in these matters, half of what I see would never get here. Bail is set in the amount of ten thousand dollars." With that, Judge Winters banged his gavel.

It took them only a few minutes to post Call's bail. When they walked out into the hall, Harry Dixon, along with Patricia Bennett, was waiting for them. Call stepped over to them. "I suppose I owe you my thanks for this."

"You just owe me a good day's work is all," Dixon shot back. "You owe Pat your thanks."

Call looked at her. It was hard to look the woman in the eye. "Thank you, then."

"You're welcome. I'm only sorry the paper couldn't come up with the money for your bail."

"The paper didn't?" Call asked. "Then who did?"

"We don't really know," Dixon said. "But I assume it's the same person who is paying for that fancy lawyer of yours."

"Good. I don't want to know. I've had enough people to thank for one day."

"I think we ought to pull you off this *Titanic* thing though," Dixon said. "I'm already getting heat from upstairs to take you off."

Call's face turned white. "Then you might as well let me go back to jail. Whoever drummed this thing up wanted me off that story; now you're just giving them what they want."

"I didn't say you couldn't work on the story."

"What do you mean?"

Dixon nodded in Patricia's direction. "Actually, this was Pat's idea. You can work on it all you want. We just can't have your name on any story connected with it, not until we've found out what we want to know."

"So who am I going to work with?"

"Someone you trust," Patricia said. "Someone people would never suspect of being capable of doing any serious investigative work."

"Oh, no." Call stuck his hands in his pockets. "Not that kid."

"Yes," Patricia said, "Morgan Fairfield."

"Look, do you two know how dangerous this thing is? What we know has put a bee in the bonnet of almost the entire police department. They're the ones that threw me in here, and they didn't do it by thinking on their own. They're not capable of that. That kid could get killed, and I like that kid."

"Dangerous stuff," Dixon said, "your liking someone, Call."

"You'll just have to keep him out of trouble," Patricia added. "You send him to the nice places and into the libraries, and you can do what you do best."

"A fine thing. I protect him while I try to solve this thing, and his name protects me. Why don't you just send me down a dark alley with a bobcat in one pocket and a skunk in the other? No one will ever see me coming."

"Well, it's either that, or you're off the story completely," Patricia said. "We're doing the best we can. I'll help you."

"Wonderful! The police want me dead or in jail, and I get help from a snotnose kid and a woman." He threw up his hands. "What more could I want?"

"Good," Dixon grinned. "Then it's settled. You bring your stories and leads to me, and anything I think ought to be printed will go out under Fairfield's name."

"This kid must really be a scratch-off as far as you're concerned. Why don't you just have him write the obituaries? Then he can practice by writing his own."

"He is new," Dixon said.

Call frowned. "Last in, first out."

After a quick lunch, Call returned to the office. The whole way there he had thought of Morgan. He'd roughed the man up in his cell, and now he had to tell him that not only could he work on the story but that his name would be the only one connected with it in the paper. He wasn't quite sure if he should tell him the whole truth, though. He wasn't quite sure if he had the stomach for it.

When he got up to the newsroom, he spotted O'Leary. "You seen Fairfield?"

The young reporter seemed shocked. He just stood there and stared at Call, his mouth hanging open.

"Surprised to see me."

O'Leary swallowed. "Yes, I am. I thought you were still in jail."

"Nah. Don't you know the *New York Herald* stands up for its reporters?" It was difficult, but Call kept a straight face when he said it. "Now, where's Fairfield?"

"I sent him down to the morgue." The morgue was where they kept all the back issues of the paper. "He said he was interested in finding out about an old story."

"Which old story?"

O'Leary shrugged his shoulders. "How should I know?"

Call started to walk away, but O'Leary grabbed his sleeve. "By the way, I heard from Dixon that the Bennett woman found this Gerry person who can vouch for you. I hear she's got her holed up at her place."

Call nodded and then turned and hustled down the stairs. The basement of the building was not only dark, but it was cold and clammy, the walls sweating while you shivered. The place had never made sense to him. Stacks of old papers, some dating to long before the Civil War, were arranged to allow anyone with an interest to dig. Of course, Call never had much interest in the past. He never felt that he had much of a future either. He had no doubt that Morgan could probably find his way around down there, though. The man was used to libraries and the dark confines of a school. He'd more than likely feel right at home in the basement of the *New York Herald*.

Call opened the door to the basement and saw a pot of coffee perking on the small stove the watchman used. The man had a desk and chair with a gooseneck lamp that shown down on an ashtray filled with cigarette butts. The idea of the watchman accidentally flicking a burning cigarette into the sea of old papers sent a quiver through Call.

He started down the corridor of news piles. Large steel shelves were labeled by year and then by section of the paper. It was a mass of confusion, however. It would take an army of secretaries many years to go through this place, and even then there would be little promise of much improvement.

He rounded a corner in the dark stacks and spotted a light in the distance. Morgan was seated on a stool with the watchman looking over his shoulder and pointing.

Call headed down the aisle. "Hey, Fairfield, what are you doing down here? If it's haunted houses you're after, I know several of them I can show you."

Morgan looked up at him. "I've already seen my share of them today." He turned his head and looked over his shoulder at the watchman. "This is Horace. He seems to know just where to find things down here."

The man wore baggy pants that folded over the tops of his shoes and drooped down to the floor on either side. Call thought that Horace might just be able to sweep the floor while walking on it. The pants were much too large for the man in a number of ways. The red suspenders he wore saved him from total embarrassment. The cap on his head was like a driving cap, slanted down at the eyes, and was made from a brown tweed. His gray mustache drooped down to a point just above his chin. He shook Call's hand while his dull brown eyes stared straight at him.

Call nodded. "Pleased to meet you, Horace. I didn't even know anybody down here could read, much less find anything."

"I like to read. That's why I work here."

Morgan looked over his shoulder at the man and smiled. "Horace seems to be quite the expert on New York society and the stock market."

Call shook his head slightly. The thought of this man knowing absolutely anything about society and the market was something he found hard to believe. "You know the market?"

"Been in it for years."

"Amazing. Made any money?"

Horace smiled. The edges of his gray mustache arched up on either side of his wide grin. They looked like the awnings of a tent. "I got me a nest egg."

"And not a little one, either," Morgan added. "You ever want any stock tips, Call, you'd be well-advised to come down here and take the matter up with Horace."

"So, is that what you're doing here? Looking for market tips?"

Morgan held up the paper in his hand. "No, these are the society pages. They're over forty-five years old—June 12, 1866." He held out the page in Call's direction for him to look over. "You ever see this woman before?"

Call took the old paper from Morgan's hand. There in the center was a picture of a beautiful young woman with dark hair. He recognized the name right away. It was Irene Saunders. "I know the name, but I've never seen her."

Horace laughed. "Not many folks have, at least not for forty-five years or better."

"Well, I saw her this afternoon. The woman's a recluse. She's sitting in that house of hers, and nothing's changed for her in all these years. She dyes her hair black just like the picture and is still wearing this same wedding dress."

"The same dress?"

"The very one."

"Unbelievable."

"I'm afraid there's much more than that. This woman has a personal interest in our story, a deep personal interest."

Call scratched his head. "How is that?"

"I'm not sure I've ever seen anyone so bitter as this woman, like a candy-coated poison pill."

"How so?"

"According to the story here, Miss Irene Saunders was left standing alone at the wedding altar at Trinity Church. All of New York society was there, everyone but the groom."

"And who, pray tell, was that?"

"Mr. J. Pierpont Morgan."

CHAPTER 22

Margaret and Gloria strolled down Fiftieth and turned right onto Fifth. Margaret wore her new black dress, and Gloria was in an emerald green gown. They made a striking pair of women, even though Margaret thought it best to be seen in clothes that could be interpreted as mourning clothes. Gloria couldn't bring herself to do that, not on a spring day in New York City. The streets were wide and bustling with activity. Cars honked their horns and taxicab drivers were screaming at the tops of their lungs.

Margaret looked down at the paper she clutched in her hand. They had reached Central Park South, and Margaret pointed down the boulevard. "I believe it's down there." They marched gallantly down the street on the other side of Central Park and were soon at the restaurant. "I think this is it, Chez Paul."

"And you really think he'll be here after what Morgan told him?"

Margaret smiled. "He'll be here. He's a man isn't he?"

Gloria shook her head. "Yes, I suppose you're right. They seem to be dictated to by something other than common sense."

"What is that to a man?"

"My dear, common sense is simply the collection of a man's prejudices and pulls by the time he reaches eighteen. Many never rise above that point. I don't think we should try to confront the man, though, Margaret."

"No, that would be useless. But I would like to try to tell him a little about the Hunter we knew and how he died. It might just prick his conscience, assuming he has one."

"That seems to be quite an assumption, my dear, given the fact that he's an actor."

They walked up to the door and stood aside as a man opened it for them. Smiling at the gentleman, they thanked him and walked in.

A man in a tuxedo rushed up to them. "May I seat you, ladies?"

Margaret looked over the crowd and pointed her finger at a far booth. "We are here to take lunch with the gentleman over there."

The maître d'hôtel turned and spotted her target. "Yes, follow me please."

They formed a line and paraded through the crowded tables, winding their way past buzzing conversations and casual glances. Finally, they stood in front of the booth Margaret had pointed out. "I am glad you could make it, Mr. Kennedy," Margaret said. "I hope you don't mind that I brought my friend."

Kennedy lifted his head and shot to his feet. He had been reading a book and quickly closed it, pushing it aside. "No, indeed," he said.

Margaret could tell that the notion of dining with two attractive women was something that appealed to Kennedy, even if he was a bit disappointed at not being with her alone.

He stepped out from behind the booth, picking up the silver-tipped cane he was carrying. "Please be seated, ladies. Garçon, could you bring us a third menu?"

The maître d'hôtel clicked his heels and scurried off as Margaret and Gloria found their places. "I am so happy you asked to meet with me," Kennedy said. "I could hardly contain my joy when you passed me the note at the party."

Margaret smiled. "I felt some explanation was in order after what my friend said to you."

Kennedy smiled. It was a pleasant if not a longing smile.

"Gloria and I were both on the *Titanic*. We both knew Hunter Kennedy."

"You mean you knew the man calling himself Hunter Kennedy."

"Yes, if you want to put it that way," Margaret said.

"So I take it that Mr. Fairfield explained the nature of his remarks to me."

"Yes, he did."

"I really don't know how to offer you an explanation. I'm not certain of why anyone would want to use my name, other than what must be a minor notoriety."

"I thought you might be interested, though, in finding out more about how this man died."

"He was a charming man," Gloria added. "We were all quite fond of him."

Kennedy's eyes wandered off for a moment, lost in thought. Then he smiled. "He must have had quite a way with the ladies."

"That seems to be a trait that runs in the Irish, Mr. Kennedy," Gloria said.

"You realize that all of us suspect the backer of your play as the one responsible for this man's death."

"Miss Webb?" He seemed genuinely moved by the idea. For a moment a flush of anger rose into his cheeks.

"Yes, Kitty Webb. She and Hunter Kennedy had a relationship that she didn't want to come out. We also think the Irish revolutionaries were at least partly responsible."

Margaret could see that this added notion had quite the effect on the man. He leaned over and lowered his voice. "Can you be serious?"

"Deadly serious, young man," Gloria added.

After ordering their food, Margaret and Gloria spent some time explaining their voyage and how they had come to know the man calling himself Hunter Kennedy. They gave a detailed account of the bomb found on board and the member of the IRA who had been arrested for setting it. Margaret watched the man's eyes widen with every mention of the Irish cause and the part it had played in what happened on the *Titanic*.

Kennedy shook his head. "I can't believe it." He seemed to be speaking more to himself than to them. "I just can't believe it."

"It's true," Margaret said. "They seemed to be after a set of diplomatic documents that just might prevent Europe from going to war. My friend Morgan was carrying them."

"He's a diplomatic courier too?"

"No, it's a long story. But the IRA was determined to stop their delivery. I even think they would have sunk the entire ship to prevent it if they had to. Perhaps that was just what they did because the documents went down with the ship."

"Who were these people? I might know some names."

Margaret and Gloria exchanged glances. They seemed to be thinking the same thing.

"Well, you know at least one of them," Gloria said. "Kitty Webb. You do work for her, don't you, not the IRA?"

Margaret watched Kennedy's eyes grow wider. Perhaps Gloria had struck a chord.

"Yes, but you said her reasons were personal, not political."

"That's correct," Margaret said. "It just seems to me that you'd be very interested in a man using your name who is murdered. I mean it might have been intended for you."

"Of course, I'm interested. I care about any murder."

He stirred his tea slowly, taking time to gather his thoughts. Margaret could see from the wrinkle in his brow that the thought of the murder left him troubled beyond what he was letting on.

"I rather think that if Kitty Webb was involved," he went on, "it was because of something she knew about him under a different name, his own name. I'm not certain we can do anything about it. This man's body, this man you call Hunter Kennedy, is at the bottom of the ocean. There is no proof—or is there?"

Margaret shook her head. "I rather doubt it. Tell us about yourself, though."

Kennedy stirred his French onion soup, mashing the piece of toasted French bread that still floated on the surface and driving it underneath the brine with his spoon. "I grew up in Ireland." He shook his head. "I suppose I was fairly typical, except for the fact that my father is a Protestant minister."

Margaret arched an eyebrow. She knew that piece of information was exactly the same as she knew about her Hunter Kennedy. It was also a fact that would not be commonly known. *Perplexing*, she thought. *Instead of answers, there seems to be more of a mystery.* He appeared to be uncomfortable talking about himself, unlike the gregarious Kennedy she had known and almost every actor she had ever met.

"I just find it hard to think that Irish patriots would do something so ghastly," he went on, "so appalling. I understand there's a war going on, at least from their perspective. But women and children were on board that ship, women and children from Ireland."

Margaret watched him. She could tell the thought of a man with his name who had been murdered bothered him a great deal, but she could also see that he was greatly troubled about the Irish patriotic movement being implicated in the *Titanic* disaster.

She thought she would turn his attention back to Hunter, in the hope of seeing some emotion. "Of course, the man we knew as Hunter was not very bookish, not like you. He set himself among people as if they were his playground, laughing and making sport with anyone, with everyone, he saw."

She saw the distant look in his eyes, almost a look of remembrance. "Yes, I know." Quickly, he caught himself. "Or I should say, I imagine. I do enjoy the classics. I read and reread them. Your Hunter Kennedy sounds like more of a people person, not one given to politics or deep thinking."

Gloria laughed. "He thought all right, but quickly. Mostly he made you worry about what he was going to say next."

Kennedy smiled. "Yes, I'm certain of that."

Margaret thought it uncanny. The man's smile reminded her of Hunter's impish smile. So much about the man reminded her of him.

He bowed his head slightly and bit his bottom lip. "And you must think me a cad. Here you've lost a good friend, and for a moment you thought it was me."

"I wonder why we never saw you on the *Titanic*, Mr. Kennedy," Gloria said.

The statement brought a shock to his eyes, but only for an instant. "What class were you ladies traveling in?"

"First class," Margaret replied. "We were all in first class, including the man we knew as Hunter Kennedy."

"Perhaps that explains it." Kennedy ladled his spoon into the soup and held it to his mouth. "I was in second class. Actors usually hobnob with only schoolteachers on a trip like that."

"I suppose you're right," Margaret said.

He shook his head. "Though Lord knows I've tried to travel first class. Most of the time, however, we do well to be working at all."

"Do you stay connected to the old country?" Margaret asked.

Kennedy smiled. "Yes, I have a number of acquaintances here. America is the melting pot, you know."

"So it would seem," Gloria offered. "And did you have friends that went down on the ship?"

"Yes, I did. In second class one makes friends quite easily."

"And who might they be?" Gloria asked.

The question took him by surprise. Margaret could see his mind at work, groping for a name, any name.

"I did stay to myself quite a bit." He smiled. "Reading, you know. I did know an engineer on the ship. He was in my lifeboat. A Jeremy Fetters. I guess you just don't realize how much you truly miss someone until after he's gone."

Margaret's mind flooded with thoughts of Peter. Even though she had planned on breaking off their engagement, the man was still a dear friend, a dear friend who loved her. She hadn't planned on the sudden rush of emotion, and she pulled out a handkerchief and dabbed her eyes with it.

Gloria slipped her hand over hers. "It's all right, dear. We understand."

Gloria cast a glance in Kennedy's direction. "Margaret had a fiancé go down on the *Titanic*," she explained. "Perhaps all this talk is upsetting her."

"I am sorry," Kennedy said. "I didn't know. I had assumed your Mr. Fairfield was more than just a friend."

Margaret's blue eyes sparkled with tears. She knew the pain she felt was the price she was paying for her curiosity toward the man. She had planned all along on talking about the *Titanic* in hopes that he would break down and tell all. She didn't believe his story for a minute. The idea of his impersonating Hunter both sickened and fascinated her at the same time. It was his reason for doing it that she couldn't quite understand. There had to be more to it than just obtaining a meal ticket. At least there had to be if this man was to emerge less jaded than he already appeared to be.

"I think we should go," Gloria said.

Kennedy looked at Margaret. "I understand perfectly. You ladies run right along. I hope we can get together later when you feel better, Miss Hastings."

Margaret's back arched, her muscles growing tense. "I find it amazing that you could work for the woman who murdered our friend."

"I am afraid I need proof of that. I can't just come out and ask her."

"She killed him in the swimming pool. Tried to make it look like an accidental drowning. Very few people still living know that little fact, only Morgan, myself, Boxhall, and, of course, the murderer."

"Perhaps I'll ask her."

"You do that." Margaret nodded. They got to their feet and made their way through the door. The fresh air felt good, and Margaret drew Gloria to a halt and breathed deeply. She looked longingly at the park across the street. "Let's go there," she said. "I'd like to see the flowers just now."

They crossed the busy intersection and in a matter of moments were watching a squirrel climb up and down a giant elm. The furry little creature seemed to climb up just so far. He would then scurry down, dance around on his paws, look at them, and then once again head straight to the upper branches.

"I wish I had something to feed him," Margaret said. "That's what he's probably waiting for."

"Let's just walk. It might help take your mind off lunch."

They began a slow walk through the park. Gloria tried hard to take Margaret's mind off the *Titanic* by talking about the trees and the flowers. The slopes were grassy and gave the place the appearance of being thousands of miles away from New York City. Of course, the honking of the taxicabs quickly brought them back to reality.

They stopped in front of a massive oak tree, and Gloria took Margaret's arm and squeezed it slightly. "Don't turn around and don't look, but we're being followed."

"By whom?"

"Two men." Gloria faked a smile. "And I am afraid we've gotten much too far from the street."

They watched an older man make his way over the top of the grassy knoll to their right. He would be the last person in sight, and suddenly they knew it.

"Let's catch up with him," Gloria said.

"Yes, let's."

They started up the long hill just as the old man dropped down over the other side. Margaret shot a quick glance back at the two men who Gloria said had been following them. They both wore shabby clothes. One was tall with a crushed hat and the other short and stubby with a leather vest.

Neither of them seemed to be intent on taking in the sights. They both had their eyes fixed on the two women. They were also picking up their pace.

When Margaret and Gloria got to the top of the hill, they looked down. The older man had disappeared. They were alone.

CHAPTER 23

Morgan and Call headed down to the docks in a taxi. "Do you really think this is a good idea?" Morgan asked.

"And why wouldn't it be?"

"It seems to be a dangerous place, especially for you of late."

"All the more compelling reason to go there, boy."

"I don't understand."

"If those bloody cowards think that they can put a scare into me and that I'll go run and hide, they are sadly mistaken. The more we turn up the heat, the more desperate they'll become. Sooner or later, they're going to make a mistake, a mistake that we'll find a witness to, a mistake that will make up the headlines of the *New York Herald*."

"The real people behind it seem to be buried under mountains of lackeys, people who'll do anything for money."

"Yes, but as long as we can pin the goods on at least one of them who squeals they'll tumble like a house of cards. Do you know how many mayors in this city we've sent into exile? Plenty, I tell you, and there just might be more to follow. Of course, these people are more difficult than elected officials. Their money never comes up for reelection."

Call pointed to an area near the White Star docks, and the driver brought the taxi to a halt. They got out, paid the man, and headed over to where the offices were located. The main office, downtown, had been flooded with people ever since word of the disaster had struck the papers. Victims were to be found everywhere, victims and grieving widows. It wasn't nearly so bad as Southampton, England, where there was a collection of orphans and widows on every block, but it had been enough to deluge White Star and bring it to an absolute standstill. The dock offices seemed to be the only place where a man could still find information without wading through a mob of sobbing women.

Call headed up the ramp with Morgan scampering along behind him. He pushed open the double doors and made his way up to the counter. Then he stepped back, pulling Morgan along with him. "Let's not do the counter. Those people have been trained to tell you no." He pointed over to where a woman was trying to pound on an out-of-date typewriter. It was a labor for her to push the keys, and she showed it, patting her forehead with a handkerchief seemingly between every word. "Let's try her."

They walked up to the overworked woman. Morgan could see that she was in her early thirties with her brown hair curled into a bun behind her tightly buttoned white blouse. Her face was red, and several curls were out of place, falling down the sides of her head.

"Good afternoon, darling," Call said. "We seem to be having quite the day of it, aren't we?"

She put both hands down on either side of the huge typewriter and blew a gust of breath up her face. It rippled a misplaced curl that had fallen down her forehead. "Yes, we are."

"I just thought I'd give you a way to make an easier buck for a few minutes of your time."

The woman's eyes widened.

Call pulled out a five-dollar bill and laid it beside the woman's right hand. "I just need some information, public knowledge stuff."

"You a reporter?"

"Yes." Call smiled broadly. "But this would just be between the two of us."

She looked around the open office area where everyone seemed to be preoccupied. Sliding her hand over, she picked up the bill and wadded it up in her fingers. "I suppose so. I need a break anyway."

"Yes, darling, we wouldn't want this job to make you old before your time, now would we?"

She smiled and pushed her hair back into place. "What can I do for you?"

"That seaman who came in on the *Carpathia*, the engineer from the *Titanic*, Fetters; can you tell me if the man had a wife or family here in town?"

"You doing his obituary?"

Call smiled. "Yes, as a matter of fact, I am. You could be real helpful and save me a lot of legwork if you tell me just what you can find out."

She scooted back her chair. "I know where the personnel files are. If you'll just wait a minute, I'll see what I can do for you."

"Happy to do that, darling."

When she walked away, Call looked back at the fellow who was manning the counter. "Now if Pat had been with us, we'd have her go to that man over there. A few words to brighten his ego might have been the charm. With us, though, we have to rely on a few smiles and greenbacks." He pointed at Morgan's notebook. "Are you taking this all down?"

Morgan tapped his index finger on his temple. "I think I've got it, got it all in here."

"Good work, my man. You just might make a go of it in this business after all."

The woman walked lazily back to her desk, a file in her hands. She sat down and opened it. Call drew close to her, looking over her shoulder.

She traced her finger down the particulars of the file. "It says here that Jeremy Fetters has a wife and three children in Southampton. But here," she pointed to another name and address, "his brother lives in Brooklyn, near the naval yard. The man's address is 321 York Street, apartment 12."

"I know the place," Call said. "You've been very helpful." He smiled at the woman. "You just take that money and buy something pretty for yourself, something that fits a woman of your beauty."

He took Morgan's arm, and both of them scurried out the door and back down the ramp. Within minutes they were in a taxicab and heading across the bridge to Brooklyn.

"Is this important?" Morgan asked.

"You've got to place yourself in Fetters' shoes that night. The *Carpathia* got in about 9:00, and Fetters was killed on the docks around midnight. Do you really think he stood around for three hours on that dock in the rain when he had a brother this close?"

The taxi took them right to the door of 321 York Street. The house, a three-story brownstone, was run-down and had shutters that hung off their hinges in several locations. Call got out and paid the driver. "Could you wait for us here? We won't be long."

The man took the money and nodded.

Call led Morgan up the steps of the building and into the dark foyer. Light crept into the place between the worn shutters, bathing the dirty walls with dark, shadowy stripes. The place smelled of urine mixed with dust. A number of letter boxes were on the wall, and Call ran his fingers down them until he came to 12. Several letters were stuffed in the box. "I'd say either our man is a late sleeper or he hasn't been here."

He moved through the foyer to the door that led to the first-floor apartments. The hallway was dark, the only light coming from a far fire door that had been left open, sending a shaft of sooty light down the worn carpet, the color of which could only have been guessed at.

They began to count the rooms as they walked down the hall, some of which had numbers. The number 6 was on their left, painted on the door. The number 8 was missing altogether. Apartment 10 had its number written in pencil, and they stopped in front of the only door that could be 12. Call knocked. "Fetters! You in there, Fetters?" There was no answer.

"Should we try the door?" Morgan asked.

"Should we? Of course. We can always leave the man a number to call and a dime to use the phone, maybe even the promise of more."

He twisted the brass knob, and the door sprang open. The smell of the place was enough to overcome all but the strong of will and stomach. The lamp was still on in the room, a flickering coal oil lamp that sent black fumes gently winding their way to bathe the dirty ceiling with soot. Clothes were thrown around the room as if a group of children had deliberately been turned loose. A piece of bread and a greasy hunk of salami sat on the table, and at the far end a screen stood between the bed and the rest of the room.

Call smiled. "Not exactly a tidy man, is he?"

"I think not," Morgan agreed. "Guess the housekeeper didn't make it."

Call gagged slightly. "And I think the man needs to open a window. You'd think he was brewing garbage."

Call took out a piece of paper and scratched his name and number on it. "We'd better leave this on the man's pillow. It might take him months to find it in the room here."

They walked over to the screen and stepped around it. Call stopped in his tracks. There beside the bed was Fetters. His shirt was soaked in blood, and the slash across his neck presented the ugly appearance of a red smile set in an unshaven face. His eyes were wide open, taking in the ceiling along with eternity.

Morgan gulped. "We're too late." He pointed to the window beside the bed. It was wide open, which was no doubt why they'd even been able to enter the room. "Somebody opened the window, though. We can be thankful for that."

"I'll say." Call reached out and touched the man's shirt. The blood was dry. "Much too late, I'd say." He looked back at Morgan. "I'd also be willing to bet that the brothers had themselves a last meeting. That's why this man died, no doubt."

"That's awful."

"I'd say these people are plenty careful of who knows what. Anyone who knows too much doesn't live very long."

Morgan looked down at the corpse. "Do you think he knew more than we do?"

"I'd say that if we knew as much as the Fetters boys, we'd be just as dead as they are."

"We'd better call the police," Morgan said.

Call slapped Morgan's forehead with the palm of his hand. "Don't be daft, man. They might have been the ones who did this. No doubt some of them know who did, if they didn't. No police. I'll call them from across the river, an anonymous call. The less they hear of my name, the better."

"I can see your point."

"Good. Listen and learn."

They backed out and closed the door, making sure no one was in the hall. They heard men talking in the lobby, talking and heading their way.

Instead of going back through the main entrance and having to confront the men coming toward them, they went out the open fire door and down the iron steps to the street. Within minutes they were back in the cab, heading for the White Star docks. When they got there, they were greeted by the sight of two men scurrying around on the lifeboats from the *Titanic*. Call and Morgan went to the edge of the dock and watched for a few moments.

"What are they doing?" Morgan asked.

"Scavengers, I'd say. There's going to be quite a market for anything with the word *Titanic* printed on it." Call put his hands up to his mouth and called out to the two men. "Hey, you two! You get out of there or we're calling the police, that or your mother."

The men stood up in the boat and looked at them. They stuffed a few articles into their pockets and jumped from boat to boat until they were at the edge of the dock that was farther away from where Call and Morgan were standing. They climbed up onto the dock and, when Call made a motion toward them, scurried off and broke into a run.

Call and Morgan walked over to the boat the men had bolted from. The sight of the lifeboats, bobbing monuments to man's stupidity and vain pride, was sad.

Call jumped down into the boat and motioned for Morgan to join him. "Let's take a quick look around, what say."

Morgan shook his head. "I don't have the least bit of interest in anything to do with those things. I can't understand why you would, either."

"You're a reporter, aren't you? This is news, isn't it?"

Morgan paddled his hand in the air in Call's direction. "You go ahead. I'll go make the anonymous phone call to the police."

"You be careful with that, boy. Say nothing. Just give the address and the fact that there's a body there. Don't give the man's name, and then just hang up. I don't want them visiting the office here. That woman could give them a description."

"OK." With that Morgan left Call. It took him some time to find a public phone. After he made the call, he walked back to the docks.

Much to his surprise, Call was still climbing over the boats. "I made the call," he shouted, "just as you said."

Call signaled him. "Get down here. I've got something to show you, something you might find very interesting."

Reluctantly, Morgan climbed down into the first boat. He made his way one boat after the other to the boat Call was standing in. "What could you possibly see that I'd have any interest in?"

Call stood up tall in the swaying boat and looked over the small flotilla. "Do you see anything here that's missing?"

Morgan turned and looked at the boats. They were bobbing with the tide, but otherwise looked peaceful and quite empty.

"Don't look for what's here, boy, look for what isn't."

"There's nothing here. They've taken everything."

"Exactly. And what was no doubt the first things to go, the things that prove they were taken from the *Titanic*?"

Morgan could see plainly that the ship's name had been removed from all the lifeboats. The paint was a different color where the plaques that bore the name, *Titanic* had been removed. "They took the nameplates off."

"That's right, boy." Call slapped him on the back. "Now look down here, and look carefully." Call squatted down near the stern of the boat and pointed to the place that had held the name. "Tell me just what you see, exactly what you see."

"I see," he began to count them, "eight screw holes."

"Good, Fairfield old man, eight. Isn't there something strange about that?"

Morgan sat down on the rear seat and thought. "Yes, now that you mention it, that is strange. The plaques would only have four holes."

"Very strange. You would think that these boats belonged to a different ship and that they switched the nameplates. Why would a new ship on its maiden voyage have lifeboats where the nameplates had been switched?"

Morgan looked up at the other boats.

"Don't bother to count them. I already have. If you were going to unscrew nameplates and then put new ones on, you might try putting them into the same screw holes, but that would be shoddy work. Of the thirteen boats here, nine of them show two sets of holes. The rest were rethreaded, however poorly, into the old ones."

"But why?" Morgan asked.

"Why, indeed."

CHAPTER 24

Margaret and Gloria ran down the hill toward the empty playground below. "Pick up your skirts, girl," Gloria yelled. "They're still behind us."

Both women lifted their dresses above their knees and did their best to keep their shoes from bogging down in the soft grass. They reached a small path just in time to see a carriage turning in their direction. The horse-drawn coach was moving slowly. Both Margaret and Gloria ran up to it. "We need to get on!" Gloria shouted.

"I'm taken, madam." The cabbie was an overstuffed man in a red jacket and black top hat. His muttonchop whiskers were white, and a semisneer came from full, almost liver-colored lips.

"Now it's taken twice." Gloria helped Margaret hop aboard the slow-moving vehicle and climbed in behind her.

The man drew the horse to a stop and, turning around, glared at them. "I said I was taken."

Margaret looked at the couple seated on the other side near the rear of the carriage. The man was well dressed with a dark suit and a hat. He was an older man, perhaps in his fifties, with gray hair and a trim gray mustache. The woman beside him was an attractive blonde who looked to be all of eighteen. Margaret leaned over and placed her hand on the man's knee. "We are being followed and are terribly in need of rescue."

The young woman looked at the man, a plaintive look in her eyes.

He shouted at the driver. "Drive on and make quick about it."

Turning around, the driver slapped the back of the horse with the traces. He then picked up his whip and gave it a pop. The horse broke into a canter and then picked up speed.

Margaret and Gloria could see now who had been following them. The two men came to a halt and stood watching the carriage pull away.

"You know those two?" the man asked.

"Never seen them before," Gloria answered.

The man put his hand on the young woman's beside him. She had her hand through the man's arm and was looking up at him adoringly. "Then I'm glad we came along when we did. You can never tell just when you'll find a policeman here in Central Park."

After a short time, the driver slowed the carriage and they continued at a leisurely pace, the horse's hooves falling on the pavement in easy melodic raps. They reached Seventy-second Street and turned left into the backside of the park mall. The flowers were beautiful, and Margaret saw that the couple had altogether forgotten their interruption. But it didn't make her feel any better.

"Why don't you pull up here, next to the angel, and let us out," Gloria said. She smiled. "Romance is something I never want to interrupt."

"Nonsense," the man replied. "It isn't often that we get to be heroes."

"Well, I think your heroics have been enough for the day," Gloria replied. "We'll just walk from here."

"As you wish." He shouted at the driver, "Pull up here, please."

The man drew the reins on the horse, bringing the vehicle to a halt. Gloria and Margaret got down from the coach. Margaret leaned back in. "Thank you both so very much. I really don't know what we'd have done without you."

They stepped back and watched as the vehicle pulled away. Close by, Margaret spotted a man with a popcorn machine. The thing was sounding off with a series of small explosions, yellow kernels bursting in a glass cage and flying in all directions. "Let's get some popcorn," she said. "I'd like to feed the birds."

"I'd just like to feed myself," Gloria said.

Margaret smiled. "I'm certain the birds can share with you."

"They'll have to, because I'm buying." Gloria stepped over to the vendor, an Italian with dark eyes and a long black mustache. She slapped a nickel down on the counter. "One bag, please."

The man picked up a shiny metal scoop. He raked it into the pile of hot yellow popped corn nuggets, and then poured them into a tall, striped bag. Handing it over, he grinned. "There you are, ladies." Picking up a metal shaker he doused the contents with salt.

Gloria thanked the man, picked up the sack, and offered it to Margaret as they walked away. She took a few from the top. "This is good and still warm."

"I was counting on that." Gloria pulled out a handful and seemed to fling them into her mouth.

They walked on for a short time and stood before the winged statue of an angel. Water was coming from its wings and pouring into a beautiful fountain with long spewing cascades. The birds were gathering. Just the smell of food from the bag was enough to draw a feathered crowd, and Margaret made sure they weren't disappointed. She scooped up a handful and started tossing the popcorn one at a time to the eager feathered residents of the fountain area.

The women couldn't remember how long they'd been there, but they soon started the long slow walk back to one of the streets that bordered the park. It was easy to get turned around in Central Park. Of course, walking in a straight line was bound to get one in the clear sooner or later.

Some time later, Gloria grabbed Margaret's arm. "They're back."

"Who's back?"

"Those men who were following us."

Margaret looked in the distance and could see two men in dark clothing heading their way down the road. They were walking at a fast pace, as if they knew where they were going, not at all like anyone bent on enjoying the afternoon. And they were going on a path straight to Margaret and Gloria. "How do you know they're the same two men?" Margaret asked.

"Do you want to wait here and ask them?"

"No, I don't."

They headed south through an area known as the Ramble. The place was a maze of trees and brush. But it had one other outstanding feature–there was no way out of the park from that direction. The path the two women took wound up facing a small lake.

Gloria pointed off to the right. "Let's go this way." They picked up their skirts and began to run.

"We should have stayed in the carriage," Margaret panted.

"Yes, we should have. Amazing how clearly we think after the fact."

"We would have spoiled those people's romantic interlude, though."

"A small price to pay, you think?"

"Yes."

They made their way down the path. Behind them they could hear the sound of what seemed to be men breaking through the bushes. The noise was close and getting closer. The path curved to their right. Soon they could see the upper arm of the lake, which stretched around them, not allowing them a path of escape.

Gloria grabbed Margaret and pulled her into the bushes.

"What are you doing?"

"If we go out there and even find a way out, they're sure to see us. It won't take them long to catch us, not with us in these dresses."

"But if they find us in here, what will happen then?"

Gloria looked her in the eye. "If they find us here, then they'll do to us what they have intended to do." She reached down and picked up a rock, clutching it in her hand.

Both women moved deeper into the undergrowth, trying their best to make their dresses disappear from the view of the trail.

Moments later, they spotted the two men prowling along the path. Both of them had sticks now, sticks they were using to beat the edges of the path, lifting the flowers and the brush and looking.

Margaret gasped and held her breath as they came closer. She could see the face of one of the men as he stooped over to look in her direction.

It was a heart-stopping moment. He was looking right at her, but did he see her?

He stood upright, and they both moved on. It was not until the women heard the slapping of the bushes up ahead of them that they were able to breathe once again.

They sat and waited for a while, waited for the sound of the two men to disappear. The noise of the beating of the bushes gradually grew dimmer in the distance. "Let's go," Gloria whispered. "Let's go back the way we came."

Margaret got to her feet. The ground where they both had taken cover was barely noticeable on her black dress, but it had left quite a series of smudges on Gloria's bright green dress. Gloria worked at brushing them off. She glanced up at Margaret. "There's something to be said about mourning, I suppose."

"I suppose so," Margaret agreed.

They stumbled back onto the path and headed for the area overlooking the lake. Moments later they were walking alongside it. "Do you suppose they'll come back this way once they realize we haven't gone the way they were searching?" Margaret asked.

"Why should they? I would think thieves could find an easier target than the one we've become."

"What if they weren't thieves?"

"I don't even want to think of that possibility."

When they got back to the fountain, the man who sold the popcorn had gone elsewhere. There seemed to be no one but the birds to greet them, and that thought alone didn't do much to ease the tension they felt. They sat down on the edge of the fountain, content for the moment to watch the water spray.

"I'm exhausted," Margaret said.

"So am I."

Suddenly they heard the sound of men running. They looked up to see the men who had been chasing them round the bend. They had evidently spotted them from a distance, and now they were bearing down on them, waving their sticks in the air above their heads.

Margaret screamed and clung to Gloria.

All at once from behind them, a man bounded out from the shadow of the fountain area. At first all they could see was a blur, a flurry of activity from a man with flaming red hair. He met the intruders head-on, his cane thrashing them on the head and shoulders. He swung the cane in his hand like a windmill in a tornado.

As he turned and cracked one of the charging men on the head, Margaret and Gloria recognized him. It was the man who claimed to be Hunter Kennedy.

Kennedy continued to swing the cane, sending the men's sticks flying into splinters. Margaret could see the look of shock on the two stalkers' faces. They seemed almost immobilized by fear.

"You!" one of the men yelled. "Why you?"

The outburst simply caused Kennedy to rap the man over the head even harder.

All the women could do was sit and watch.

The two stalkers backed up from Kennedy. They first stared at each other and seemed to swap looks of bewildered amazement. Then they reached into their belts and pulled out knives.

The women watched as Kennedy twisted the handle of his cane and drew out a long, gleaming sword. He swung it in midair, the sound of the blade making a whipping noise. Now the confused stares of the two stalkers turned into looks of horror. In unison, they turned and ran.

Kennedy watched them run away. He whirled and walked to where Margaret and Gloria were seated. "Are you ladies all right?"

"We are now," Gloria panted.

"I'm glad I decided to follow you."

"We are too," Margaret said. "I don't know what we'd have done without you."

They heard the sound of running footsteps, and all three of them turned around. It was Ed Leslie, the theater manager. He was slightly out of breath when he stopped in front of them and bent over, his hands on his knees. Looking up at them, he panted out a smile. "Boy, am I glad you were here, Kennedy." Turning around, he pointed to a hill in the distance. "I was up there when I spotted what was going on, but I'm afraid I would have been too late."

He stared at Kennedy. "I was actually trying to find you, Kennedy. The theater is paying off today, but you have to go to the cashier. I spotted you going into the park and hoped I could catch you. Now I'm glad you were ahead of me and I didn't."

"We all are," Gloria said.

CHAPTER 25

The *Mackay-Bennett* arrived on the scene of the disaster at around 8:00 P.M. on the twentieth of April. The seas were rough, which was expected. Lardner had hoped for waters similar to the night the *Titanic* had gone down, but those conditions seldom happened. On that night the Atlantic had been a flat calm, with virtually no wind. It was like a millpond with oil poured over the surface. Such a sea made it difficult to spot an iceberg. No waves would be breaking over the surface of the berg to attract a lookout's attention.

The moon had also been new that night, with only the light of the stars suspended high above to shine on the surface of the Atlantic. A man might be looking straight ahead, and if the berg had been a blue berg, having recently turned over in the water, he might not see it at all. He might just be able to see the stars disappearing in the distance without knowing that it was a mass of ice on the water swallowing them up. Such a thought sent shivers up Lardner's spine.

He turned to the helmsman. "Stop all engines. We're here."

The man rang up the orders on the telegraph to the engine room below, and within moments the *Mackay-Bennett* was gliding over the surface. The engines continued to chug, but at a far reduced murmur.

Charles Hitchens, the first officer, stepped onto the bridge. He looked at the telegraph. "Do you think that's wise, sir? Shouldn't we be making some headway to keep the gentlemen down below more comfortable?"

Lardner knew at once the man was right. By merely sitting in the water, the chop would tend to make the *Mackay-Bennett* bob in the current and sway with the rocking motion of the waves against the ship. Forward movement, however slow, was preferable for people cooped up in the belly of a vessel at sea. In this case that would be threateningly true. Forty morticians would have their stomachs aggravated by the job they had to start in the morning without having those same bellies retching the night before.

Lardner stepped to the closed window that looked out on the sea. "You're right, Hitchens, of course. I just wanted a moment to look over the place, just to burn it into my mind. All those people dying, and right here. It still doesn't seem possible."

"No, sir, I suppose not." Hitchens stepped up next to Lardner.

The ocean was littered with growlers, small icebergs that posed little threat to ships the *Mackay-Bennett*'s size. Pack ice also littered the water, and what little moon there was now showed the stark white surface as the pack ice bounced over the waves of the dark Atlantic. In the distance both men could see several large icebergs, formidable castles of doom set against the night sky.

"You'll have to keep a good watch on tonight, Charlie. You take four hours and then wake me."

"Aye, sir."

Lardner looked back at the helmsman. "All ahead slow."

The following morning began with tea, scrambled eggs, sausages, tomatoes, and muffins. The crew ate it with seeming joy, each man trying hard to push out of his mind just what it was he was doing on board the *Mackay-Bennett*. They bantered about the fate of the Canadian Navy and the soccer team that Halifax was putting together. A few of the funeral directors joined in. While these men were already jaded to their handling of the dead, the motion of the sea had done much to undo what otherwise would have been stoic resolve.

Captain Lardner stirred cream into his hot tea and sipped it, allowing the steam to roll over his lips. He liked his tea hot and his eggs cool. It was something the men in the mess had become accustomed to. He looked across the table at the three ministers who would be performing burial services throughout the day. "Would one of you gentlemen honor us with a small service before we go up on deck?"

The three clergymen looked at one another. In Lardner's estimation, rank seemed to play a more important part in heaven than anywhere on the high seas. The two younger ministers focused their attention on the older man. He was a Presbyterian, and while it was doubtful that many of the victims shared his theology, it was plain to see the other two ministers on board looked to him for approval.

"I think Pastor Antisdale should speak for us," the youngest of the men said. He nodded in the direction of the oldest of the group. "He's had much more experience than we've had."

Lardner got to his feet and tapped a spoon on a glass half full of tomato juice. It stopped the conversation. "Gentlemen, we're going to hear a few words and be led in a prayer." He motioned to the oldest minister. "We're yours to command, Reverend."

The old man got to his feet. He had a shock of uncombed white hair and a large, drooping, white mustache. When he opened his mouth, however, he got everyone's immediate attention. His voice was a deep, rich baritone, and doubtless it could have carried across the waters and been heard back in Halifax if that was what the man had intended.

He opened his Bible, but when he spoke from it, never once did his eye refer to the page before him. "The psalmist writes in Psalm 46, 'God is our refuge and strength, a very present help in trouble. Therefore will not we fear, though the earth be removed, and though the mountains be carried into the midst of the sea; though the waters thereof roar and be troubled, though the mountains shake with the swelling thereof. Selah. There is a river, the streams whereof shall make glad the city of God.'"

He closed his Bible and lifted both hands. "Today we celebrate the river in the city of God. We will never forget the time of trouble, but neither will we fear it. We must always be mindful of the heart of the sea, but it is the heavens that soar above it, and in Christ that is where our souls depart this life for."

The old man then bowed his head and led the entire assembly of crew and morticians in the Lord's Prayer. It produced a stillness in the galley, a stillness that not one of the men would ever forget.

Lardner got to his feet. "Thank you, Reverend Antisdale. This is perhaps the quietest our hearts will be all day." He then looked at the crew. "All right, men, we have much work to do today."

With that each member of the crew slowly got to his feet and began to file toward the stairs that led up on deck. The funeral directors followed, and Captain Lardner brought up the rear with the small collection of ministers.

On deck the cable ship's boats were lowered. It was a painstaking job with heavy seas fighting them all the way. The crew, supplied with hooks and nets, manned the boats. Everyone knew full well that after almost a week at sea many of the bodies would be in poor condition. Some would bear the marks of injury sustained during the sinking, and others would be victims of sea life.

Lardner went to the rail to watch the retrieval of nearby bodies. The men on one of the first boats over the side stirred at a mass of wreckage and fished three bodies out from among the debris. The fourth body, however, was the most difficult, even though it was the lightest of all. The crew members on the boat pulled the small body in, then sat down to cry. The body was that of a fair-haired boy who appeared to be no more than two years old.

Lardner turned to Hitchens. "Make certain that the wireless sends reports of any identified bodies just as soon as we can make confirmation."

Hitchens nodded. "Aye, sir."

The men with the small boy's body rowed back to the ship. The boat was in no way full, but Lardner could see that they weren't able to go any further, not just then. The rough and tumble, hard and jaded seamen rowed the boat, wiping the tears away from their eyes.

As each body came on board, a number was stenciled on a square of canvas. Personal property was labeled with that same number and placed in a small bag that would accompany the bagged body. Many of the bodies were stripped and searched for tattoos or birthmarks should there be no other means of identification. The bodies were each identified according to hair color, height, weight, and age. It was hoped that the details contained in the descriptions, along with the contents of pockets, jewelry, and a description of clothing could be used later on to make positive identification. The boy was simply and tragically marked, "No identification, no effects." His body would be embalmed and taken back to Halifax.

Lardner watched from the rail, fighting the feeling of tears that at times seemed to overwhelm him. One member of the crew walked from body to body, checking off a name on his list of passengers and crew when and if a name could be found.

One of the crew members called out, "Captain, you'd better come and take a look at this."

Lardner left his post and walked over to where the crew member was standing over the body of a *Titanic* stoker. The man was dressed in black except for his white life preserver. He had a brown beard and dark brown hair. "We'll search this man for identification, but he had something on him that wasn't his."

"What?"

The crew member passed Lardner a leather notebook that was bound in carefully cut and stenciled black leather. The name Thomas Andrews was emblazoned in gold on the outside.

Hitchens stepped over to look. "Andrews—wasn't he the ship's designer?"

"Yes, he was." Lardner looked down at the stoker. "But this isn't Thomas Andrews."

"Maybe Andrews gave it to the man before the ship went down, for safekeeping."

The irony of the situation was not lost on Lardner. He looked down at the corpse. "I'd say he kept it very safe."

CHAPTER 26

Morgan and Call marched to Dixon's office and stood outside the door. It took some doing to stand there. Dixon had just tossed a reporter out, almost literally. He did it like most other ejections—preceded and followed by curses and insults.

"Is this a good time?" Morgan asked. The reporter walked away, mumbling curses to himself and shaking his head.

Call pushed his hands down into his pockets. "Might be a great time. Maybe the old man has it out of his system. Who knows, deep inside he might even have a conscience. There's nothing like getting your way with someone who has guilt."

They knocked lightly on the door and pushed it open.

Dixon was scratching a few notes on lined paper. He looked up at them, an unlit cigar clinched firmly in his teeth. "Well, what do you two want? Haven't you caused me enough trouble for the day?"

"Did you get my story?" Morgan asked.

Dixon looked down at the paper he was writing on and continued to scribble. "I got it."

"Well?"

Dixon looked up. "Well, what?"

"Did you like it?" Call had been in jail when Morgan had written it, so Dixon had gotten it fresh from Morgan's typewriter. There had been no built-in censor, and Morgan wanted very badly to find out what Dixon thought of his writing. He also wanted to get his reaction to the headline of the piece, "Murder on the *Titanic*." The story detailed his account of the murders that took place on the *Titanic* before it struck the iceberg, and it included the IRA plot to blow the ship up. He knew he seemed anxious for the old man's approval, but that was only because he was.

"You're not going to Washington for the hearings next week, Fairfield. So just plan on staying here and finding yourself a place to live besides the Waldorf Astoria."

"Why not?"

Dixon gave off a sarcastic half grin, half grimace, closing one eye to half-mast in that way of his that registered scornful disbelief. "Because you're just a cub reporter. No matter what you think, you don't own or run this paper yet. You also don't decide what to write your stories about. I'm the city editor. I make those decisions. This isn't some sixth-grade writing class where we're trying to produce something for your mommy."

He looked in Call's direction. Call had a smirk on his face like someone watching a predictable disaster at a family reunion. It wasn't often when love and hate could be blended in such equal proportions, but when it came to the way Harry Dixon treated his reporters, there always seemed to be a perfect balance. Apathy would have been an improvement. "What are you staring at?"

Call chuckled. "You. I'd like to see you teaching sixth graders."

"And I'd like to see you sober."

Call raised both hands. "Haven't had a drop all day. You see what a good teacher you are?"

"Well, just step into my office and look over my shoulder. I teach schoolchildren every day, all day." He glanced back and forth between Morgan and Call. "So have you filled the kid in on what he's to do to keep your behind out of a sling?"

"I explained some of it, how I'm writing the stories, and how some of them will have his name on them."

"He still didn't tell me why," Morgan said.

"Because you're easier to fire," Call chuckled.

"Now that's not exactly it," Dixon said, "and you darn well know it." Dixon pulled the cigar's soggy stump from his mouth and pointed it at Call. "'Cause if this man keeps writing, he's a target for somebody. We still haven't figured out who, but the list is probably quite long."

"And now I'm supposed to be the target?" Morgan asked.

Dixon waved the cigar. "You'll do fine. Like I said, you're a cub reporter. Nobody expects you to know anything, just spell the names right. Besides, the front office wants Call here off the story. Some of them want him off the paper."

"Why don't you just leave his name off it altogether?" Morgan asked.

"Having a name on it draws some fire. I'd rather have them firing at you. You're new, they don't know you, and frankly, they don't much care."

"So the story Call's working on about Fetters is something I have to put my name on?"

"You're catching on, boy. That's about the size of it."

"That doesn't seem right," Morgan said.

"What do you want me to do, spike it?"

"That's never bothered you before," Call said.

"Maybe not, but this story of yours is still connected to the *Titanic*, and that's big news. Morgan has become our—how shall we say it—*Titanic* reporter."

"One you're not even sending to Washington to cover the hearings," Morgan added.

"That's because the real crime story is this Fetters thing, him coming off the *Titanic* and all, and we can't attach Call's name to it. I don't even want him close to it. I don't want people to even think he's working on it. Besides, I've got other reporters I'm sending to Washington."

"O'Leary?" Call asked.

"I tried to do that, but for some strange reason he declined. Some men just hate sitting in large rooms with people they don't know at their elbows all day while they take notes. Imagine that."

"Well, he does seem to be interested in our story," Morgan said. "He was asking me a bunch of questions about it."

"You didn't tell him anything, did you?" Call asked.

"I may be a cub reporter, but I'm not stupid. It's our story."

Call grinned at Dixon. "I did find out something about the *Titanic*. Something everybody else has missed."

"Are you talking about those lifeboats?" Morgan asked.

"Yeah, sure."

"I think you're nuts," Morgan said.

"Oh, nuts am I? Now what brand-new ocean liner goes out on her maiden voyage with used lifeboats?"

"What's this?" Dixon asked.

"The plaques that carried the ship's name were switched on the lifeboats from the *Titanic*."

"Anyone could see that lifeboats were the last thing the people who outfitted that ship ever thought about," Morgan said. "If they'd just given it a modicum of thought, 2,200 people wouldn't have died."

"I like the angle," Dixon said. "Work it."

"These companies switch parts all the time," Morgan said. "I don't know what you intend to prove by that. We're just talking about a few screw holes."

"I just report the story, I don't prove anything. But you sound like a spokesman for the company. If that's their explanation, let them say it."

"But my name's going on this story, and it just sounds absurd to me."

Dixon glared at Morgan. "With what you turned in to me, I wouldn't be the one to talk about nutty stories."

Just then a reporter stuck his head in the door. Bruce Elliott was a bright man, bright enough to know he should never walk into the boss's office without being asked. It was something he not only never did but something he had no desire to do. He had a thin face, dull brown eyes, and a sharp nose. "Are you busy?" he asked.

"Why, never too busy for you, Bruce." Dixon used the syrupy sweet voice he reserved for an explosion to follow. "Of course I'm busy," he barked. "When I'm sleeping, I'm busy sleeping too."

"I just have something I thought Call and Fairfield here might be interested in." He gulped. You could see the man's Adam's apple bobbing under his high starched collar. "I showed it to O'Leary, and he told me I should find the two of them and bring them into it." He stepped into the office sheepishly, dragging his feet. He looked down at the piece of paper in his hand. "I was over at the police station a short time ago when this came in. I recognized the name right away."

Call pulled the paper out of the man's hand and read it. He showed it to Morgan. "A murder over by the navy yard. Man named Fetters."

"Do you think he might be related to the man you're looking into?" Elliott asked.

Call shrugged his shoulders. Morgan could see that the last thing Call wanted was for Dixon or anyone else to know that he'd been near a crime scene and left it unreported. He could also tell by the look that Call flashed at him that he wasn't a bit certain Morgan would be savvy enough to keep his mouth shut.

"He might be," Morgan answered. Call seemed relieved.

"Then you two better look into it," Dixon said. He placed the cigar back into his mouth and started back to work.

Elliott pointed at the piece of paper. "It's got an address on it, someplace on York Street."

As Morgan and Call reached the door, Dixon suddenly jerked his head up. "Not you, Call. We'll send Fairfield. I don't want to attract any more attention to you. There'll be cops crawling all over the place, and there's no sense in having your puss anywhere you'd be seen, at least not yet."

They stepped out of Dixon's office. "You better take Elliott with you." Call smiled at Elliott. "Might as well have as many moving targets on this story as we can get."

CHAPTER 27

Morgan and Elliott caught a cab in front of the building and headed straight for the Brooklyn Bridge. For once, Morgan knew right where they were going. Most of the time he'd been completely lost in New York City, but now he was the one who'd give the directions. It didn't take them long to pull up outside the apartment building. The black hearse belonging to the coroner was there. Morgan and Bruce Elliott got out, Morgan paying the man and jotting down the fare so that he could reimburse himself from petty cash.

As Morgan paid the driver, his gaze focused momentarily on the other side of the street. He noticed a man in a coat, his hat pulled down. The man was in the alley, but when Morgan looked at him, he jumped back behind a stack of boxes. *Odd*, Morgan thought.

Both Morgan and Elliott raced up the stairs and into, what was to Morgan, the familiar dark and seedy lobby. His eyes were drawn to a large piece of wallpaper that hung from the upper portion of the wall. It fluttered in the breeze of the open door, looking like a large shark on the end of a fisherman's line. The portion that had been on the wall wasn't the least bit white, as one might expect, but smeared brown by a glue that refused to work.

The men from the coroner's office were coming through the door from the first-floor apartments carrying the body. They had to step carefully through a pile of boxes and discards that stood between them and the front door. Morgan spotted Clifford, the medical examiner he had met at the morgue, following the litter. The man in front of the stretcher worked at negotiating the obstacle course. The last thing he wanted was to fall and have the corpse flopping on top of him on the grimy floor.

"We meet again," Clifford said. He put out his hand and stopped the stretcher bearer in the rear. "Where's Call?"

Morgan shrugged. "He's working on other stories now."

"Something hotter, I take it."

"I guess so."

Clifford shook his head. "The man's a regular bird dog. He just keeps his nose to the ground, sniffing all the time."

He motioned and caught the attention of the bearer in the front. "Let's set him down for a moment." Morgan could see the stretcher bearer roll his eyes. In unison they positioned the stretcher on the floor. This wasn't a task they were very happy with prolonging. There was an unmistakable odor of death to the body, and Morgan couldn't blame them at all for wanting to get back to the morgue as quickly as possible to get this thing out of their hair or at least out of their nostrils.

Clifford crouched down beside the covered body. "Why don't you take a good look at this and tell me what you think. We found him in bed."

Morgan's reaction was delayed, as if he wasn't sure what Clifford had said. "The bed?"

"That's right, lying comfortably in bed, just as pretty as you please."

"I'm not a great expert with these matters," Morgan said. He looked back and caught a glimpse of Elliott. The man was stepping closer for a look, but there was an air of timidity in his inch-long steps. He had also taken out a handkerchief and was using it to cover his nose. "This is

Bruce Elliott. He's a reporter." Morgan smiled. "If you have any cologne on you, Bruce, I'd try soaking that hankie of yours in it."

Elliott smiled. "I'll do that." He pulled a small bottle of bay rum out of his pocket, sprinkled it onto the handkerchief, and once more covered his nose.

Clifford smiled. "Nice to meet you, Elliott. I don't see much of you at the morgue." He stuck out his right hand to shake Elliott's, but Elliott offered his left hand, keeping his right hand with the handkerchief firmly clasped to his nose.

Elliott gulped and smiled, swallowing as he did. "Not my idea of a good time."

Clifford shrugged. "Just a job I guess." He pulled back the sheet, and Morgan took a closer look. He hadn't seen that much when he was here with Call, only enough of a glance to know the man was dead. Of course, Call had been so intent in looking that Morgan had barely been able to see around him.

Morgan picked up the man's left hand. There were wounds on the palm and a small cut near his pinkie. His right hand was balled up and stiff.

"We saw that. Does that mean this man was left-handed?"

"Not necessarily. These are defensive wounds, however. The man put up a fight against somebody coming at him."

"A fight?"

"That's right. There was a struggle."

Clifford stroked his chin. Morgan could see the wheels turning in the man's mind. "Makes you wonder, doesn't it?" Morgan asked. "Just how a man could put up a struggle and wind up lying comfortably in bed, 'just as pretty as you please,' as you put it."

"That is peculiar."

They looked down to the spot on the man's neck that was obviously the exit wound. There was also a deep entrance wound. The entrance wound was on the right side of Fetters' neck with a deep cut leading to the exit wound on the left. Clifford pointed it out. "This our left-handed killer?"

"I'd say so, given the fact that we know Fetters here was attacked directly."

"What an odd thing, two men named Fetters killed on the same night by the same man miles away."

"You'd have to say they were connected, wouldn't you?"

"I don't think there's any doubt about it."

"And it would have to be someone who knew where our *Titanic* engineer's brother lived."

"Yes, it would."

Morgan pulled the man's shirt out from his pants and turned him over slightly. "That's interesting." He looked up. "Can we go have a quick look at where this man was found before I tell you what else I think?"

"Sure." Clifford looked at the two men assisting him. "Just hold him right here. He isn't in that much of a hurry, not anymore."

They walked to the door that led to the hallway, and Clifford held it open for Morgan and Elliott. "It's down here."

Morgan could see the uniformed officer outside of Fetters' door. They walked down the hall and, nodding at the man, stepped inside.

A uniformed officer and a plainclothes detective were sifting through the room. They held up each article of clothing and went through any pockets they could find. The man in the street clothes turned around and smiled at Morgan. It was Ryan. "Fairfield, fancy seeing you here."

Morgan shrugged. "Just doing my job, like you." He looked back at Elliott. "This is Bruce Elliott from the paper."

"I didn't expect to see you." He smiled. "Where's Call?"

"Working his own story, I guess."

"Shame," Ryan said. "I miss him."

Morgan smiled. "And I think he's trying to keep it that way." He pointed at the uniformed officer who had started digging through a trunk. "Quite a search you've got going, Ryan."

The sergeant smiled. "Got to do good police work."

"Wouldn't you normally take this stuff downtown?"

"We probably will. We just thought we'd give it a swift examination first." He waved his hand at the room. "There's nothing but a bunch of junk here."

"Any suspects yet?" Morgan asked.

Ryan shook his head. "Two men were seen going down the fire escape earlier today, but the man was obviously killed earlier."

The three men stepped over spots of dried blood near the middle of the room. Morgan hadn't seen them the first time he and Call had visited the place, but Ryan had all the lights on. The strewn nature of the room was even more visible. They walked around the screen that sheltered the sleeping area from the rest of the room, and Morgan felt the mattress. There was some blood on it, but the largest area of spilled blood was next to the bed on the floor. The mattress was thin, with hard springs forming the bulk of what there was to sleep on. "That must have been hard to sleep on," Morgan said.

"He's sleeping fine now," Ryan replied.

Morgan gave him a quick look. There was a broad smile on the man's face. "I suppose he is." He motioned to Clifford. "We better let you get back to your job. Maybe Elliott and I will come back later."

The three men stepped out in the hall and made their way back to the lobby. When they got to the stretcher, Morgan picked up the sheet once again. He lifted the man's shirt. "You found him on his back?"

"Yes, we did."

"You see any signs that he was lying on those springs in there?"

Clifford looked at the man's back and shook his head. "None at all."

"Kind of unusual, wouldn't you say?"

"Now that you mention it, I would say that. I mean, if the man was killed on his bed and died there, I suspect we'd find more indentations in his skin."

"Exactly. This man died and laid in that room beside the bed for some time before somebody came and moved him to the bed. Rigor mortis had already taken hold before Fetters was moved."

"That's odd. It sure looks that way."

"Why would anybody do that?" Elliott asked.

"That's the question," Clifford said.

Morgan laid the man's shirt back into position and covered him with the sheet. He looked back at the hallway. "You saw the condition that room was in."

Both Elliott and Clifford nodded.

"Maybe whoever it was who killed him didn't find what he was looking for," Elliott said. "Maybe he came back and moved him, hoping he had landed on it."

Morgan smiled at the man. "That's good thinking. I believe you're right." He looked down once again at the covered corpse. "Let's take one more look." He lifted the sheet and picked up the man's right hand. It was clinched tightly, and Morgan began to pry the man's fingers open. The fingers were stiff and came open one at a time with a great deal of effort. Slowly he opened the man's fingers, and there in the palm of his hand was a piece of paper.

Clifford picked it up and read it.

"Can I see that?" Morgan asked.

Clifford held it to his chest. "I'm not sure. This is the property of the coroner now."

"And I helped you to find it. It won't go beyond the three of us."

"Oh, all right." He handed the paper to Morgan.

Morgan read it. "It's a phone number." He showed it to Elliott, who whistled.

"You recognize that number?" Clifford asked.

"Both of us do," Morgan said. "It's the number to the city desk of the *New York Herald.*"

"What do you think about it?"

"I haven't a clue," Morgan said.

"Me neither," Elliott agreed. "I'm mystified."

CHAPTER 28

As Call stirred his tortellini, Fredo Giuseppe sat across from him. "You'll like that," Fredo said. "It has some nice sausage in it." He waved his hand around the room like a man showing off his house and trying to impress his mother-in-law. "Dis is a family business, and they do the things you'd expect from a family."

Call looked around. The wallpaper was well done, pink with red roses on it. The black-and-white floor tile was so clean it sparkled, and the tables had carnations in vases. There was a personal touch to the atmosphere. He pushed his fork into the tortellini, swishing the pasta around to mop up more of the tomato sauce, and then put the entire thing into his mouth. His eyes brightened from the small bite of the sauce. "This is good. You sure know Little Italy."

Fredo smiled. "Of course, I do." He leaned back and grinned, thumping his chest. "What do you think I am, a nobody?"

The owner of the restaurant walked with a shuffle into the room, smiling and bowing to patrons as he passed them at their tables. Call thought he looked much like a bowling pin. The man was large around the waist, tapering slightly at the hips and winding up on short legs and small feet. His head was bald with a slight fringe of black hair over his ears. Call smiled at the thought of the man's apron as the stripe painted around the middle of a bowling pin.

The man flung out his arms, as a mother would greet a child coming home from school. "Fredo." He spoke an Italian phrase. "I'ma so very happy to see you."

Fredo got to his feet, and the two men kissed each other on the cheek and hugged. Fredo looked down at Call. "This is a friend of mine. Call. He is a newspaper reporter."

The man looked Call over. "No policeman?"

Call smiled. "No, I'm a reporter. That means I pay."

"It certainly does," Fredo agreed.

The man laughed. "Well, then, we're gonna hafta be very, very good to you."

Call stuck another forkful of the tortellini in his mouth. He smiled and chewed. "You are being good to me. But you're not going to try to hug and kiss me, are you? The food's enough so far as I'm concerned."

"Good, good, I'm very glad." He put his hand on Fredo's shoulder. "Any friend of the sergeant here is a big friend of mine. You gentlemen enjoy yourselves. Stay as long as you like, and eat as much as you want."

The man's eyes danced in his head. He turned and made his way back to the kitchen, nodding at the patrons he passed.

Fredo cut a bite of his veal. "It does pay to have friends, Call." He pointed at the retreating man with his knife and fork. "You could do to have a few, you know, people you don't pay to try to like you."

"I make friends when I need to."

"Sure you do, but are they there when you need them?" He made a circling gesture with his hand. "I don't think so."

Fredo always made it a habit of talking with his hands. A gesture found its way into each and every sentence. Call figured it was an Italian thing to do. He doubted if the man could talk if his hands were tied.

Fredo motioned toward Call with his knife. "Now take O'Toole, for instance. You're never going to find out anything from him. He has friends, so he doesn't need you. He needs them. He has family and he has a city. Why should he risk anything, including his job, to do anything for you?"

"I'm pretty sure he saw the murders. I'm also sure that whoever it is who's behind this got to him."

"OK. You know all you're going to know." He slashed through the air in a downward motion. "The Irish Tommyknockers are behind this. We know that. O'Toole and a bunch of the force are beholden to those people. After all, they're Irish."

He set down his fork and pointed at Call. "You'll get nothing by going after them. They're tighter than a drum." He then waved at Call in a sweeping direction. "Besides, the murderer isn't your story here. You want to know why?"

"You find out why, and you'll find out who's behind this. Don't think of the IRA or the," he uttered a word of Italian slang, "New York Tommyknockers as the murderers. They're the weapons. Somebody else holds the weapons, and somebody else pulls the trigger."

He picked up his fork and continued to cut his veal. "The real killer might not be Irish at all."

Call started eating. "He might even be Italian."

Fredo smiled at him. "He might." He stuck a piece of veal into his mouth. "In fact, the smarter you say this person is, the more you might be right about him being Italian."

"I've just got to find out what Fetters knew about the *Titanic*."

Fredo pointed his fork at Call and smiled. "That would help."

"Read the mind of a dead man."

"You got it." He pointed his knife at Call. "It's something we have to do all the time. But what makes you think this has anything to do with the *Titanic*?"

"Look, I've been on the crime beat for some time. I've never had people try to kill me before no matter what they thought about my articles, and I've never been thrown in the slammer on trumped-up charges."

"And you think it's because of this *Titanic* thing?"

"It's the story we're working on. Fetters came off the *Titanic* and the deeper we dig into him and what he knew, the more smoke and fire we run into. This is the biggest story of the century. Companies will rise and fall with the investigation, and men's lives will be ruined. Sailors are killed all the time, but why Fetters? He must have known something."

"I see your point."

"The man's brother was even killed about the same time. That's just too much of a coincidence."

Fredo mumbled, his mouth swimming in veal. "I suppose so."

"Meanwhile, I'll have your protection, right?"

"Yes, you will. I'll put some of my men on the cops you've told me about. They'll watch where they go and who they talk with. You're perfectly safe with me. You have my guarantee."

The restaurant owner walked into the back dining room where Call and Fredo were seated. He had an open bottle of wine in one hand and three glasses between the fingers of his other hand. "I have a nice'a bottle of vino here for you. You try."

He set down the glasses and poured the wine.

"Who's the third glass for?" Fredo asked.

The man smiled. "Why, for me, of course. You don't think I'd serve my customers anything that I wouldn't drink, do you?" He picked up his glass of wine and held it out. "Salute."

Call and Fredo heard a commotion in the front dining room. It sounded like tables were being overturned, and it was plain to see the noise disturbed the owner. He lowered his glass. "What is that?"

Two men wearing hats and long trench coats walked through the door and into the back dining room. One had a red beard with green eyes, and the other was a clean-shaven, dark-haired man. When they spotted Call and Fredo in the back of the room, they reached under their coats and pulled out double-barreled shotguns.

Fredo grabbed Call and pulled him to the floor.

Lifting up one foot, Call shoved over the table, sending glassware and food to the sparkling black-and-white tile.

The first two explosions rocked the room, echoing from wall to wall and rattling the pictures. Large chunks of the table splintered off the top, sending needlelike particles of oak flying. The table jerked backward as a third blast was fired dead-on.

The restaurant owner lay sprawled on the floor in front of them. The man still had the wineglass in his hand. It was unbroken, but he appeared to be dead. Fredo drew his revolver and peered around the edge of the table. He fired and then ducked back behind the table just as a fourth shot was fired from the scatterguns.

Fredo pushed the revolver back around the edge of the table and fired three shots in close succession. The shots were followed by the sound of the two men running and the screams of patrons from the front dining room.

Fredo opened the gate on his pistol. He ejected the spent cartridges and, reaching into his pocket, stuffed fresh rounds into the now empty chambers. He got to his knees and peered around the table.

Call got to his knees beside the man. "So, I'm perfectly safe with you? I have your guarantee, do I? Seems to me the question is, are you safe with me?"

Fredo shook his head. Call could see the dull look of disbelief in his richly brown eyes. "This is big. I've never seen a police sergeant attacked this way."

"Makes you think those people just don't think they can be caught, doesn't it?"

Fredo got to his feet, his gun still pointing toward the door. "I'd say they have lots of confidence." He looked back at Call. "You better get out of here and leave this to me. I don't want you anywhere around when the cops on the beat get here."

"And what about you?"

"I'll stay here and make my explanations. I just won't tell them everything I know." He shrugged. "What good would it do?"

Call stumbled to his feet. He watched as several diners tried to poke their heads up above their tables, fear and hysteria registering all over their faces.

"You better do one more thing too. I don't care what that lawyer of yours told you, you better carry that gun of yours."

"I will."

"I'd do something else too."

"What's that?"

"I'd give that young friend of yours a warning. Whoever it is that's behind this isn't going to stop with an Irish cop just arresting someone, not anymore."

CHAPTER 29

Morgan sat in the small French restaurant. He pushed his feet out and studied his new oxfords. It would take a while to put himself in a new wardrobe, and he hoped it wouldn't be as painful as these new shoes were.

The tables and chairs were wicker, painted white. Morgan could see the place was doing its best to adopt a spring look. The booths next to the walls were framed by a wooden trellis. Lush vines were woven through the spaces, and, although the leaves were paper and the red and deep purple grapes were no doubt wax, they made for a lush, dreamy setting reminiscent of an outdoor garden. Roses were in the middle of each table, and napkins were folded in the shapes of birds. He was hungry. He had skipped lunch, and now the cloth napkins were even beginning to look like turkeys to him, inedible but tempting.

He took out his watch and pried it open. Margaret was almost forty-five minutes late. He'd already been told by more than one man that marriage meant a lifetime of waiting. He figured if it was something he was going to have to do, he might as well make the best of it. Taking out his notebook, he began to scribble notes on what he knew about the story he and Call were working on. He always seemed to think best with a pen and paper in hand.

Moments later he looked up to see Margaret and Gloria standing at the door. What surprised him was the fact that Ed Leslie, the man who managed the theater, was also with them. Morgan got to his feet and waved. He forced a smile. The romantic interlude he'd planned for Margaret was turning into a dinner party of four.

They spotted him and walked to the table, led by the maître d'hôtel. The man held a stack of menus in his arms. With a broad smile, Morgan kept up the pretense of his delight at seeing the others. "Good to see you all. I'm happy you could join us."

"Fiddle-dee-dee," Gloria said. "Normally I wouldn't have come within miles of you two tonight, but Margaret and I had some experiences today that we didn't think you should be left out of."

"Please," Morgan said, "have a seat." He could see that Margaret was almost trembling, though she was trying hard to look at ease. He took her hand and guided her to her seat. "Are you all right?"

"I will be."

Gloria and Leslie took their places across the table, and Gloria continued her report. "Margaret and I had lunch with Kennedy today."

"Did he say something to upset you?"

"No," Gloria responded. "He was the perfect gentleman."

"And our hero as it turned out," Margaret added.

"Yes, he was," Gloria went on. "That was afterward. Margaret and I took a walk through the park and were followed."

"By whom?"

"We don't know." Gloria took some time and described the two thugs and their rescue by the man calling himself Hunter Kennedy.

Morgan put his arm around Margaret and pulled her closer. He could feel a series of cold shivers running up her arms. "I'm sorry you were upset. Maybe you two ladies shouldn't stay in New York."

"We're just glad Mr. Kennedy came along when he did," Margaret said. She was trying to be brave.

"He acquitted himself quite well, too, you'll be happy to know."

Ed Leslie leaned over the table and shoved a badge in Morgan's direction. "I was following Kennedy after he had lunch with these two ladies. I'm with the Secret Service. I've already shown my credentials to these good ladies."

Morgan picked up the badge and looked it over carefully. He gave it back to the man. "I'm happy to see you're not with the New York City Police Department. I've had more than my trouble with those people, and I can't tell whose side they're on."

Leslie smiled. "I can understand that, Mr. Fairfield." He folded the badge's leather case and dropped it into his coat pocket. "We're working on that too."

"There is something you need to know about our lunch with Kennedy," Margaret said. "Gloria and I were talking about it before we came in."

"Yes," Gloria said. "It might be important." She looked at Margaret. "Given what happened to us, we really don't want to speak evil of the man, but it seems the only friend our Mr. Kennedy could remember from his voyage on the *Titanic* was the engineer, Jeremy Fetters."

"That is the man whose murder you're investigating, isn't it?" Margaret asked.

"Yes. Quite the coincidence I'd say."

"Kennedy said he traveled second class," Gloria added, "which was why we never saw him. I suppose that's possible."

Leslie smiled. "Actually, that's not possible. I've been following him for weeks, and he's used many names. When he showed up here as Hunter Kennedy, I became the theater manager. It gave me an excuse to keep a close eye on him and watch who came and went." He looked over at Margaret. "Of course, I became interested in why Miss Hastings wanted to see him. I suppose I'd like to think of his actions in the park today as common decency."

"I'd say it was a good thing for us," Gloria said.

"And why have you been following this man?" Morgan asked.

"I can't tell you everything, but we suspect his involvement in gunrunning for the Irish cause. Off the record of course, Mr. Fairfield." Leslie smiled.

Margaret looked at Gloria. "That would explain his reactions to our discussion of the IRA."

The four of them ordered from the menu and spent the next hour talking over the day. Gloria and Margaret did their best to recount the conversation with Kennedy. "I did get the impression that he was somewhat disillusioned with the Irish patriotic movement," Margaret added, "and the part they might have played in the tragedy. Perhaps he is a decent man, after all."

Leslie looked at Morgan. "From what the ladies tell me, you have some information that the War Department should know."

"Yes, I do." Morgan hadn't been able to recount his experience on the *Titanic* and how he had come to gain and then lose possession of a top secret document. He was now the only man alive to have seen the letter meant for President Taft.

"I know I should sit down with some authority and tell them just what I know," Morgan said, "but I've been thrown into this thing. I haven't been able to even think about anything else." He rubbed Margaret's hand lightly and looked into her eyes. "Even people who mean all the world to me."

"Well, hopefully we can wrap this up soon," Leslie said. "We know Kennedy has been running guns, and we know he has a shipment ready to go soon. What we don't know is who is going to carry it and when."

"Would Fetters have known that?" Morgan spoke without thought, almost to hear himself think out loud. "No, that's my whirlpool, not yours."

"Who is this Fetters?" Leslie asked.

"He was an engineer who survived the *Titanic* only to be murdered on the docks of New York. His brother was murdered that same night, so we figure the man must have seen him and told him something very dangerous."

Margaret gave a deep sigh. "Oh, Morgan, this does sound dangerous."

Morgan could see the look of concern in her eyes. He patted her hand to reassure her. "I think I'm all right. Everybody sees me as a cub reporter who doesn't know enough to come in out of the rain. And that's just what I want them to believe." He smiled. "For a while, anyway."

"The ladies told me about the IRA bomb on board the ship," Leslie said. "There may be some connection there. I'd be careful if I were you. There may be people who know you have knowledge of that."

"Only one of the officers from the *Titanic*. I don't really think Boxhall's going to say anything to anybody, though. Besides, he's in Washington now."

"You be careful, all the same," Leslie said.

Morgan nodded, looking at Margaret. "I'll be the soul of caution."

Morgan paid the check, and they walked to the door. Gloria and Leslie stepped outside to allow Morgan to have a moment of privacy with Margaret.

"I need to move out of the Waldorf and find a place tomorrow," Morgan said. "I thought you might want to help me look. You women seem to have an eye for things that I'd simply ignore."

"I'd love to help." Her eyes sparkled for the first time all night.

He held her hand tightly. "Wonderful. Then it's all settled. I'll turn my article in tomorrow morning and do what I can on this story to keep the paper satisfied. Then I'll look for you."

"Are you going to walk back to the hotel with us?"

"No, I think not. I need to see Call tonight. I'd planned on taking a taxi to his place and then getting back to the hotel late."

"Morgan, don't make me go through this again. I couldn't take it."

"Go through what, darling?"

"I've just lost Peter. I'd be totally devastated if something happened to you." She gripped his hand tightly. "Please be very careful."

"You just pray for me. I'll be fine."

She nodded. "I will. I am praying for you all the time."

Morgan stroked her face gently with his finger. "My dear, it's the Lord's tender mercy that brought me back to you. He can't allow that to happen only to take me away again."

She rose up on her toes and kissed him tenderly. Then, turning around, she joined Gloria and Leslie for the walk back to the hotel.

Morgan stepped out onto the sidewalk and watched her walk away. He was so intent on not losing sight of her that he didn't notice the two men who walked up behind him. He didn't notice them until he felt the hard barrel of a gun in his ribs. He froze.

"You're coming with us," one of the men said.

"I have money," Morgan turned to look at the man, "if that's what you want."

"Right now we just want you," the second man said.

They took hold of Morgan and slowly turned him around. A black car was parked in the alley, and they marched him straight to it. Morgan noticed the one man as he opened the back door for him. The man was tall and thin; he had a trim black mustache and dark eyes. He was well dressed in an overcoat and homburg.

Morgan slid into the seat, and the man jumped in beside him. He, too, held a gun pointed in Morgan's direction.

The other man, the one who had shoved the gun into his ribs on the street, was a clean-shaven, rotund man. He wore a cap and jacket. He jumped into the driver's seat and threw the car into gear.

Morgan watched as the lights of New York surged past his window. "Where are you taking me?"

The driver sneered over his shoulder. "Someplace where we can have a little talk, just the three of us."

"What about? I don't really know anything."

"You seem to know quite a bit," the man in the backseat said. The man's eyes were fixed on him, as if he were trying to read Morgan's mind.

"Most of what I know is what happened to me on the *Titanic*, that and things you could find in a schoolbook."

The driver laughed. "Schoolbook! That's rich."

A short time later the diver turned the car into a schoolyard. He turned off the engine and looked around at Morgan. "Here's your last school. We'll just find out what you have in that schoolbook learning of yours."

The man in the backseat got out and held the door open for Morgan. When Morgan got out, the man pushed him in the direction of the playground. Morgan could see the swings and a number of teeter-totters outlined in the black sky. They stood there, empty of laughter, empty of play. He walked onto the sandy ground.

"That's far enough," the driver said. He was holding a small revolver, and Morgan could see the man's eyes now. They were an icy blue, almost like the blue berg that hit the *Titanic*. They were deadly and determined, and they sent a chill up his spine.

"Yes," the second well-dressed man said, wagging his own revolver. "I think this is far enough."

"What would you like to know?" Morgan asked. "What could I possibly tell you?"

"We don't really want to know anything from you," the driver said. "We just want to know how you'll die."

The well-dressed man waved his gun. "Get on your knees, young man."

"Are you serious?" Morgan asked.

"Deadly serious," the man replied.

CHAPTER 30

Patricia Bennett lived comfortably in a large brownstone building. The upstairs contained four bedrooms, three of which were constantly empty. Her own bedroom faced the busy street. She'd grown accustomed to the noise, unable to sleep without the constant clatter of traffic on the street below.

The water in the pot on the stove was boiling, the eggs rising and falling with the foam that threatened to overflow at any moment. She reached over and turned down the gas. Taking the pot off the stove and putting it in the sink, she ran cold water into the boiling eggs. Within minutes she was stripping off the last of the shells. She dumped the eggs into a large bowl and added mayonnaise, a couple of spoonfuls of pickle relish, and a dollop of yellow mustard. Setting the loaf of bread on a cutting board, she ran the serrated blade over the bread and cut it into a number of fresh slices. Egg salad sandwiches were a simple meal, and they were easy to make. They were probably also the best meal the Farier woman had eaten in quite some time.

Patricia set the small table in the kitchen and poured milk into two glasses. The red checkered cloth and white napkins made a nice touch. Her eyes drifted over the kitchen until she spotted the last thing that would make the meal complete. Walking over to the windowsill behind the sink, she picked up a jar with lilacs in it. The purple flowers would brighten up the table, and she had a feeling it would be needed.

The lights were bright overhead, but that was all right. This woman who was now her houseguest cried out for bright lights, anything that would take her life out of the shadows.

Through the hallway was an open living room, large French doors ajar. It was warm and cozy, with muted brown furniture that would have seemed masculine to anyone but Patricia Bennett. She liked things that were strong and solid and soft to the touch only if you dared to feel it. It was the way she saw herself.

"Whew-ee."

Geraldine Farier had to be only in her forties, and for the first time she even looked it. The bath and shampoo had taken at least ten years off her age. Patricia watched the woman come down the stairs. She was wearing one of Patricia's old robes, pink terry cloth with a hood. The puffy pink slippers practically came off her feet with each step.

Gerry scrambled her hair with the tips of her fingers, feeling for the roots. "I left me some mighty dirty water in that tub up yonder."

"Just think, that was all on you." Patricia put her hands on her hips and smiled. There was something about seeing someone change that felt more than a little fulfilling, even if it only took a good bath to do it.

The woman smiled, showing her missing and blackened teeth. "I guess I growed pretty used to what I had on me, even if it was mostly dirt."

"We all get accustomed to things as they are."

"I ain't putting you out none, am I?"

"Being alone is what I've become used to. I'll adjust, same as you."

"Well, I surefire hates to put folks out. You got your own life to lead here without old Gerry. What will your gentlemen callers think?"

Patricia pulled the chair out for the woman. "I'm afraid there aren't any gentlemen callers, so you don't need to worry about what they think."

Gerry sat down and scooted her chair forward. "No gents in your life? How's that, pretty woman like you?"

"I have no time for them."

"No time? I ain't never seen me a woman with no time for the menfolk."

"Well, you're looking at one now." Patricia motioned to the food in front of the woman. "You better eat your sandwich. It'll get your strength up."

Gerry picked up the glass of milk and held it up to her eyes, inspecting it. "This here's milk, I take it."

"That's right, fresh too."

"Ain't you got nothing more in it?"

Patricia shook her head. "Nope. Everything you see there comes from the cow."

Gerry put down the glass. "Ain't you got no wine? I'd a figured a woman in a nice place such as this would have her some spirits about."

"I have plenty, but I think you've had enough."

"I ain't had me nothing to drink in a spell now."

"And what would a spell be?"

Gerry rolled her eyes and stroked her chin. She had a contemplative look, as if she were trying to solve a puzzle. "Must be hours by now."

"Good, then you're sober. That's just the way we want to keep you—sober." She again pointed to the sandwich. "Eat up."

Gerry picked up the sandwich and held it in front of her face. She glared at Patricia. "Maybe iffen you had yourself a man you wouldn't be so hard on an old girl like me."

"Hard on you? I took you shopping for some decent clothes, brought you to my home, and gave you a bath. Then I fixed this supper for you, one that you're not eating."

Gerry took a big bite of the sandwich. "Ain't give me no spirits, though." She said the words with her mouth full, spewing egg salad onto her plate and the table as she spoke.

"No, and I don't intend to. You have to be sober for Call's trial."

"Call's trial. I can't figure out why you wouldn't just leave me be if that's all you wanted." She pulled the sandwich away from her mouth and opened the top of it. "You got some pepper?"

"I think so. Just a moment." Patricia went to the kitchen counter and took down a set of cut glass salt and pepper shakers. She walked back to the table and set them down in front of the woman.

Gerry picked up the shakers and held them up to her eyes. She turned them around to see the colors and then held out the pepper. "This pepper?"

"Yes, it is."

"I ain't never seen me nothing fancy like this before. A gal don't know what she's shaking out till it hits the food."

She shook a coating of the black pepper onto the yellow sandwich. She closed the sandwich and patted it down as if to drive the taste in deeper. "I like me some zip in my food. A gal's got to keep her taster alive and kicking, ya know."

"Yes, I'm sure. Now, why else would I bring you here?"

Gerry took another bite of her sandwich. "That's better." She grinned, showing the missing spaces in her mouth. "I spose I thought you needed a cleaning woman. I done that before, but never for nobody who wouldn't turn me out for a snifter full of gin now and then."

"No, I don't need a cleaning woman. I never spend enough time at home to get the place very dirty, and what I do, I clean up myself."

"Fancy working woman like you?"

"That's right, fancy working woman like me."

"And no man?"

"That's right. No man."

"Ain't you never had the sweets for Call? I mean, if he's the reason you brung me here, I'd think you had some heart thoughts on the man from time to time."

"He is an employee, and I'm his boss. We try to protect our own. If you know something that can keep the man out of jail, then I want to make sure you get to court in one piece to say what you have to say."

"You're his boss?" Her eyes widened and her jaw fell slack, showing a layer of unchewed egg salad.

"Yes, in a way I am."

Gerry took another bite. "Durned if that don't beat all. I got me a rich gal who works, who don't have the sweets on no man, and who does her own housework." She shot Patricia a cockeyed look of curiosity. "I reckon I done gone and seen it all."

"I suppose you have." Patricia took a bite of her own sandwich and then pointed at Gerry's. "Is that OK?"

Gerry grinned. "It is now." She picked up her glass and held it up to the light, trying her best to see through the white liquid. Shrugging her shoulders, she gulped it down.

When she set down the glass, Patricia could see a faint white mustache around the woman's upper lip. She picked up her napkin and reached over the table in Gerry's direction.

Gerry backed up. "Here, what you doing with that thing?"

"You have milk on your mouth."

"I'll wipe it my own self." The woman frowned and, picking up her own napkin, matted it to her mouth.

"Hard to let people help you, isn't it?"

Gerry dropped the napkin on her plate. "No more than it is for you."

There was a knock at the door, and Patricia got to her feet. "I wonder who that is? I'm not expecting anyone."

Gerry grinned. "Maybe it's a gentleman caller."

"I doubt that."

Patricia walked into the hallway and toward the door with Gerry at her heels. She stopped at the door. "Who is it?"

The voice was squeaky but clear. "Flowers for Miss Patricia Bennett."

Gerry clapped her hands. She was almost bouncing up and down. She leaned closer to Patricia. "See, you do have yourself a gentleman friend."

Patricia stepped back and reached into a bureau drawer. She pulled out a revolver.

"You ain't going to shoot him, are you?" Gerry asked.

"I don't have gentlemen friends, and I'm not sick."

Once again the door sounded with a series of knocks. "Flowers, Miss Bennett," the voice sounded.

Patricia opened the gate on the chambers of the revolver and checked to see if the gun was loaded. She flicked her wrist, snapping the thing back into place. "Just a moment. I'm opening the door."

She turned the knob on the dead bolt of the door and slowly cracked it open, just as far as the chain on the door would reach. Peeking through the crack, she spotted the deliveryman. He was of average build with a shock of black hair curved over his forehead. He was dressed in white. A white cap with a shiny black bill was on his head, and he was holding a bouquet of red roses. He held them out and smiled. "Flowers for Miss Bennett."

Gerry was jumping up and down behind her. "Wow-ee. I ain't never seen me no delivered flowers before."

Patricia put the gun down on the table next to the door. Reaching up, she slid the chain off the door and opened it wide.

The man looked back at the street in both directions. Patricia panicked, but it was too late. He pushed a revolver out from behind the flowers and began to fire. Patricia felt the sting of the first bullet. She dropped to the floor like a rock and lay there as the man continued to shoot. When she heard the click of the empty revolver, she felt the roses land on top of her. Then everything went black.

CHAPTER 31

Morgan slowly got down on his knees, looking up at the well-dressed older man. The man was calm as he held his pistol, almost as if he were inspecting a tree that had fallen on his driveway. Morgan would have expected him to show more emotion in a situation like this some degree of anger or irritation. As it was, there was a matter-of-fact look, a distance that the man's brown eyes drifted off into. From all appearances he didn't belong in a place like this, doing a thing like this. Of course, Morgan held the same opinion about himself. He'd just been doing his job. He didn't know these people, and he still had no idea of what they were doing and just what they were trying to cover up, if anything.

"You know I have no idea who you people are or why you're doing this," Morgan said.

The driver, who had his own gun out, was more animated than his friend. He shook his gun in Morgan's face. "That's just the way we like it, and that's just how we're going to keep it."

"Is this all about the Fetters thing?"

The well-dressed gentleman looked over at the driver as if to give him a signal.

"It's about more than that," the driver shouted. He looked over at the well-dressed man and shrugged his shoulders. "What harm can it do? He's gonna be dead anyway."

"Is it about the *Titanic*?"

"I don't rightly know everything," the driver said. "Let's just say we got ourselves some people who'd rather not see you around to dig up any more dirt. You're like a dog nipping at their heels, one they'd rather be rid of right now."

"So that's it. I'm an irritation."

"Yeah, that's it, a powerful irritation."

The gentleman stepped around in front of Morgan. "If you are a praying man, I would suggest you make the most of it."

Morgan bowed his head as the man walked around to his rear. This was going to be one simple shot in the back of the head, and Morgan knew it. He had little fear of dying. He knew full well just where he'd be going; he'd been taught that since he was a boy, and as a young man he'd come to believe it. He would be facing Jesus, not as his judge but as his Savior.

He began to pray silently. *Lord, I commit my soul to Your safekeeping. Please let Margaret know that I love her, and take care of her. You have my total trust, even in the midst of this.*

"You gonna do it?" the driver asked the other man.

"Be my guest," the gentleman replied.

Morgan heard the cock of a pistol. The next sound he heard was the explosion of a gunshot behind his head. It left his ears ringing, but his heart was still beating wildly. The man who had been his driver dropped to the ground beside him.

The gentleman put his hand on Morgan's shoulder. "Get up, young man."

Morgan slowly got to his feet, trembling like a leaf. He was much too stunned to even speak.

"I'll give you a ride to where you're going," the man said.

"I d-d-don't understand."

"You don't need to understand. You just need to do what you're doing."

Morgan shook his head. "I don't even understand what I'm doing."

The man chuckled slightly, dropping the pistol into his pocket. He reached down and picked up the revolver the driver had dropped and handed the gun to Morgan. "You had better keep this. You might need it sometime when I'm not around."

Morgan held the pistol. It was heavy, and he felt awkward even handling it. Only moments before it was supposed to have been the instrument used to take his life, and now this man wanted him to use it to possibly take the life of someone else. He shuddered at the thought.

They walked back toward the car, and the man put his hand on Morgan's shoulder. "Are you all right?"

Morgan's knees were still shaking, and he was walking in a wobbly fashion, as a drunk. "I may never be all right again."

"I am sorry I let it go that far. I just had to make certain we were not followed, that no one was watching."

"Who are you?"

The man shook his head. "I'm afraid I can't tell you that. Let's just say that I'm a friend of a friend."

When they got to the car, Morgan got in the front seat and the man started the ignition. The black car sputtered to life. The man slipped it into reverse and backed out of the grassy area beside the school. Morgan could see the name on the building—Holmes Elementary School.

Morgan and his would-be killer were both silent for most of the trip back into the city. The silence was deafening, but it only fueled Morgan's curiosity. "Tell me something," he said. "What is it really like to hold a man's life in your hands?"

The man looked over at Morgan, studying him. "No, you tell me something first."

Morgan nodded slightly.

"How does it feel to hold everything a man ever was and everything he hopes to be in your hands?"

"I don't understand your question."

"You are a reporter. When your story is printed, people believe it. But what if you are wrong? Do they hear that? No, they don't. They only remember what was printed in the paper. In the meantime, all that a man ever was is dragged through the mud. He has no past, no wife, no children, no church, no good deeds to think about. He has only what you have said about him. And he has no future. Do you really think that what I do causes more damage to a man's total life than what you do?"

Morgan bowed his head. "I'm not sure."

"That's OK. You're much too young to be really sure about anything. You just better make sure, though. You better make sure that what sounds like an exciting story to you is the truth, the totality of the truth. You leave anything out, and you could very well ruin an innocent man's entire life."

"I see what you're saying."

"Make sure you do."

The man spotted the address Morgan had given him and pulled the car over. He reached over Morgan and opened the door. "Here we are, Mr. Fairfield."

Morgan got out and leaned back into the car. "I don't know what to say, but thank you."

The man waved the gesture off. "Just keep doing what you're doing." He lifted his index finger and shook it. "Just make certain that you get it right."

Morgan swallowed hard. "I have been given my life back twice, once when the *Titanic* went down and a second time tonight. That happens to very few men."

Leaning over, the man slammed the door. He reached out and took Morgan's hand. "Then God must have a place for you." He then threw the car into gear and sped off.

Morgan watched the car as the taillights disappeared into the darkness. He looked up at the house where Call lived. It was a small brownstone with two sets of stairs. The numbers on the two short pillars that anchored the sets of stairs gave the addresses, 892 and 892½. He climbed the stairs that led to the half address, hoping the man had a whole chair he could sit in. He was suddenly feeling very fatigued.

Morgan stepped up to the door and knocked lightly. It was all he had the strength to do.

Call's voice answered from behind the door. "Who is it?" There was a tone of anger to it.

"It's me, Morgan."

Morgan heard the chain pulled off the door, and then Call opened it. He had a gun in his hand. He quickly put the pistol down and, grabbing Morgan, pulled him in. "I'm so glad to see you boy, very glad."

Morgan practically collapsed in his arms. His legs were suddenly shaky once again. Call helped him to a chair. Knocking a stack of papers to the floor, he lowered Morgan into it. "What's wrong?" he asked.

Morgan's face was now white as a sheet. "You'll have to make the anonymous phone call tonight."

Call bent over to look Morgan in the face; his hands were on his knees. "What happened to you?"

Morgan and Call spent the better part of the next hour over a pot of hot tea. They exchanged stories, each story seemingly topping the last. When Call got back from making the phone call to tell the police where to find a body at the schoolyard of Holmes Elementary, he pulled up a chair across from Morgan.

"It wouldn't do to have kids show up for school and find that tomorrow," Morgan said.

"No, it wouldn't."

The phone rang, and Call got up to answer it. Morgan watched as Call's face turned red and then white. When Call hung up, he walked to the coatrack and pulled down his topcoat. "We have one more place to go tonight," he said. "That was Dixon on the phone. Somebody showed up at Pat's house tonight to deliver flowers."

Morgan shook his head. "No."

"Yes. The man shot both Pat and Gerry, the witness she was protecting. They're both alive, though. Gerry's barely hanging on. They're at the Sisters of Mercy."

CHAPTER 32

Sisters of Mercy Hospital took up nearly an entire city block. A slow sputtering rain had started. Streetlamps glared with a dull yellow, the misty rain sprinkling through buttery shafts of light. As Morgan followed Call down the sidewalk and to the sweeping marble stairs, he sent up another prayer of thanks. He had no desire to be ungrateful that God had given him his life back a second time. Morgan and Call took the steps two at a time and pushed their way through the oversize doors and into the lobby.

The hospital had a number of plants blooming in clay pots. Papers were strewn about the empty chairs, and half-finished cups of coffee sat cold and long forgotten on several tables. A father sat in one chair in the corner, doing his best to quiet a crying child. Morgan wondered if the baby was crying for its mother.

Call spotted the nun behind the counter. He stepped back and spoke in a low tone to Morgan. "Wait right here. Women are my specialty, but this is a little different."

He made his way to the desk and immediately caught the attention of the nun on the other side. The woman was sour in expression, and he could tell immediately that no amount of coddling or flattery would work to get them in past visiting hours and past this guardian of proper procedure.

"May I help you, sir?" she asked.

Call seemed a bit flustered. He flashed a meager smile. "I do hope so, Sister. I'm Reverend McCall, and this is Reverend Fairfield. We are here to see two very sweet ladies who are members of our parishes."

The woman stroked her chin and produced what for her might be a smile. "And just who might they be?"

"A Miss Patricia Bennett and Miss Geraldine Farier. They were both brought in a short time ago. Could you tell us where we might find them?"

The woman looked Call over. Pretending to be a minister was something new to Call, and he didn't quite know if he and Morgan looked pious enough to play the part. They also weren't wearing clerical collars, embellishments that must be standard with the Sisters of Mercy. "We're Baptists," he added quickly.

"Oh, I see. Well, let me look, Reverend." She picked up a clipboard from the desk and ran her finger down the list of names. "I see here that Miss Farier is still in surgery, but Miss Bennett is in room 704."

She pointed down the hall. "The elevators are down the hall to your left."

"Thank you, Sister." Call bowed slightly, almost apologetically. He looked back at Morgan and waved him forward.

As they walked along the corridor, Morgan frowned. "A minister?" he asked. "Now you have me playing the part of clergy?"

Call stopped at the elevators and pushed the white button. The large arrow pointing to the number nine started to drop. "What better job for you, Fairfield? You're just about the most righteous person I know."

"You have a very limited circle when it comes to righteous people."

Call smiled. "You got me there."

The elevator stopped, and the doors were opened. Morgan and Call got in. "Seven," he said to the elevator operator. "Tonight was supposed to be the night when the people we're looking for punched all our tickets at once," Call said, lowering his voice. "No more hassle, no more questions." He rocked back and forth watching the needle climb. "Just quick, get the bad blood done with."

The lift, as it was called, was more like a large bird cage. Call and Morgan could see the cables and the wheels turn and could feel the gust of a breeze as it whistled through the elevator shaft.

"I'd think there would be plenty of questions."

Call smiled. "Why? Somebody shoots a cop, and a reporter gets in the way. Somebody robs a newcomer to the city and decides to do him in. Some jealous lover kills a single woman and leaves flowers. Sounds like a typical weekend night in New York City, if you ask me."

"Right," Morgan smirked, "and all of them connected to this story in the *New York Herald*. Not likely."

"I don't think they'd have to worry about a bang-up job by the men in blue."

The doors in the elevator opened, and Morgan and Call stepped out into a long, semidark hallway. Several tables were scattered around the hall, some with cold food on them and others with medicine. Darkness had frozen the place into a dull gray. Morgan and Call walked toward the brighter light down the hall.

"How did they know about this Gerry woman at Patricia's house?" Morgan asked.

The question stopped Call in his tracks. "Somebody at the paper told them."

Morgan grabbed Call's sleeve as he started to walk away. "There's something I didn't tell you. It might be very important."

Morgan had Call's complete attention.

"When I went back to Fetters' brother's place, somebody had moved the body, somebody who came right after we left."

"Who?"

"Why is a better question."

"OK, wise guy, why?"

"They must have been looking for something. They had to move the man's body to make sure he hadn't fallen on it." Morgan smiled for the first time that evening. "And I found what they'd been looking for. It was balled up in the man's right hand."

"What was it?"

"The phone number of the city editor's desk at the paper."

"The *Herald*'s number?"

"That's right. The main switchboard number. Fetters must have had a contact on the paper that he wanted to reach, maybe some sort of emergency number he'd been given. If whoever did this thing tonight got the information about where this Gerry woman was, they had to get that from someone at the paper. Who would have known that?"

"I didn't know," Call said. "Did you?"

"No," Morgan answered.

"Maybe only Patricia can tell us that, or maybe Dixon."

"You don't think he had anything to do with this, do you?" Morgan asked.

"I think we'd better keep this under our hat for the time being. The only people we can really trust are the ones being shot at." Call used his thumbnail to pick at his teeth, something he liked to do when he was thinking a matter over. "Maybe it's someone who just doesn't think he's being paid quite enough."

Morgan bit his lip. "Or someone who doesn't feel quite satisfied with how far he's risen."

"Could be." Call shook his head. "We'll have to think on this matter. One more thing bothers me, though."

"What's that?" Morgan asked.

"I can't figure out why they'd go to so much trouble to rub out Geraldine Farier. The woman doesn't know much, only that she saw me. I don't think they'd try to kill her to give me a jail term. It would be easier simply to kill me, as they tried to do tonight."

"Maybe she knows something that you're not aware of," Morgan said, "something that even she is not aware of?"

Call's eyes brightened. "You could be right there, Fairfield." He smiled. "You know, for a college boy, you're not so dumb after all."

"Thanks, I think."

"Let's just hope the old lady pulls through surgery."

They walked a few more paces until they came to the room marked 704. Call slowly pushed the door open. A small lamp was glaring in the darkness. It sat on a table covered with syringes, bottles, and other medical paraphernalia.

The sight of Patricia on the bed was hard to adjust to. The woman was quiet and still, so unlike her. The sheet was draped over her like a hastily erected tent. A chart hung on the iron grate that made up her footboard.

Call looked nervous. "I guess we shouldn't be here," Morgan said. "There's no doctor to talk to."

"That's not what I'm worried about." He stepped over to Patricia's side. "Someone tried to kill this woman tonight, and there are no police stationed outside her room."

Morgan stepped up to the bed. "I think right now I'd be more worried if there were."

Call pulled up a chair and sat down. "You better go on back to the hotel now." He pulled the revolver out of his pocket and set it on his lap. "I'll sit with her tonight."

CHAPTER 33

Morgan was at the Sisters of Mercy the first thing the following morning. He seemed to blend in with the crowd in the lobby. Children were tugging at the hands of their parents, older people were waiting for the first sign that anyone was interested in their cases, and young parents were walking out, some with newborn babies in their arms. Morgan made his way to the elevators and stood in the back of the waiting crowd, watching the slow-moving needles as they clicked their way to the first floor.

Crowding his way into the second elevator that arrived, he listened as people spoke their floor number. He tried to make certain that number seven had been mentioned. The cage closed and slowly lurched its way upward. The sixth stop was the seventh floor. He pushed his way out, feeling sorry for those he'd left behind.

The corridor of the seventh floor was busy and brightly lit, yet it had an unmistakable hospital odor. It smelled like iodine-soaked cotton balls that had been sitting in the sun for a week. The smell filled his nostrils with sickness, not health.

A number of nurses ran from room to room. In reality each was walking, but the haste Morgan saw in their movement caused him to think of a determined, long-distance runner full of equal parts of fatigue and determination.

He came to the door marked 704 and pushed it open. Patricia was sitting up, awake. Call was still slumped in his chair, and Harry Dixon was standing over Patricia doing his best to look and sound civil. Morgan knew that was hard for the man. He was used to giving orders, not taking them, and this was not his domain. "I'm glad to see you've got your eyes open this morning," Morgan said. "We were worried about you last night."

Call lifted his head up. He gave Morgan a blurry gaze. "Get some good sleep, kid?"

"I got some sleep. Looks like you could use some."

"Both of you should go and rest," Patricia said. She lifted her arm. It was bandaged and in a sling. "I'll be all right. The doctor says I'll be out of here in a couple of days."

Dixon stepped around the bed. "Call tells me you had quite the scare last night."

"We all did. Mine wasn't nearly so bad as Pat's here though. How is this Gerry woman?"

"Pretty bad," Dixon replied. "She came through the surgery last night but hasn't regained consciousness. Doctors sound pretty guarded."

Patricia shook her head. "I shouldn't have opened that door. I knew better, but I did it anyway."

"Did she say anything to you while she was there?" Morgan asked.

"I already asked her that," Call said. "I told both of them our thoughts on the matter, and it's something we can't quite figure out. It doesn't make sense, somebody going to that much trouble to keep me in jail."

"You do seem to be a hard man to kill," Dixon said.

Call got to his feet. He gave Morgan a slight push as he headed for the door. "Let's go check on Gerry. Maybe the doctors know more."

Morgan and Call walked down the hall from Patricia's room to a room in the corner across from the busy nurses' station. A uniformed policeman was in a chair beside the door. His chair was leaning comfortably against the wall, and the man was reading a paper. He pushed the bill of his cap up, staring at them. A lit cigarette dangled from his lower lip. "You want something?"

"Nice to see a cop who can read," Call said. "We're friends. Reporters from the *Herald*."

The man brought his chair down on all fours. He picked up a clipboard on the table next to him. "Sorry, can't let you in. Just for doctors and nurses right now."

"And for other cops, I imagine."

The man once again leaned his chair back against the wall. "I imagine so."

Call turned around and walked down the hall with Morgan. "I don't like it, don't like it one bit. It's like the fox guarding the henhouse. That woman knows something, and whoever it was who tried to kill her seems to be the only one who knows what it is."

Just then, Morgan saw Call's face really fall. Heading down the hall in their direction was Sergeant Ryan. The plainclothes detective had a smile on his face. He was wearing a dark gray suit and looked like he had just stepped out of a storefront window. His red hankie peeked out from his pocket, and the gold fob chain on his pocket watch snaked across his vest. Ryan pushed his fedora back. "Morning, gentlemen. I didn't expect to find you two here."

"I'll just bet you didn't," Call said. "I guess you'll be pulling guard duty today."

"For a while, I guess, though I don't see much sense in it. That thing last night was obviously a case of mistaken identity. Nothing to get too upset about. No need for you to be here."

"Don't mind us. We'll just stick around to make sure Patricia doesn't have any more unexpected visitors."

"Suit yourselves." Ryan started his walk back down the hall. He had a devil-may-care attitude about him, an attitude that Morgan didn't much care for.

They spent almost an hour in Patricia's room before Bruce Elliott showed up; leaving him there, Morgan, Call, and Dixon made the trip back to the office.

Call and Morgan went to the corner used by the crime writers. The morning edition was on the desk, and Jake O'Leary had a broad smile on his face as he was reading his copy.

Call pointed to Morgan. "You better get on to your story."

"Why bother?" O'Leary said. He turned the page. "They might not let it go, anyway."

"What do you mean?" Morgan asked.

The man lowered the paper, a big smile on his face. "I don't see your story here."

"Let me see that." Morgan snatched the paper out of the man's hands. He riffled through it, looking for his story on the *Titanic*. The man was right. It hadn't been printed.

"What's wrong?" Call asked.

"My story of murder on the *Titanic* was spiked."

"You're kidding?"

"See for yourself."

He handed the paper over to Call, who began to slowly turn the pages. "The man's right." Call lowered the paper and stared at O'Leary. "One of the few times he's ever been right."

O'Leary laughed. "I'll be here long after you're in prison, Call. In fact, you may be my next crime story."

"Very funny." Call took hold of Morgan's coat sleeve. "We better go see the chief. I've got something to talk with him about anyway, and it's obvious you do too."

"I sure do."

Moments later they were knocking at Dixon's door and not waiting for a response. Call opened the door and walked right in, followed by Morgan. "Fairfield and I have a couple of matters we need to take up with you, chief."

"I was just with you two. Can't I have some peace and get some work done?"

"I think you've got some explaining to do to the kid here, chief."

"Explaining about what?"

"His story. You spiked it."

Dixon focused his attention on the work on his desk. He picked up his pen and began to write.

"You want to explain yourself?" Call asked.

Dixon put down his pen. "Are you talking for him now? That his story or yours?"

"It's mine," Morgan said, "and I want to know the answer to that question too."

Dixon went back to his work. "You write me a real story, and I'll print it."

"That was a real story. It really happened. I was there."

"Find me some corroborative witnesses, somebody who can back up what you're telling."

"Boxhall's in Washington. I do have Margaret here in New York, though."

Dixon looked up. "Oh, fine, I got a reporter's girlfriend says he's telling the truth. That's going to go over real great. You act like we have some kind of short story workshop going here. We just print the news, not some passel of speculation you may have about the Irish Republican Army. And right now, I certainly don't want to take some woman survivor from the *Titanic* and accuse her of killing a man that's currently appearing in a Broadway play."

"But it happened. I was there."

"So you say. Go to the police. Get me the proof. I'll print it when you've got it." He looked at Call. "Now what problem of yours do I have to massage?"

"I'm worried about Patricia."

"Worried about what?"

Putting his fists down, Call leaned over the desk. "They tried to kill that woman. For all they know, Gerry told her what she knows, and we still don't know what that is. Do you really trust the police to protect her? They're coconspirators. Morgan here was almost killed last night, and so was I."

Dixon pushed his chair back. "What do you want me to do?"

Call put his finger in the air, pointing at the ceiling. "I want you to go upstairs and get approval for some armed guards for those two women. Remind the big guy it's his niece we're talking about."

Dixon got to his feet. "All right, all right. I'll do it." He pointed at Morgan. "Now you, young man, go write me a story I can print, and the both of you better go solve this thing. And make me believe it."

CHAPTER 34

There was a newness to the day that not even Harry Dixon could have spoiled for Morgan. He'd been given another chance to live and from a total stranger. Morgan walked through the large glass doors of the Waldorf. The air outside smelled fresh, like the fallen rain. Inside the Waldorf, it smelled like the rich Persian rugs that adorned the marble and tile floor. There was an odor of money about the place, old money locked in deep vaults.

He had already gotten several leads on apartments near the *Herald*. He glanced around the lobby and spotted Margaret seated with Gloria. Margaret was wearing a stunning black dress, and she had on a swooping black hat that dropped to eye level. He raised himself to full height and walked toward the two women, who were sipping tea. The flowered teapot sat in front of them on a table that had been set with silver. "I hoped I would find you here."

Margaret and Gloria looked up at him and smiled. "We were just talking about you," Margaret said.

"Is that a good thing?" Morgan smiled. He'd never been more happy to see her. There was something about life on this day that seemed borrowed to him, that made everything and every comment spoken seem like a gift.

"That's a very good thing," Gloria said. She put her hand on Margaret's and patted it slightly. "When a woman can't talk about anything but the man in her life, it means only good things for the man."

"Do you mind if I sit down?"

"Please do," Gloria said.

Morgan sat in the floral print chair and looked at Margaret. Telling her what had happened to him the night before was the last thing he wanted to do. She was worried enough as it was. "I got my story in and even picked up a few leads on apartments from the paper."

"That's good," Margaret said.

He looked at Gloria. "Will you be joining us today?"

"Not on your life. I'm going to start some ferocious shopping today, rebuilding what was lost of my wardrobe." She smiled at Margaret. "I couldn't even interest Margaret in that. Of course, I didn't try very hard. When a man says that he actually needs a woman's help, then there is little left to be said."

"I do need her help. I've never noticed what living arrangements ought to be like; I just lived wherever I was put and never had much choice in the matter. If I wasn't living at school in the dormitories, then I was in my loft at Aunt Dottie and Uncle John's house." He shook his head. "I suppose if you've never had to make a decision, then when you finally have to it can be overwhelming. I'd just as soon throw the landlord the money in a paper bag without ever looking the place over."

"Men can be quite helpless about some things," Gloria said.

"You are welcome to come along."

"Don't worry about me. I have plenty to do. I'm sure I'll terrorize the stores."

"Now that is something I hate to miss," Morgan said.

"You see, Margaret, the man is perfect. Any man who would agree to shop is someone you wouldn't want to let get away."

Margaret slid her hand over to Morgan's. "Yes, he is perfect."

"Just pardoned," Morgan said, "not perfect. I would say that it's a perfectly beautiful day, though. It will be a nice day for a walk, so I hope you wore comfortable shoes."

Margaret looked down at her feet. "The most comfortable I could find. Of course, that isn't saying much. Sometimes I get the idea that women's shoes have been designed by bitter old men just to torture us."

She stared down at the golden carpet with its large red and yellow peacocks. "Isn't this carpet beautiful? There are times when I think we don't fully appreciate what we're standing on." She looked out over the lobby of the hotel. "So many of them, and so beautiful."

"Not perfect, though," Morgan said.

"Why not, pray tell?" Gloria asked.

"The men and women who tie these rugs can work for many years on just one. They create a work of art, but they make certain that it's never perfect. Something to do with their religion, I think."

"I've never heard of such a thing," Gloria said.

"It's true. They work at making it look perfect to anyone to see but themselves. They purposely tie some knots to create a flaw. Of course, no one knows where the flaw is but the rug's creator."

"How interesting," Margaret said. "Isn't he smart?"

"He certainly is. And how did you come to know this, Morgan? I've never heard this before."

"I studied in school near a shop that specialized in Persian rugs. Sometimes, when I was studying for an examination, I would need to clear my head and think of something else, anything else. I would go in there, look around, and just ask questions. One of the old traders told me the story. He even showed me some of the flaws he had found. If he hadn't pointed them out, I would have never known."

"Fascinating," Gloria said. She rested her head on her hands, drinking in the conversation.

"They think that no matter how hard we try we can never achieve perfection. This is true for Christians, as well. We live with our imperfections as part of God's design. It's almost a signature of His ownership. When the Persians make their rugs, they try to make certain that no human can ever boast about something that comes from his own hands and claim it to be anything but tarnished. We'd do well to learn from that. Some of us can't live without perfection."

"How about you, Morgan? Can you be merely human?" Gloria asked.

Morgan laughed. "Yes, I'm afraid I'll have to. Any time I feel otherwise I merely have to go to work where I'm treated like an imbecile. Cub reporters are the lowest form of animal life in a newspaper office. I even had a story of mine killed that was supposed to be in today's paper."

"Which one was that?" Margaret asked.

"The one I wrote about the murders on board the *Titanic*. The city editor thought it was too far-fetched."

"I would have found it hard to believe myself," Margaret said.

"Well, there you are. Harry Dixon did, too, and he doesn't love me, not by a long shot. So, you see, it's quite easy for me to be reminded that I'm a blemished creature. I did try very hard at being perfect at one time, but no more. No man that has been given his life back twice can ever truly feel that it belongs to him."

"Twice?" Margaret asked.

"I think we should get on with our house hunting," Morgan said. He'd let the thought slip about getting his life back twice, and he hoped Margaret wouldn't keep asking him about it. Lying to Margaret was something he knew he could never do.

They spent the next several hours moving through Morgan's list of row houses, apartments, and brownstones that covered the spectrum in terms of prices, comfort, and convenience to work. But it was the red brick cottage in Greenwich Village that caught Margaret's eye.

The outer walls were covered in ivy, and there was a shady inner courtyard. Stones bordered flower beds in bloom, and a vegetable garden was out back. The windows had green-painted frames. Inside, there was not only a living room but a small library so cozy that it made Margaret want to collapse into the overstuffed chair and read. The kitchen, painted a bright, sunny yellow, and bath were adequate. The bedroom had double closets, which were quite the latest in design. And the back bedroom could easily become a sewing room.

The landlady was a woman of about sixty who lived across the street with her son and his wife. She was of medium build with a gray bun neatly pinned in place behind her head. She followed the two of them everywhere throughout the house. The rent money from the cottage would help her find a place in Florida for the winter.

Margaret wrapped her arm through Morgan's. "I love it," she said. "We, I mean, you could be very happy here."

The older woman smiled. "You could even make the back bedroom into a nursery."

That made Margaret blush. Morgan smiled. "How much is it?"

"The rent is thirty dollars a month."

Morgan gulped. As far as he knew, he would only be making twenty to twenty-five dollars a month from the paper. He knew he could always use money from his trust fund. The interest alone would give him an enormous sum, but he wanted to live on his own earnings and not feel that his parents were caring for him, even though they both were dead. "That's a lot," he said.

The woman could see that Margaret felt depressed at Morgan's words. "Why don't I leave you two alone to talk it over?" With that, she stepped outside.

Margaret looked up at Morgan. "I know that's more than you intended to spend."

"Twice as much."

"And I know you want to stand on your own feet."

Morgan nodded.

"I'll leave the decision with you. We could be happy here for many years to come, and I'm sure you won't always be a cub reporter. With what you're doing now, they can't keep you from being a front-page reporter. But it's up to you. I'll respect your decision, no matter what it is."

"It's probably my pride doing the thinking. I'm wanting to be the perfect rug with no flaws, standing on my own two feet without my parents' money in the bank."

"But it's your money now, even though it came from them. They entrusted it to you, knowing you'd use it wisely."

Morgan bowed his head. "I've already spent ten thousand dollars on a matter of pride, I suppose."

Margaret looked shocked. "Ten thousand dollars?"

"Yes. I am the one who put up the money for Call's bail. The paper wouldn't go that high. They got the lawyer, and I paid the bail. It's something he can never know about, though. The man's pride would kill him."

"I see. You want to protect him from his pride, but who will protect you from yours?"

Morgan patted Margaret's hand. "No one but you, I suppose."

"All right. I just want you to think this over. Make no decisions today. Just think about it in your own heart and decide. Whatever decision you make will be fine with me."

CHAPTER 35

The day was much too nice for another taxi ride, so Morgan and Margaret walked instead. Vendors were selling everything from pretzels to hot dogs on the street, and children were walking with their parents. Most of them in the downtown section were well behaved, waiting for that promised ice-cream cone, no doubt.

Morgan stopped and looked up at the street sign. West Ninth, just two blocks from Washington Square. "There's someone who lives down this street that I'd like for you to meet."

"Who is it?"

Morgan smiled, his eyes twinkling. "The Witch of Wall Street."

"A witch? Be serious."

"I doubt that she's actually a witch, but I am serious. That's the name that people call her."

"I think that's awful."

"The woman's made quite the fortune in the stock market."

"And you are getting stock tips from her?"

Morgan laughed. "Now who isn't being serious? Can you really see me playing the stock trading exchange? I'm much more of a money-in-the-bank man. You know me. I'll play it safe every time."

She squeezed his hand. "Mr. Reliable. I like that. How do you know the woman's at home? Maybe she's at her bank or on the trading floor."

"She's home. The woman never goes anywhere. She hasn't even stepped out of her house for forty-five years."

"That's strange."

"I think you will have to meet Miss Irene Saunders to believe her. *Strange* is the operative word—strange and bitter."

They started their walk down West Ninth Street. "Why is she so bitter? It doesn't seem to me that bitter people live all that long."

"I've really told you too much already. I did some research on the woman after I met her, and I'd rather she not even know that. I'm not sure I want her to know that she aroused my curiosity that much. I don't want to taint your opinion of the woman, Margaret. I'd like you to see her through your eyes, not mine. I do trust your intuition, and, frankly, I'm looking forward to finding out just what you think of the old girl."

"Amazing how a man will acknowledge a woman's intuition but never her brains."

The remark caught Morgan completely off guard. "Why, Margaret, I know you're smart, very smart. I just think that sometimes you have a sixth sense about some things, especially about other woman. Women seem to be a complete mystery to me, and if I can't rely on you for insight, who can I turn to?"

She smiled. It was a knowing, thoughtful smile, though, and Morgan knew there was something behind it. "It does take brains to know people. I don't think I'd trust anyone's intuition to know what I'm all about."

Morgan shrugged. "I'm sorry. I think I was simply repeating what others have said without thinking the matter over."

"You're a reporter. You need to think something through before you say it or write about it. Do you think this woman has grown wealthy in the stock market from intuition?"

Morgan laughed. "Some think she consults a Ouija board or conjures up potions in some black pot she keeps in the backyard."

Margaret started walking. "Men, I'm sure, who want to find some explanation other than the woman's mind. And don't you work for a woman, this Patricia Bennett?"

"Not directly, but she does have a higher position on the paper, far above me."

"All because of her intuition, I suppose."

Morgan was getting frustrated, but he tried to hide it with a broad smile. "OK, you win. I've always heard that a man uses what little intuition he has to confirm his thinking and a woman uses her thinking to confirm her intuition."

"I think you misquoted that."

"I did?"

"Didn't you mean to say that a woman uses what *little* thinking she does to confirm her intuition?"

"Well, it's not my saying, I won't defend it. Margaret, I have such a deep respect for you in every way, including your mind. Let's just put it this way: I'd like to get your thinking on the Saunders woman without clouding your judgment by my own. Can I say that and climb out of the hot-water tank?"

"Yes, of course you can. I don't mean to pick on you. It's just that sometimes you speak without thinking. I may love you and forgive it, but others will not."

"My education goes on," he smiled.

They soon came to number 396. Morgan stopped, looking at the huge gray house. "Here we are. Impressive, isn't it?"

"And scary."

"Well, just what would you expect from the Witch of Wall Street?" They started up the stairs and stopped on the landing. Morgan pulled the chain next to the green door, activating the deep chimes that rang out "Bless Be the Tie That Binds." The music caused Margaret to shiver slightly. Morgan could feel it in her grip.

The door opened slowly, and once again Morgan was face-to-face with Mortimer, the butler. This time it was different, however. The man squinted a slight smile and nodded. "Please come in, Mr. Fairfield. Miss Saunders is expecting you."

"She is?"

"Why, of course, sir. Please follow me, and I'll announce you."

They tagged along after the man, Margaret looking at the swords fanned out along the wall, along with several paintings done by the Dutch masters. She leaned over and spoke to Morgan in a whisper. "Did you tell her you were coming?"

"Of course not."

"Then how did she know?"

"The woman seems to know everything."

The house was dark, something Morgan assumed was quite usual. The butler stopped at the familiar doors leading into the smoking room and pulled them apart. "If you would kindly wait here for a few moments, I'll tell Madam you have arrived."

They both walked into the room and watched as Mortimer smiled, drawing the doors closed. Margaret walked into the middle of the room, staring overhead at the impressive chandelier. "This is amazing."

"I need to show you something." He took her by the arm and led her to the far wall with its grouping of muskets. He left her there for a moment to take in the sight of the photographs flanking the display, all dead men in their coffins. The coffins were ornate, the photos obviously taken at rich men's funerals.

Margaret looked over the sight, taking great care to see each and every face in the photographs. "I think I've known a couple of these men," she said.

"I believe it. No doubt they've been guests in your home at some time. Your father does make his rounds with people of power and wealth."

"Why would she do such a thing?"

"That's what I'd like to find out from you." He took her by the arm. "You need to see the photos on the other side of the room, the ones you walked by."

Margaret turned and looked at the array of muskets forming the familiar sunburst pattern on the opposite wall. She walked over to them, more cautious this time. Standing in front of the groups of pictures, she trained her eyes on the sleeping children. All of them seemed to be resting in quiet repose. Some held small teddy bears or toys, others had flowers in their hands, all had their eyes closed. "These children are all dead," she said.

"Are you sure?"

"Of course I am. What children do you know who could possibly sleep with a bunch of cut flowers in their hands? Toys and stuffed animals, possibly, but flowers? No." She turned, glaring at Morgan. "What monster or beast would do such a thing and for what reason?"

Morgan shook his head. "I have my own ideas, but I couldn't say for sure. You've seen this house, dark and forbidding. The guns and swords have been used in the past to frighten visitors and impress them with the power of the owner. Maybe these photographs serve the same purpose. Perhaps the woman is subtly trying to communicate that she has the power of life or death over a man. Of course, maybe it's only one man she has in mind. Did you see the empty frame on the other side of the room, the one at the very top?"

Margaret turned around. She could see the empty frame atop the display of firearms. The frame was gilded, impressive, and empty.

"You see, it's almost as if she's waiting for another funeral. I'd be willing to bet the woman would, and could, pay big money for the photo of the man she has in mind for that one."

"No doubt." Margaret stepped away from the children and into the middle of the room once more. "I can say that she's succeeded in one thing. She's frightening me to death, and I haven't even met her."

The rollers on the bottom of the doors slid open, frightening Margaret even more and practically causing her to leap into Morgan's arms. Mortimer the butler stood in the doorway, his chin lifted. "Madam will see you now."

"Fine, lead on."

The man stepped out into the hall and, instead of once again going into the foyer and across the foot of the stairs, he turned and led them through the house. The walls were covered with paintings and photographs of men and women long since dead and gone. Morgan looked into the faces they passed. It seemed obvious to him that they were the highbrow members of the woman's long-lost family. Each face looked back at him, almost giving him a warning.

He stepped out into a lush, almost bright greenhouse. The place was misty and humid. It brought a drop of sweat to the back of Morgan's neck, mixing with his hair subtly and then winding its way on a path between his shoulders and into the small of his back.

The air was sour with the aroma of decomposition. Waist-high wooden tables were filled with flowering pots of orchids, begonias of every color, blue hydrangeas, and a mixture of scarlet, white, and pink impatiens. Between the tables was a winding walkway made up of wood chips, mulch, peat, and topsoil, with shovels, pitchforks, and hoes leaning against the boxlike tables. The plants were in full bloom, spilling their colors over the sides of ruby red terra-cotta pots.

They followed the man down the long row, stepping out into a lush garden complete with a babbling brook. The water rose, pouring over a rocky formation at one end and snaking its way through the glass enclosure into a pond filled with blooming water lilies. One lone white duck paddled its way through the murky water. It seemed lonely, just like the woman of the house.

At one end of the enclosure sat the Lady Saunders, complete with her wedding dress and tiara. Margaret reached out for Morgan's hand. The sight would have frightened anyone. The woman sat in a large padded wicker chair in front of a glass-topped white wicker table. A matching couch was in front of her, obviously the place where Morgan and Margaret would sit. On each side of her were two of the largest black rottweilers Morgan had ever seen.

She signaled them forward. "Please be seated, Mr. Fairfield, and you too Miss Hastings. Mortimer, would you bring us some tea?" The woman inched forward so that her toes touched the floor. "I am happy to see that you are well, Mr. Fairfield."

"Why shouldn't I be?"

She smiled, but Morgan wondered just what this woman knew and how powerful she really was. Her powdery skin cracked slightly with the smile, showing the wrinkles around her eyes that she evidently made every effort to conceal. Her lips were painted a ruby red. They seemed to shine against the backdrop of her baking-powder-colored face. "We do have a dangerous city. And I am pleased that you brought your lovely lady to see me." She looked intently at Margaret, fixing her eyes on her black dress. "You seem to be in mourning, my dear."

"My fiancé was killed on the *Titanic*."

The news seemed to stun the woman. She blinked her small beady blue eyes and then gently eased her shoulders backward. "I am sorry to hear that." She reached her hand down and gently stroked the head of one of the dogs. It made little difference to the beast. His black eyes remained trained on Morgan.

"So many people died," Margaret said, "so very many people."

"These things are all written in heaven. No one dies before his time."

"I can't agree," Margaret said. "Peter died long before his time. He was a man of great promise."

"But, my dear, what might that have meant to you and Mr. Fairfield here? Believe me, these things are for the best. You may not see it now, but you will. I assure you, you will. This was an act of God. But some people do suffer because of the actions of the cruel, and that is never right."

She shook her head. "That type of pain can go on throughout a person's lifetime, the constant reminders, the remembrances of what was and what will never be. But those are the actions of men, not acts of God."

"An interesting difference," Morgan said.

Those few words from Morgan brought the rottweiler closest to him to his feet. The beast seemed to be fixated on him, looking at his eyes. It was unnerving.

"Isn't God sovereign over the actions of men?" Margaret asked. "How can someone do something that God himself doesn't permit?"

"God is kind, not cruel." The woman's voice rose to a shrill pitch. Anyone could sense the emotion in her voice. "Man is the sinner here. There are times when men abuse the freedom and privilege they have in order to violate the innocent. When that happens, it becomes our duty to punish the perpetrator of such a thing, no matter what the cost."

"Sometimes the cost is much too dear," Margaret said. "If it costs someone his soul through bitterness and hatred, then I would say the price is far too steep. It's far better to forgive someone than to hate him."

Mortimer served the tea, and the old woman poured a stream of cream into hers, stirring it into a cloud of red and tan. Picking up a carved lemon, she wrung the contents into the cup. Holding it to her lips, she sipped slowly. "Bitterness can be a sweet cup to some people, my dear. Just the thought of justice some day is enough to sweeten the harshest lemon."

Morgan turned the conversation to flowers. He was ready to do almost anything to keep Margaret from arguing with the woman. It seemed to be risky for him to talk, though, because each time he opened his mouth to speak, one of the dogs would mutely growl and get to its feet. "I think we should be going," he said. "We've been shopping today for a place for me to live."

The woman smiled. "We have plenty of room here, Mr. Fairfield. Mortimer would be more than happy to rent you a room."

Morgan put his hand on Margaret's. "I think that wherever we choose, it will more than likely become our home."

"Oh, I see," she smiled. "In that case, choose wisely. Make certain that you make your lady happy first of all."

Mortimer showed them out through the front door. They walked to the street, and Margaret turned around to look at the house. "She's watching us."

"Who?" Morgan turned around to see. He could see the figure of the old woman staring out the window of a front room he hadn't been in. Then, just as suddenly, she vanished.

They began to walk down the street. "That woman was behind the window watching us," Margaret said. "She has a great deal of bitterness inside, so much so that I almost forgot about what she was wearing and what she looked like. It was that overpowering."

"Did you get the sense of control the woman carries with her, almost as if by lifting her finger she could turn the course of the stars."

"Money can do that to a person."

"And what did you think of her photograph collection?"

Margaret stopped and looked back at the house. "I think the pictures are of husbands she never had and babies she never bore. Every one of them is a brick in a wall of bitterness. The thing I wonder about is that last empty frame. Who do you think she intends to occupy that space?"

"I think I have a good idea," Morgan said.

PART III
CHILD OF THE SEA

CHAPTER 36

Ed Leslie stuck his head in the dressing room door. "Miss Webb is in my office to see you. You asked her to come by?"

"I most certainly did." Kennedy continued to dab on his pancake makeup. The dresser was littered with cotton balls, all smudged in various shades of tan, flesh, and gray. Bright lights hung over the mirror, creating a reflective glare that lit up the man's face like a flaming torch. His face seemed to glow with a soft flesh color. He gently stroked his chiseled chin with a smear of color on the end of a wide brush.

"Well, you better go see her. She is supplying the capital for the show, you know." Leslie pulled his watch out from his vest pocket and pried open the lid. "You have a half hour before curtain. I suggest that whatever business you have with Miss Webb you take care of now."

Kennedy got to his feet, smiling at the mirror and running his hand across the locks that curved down close to his forehead. "The business I have with Miss Webb should take only a few minutes." He picked up his jacket and slung it over his shoulders so that it fell around him like a cape, the arms dangling at his side.

Leslie followed him out into the hall and down the corridor that led to his office. He watched the man open the door. "I'll just wait for you."

Kennedy smiled. "Oh, don't worry. You act like my mother."

When Kennedy closed the door, Leslie slipped into the small room next to the office. He crossed the room and took a picture off the wall. Behind it was a glass that looked out from a mirror in his office. From there he'd be able to see everything and hear every word spoken. He watched as Kennedy crossed the room and took the woman's hand. She was seated in a large leather chair beside his desk. She smiled and nodded her head at the man.

"I'm glad you could meet with me," Kennedy said. He pulled up a weathered wooden chair. "Do you mind if I have a seat?"

"Of course not. Please do."

Kennedy smiled and took his seat. "Thank you. This won't take too long."

"If this is about your salary, I'm not prepared to offer you any increase at this time. The show simply hasn't been playing long enough to judge what our crowd size will eventually be. We are fortunate the *Titanic* hearings have moved to Washington, though. It might give us a bigger crowd."

"Yes, we are. I must say I'm a bit surprised you aren't there. Shouldn't you be a witness?"

Kitty Webb wore an attractive blue dress. The silk was wound tightly around her body, showing off its natural and very beautiful lines. Her hair was pushed up on her head, and a small hat was pulled down to a place on top of her ears. Her teeth seemed to sparkle as she smiled. She laid her hand gently on her chest. "Me? My, no. I should think not. There are plenty of others there to tell the story of what happened without my involvement."

Leslie could see the woman shift in her seat. She was feeling obvious discomfort, though he could tell that she was doing her best to disguise it. She was also looking away in quick stabbing glances from Kennedy to the carpet on the floor.

"Oh, you're being much too modest, Miss Webb. From what I understand there are many things that happened on the *Titanic* that only you can explain. I'm certain your testimony could create quite a stir."

"I know nothing beyond the average survivor."

"Of course you do. You know, for example, that I am not Hunter Kennedy."

That brought her gaze to full attention in Kennedy's direction. "Is that true? You're not Hunter Kennedy? Now why would I know that?"

"For a number of reasons." He smiled. "You see I knew Hunter quite well. I knew enough about him from his letters to know the highlights of his life: the plays he was in, the women he loved, at least some of them. I certainly knew about you."

"I see."

"Yes, I'm sure you do. He spoke of you many times. He also told me that you had, how shall we put it, left him in the lurch to pursue a climb toward wealth—wealth purchased at the expense of your honor."

"My romantic life is none of your business, Mr. Kennedy. When I stopped seeing Hunter, it ceased to be his business as well. Unfortunately, that was something the man could never quite accept. He was immature enough to believe that when a woman spoke to him of love it meant some kind of eternal bond that could never be shaken."

"And so you left Hunter for money, even though Benjamin Guggenheim was a married man."

"I left Hunter because I fell in love with someone else."

"A man old enough to be your father."

"Age had nothing to do with it."

"Only money, I suppose."

Kitty's fingers tightened around the arms of the chair. She dug her nails in deeply. "What I do and who I do it with is my own business. It wasn't Hunter's, and it certainly isn't yours." She jumped to her feet.

"What happened? Was he so jealous that he threatened to expose your relationship with him to Guggenheim?"

"He was jealous," she barked. "Insanely jealous."

"And therefore dangerous, too, I take it."

"I didn't say that."

"Dangerous enough for you to kill him?"

The question took her by surprise. She sat back down and scooted forward in her chair, staring straight into his eyes. "Who told you such nonsense? Was it that pesky reporter Morgan Fairfield? The man's a menace. He will say or do anything for a story, even if he has to make it up. I am sorry about Hunter's death, but I had nothing to do with it. He slipped and fell in the swimming pool and drowned, and that was it."

"How did you know that?"

"Everyone knew that."

"Not everyone." Kennedy's smile had a wicked nature to it, like a cat who has cornered a trembling mouse. And like a cat, he could afford to softly pad his way forward, relaxed on the outside but coiled like a spring on the inside.

"The captain knew it. Fairfield and Miss Hastings knew it. One of the ship's officers, Boxhall, knew it. The doctor knew it, and the murderer knew it. That would be you, Miss Webb, the murderer."

She breathed a deep sigh. Reaching out with her hand, she gently touched his. "If this man was your friend, you must be grieving. I am too. I lost people whom I loved dearly, including Hunter."

She ran her hand up his softly. Her eyes moistened ever so slightly, and she looked deeply into his. "I heard about Hunter from Benjamin. I really can't say where he came by the information."

"Fine. That seems to be just like you, trying to throw suspicion on a dead man, a man who can no longer defend himself."

She pulled her hand away, reaching into her purse. "I can see that you've got your mind made up here. You seem to be so full of hatred and bitterness that you simply can no longer accept the truth." Pulling out a silver and gold cigarette case, she opened it and withdrew a perfumed cigarette, tapping it on the outside of the case.

Kennedy's eyes widened. He grabbed her wrist, twisting it. "Here, let me see that." He grabbed the case out of her hand before he released his grip on the woman.

She began to massage her wrist as he looked over the case. There on the inside were etched the words, TO THE LOVE OF MY LIFE. It was signed, KITTY. "This belonged to Hunter. He wrote and told me about it. You gave it to him."

"What if I did?"

"And he threatened to expose you with it, didn't he?"

"Why would he do a thing like that? Hunter was a gentleman, unlike you. He gave it back to me."

"You mean you took it off his body."

"I mean no such thing." Her eyes hardened, and there was a calm hostility in her voice. "You evidently don't understand the power I have over you and this play you're in. You may be a broken-down, two-bit, out-of-work actor, trading on Hunter's celebrity status at the moment." She held up her hand and snapped her finger. "But just like that I could close this show and put everyone in it out of work, including you."

"I may be a two-bit actor, but I'm not a murderer."

A smiled curled over her lips. It was a sly, knowing smile that seemed to say, I have found your soft underbelly. "Oh, is that right? From what I hear from some of my friends, you have been using your status to raise money for the Irish cause. Doesn't that make you an accomplice to murder?"

"That matter is entirely different."

"I wonder if the authorities would think so? You know, I could be a great deal of help to you. I could even be persuaded to give you, shall we say, a thousand dollars? What you did with that would be your own business."

"Now a bribe? Blood money for Hunter?"

"No, we'll just call it a contribution to the cause. No one would have to know."

Kennedy got to his feet and stood behind his chair. "You are a cool one, Miss Webb. You deny it. You try to seduce me, threaten me, and then bribe me. It seems there are no boundaries you will not cross."

"Suit yourself, Mr. Kennedy, if that is your name. I've tried to be reasonable. Just remember what I've said, however. I am now a woman of means. I won't forget you."

Kennedy walked toward the door. He turned around. "And I won't forget you. I'm not exactly without connections on these shores, you know. Powerful men owe me favors. I'm certain that a little bit of justice I might request wouldn't go unheeded."

"What do you mean by that?"

"I have only to say the word. There are other ways to find justice than in the courts."

CHAPTER 37

The street was dark in front of Sisters of Mercy Hospital. Only the amber, cone-shaped cylinders of light from the streetlamps fell on the dark pavement and sidewalk. Cars sputtered by on the street, their headlights like Paleozoic lightning bugs from another time, with bright eyes and oversized black bodies coughing and spitting up the smell of gasoline.

Two men walked hurriedly along the sidewalk. Both of them wore hats pulled down close to their eyes, and the taller of the two had a long scar that meandered down his left cheek, coming to a halt just below his chin. Their clothing was white hospital attire, somewhat shabby but well hidden by the overcoats tied around them. The only thing that was missing were the white shoes; theirs were black.

They got to the corner of the building, and the man with the scar pointed to the fire escape. The ladder contraption zigzagged down the side of the dark building, a rust-colored snake that hugged the red brick and gray concrete.

The two made their way through the tall hedges to a place near a large collection of garbage cans, where rustling and small noises caused them to focus on the small glowing eyes of rats who were seeking their midnight snack amid the sumptuous leavings of the day's garbage.

The smaller of the two men kicked one of the cans, sending the rats scurrying along the side of the building and into the heating ducts.

The tall man with the scar looked up at the bottom rung of the ladder overhead. He jumped up and grabbed it, hauling it down with a series of loud rattles. Pushing his foot onto the bottom rung, he nodded at the other man.

The men climbed through the rusted steel maze. The fire escape had been painted a burnt orange, which only partially concealed the rust that had begun to form on the ladder itself. Each floor they passed had a landing with an opening that led to the floor below and the floor above. The green doors leading from the grated metal platforms had no markings, so they counted them as they climbed. At the seventh level, a small white towel stood out from the latch on the door, its blood-stained corner flagging the place where the men were to enter the building. The towel covered the latch used to lock the door, and the tall man with the scar yanked it open.

They stopped at the entrance to the corridor and pulled off their hats and coats, dropping them into a pile by the fire door. The tall man pointed to the main hallway, and they moved past numbered rooms, stopping occasionally to listen to the nighttime gurgles and coughs of the patients asleep in dark beds.

Rounding the corner, the tall man held the smaller man back and looked down the adjoining hallway. He spotted the uniformed cop at the end of the hall and the second policeman who wore a suit. It was the second policeman who looked back down the hall and spotted him. The policeman flashed a slight smile at him and nodded.

CHAPTER 38

Ryan had been waiting, nervous on the inside but talkative and flirty on the outside. He'd worn one of his best suits, his blue one. The cuffs weren't worn. Even the bottom cuffs on his pant legs, where the laundry seemed to wear the crease in their attempt to get it stiff to the touch, were still smooth. His shirt was a brilliant white, so bright with starch and bleach that it could still dress the store window at Macy's. His hair was neatly parted, and the lilac water he wore almost cut through the thick smell of the hospital floor.

When he spotted the man at the end of the corridor, he sprang into action like a hungry snake, moving slowly and determinedly, his eyes fixed on his prey. He turned his attention to the two nurses who sat behind the counter. One was a young woman with flaming red hair. The freckles on her face could have made her pass for a schoolgirl were it not for the starched white uniform she wore. The older of the two women had mousy brown and gray hair with a large, wedge-shaped nose. She would be the more difficult of the two women to handle.

He meandered over to the counter. "How long have you two ladies been working here?"

The young woman smiled. "I've only been here a year, but Maggie's been here forever."

"Not forever," Maggie barked. "Long enough to know what I'm doing."

"And I'll just bet you know more than many of the doctors," Ryan said. He knew enough not to try to appeal to the woman's femininity. A woman of this sort responded to pride, and there was no greater job satisfaction than to hear that you knew more than the people you'd been assigned to assist.

She smiled. "A lot of them I do."

"I bet you can even tell me when that Farier woman is going to wake up, if ever. The doctors say they don't know, but I'll bet you do."

"I watch the patients closely. The doctors just stop by on rounds."

Ryan looked up at the oversized clock on the wall. "Speaking of that, when are their next rounds?"

"Not until 8:00 tomorrow morning, and maybe not even then. Most get coffee and then talk and flirt with some of the nurses if the nuns aren't looking over their shoulders. Men—you know how they are."

Ryan shot a quick glance at the young nurse and smiled. "Oh, yes, I imagine you ladies have to put up with that quite a bit."

The older woman shot out her bottom lip. She twitched her head in the direction of the young nurse. "Vicky here does. She's fresh meat at the hospital."

"What a way to put it," Vicky blurted out. "I didn't come here to date doctors."

Maggie got up from her seat and walked over to the coffeepot. "Oh, is that right?" She poured herself a cup of steaming black coffee. "Don't tell me Dr. Patrick hasn't caught your eye."

Ryan watched as the young woman blushed. The skin beneath her freckles turned a rosy pink. "Who is this Dr. Patrick?" he asked.

Maggie turned around, sipping the steaming brew. "He's the talented surgeon on our floor, the one who gets the 'yes sir,' 'no sir,' 'that's a good point, doctor.' The girls here act like they're in the Holy of Holies when they walk the rounds with him. All that reverence is sickening. You'd think they'd never seen another human being in pants before."

Ryan smiled. "Well, I'm sure glad you ladies know your business." He wanted to make certain he didn't lump the lovely Vicky in with Maggie's roundup of the brainless nurses who were only out to try to land a doctor's attention. "They must put only the most dependable people on at night, nurses who don't need a lot of supervision. I know that's the way I'd handle it."

Maggie sipped her coffee and looked at him with steely eyes over the rim of her dirty white cup. He wasn't sure if she was buying all the compliments he was handing out. It was obvious the woman was worldly-wise. "We don't need a lot of attention." She glanced at Vicky. "At least some of us don't."

"And when do you make your next rounds?"

Maggie turned and looked back at the clock. "One of us ought to be doing them right now, at least the first half of the floor."

"Will you be doing the first half? I know we'd like to see just how it's done right." He was hoping against hope that the woman's ego wouldn't put off showing her skills to the only men around to watch. She might not be a likely candidate for flattery, but she was, after all, still human.

She put down her coffee cup and then stared at Vicky, who wasn't moving. "I suppose so. You can come along if you want to watch."

Ryan cleared his throat. "I think I'll send Alexander here along with you. It'll do him good to get the blood flowing to that head of his. I can watch you the next time."

"As you wish." She picked up her clipboard and began to load a tray of supplies.

Ryan walked over to where the uniformed cop was still sitting. The man was thumbing through a magazine. "Go with the nurse here on her rounds. See if there's some pointers you can pick up on how to take care of people."

"What?" The man brought the front two legs of his chair to the floor with a thud. He was a cop with ten years experience on the force. Normally he walked the beat, and this was a job that involved sitting. It was something he'd been looking forward to. "We're supposed to watch these here two rooms."

"I'll take care of that. You just go with her, as I said. You can never tell when that wife of yours is going to need some home care, and you just might pick up something."

Alexander got to his feet. The man was tall and lanky, just over six feet but no more than a hundred and seventy pounds. His blond hair made him appear almost boyish, but ten years on the streets of New York had made him a man. He held out the magazine he'd been reading. It was the *Police Gazette*. "I was hoping to get through this crime story."

"Don't tell me that. You were looking at the pictures of those women in tights." Ryan jerked the magazine out of the man's hand. He looked at several of the pictures and then rolled the magazine into a tube. "You can get back to that when you finish the rounds with nurse Maggie here."

"Aw, all right." He laid the magazine down in the chair and buttoned his jacket as Maggie rounded the counter.

"You ready?" Maggie asked.

"I guess so." Alexander gave Ryan a bone-chilling look. He wasn't very happy about leaving his post and was even less happy about laying down his magazine with the pictures of shapely women to follow a dumpy-looking nurse down the dark halls of the seventh floor. "Lead on, nurse. I'll follow, though I don't see the sense of it."

They both began to walk toward the corner of the hall. "You will," Ryan said. "Your wife gets herself sick, and you'll thank the good nurse here for showing you how to take care of her." Ryan had seen the two women make their rounds before, and he was counting on them to be creatures of habit. The first of the rounds went around the corner to the hallway behind the nurses' counter. That would put them out of sight of the two rooms the cops were supposed to be guarding. And if Ryan's expectations were correct, it would be over forty-five minutes before they returned. That would be more than enough time for the two men in the hall behind him to do their dirty work and get back out of the building.

Reaching into his pocket, he pulled out a pearl-handled pocketknife and glanced quickly at the young nurse. The woman had turned her attention to reading the charts on the desk. She wasn't a beautiful woman, but she was pretty. He opened the blade on the knife and stepped closer to the counter. He held out his left hand and slowly raked the blade over the back of his hand, sending a small flow of blood down between his fingers. Closing the knife, he dropped it back into his pocket.

He stepped over to the counter, smiling. It was a warm smile, full of charm. He bumped the counter with his bleeding hand, then looked down at it. "Darn, I seem to have cut myself on the metal edge of this counter of yours." Grabbing his hand, he held it out, watching the drops of blood fall on the white and gray checkered tiles.

She leaped to her feet. "Let me take a look at that."

Moving around the counter, she spotted the bleeding. "You did. Let me see that." Taking his hand, she gently pressed on the wound, slowing down the flow of blood. "I'd better put something on that."

"I'd appreciate it."

She took him by the hand and led him around the counter. "We have a treatment room back here, but I don't know if I should leave my post."

Ryan cast a glance down the hall. He could see the spot where the man was still peering around the corner. He raised his voice, hoping the man would hear. "It'll be all right. We can go back there for a bit. Nobody's around."

She looked up at him. "All right. You hold this and follow me."

He smiled and followed her around the counter and past the row of charts that hung on the wall. Shadowing her into the back room, he closed the door behind them. "I'm a lucky man to have a nurse to see to me."

She pushed the arm of his coat higher and unbuttoned his sleeve. Then she held his hand underneath the spigot on the sink. She soaped his hand, rubbing it gently and slowly washing the wound. "You're fortunate this is a clean cut."

"I am?"

"Yes, you are." Picking up a soft cloth, she blotted the hand dry. "Some scratches can be deep and nasty looking, but this looks like a smooth, clean cut. It ought to heal fast."

Ryan leaned close to her. "Now tell me about this Dr. Patrick."

"There's nothing to tell, except in Maggie's mind. I really don't date doctors."

"What about policemen? Do you have a rule against dating them?"

The woman gave a coy smile. She edged closer to him. It was what he'd hoped for. "No, I don't have a rule about that."

"Good." Ryan looked down to where she was applying a swab of iodine. "Man like me needs to know a woman who can take care of him."

She smiled up at him. "Yes, I suppose you do."

"You know I worked really hard at getting those two away from here."

"You did?"

The smirk on his face grew wider. "Of course, I did. You're a beautiful woman and, after all, I'm a man. I may be a police sergeant, but I don't have ice water flowing through my veins."

"Well, now, we can both see that. You bleed red just like the rest of us."

CHAPTER 39

The group that Call led through the door of Sisters of Mercy Hospital would have attracted attention during the busiest time of the day, but at night it brought everyone, including the nun at the front desk, to their feet. Jim Nance, the *Herald*'s attorney, stopped at the desk to explain. Call led the rest of the group to the elevators and pushed the white button. By the time the cage had descended to the first floor, Nance had rejoined the crowd. "She didn't understand," he said, "but there wasn't much she could do about it."

Call looked back at the burly men forming the bulk of the group and smiled. "I don't suppose she could."

Fredo stroked his black mustache, a twinkle in his eye. "There's nothing anybody can do about it now. You've seen to that."

They stepped into the elevator, and in a matter of moments the lift was rising through the belly of the building on its way to a confrontation with authority on floor seven. When it came to a bouncing stop, they stepped out into the hall. The group made its way down the long corridor to the nurses' station at the other end.

Call could see the light from the desk at the far end of the hall and the empty chair that sat beside the room Gerry Farier lay in. It brought a sense of panic to him, and he quickened his pace. He looked back at Nance. "I don't like this. I don't like this at all. The place looks deserted."

When they got to the end of the hall, Fredo pointed to the men in their group and then to the rooms across from the desk. "Stand by those two rooms, 704 and 708."

Call rounded the empty counter, hoping he wouldn't find the body of a nurse on the floor. He was relieved to find the floor bare and empty. Then he heard murmurs from the room behind the counter. He walked over to the door, twisted the knob, and opened it.

"What are you two doing here?" he asked. He could see Ryan with the nurse backed into a corner. "Why aren't you out there watching those two women?"

Ryan backed away from the woman, his face flush with anger. "What are you doing here? Visiting hours are over." He stepped over to Call and pushed him back out through the door. "You've got no right to be here. Get out, and get out now. This is police business."

"I can see pretty plainly just what your police business looks like, and I don't like it."

Ryan spotted Jim Nance, Fredo, and the other men. "Who are these people?"

Nance pulled a piece of paper out of his pocket and stepped over in Ryan's direction. He handed it to him. "These men are detectives hired by the *New York Herald.* They are licensed to carry firearms. This is a court order signed by Judge Hiram White, allowing these men to guard the two women listed. If you try to interfere in any way, you will have to be in Judge White's court tomorrow morning to show cause. Am I being understood?"

Ryan gulped. He read the court order carefully. "Yeah. I got it."

Fredo grinned and shrugged his shoulders. "I'm just here to make sure the court order gets obeyed, that's all."

Call felt better about bringing the Italian policeman with them. The local police on the scene could always have stalled a court order, but with one of their own on the scene to back it up, they didn't have much choice. He stepped over to room 704 and opened the door. The room was black, but he could see movement by the window. "Patricia?" There was silence in the room. "You awake Patricia?"

His eyes gradually grew accustomed to the darkness. He felt a cool breeze and watched the gauzy curtains ripple like a wave on the high seas. The window was open. He thought that odd.

Call moved toward the window, and suddenly from the corner of the room a shadow came to life. Running at Call, the man hit him full force, knocking him onto the floor. Call slid across it and got to his elbows as the man delivered a vicious kick to his ribs. The pain shot through him like a knife, air rushing from his lungs. He rolled over in agony as he watched another man separate the curtains and step out onto the ledge outside the window.

The man standing over him in the darkness delivered another swift kick. The violent sting seemed to blur Call's vision. He gave out a grunt followed by a cry of anguish. When he rolled over, he watched his attacker step through the curtains and join the first man in his escape onto the ledge. Seconds later, the lights came on and Call looked up to see Fredo and one of the detectives.

"What happened?" Fredo asked.

Call could hardly breathe. He pointed to the curtains blowing in the open window. "There," he croaked. "They went out there." Fredo rushed to the window as Call rolled over slowly and got to his knees.

"They're out on the ledge," Fredo said, "two of them."

Call worked at getting his feet under him, first one, then the other. Fredo stepped back over to him and helped him up.

They both looked over at the bed. It was empty.

The young nurse stepped into the room, wringing her hands. "Is everything OK?"

"Where's Patricia Bennett?" Call asked.

"We moved her to 706 this evening to give her a more private room."

"You moved her before the sergeant out there got here?" Fredo asked.

"Why, yes. Since the police were standing guard between 704 and 708, we felt that 706 would be safe too. We didn't have time to inform the sergeant before rounds. Why do you ask?"

Call nodded at one of the detectives. "You better go see to her. Make sure she's all right." He looked at Fredo. "I got to go after those men. They were here to kill Patricia, then probably Gerry."

"You can't go out there," Fredo said. "I'm surprised you can stand on your feet. Those men are walking along the ledge to get to the fire escape."

"Then we better go get them and fast."

They moved out to the hall, Fredo running to catch the elevator as Call did his best to keep up.

Call pointed to the stairs. "I don't think we have time to bring the lift up. We better take the stairs."

Fredo headed down the stairs, shouting over his shoulder. "No way, my man. You wait right here for that contraption. You'll only slow me down."

Call could hear the man running on the stairs and knew Fredo was right. He'd never have been able to keep up the pace.

When the elevator finally arrived, Call stepped onto it. At that hour it was a straight shot to the bottom floor, and Call was thankful for that small favor. He listened to the slow buzz of the motor and the clanking of the cage as it passed each floor. It bounced to a halt at the bottom, and Call jerked the cage door open and headed down the hall. He passed by the nun who was still standing guard at the counter. "Which way do I go to get to the fire escape outside?"

"You're already on the bottom floor." The woman seemed puzzled. "There is no fire."

"I know that. Just tell me, and tell me quick."

Pointing to the hall that ran from the front door to the side of the hospital, the woman spoke in a reluctant tone. "It's down that way and out the doors, but there is no fire."

Call made his way out the side entrance in time to hear footsteps on the sidewalk next to the street. It was the sound of men running. Holding his ribs as he loped through the tall shrubs, he did his best to catch up.

Down the street he could see Fredo chasing the two men. They burst into the light from the overhead streetlamps only to disappear into the darkness beyond. Fredo was outnumbered, and Call already knew the men he was chasing were dangerous.

He saw the two men cross the street with Fredo at their heels. Just on the other side, Fredo made a flying leap, tackling the man in the rear. The man up ahead ran a few more steps and then turned around. Call gave out a loud cry. "Police! Stop, police!"

Call's voice sounded like a fellow cop coming to the rescue, even though there was really very little he could have done. The man up ahead once again took to his heels and ran off into the darkness. When Call got to the two wrestling figures on the ground, Fredo had already turned the man over on his stomach. He had his knee in the man's spine, pulling back on both of his arms.

Call bent over the two figures, panting and in pain. "You all right?"

"Oh sure, I'm fine." Fredo looked back at Call and grinned. "Better shape than you are." He yanked back on the man's arms, causing the prone figure to cry out in pain. Reaching to his belt, he took out a pair of shiny handcuffs and clamped them shut around the man's wrists. He stood up and jerked the man back to his feet. "At least we got one thing out of this." He jerked the man to attention. "A suspect."

"Yeah," Call said. "Only problem is, what jail are we going to take him to? The cops in this city aren't exactly our friends." Call smiled. "Present company excepted."

"You got a point there." Fredo spun the man around to take a look at him. "Maybe I'll just have to find out what I can from him before I call the collar in." He smiled. "He'll come out the worse for wear, but we may get something."

The short and squatty man had a close-cropped black beard and a pug nose. His dark, panic-filled eyes darted from the street to the darkness beyond.

"Don't you go to looking for help anywhere," Fredo said. "You're mine now. That buddy of yours has gone and left you high and dry." He grinned. "He left you in my hands too; and if you think I'm calling the precinct to turn you over to them, you better think again. You and me are going to spend some time together first." Fredo occasionally talked down to a man when he wanted to make his point clear. He nodded in the direction of the tall shrubs beside the hospital. "Probably over there in the bushes. I think you're going to have some injuries during this chase of ours."

The man seemed to melt at the prospect. Fredo pushed him into the street, holding on to the chain that separated the man's wrists. "You better get back up to the seventh floor," he said to Call. "Check on that Patricia woman."

"Are you going to need some help seeing to this man's injuries?" Call asked. "Should I send one of the private detectives down?" They crossed the street.

"Oh, we'll be fine." He smiled. "At least I will. I'll come up in a while and let you know what I find out. Then we'll call the patrol wagon. By that time I won't much care what happens to our friend here. He may even need to see one of the doctors."

When Call got back to the seventh floor, Ryan and the uniformed cop were just leaving.

"You catch whoever that was?" Ryan asked.

"Read about it in the *Herald*," Call said.

Ryan and the cop stepped into the elevator. "Fine thing. By the way, that young cub reporter is down the hall looking for you. I told him you were out getting yourself killed. Maybe next time."

Call watched as the cage door closed on Ryan. "Maybe next time you'll come and try to do it yourself," Call said.

He turned and walked down the hall. Morgan was waiting at the nurses station. He looked concerned, but there was something else written on Morgan's face, the hint of a smile. "Is she all right?" Call asked.

"She's fine. She's asking about you, though. Before you leave here, you better go in and tell her you're OK."

Call nodded and started toward the door, but Morgan grabbed his arm. "Just a second. I found out something you might want to know."

"Like what?"

Morgan smiled. "Like why those people might want that Gerry woman dead."

Call stepped closer. "I'm all ears."

"Well, don't think it has anything to do with you or that trial of yours. Like you said yourself, they could always kill you if they wanted to bad enough."

"They've already tried that. Well, what did you find out?"

"I just thought that we didn't know enough about that old woman, where she's been and what she does these days. I went to Patricia's place and did a little digging through the old lady's things. I came up with this." He handed a piece of paper to Call. "It's a pay stub. It's not for much, but the important thing is where the woman's been working."

Call looked at the slip of paper. It was indeed a pay stub for $17.73, from the White Star Line. "Glory be," he said.

"I called them today," Morgan went on. "The woman works from 4:00 P.M. till midnight sweeping and mopping their office on the docks. That's why she was at that bar the night you came in. I figure she may have seen something or someone there the night Fetters was killed. Who knows what's in the mind of that woman?"

Call nodded, staring at the small piece of paper. "Who knows?"

CHAPTER 40

The *Mackay-Bennett* had put long hard hours into the recovery of bodies from the *Titanic*. It rolled with the heavy seas, sending anything that wasn't tied down banging into a bulkhead below deck. The pitch of the ship as it made its way through the darkness rose steeply and then slid down into the trough of the large waves. Fog had cloaked the vessel in a shroud all day, and when darkness came, visibility was impossible. The horn, sounding like the lonely cry of a mourner, sent out a warning to any ships that might be passing nearby. On the *Mackay-Bennett*, this seemed more than appropriate; it was, after all, a death ship.

Captain Lardner sat at the desk in his cabin, making notes in his log. The logbook was something no captain would be without, and it was certainly something he wouldn't lose or leave behind. Lardner wondered just what Smith had done with the log from the *Titanic*, what the captain had been thinking about. Such a thing would be invaluable now. It would provide the answers to many of the questions people were asking. So far as Lardner was concerned, keeping the logbook had been a part of Smith's duty, duty he had failed to perform.

To some it might seem to be understandable. A man in command of the greatest ship afloat, an unsinkable vessel, headed to the bottom with over 2,200 lives in peril could be forgiven for not securing a book. In Lardner's mind, however, that made Smith's lack of thinking even more inexcusable. If a man is in command of a situation he can't control, he owes it to himself to take charge of a simple thing he can.

Lardner glanced at the photograph of his wife and four children on his desk. They were each in their Sunday best and doing what they could do to maintain a stern and serious composure. They were the very model of a captain's family, all except for little Alice. She was young, though, and the smile plastered across her face could be forgiven. She had been enchanted by the photographer and the black tent he huddled under to take the picture. He smiled at the thought of the girl. Perhaps it was best. Just when he needed a smile she gave it to him.

For Lardner, a man's family came back to a question of duty. They were his, and while his first obligation at sea was to his ship and crew, on land it was always to his family. He hated to be away from them, especially on a mission like this. There was no glory or honor to the job, only picking up the human debris left over from men who had failed to perform what they had been trained to do. There was blame to be had for the *Titanic*'s floundering at sea. He was sure of it. It was something he hoped could be found out at the British Board of Trade's hearing. He had very little confidence in what the Americans might discover. To him the United States, with its collection of politicians, was nothing more than an ignorant mass led by a group of publicity seekers.

He looked over at his bunk. The small bed sat on a teak platform with storage shelves underneath. Thomas Andrews' leather-bound notebook lay on the tightly made bed. Andrews had made certain to give it to a crew member with a life jacket on. At least the man had the foresight to protect what he'd been working on. Lardner shook his head. He only wished Smith had done the same thing.

His eyes drifted over the room. By most standards, Lardner's cabin was meager, especially for a captain. It had one porthole with a small curtain suspended on a brass curtain rod. The teak walls had been polished.

He kept them that way. Even if the place was tiny, he kept it neat. The fact was, he kept it neat because it was so small. There was room for nothing other than the things he had to use. Even his bookshelf had only three volumes: the King James Bible, a collection of poetry by Dickens, and a copy of Tennyson's *Idylls of the King*.

He dipped his shiny silver fountain pen into the inkwell, pulling back on the small brass latch to extract the ink from the well. The jet black goo flowed into the reservoir in the handle of the hefty pen. Shaking the loose ink onto the piece of blotting paper under the log, he began once again to write.

> By April 23rd we had eighty bodies on board. We received an additional supply of canvas and burlap from the Allen liner *Sardinian*, which passed through the area. Today has been a day of heavy fog and high seas. Nevertheless, recovery operations began at 4:30 A.M. and continued straight for fourteen hours. Eighty-seven additional victims have been recovered, searched, and tagged.

He heard a knock on his door. "Come in."

The door opened, and first officer Hitchens stepped in. The man, like the rest of the crew, looked haggard and worn. Circles were beginning to form under his eyes. Lardner admired the man. Hitchens desperately wanted his own command, and Lardner was going to see that he got it. The man was deserving. He was keen in not only seeing the right thing to do but in executing orders to get a matter solved. The man's tie was hanging from his collar, two black strands of disheveled silk. "I have a wire for you, sir."

Lardner put down his pen and took the message. It read: "Received your request for relief and supplies. We have chartered the cable ship *Minia* owned by the Anglo-American Telegraph Company. A coffin shortage has delayed her sailing, but she will depart tomorrow fully stocked with ice, coffins, grate bars, and embalming supplies." It was signed by A. Kingsly, director of White Star operations in Halifax.

Lardner handed the message to Hitchens and watched as he read it. He could see the look of some relief on Hitchens face. Any help would be welcomed. Theirs was a thankless task, and that was always the kind you wanted to share with someone else, anyone else.

Hitchens passed the telegram back to Lardner. "Why grate bars?"

Lardner folded the message and put it into the binding of the log. He would copy it there later. "They're iron blocks of grating like the kind you would use on a heavy drain. We'll use them to weigh down the bodies we bury at sea."

Hitchens nodded. It made sense to him. The grates would make perfect weights, allowing the water to pass through them yet heavy enough to sink the bodies quickly. "I take it that the third-class passengers will be buried at sea."

Lardner nodded. "You take it right, along with members of the crew."

"Non-officers, of course."

"Of course." Lardner knew Hitchens' bent toward making things equitable. It was one of the things that made him a favorite of the crew, that and his efficiency. The man was enough of a Canadian to be unimpressed with people of rank and power, but still British enough to abide by the class distinctions that seemed to permeate the empire.

Hitchens stared at the Captain. "Do you still have that message our radio operator intercepted, the one from *Titanic* to *Pirrie?*"

Lardner stuck his hand in his pocket and pulled up the piece of paper.

He opened it. "I'm not sure anyone should read this—ever."

"Can I see it again?"

Lardner handed it over and Hitchens read.

> Disaster inevitable—stop. You can forget about the old girl now—stop. Good thing J. P. took up sick—stop. Make certain ships are in position—stop.

He looked up at Lardner. "Why would Henry Wilde, the *Titanic's* chief officer, send such a message?"

Lardner took the message from Hitchen's hand and stuck it back into his pocket. "We may never know. Wilde went down with *Titanic*."

Hitchens pointed over to the Andrews ledger that lay on the bunk. "Have you read that thing?"

"Not yet. I've been too busy."

"Aye, sir. I can understand that."

Larder motioned over to the bunk. "Why don't you have a seat. You look tired. You can look it over if you like."

Hitchens began to turn the pages on the ledger. Lardner watched the man as he ran his fingers over the drawings made by Andrews. Even though he was fatigued and had no doubt reached his last ounce of energy long ago, Hitchens could be counted on to make a thorough inspection. That was the way of the man, especially with something he had an interest in seeing. "I guess the *Titanic* and her sister ship the *Olympic* were a lot alike."

"Practically identical, from what I hear," Lardner responded.

"I take it then that that is why Andrews made these curious notes here. He has some question marks."

He handed the ledger over to Lardner. The question marks caught the captain's attention right away. He read the words next to the sketch. "Forward half of A deck, enclosed. Why was this redone?" He then skipped down to the bottom of the page and read. "Ask Pirrie about the change in the B deck windows. Other changes made to partitions. Looks like sister in disguise." The last notation was followed by a series of question marks.

"Did you read the bottom of the page?" Hitchens asked.

"Yes." The idea of the *Titanic* being her sister ship in disguise sent a sudden chill up his spine. He wasn't going to react to it, though, at least not in front of Hitchens.

"What did the man mean by that?"

"It sounds like Andrews found something that shouldn't have been there." To Lardner it sounded worse. It almost sounded like Andrews had been making an accusation and one that he was going to take up with Lord Willam James Pirrie, the chairman of Harland and Wolff. They had constructed both the *Titanic* and her sister ship *Olympic*, and Andrews, after all, worked for them.

"Like what?"

"Changes made to the *Titanic*, changes that he didn't approve."

"Curious."

"Very. The man was the ship's architect. If anyone could spot something that shouldn't be there, it would be him." Lardner turned the page. What he saw next surprised him. It was another question written in Andrews' hand. "Was this work done when the *Olympic* was brought in for the new propeller?"

Lardner laid the book on his lap. He remembered reading in the newspapers that the *Olympic* had thrown a propeller at 20 knots and had been taken back to Belfast for repairs. He also remembered that it had taken the shipyard much longer to install the new propeller than was originally planned. It had taken nearly a week instead of the usual one day. He handed the book back over to Hitchens. "Read that page."

Hitchens read it. His eyes widened when he read Andrews special question. "I don't understand this. Why would Andrews talk about the *Olympic* brought in for refitting? Isn't he writing about the *Titanic*?"

"That would seem to be the question," Lardner said, "at least in Andrews' mind."

"Shouldn't he know?"

"If anyone would, it would be Thomas Andrews."

Hitchens closed the book. "What are we going to do about this?"

"We are going to do our duty." Lardner could tell at once from the expression on Hitchens' face that the question of duty in this case was a muddy one.

"And what is our duty?"

"Our duty is to recover bodies and return them, along with anything else found at sea, to their rightful owners."

Hitchens stared down at the leather book. "And just who is the rightful owner of this book? The man is dead."

"I would say the proper owner is the White Star Line, and if you ever expect to command a vessel of your own, you had better say so too. When we return to Halifax, that book goes to the White Star office."

CHAPTER 41

It was early the next morning before Patricia opened her eyes, and Call was there beside her, sleeping in a chair. "Have you been here all night?" she asked.

He lifted his head groggily. The stubble on his face was noticeable, and his suit was more than a little rumpled. "Is it morning already?"

The first rays of the sun were starting to peek around the curtains, giving the room a pea-green haze, the color of the paint on the walls. "I suppose it is. And you've been right here?"

Call stretched. "What makes you think that? You know me. I get on the job early, long before you put your toes in those fuzzy slippers of yours."

"Oh, funny man. You're usually so hung over you don't see the light of day until it's directly overhead."

"Well, here lately the only alcohol I've been smelling is the stuff they're using on you. I can't say that I haven't been tempted by it, but I'm holding out hopes that you can buy me a round of the real stuff at Jasper's Place."

"Jasper's?"

"Oh, I forgot. That's usually reserved for real reporters. It's the bar around the corner from the *Herald.*" He grinned. "I think maybe they'll let you in, though, if I put in a good word for you."

"Fine." She grinned. "I'll let you keep working at the *Herald*, and you can get me into a bar."

Call got to his feet. "It's good to see you smiling, Patricia. We've been more than a little worried about you."

"How's the Farier woman?"

Call shook his head. "Darned if I know. The doctors haven't been around yet this morning, and I don't think this place knows anything until those people tell them they do." He straightened the sheets around her feet. "Sort of opposite the newspaper business. Where we come from, the people upstairs stay in the dark until we tell them the sun's up."

Patricia laughed. "As I said, in your case, that's the middle of the day."

Call really didn't mind Patricia's ribbing him. If the truth were told, he kind of enjoyed it, especially this morning. It showed the woman's mind, along with her sense of humor, was in full force. He stepped up next to her and put his hand on hers. "You know, I never could figure out why you and I never became an item."

"I guess I never had any designs on you," she replied. "Just that you get that behind of yours off a bar stool."

"And you really think it would have made any difference if you'd had designs? Don't I get a say in this?"

She laughed. "Not much of one. You're good at your job, Call, but you'd better leave the feelings part of life for someone else to decide."

"Someone like you, I suppose."

"It would be a step in the right direction."

Call shook his head. "I guess I've never had much reason for a relationship that ever saw the dawn."

"Friendships last forever, Call. Don't you think a man and a woman can be friends?"

"I think we are. Of course, we stay friends because we respect each other. If you had to put up with me outside the office, though, I think your tolerance would be sorely tested. There're only so many times a man can ask for forgiveness and even fewer times a woman can give it. I don't ask for it very well, even the first time, and I have a feeling you're not very good at giving it out."

"So that's it, I suppose. We both like each other, but we just can't put up with imperfection."

"I suppose that about says it all."

"Makes for lonely times."

Call shook his head. "I've never gotten the impression that you were a lonely woman, Patricia."

"It's not something I like to advertise." She smiled. "I work it out at the newspaper. A woman's got to work harder than most, got to take fewer days off, and got to seem less susceptible to pain than any man who's ever around her."

"I guess we both have our own ways of dealing with pain and loneliness."

She smiled. "Yes. I work it off, and you drink it off. Seems a shame, though, two people who can neither ask for forgiveness nor give it."

There was a gentle rap at the door, and Morgan pushed his head through. He smiled. "Am I interrupting anything?"

Patricia and Call both exchanged smiles. "No, I guess not," she said.

"Patricia and I were talking about forgiveness, Morgan. Is it any easier for you than it is for us?"

Morgan shook his head. "I suppose it's always easy if there's not much to forgive. Stepping on somebody's toes is so much easier than breaking their heart. But the little things are important too. They give you practice for the big things."

Call smiled and looked over at Patricia. "You see, practice makes perfect."

"I think forgiving yourself is the hardest thing to do. Me surviving the *Titanic* while better men didn't, that stays with me. I wake up in the middle of the night, just thinking about it."

"You did the best you could," Patricia said. "That's all anyone could ask."

"Maybe so, but it wasn't good enough. It couldn't save Peter or Hunter."

"Friends of yours?" Call asked.

"Yes. And I suppose it always comes back to haunt me. If I'd done something different, been different, then things would have turned out different. That old woman I've seen here in town, the Witch of Wall Street, she's a bitter woman. I think she blames a certain man for what's happened in her life, but really she's blaming herself. If she'd been a better person, or been more attractive or charming, then she wouldn't be so alone with herself, her dogs, and her servants. Something like that never leaves you because no matter where you go or what you do, the source of your bitterness is always there in the mirror. It's something you can't shake."

Once again the door opened. The morning nurse marched through, a nun with black hair and a narrow, beaklike nose. She shook a thermometer and stuck it into Patricia's mouth.

"How's she doing?" Call asked.

"Pretty well, considering." She looked at Morgan. "That woman next door you asked about, she's regained consciousness."

Call looked over at Morgan. "I guess we should ask her some questions before the cops get to her."

"Might be a wise thing to do."

Call nudged his arm. "Pretty smart of you to go through her things and find that pay stub."

"The woman's a pack rat. Maybe collecting paper is something she's used to in her job. She has scraps that go way back, odd things, even pictures."

"Do you have the rest of her leavings?"

Morgan patted his coat pocket. "I've got a pocketful of things from that woman."

"Let me see. Why don't you lay them out on Patricia's bed here?" Call looked at the woman. She seemed so helpless with the thermometer protruding from her bottom lip. "You don't mind do you, Pat?"

He could see the use of the name *Pat* irritated her. The name *Patricia* was the last vestige of being a woman that she appeared to cling to, something that distinguished her from all the men she worked with. It was a badge she clung to, kicking and screaming to be a woman in the man's world of the newspaper business. He'd used it deliberately, taking great delight in the fact that she couldn't respond with the glass tube hanging out of her mouth and the nun standing guard over her.

When the nun reached for the thermometer, Patricia practically spit it out. "You people don't listen much, do you?"

"What do you mean?"

"It's Patricia, not Pat."

Call watched as the nun wrote things down on Patricia's chart. The woman was trying very hard to appear disinterested, but her slight smile was betraying her.

"I read a study a couple of weeks ago," Patricia went on. "It said that on the average men use twenty thousand words a day and women forty thousand. I figure it's because we have to repeat everything at least twice. You men could be sitting someplace and if there was a fire and I yelled fire, you'd still be sitting there. I'd have to yell fire again and then shake you."

Call patted her foot under the covers. "You see, forgiveness is a hard thing."

"Especially when someone never changes."

Call patted her foot once again, a big grin settling over his face. "Oh, I'll change if you will."

Patricia grunted. "Fine thing when there's only one of us who needs to."

Morgan had laid the various scraps of paper out on the bed, and Call stepped around it to inspect the things Morgan had found in the woman's things. Call pushed several pieces of paper aside—a couple of addresses, the top of a box with a woman's name scribbled in pencil on the back of it, and a wrinkled photograph of several small children. Then he found something familiar. It was the piece of paper Bain had written on at the Brass Rail. Call picked it up and unfolded it. "Amazing." He handed the note to Morgan. "Now here's a collection of the three most unlikely names you're going to see in a long while."

Morgan read the names.

"Recognize any of those?"

Morgan handed it back. "Of course. One of them is my great uncle."

"Your great uncle?" He handed the piece of paper over to Patricia. "Which one?"

Morgan's face fell. "Well, I've never heard of Jimmy Kirk or Oscar Solomon."

"J. P. Morgan? You're related to J. P. Morgan? What's a blue blood like you doing working in a newspaper office?"

"I don't like to throw that around, and just for that reason."

Call took the paper from Patricia. "Well, I can see that we're going to have to pay the great man a little visit." He shook the paper. "You see, that woman in the next room took this off me after that cop knocked me unconscious and went to look for a patrol wagon. More than likely, she took my money too. Either the cop or somebody else took my gun and killed Bain with it."

"Who wrote the names?"

"Bain did. I asked him who was responsible for Fetters' murder. Buffaloed him, I did. The man thought I already knew the answers."

"And you expect me to believe the word of a dead killer?"

Call stuck the paper in his pocket. "I'm not sure if I believe it myself. All I know is that these names are all we have to go on. That sort of settles it in my book. A man's got to dig where he finds ground."

"Just be careful with that," Patricia added.

"Oh, we will. I don't think this necessarily explains why they tried to kill that woman, though. We better go and ask her about that."

The two men walked over to the next room, passing between the two armed guards standing at the door. Gerry was awake, and the nun was allowing her to sip her first orange juice through a glass straw. When Gerry saw Call, she grinned, showing her blackened teeth. "You hangin' 'round to say good-bye to old Gerry?"

"You're too mean to die," Call said.

The nun wiped Gerry's mouth and left the room.

"Fine thing when a body can't even wipe her own mouth." Her eyes twinkled when she looked at Call. "You think you could find me a plug of tobacco?"

"Oh, sure. You can't wipe your mouth, and you want to fill it with tobacco juice. These people would never let me in if I brought you that. I do have something else to show you, though." He took the paper out of his pocket and showed it to the woman. "You took this off me that night?"

Gerry shot out her lower lip. "I suppose I did. Figured them people was going to clean you out anyways, and you said you wuz workin' on a story. That other woman you wuz talking to went through your pockets too. She was turnin' 'em inside out when I got there."

Call waved the paper. "I don't care about the money, but I do care about this. I got to ask you something else too. Whoever tried to kill you didn't do it because they thought you had this on you. You were working for the White Star people. Is there something you heard or somebody you saw that you shouldn't have?"

"I might have." She had a coy, rather sheepish look on her face.

"You want to tell me what that was?"

Her eyes sparkled. "I might for a plug of tobacco."

"All right, you win. We save your life and it isn't enough, is it?"

"What's a woman's life if she can't have a smidgen of pleasure out of it?"

"All right. All right. I'll get you your tobacco—and a brass band to deliver it, if you like. I just need to know what you saw or heard."

"I can't say for sure, but the night all those people came in, the night that man was murdered, I heard somebody on the telephone. That was a bit odd, 'cause it being so late, folks don't use the phone."

"Do you know who it was?"

"A man in a suit. Had a mustache that curled up. He worked for White Star and he come in on that boat."

"The *Carpathia*?" Morgan asked.

"I guess that was it."

"Was his name Ismay?" Morgan asked.

"Yep, that was it, cause he said 'Ismay here.' He was talking to another fella, and I was mopping up the office. He didn't see me. The quickest way to have folks see right through you is to pick up a mop. He said a bunch of stuff, but the thing I remember most was him saying, 'We didn't want all them people to die.' He kept talking about the ship going down."

"The *Titanic*?" Morgan asked.

"Nah, I'd a remembered that. It was some other ship's name."

"Was it the *Olympic*?" Call asked.

"Yeah," she became animated. "That was it, the *Olympic*. I remembered it 'cause it made me think back on my school days and some of them stories the teacher had us read."

"Can you recall who he was talking to, any name you might have heard?" Call asked.

"T'weren't really a name. More like letters."

"Was it J. P.?" Morgan asked.

"Yep, that was it. He called the man J. P. Course, then the feller saw me there and got real befuddled like. He asked me what my name was and why I was there."

"You told him?" Call asked.

"I sure did."

CHAPTER 42

Ed Leslie bounced out of the taxi, ran around to the other side, and opened the door for Margaret. He'd gone to the Waldorf to try to find Morgan and instead had run into Margaret and Gloria coming back from the memorial service given for Peter by his American relatives. He stuck out his hand, helping her out of the vehicle. "You sure Morgan is here?"

Margaret stood outside the taxicab and looked up at the large gray building that housed the *New York Herald*. "This is where he said he'd be. He was so busy today that he was going to work on his first-person *Titanic* article late tonight. I really wanted to see him after Peter's service today, but I am glad you came along when you did. I don't think I feel very safe on the streets this late at night."

Leslie paid the driver and stepped back to where Margaret was still looking at the lights in the windows of the newspaper office. "I bet it's closed," he said.

"I'm certain it is, but Morgan told me where he gets in after hours. We have to go around to the back."

Margaret had changed from her black dress to something more suitable for traveling when she boarded the train with Gloria to come back to New York City. She was wearing a muted green skirt with a row of bone-colored buttons down the front and a cream-colored blouse with ruffles that cascaded from the neckline to the top of her full skirt. The jacket was a matching green, and the small pillbox hat a salmon color.

The service had gone well. Unfortunately, there had been no reports of Peter's body being found, so the group had a framed photograph of the man instead. Her mind was full of the thoughts she had pushed away while with Peter's relatives, thoughts about Morgan. She was worried about him and couldn't escape the feeling that no matter what he had told her, he was in danger. The idea curled around her brain like a python, slowly squeezing out any other thought.

Leslie and Margaret moved around the corner and into the alleyway behind the *Herald*. A long, flat dock had stairs leading up to two large doors used for loading supplies and equipment and to a smaller door. They could hear the hum of the presses inside, a noise that Morgan said never stopped. Margaret pointed to the small door. "There. That's the door that Morgan said they keep open at night. It's used by the men on the graveyard shift. In spite of the way the place seems, a newspaper never sleeps."

Ed Leslie headed up the steps with Margaret behind him. The alley was deserted and dark in both directions. "I'm glad you let me come along with you," he said. The man had his hand on the door, but with the noise coming from inside they both knew that hearing each other would present a problem.

"I am too. I really don't think I'd have felt safe alone here, but I need to see Morgan. I just couldn't go to sleep tonight and not know where he is."

"It must be difficult for you to lose someone and then have someone else that you care about in real danger."

"Do you really think that's true?"

"What?"

"That Morgan's in danger."

"Miss Hastings, I don't want to alarm you needlessly, but from what I've seen so far, I think we're up against something quite sinister and ruthless. The operatives of the Irish political movement in this city are quite formidable. They have a small army, even in the streets of New York, and a vast array of informatives."

"But why Morgan? What could he know that they want to prevent?"

"From what you've already told me about their work on the *Titanic*, and given the fact that it's such an explosive story right now, I'd say they would go to great lengths to prevent its publication. They raise a great deal of money here in America, and the publicity would hurt their cause. I also think there's someone behind them, someone who wants to stop any deep investigation into the *Titanic* disaster. Your friend Morgan Fairfield represents a gun to the head of that person or that corporate interest."

Leslie's words sent a chill up Margaret's back. Everything she'd seen told her the man was right.

Leslie twisted the knob and opened the door to the pressroom. Noise erupted and belched out the door to the alley. Leslie and Margaret walked past row after row of large rolls of paper. The air seemed to be stuffy, a misty gushing of paper particles mixed in with the strong smell of oily ink. To their right, several layers of spinning paper drums whirred with earsplitting rumbles. The sheets of paper disappeared above, only to return below, printed. It was all they could do to stand there, but there was a fascination with the process of mixing massive solid objects with gyrating noise and seeing the printed page as its product.

Leslie leaned back and bellowed into Margaret's ear. "Awesome, isn't it?"

"Yes," she screamed. "It's amazing." There was something about the power of the press that had always seemed metaphoric to Margaret. She had been told about its power to sway people, to move a generation to action, to war, to charity. But this was the first time she had seen the pressroom of a large metropolitan newspaper. Here the term took on a different form altogether. This was raw power, a visual demonstration of what had always seemed poetic.

Leslie was wearing a khaki-colored suit with brown leather buttons. They were a perfect match for his dark brown hair and mustache. He stepped in front of one of the enormous wheels of spinning paper. Margaret thought the image of him standing there was somewhat striking, as if the man's body blended perfectly into the speeding drums. He stepped around the drum and instantly jumped back, signaling Margaret to keep out of sight.

She crept toward him as he bent low and once again stuck his head around the drum of paper. "What is it?" she shrieked.

Leslie stood up straight. "Hunter Kennedy's back there." He said it in his loudest voice. "He's back there with three other men, and one of them's a cop."

"A policeman?" Margaret yelled.

"That's right, fancy blues and all." He swallowed hard, trying his best to clear his throat for more yelling. "You better go up those stairs and find Morgan. I'll try to get closer and see if I can hear anything."

"Not on your life," she hollered. "I'm staying with you. Besides, if there's a policeman, how dangerous can it be?"

Leslie put his hands to his mouth to try to amplify the sound. "Very dangerous. He could be the worst of the lot. I think you should go upstairs and leave this to me."

Margaret shook her head furiously. No matter how dangerous Ed Leslie thought the men were, she had no intention of leaving him alone. She also didn't look forward to wandering through the building at night, especially since she wasn't sure if Morgan was in fact there. Too many things could go wrong, and if something did, she wanted to be there and not somewhere else, waiting and wondering.

"All right," he bawled out. "Just keep behind me and out of sight. If anything goes wrong, you make a run for the door and I'll hold them off."

She meekly nodded.

The two of them rounded the massive roll of spinning paper and headed past the row of machinery as it cut and separated the paper. The stamping of the large blades, rising and falling in precise thuds, shook the floor and sounded like the marching of giants through an empty bowling alley.

Margaret could see the four men in a corner of the room as she and Leslie passed by spaces in the machinery. The men appeared to be animated, bellowing at one another at the tops of their lungs. At first she thought this to be a strange place for a meeting, but then she realized how perfect it was. No one of any importance could be expected to walk by this place at this hour; and even if anyone did, who could possibly overhear them?

Margaret grabbed Leslie's coattail. She mouthed the words, "I know that man." She referred to a man with a shock of red hair and wearing a brown tweed jacket. The man had his hands in his pockets, revealing bright red suspenders.

Leslie stooped down, out of sight. He formed his words right back at her. "Who is he?"

She shrugged, shook her head, and formed the words, "I don't remember."

Rounding the end of the large machine, they crouched and watched for a few moments. The larger of the men turned around, and instantly Leslie recognized him. Margaret knew it by the expression on Leslie's face.

Suddenly, bells began to ring overhead. They drowned out the noise of the machines, something neither of them thought possible. And then as if by magic, all the machinery stopped. The clanking and stamping sputtered to a halt, and the drums froze in place. The only sounds left were the echoes of the din that had filled the large room only a moment before and the men's voices in the corner.

"So, the Francis?" Kennedy yelled, "At 11:00?"

"That's right," the largest of the men yelled back. "11:00."

The silence soon became oppressive. It stopped the men in midconversation, and in unison they looked around the room for signs that the noise would start again.

Margaret took one step back, her heel hitting an empty ink can with a sharp blow. The can rattled an echo across the room.

The policeman drew his revolver and turned around. He had medals on his oversize chest, and his face grew red as a beet. "Who's there? Is somebody there?"

Leslie grabbed Margaret by the arm and pulled her toward him. They stooped to hide behind a large piece of equipment. Leslie dragged her toward him and started to move back to the door. They could hear the sound of the group as the men fanned out, all of them moving in their direction.

"I said, who is there?" the man roared out a second time.

Margaret and Leslie started to move quicker, keeping the machinery and the bales of paper between them and the men. Leslie found a space between the rows of paper and darted into it, pulling Margaret along with him. Now they had open space between them and the door, and as one they began to make a run for it. When they yanked the door open, the policeman rounded the corner and had them in view.

The man waved his gun at them. "Stop, police!"

Leslie pulled Margaret out the door, and they scampered over the loading dock and hit the steps running. When they made it to the street, Leslie looked for the brightest lights and they sprinted toward them. They rounded the corner and ducked into the first door they found with lights on. It was a coffee shop.

Collapsing into the first two empty seats, Margaret panted slightly. They picked up menus and did their best to shield their faces from anyone who might look into the window. It was a wise decision, because only a moment passed before two men looked through the window for signs of movement. Finding none, they moved on down the street.

Margaret lowered her menu. "That was close."

"Yes, it was. Very close."

"What did they mean by the Francis at 11:00?"

"I'm not sure. There is an old hotel called the Saint Francis. That might be it."

"Or a restaurant," Margaret added.

Leslie's face brightened. "Yes, that could be. I'll have to check the directory."

"Did you recognize those men?" she asked.

"Three of them: Kennedy; a man named O'Brien, who controls the Irish mob along the East Coast; and a captain with the New York City Police, a man named Connor. None of them belong in a place like that. You said you thought you knew the fourth man?"

"Yes. I've seen him before. I just can't place where or with whom."

"Perhaps you've seen him with Morgan."

"Yes. I'm sure of it. I just can't recall where."

CHAPTER 43

The note Morgan still had clutched in his hand was more than enough excuse to see the man he knew he had to see. It read, "Please drop by to see me this morning. We need to talk." It was signed J. P. Morgan.

Call insisted on coming along. He'd never seen J. P. Morgan, at least not close up. Morgan could tell that Call's insistence was also based on the suspicion that Morgan just might let the powerful robber baron intimidate him. While it bothered him that Call felt so little trust in Morgan's backbone, he knew the man might be right. Even as a small boy, just the sight of the old man made him feel like he was still in short pants.

Call gave Morgan's arm a slight pat. "I'm glad you let me come along. I know the man's a relative and the two of you might talk about family matters, but I'll be there just in case you need me."

Morgan nodded and kept his gaze fixed on the street through the cab driver's window. He'd been to his great uncle's house a few times as a boy, and the street was beginning to look familiar. It was in the Murray Hill district, a very quiet neighborhood with elm trees lining the pavement. The only other times he'd been to J. P. Morgan's house was when he had been accompanied by his nurse, Lilly. He'd been too young to pay that much attention, but Lilly had told him a few things in her letters. J. P. had been trying to keep track of him after his parent's death, taking stock of the family's investments. It had always made Morgan feel that he was a prize colt in the stable. He was expected to be a boy, but only so far.

The cab pulled up outside the large brownstone house at 219 Madison Avenue, and Morgan and Call got out. Call paid the driver, who sped away, leaving them feeling like a pair of sheep waiting to be sheared. And a slaughter of the lambs was just as likely.

They climbed the stairs, and Morgan rang the bell. The white button was set in polished brass, which appeared to be an emblem. The large, red double doors were flanked by flowering plants. The bell was soon answered by a very tall, sturdily built butler. The man's face was milky white, and his light blond eyebrows offered little in the way of color. "Good morning, gentlemen," the man said in a very crisp English accent. "May I help you?"

Morgan glanced at Call. "Morgan Fairfield, and a friend."

"Certainly, sir. Please follow me."

The interior of the house was a rare combination of elegance and taste. It lacked the clutter one might expect from a man who had the money to satisfy whatever his desires. The floor was marble, and an extensive white stairway wound its way to the upper stories. Morgan and Call passed some expensive paintings from the great Dutch masters and a few medieval Italian paintings depicting biblical scenes. Ceramic vases and alabaster busts stood on ornate marble pillars, stoic and solitary in their posture. The butler stood beside a heavily paneled door and swung it open to reveal a dimly lit room. Morgan and Call stepped inside.

The ceiling was high, and the walls of the room were paneled with a semiblack mahogany. Morgan remembered that the old man's study was known in New York society as the "Black Library." He had always thought it was because of the evil deeds hatched in the place, but now he could see that it was for more than that. The place was indeed black, and if it were not for the small silver lamps glowing in the corners of the room and the large brass lamp on the old man's massive desk, it would have been like standing in the middle of the darkest night.

The fire in the fireplace burned a bright but low flame. Ornate and luxurious carpets covered the floors, and tall bookcases lined the walls, each filled with leather-bound rare editions. The old and rare books were the best that money could buy and represented a great deal of time spent by the man crawling through the libraries and abbeys of Europe. Morgan knew full well that some of the most important meetings ever held in New York, and indeed in the United States itself, had been conducted in this very room.

Two men stood in front of the fireplace. One of them, Captain Connor of the New York Police Department, Morgan already knew. The man's badge and shiny brass buttons gleamed in the flickering fire. His lantern jaw looked rock steady, even though Morgan could see he had suffered a cut that morning from trying to shave too close and had tried to stop the flow of blood with a tiny glob of paper. The other man was tall and wore an expensive, well-cut suit. His gray mustache was neatly trimmed, and his hair, streaked black and gray, was neatly parted down the side and had a slick sheen. Seated on a dark red leather couch beside the fireplace was a man in a purple cassock, and alongside him was another man in a black suit. Both wore clerical collars.

J. P. Morgan sat at his desk, scribbling out some notes. Morgan thought the collection of men in the distance, watching the great man think his way through a pile of papers, made for quite a scene. John Pierpont Morgan, a large man, would have been a formidable individual from any perspective. His pressed black suit and sparkling white shirt made quite an impression. His face, except for his nose, was still rather handsome for an older man. J. P. Morgan's nose was large and bulbous, cracked and deformed by serious long-term boyhood acne. He looked up, his small beady eyes sparkling from the puffy confines of his white-bread face. Signaling with his meaty paw for Morgan to step forward, his lips broke into a slight smile. "Step forward, boy. I want to get a better look at you."

Morgan took several cautious paces forward.

"You have grown, my boy. England and Oxford must have agreed with you."

Morgan couldn't shake the image of himself as a little boy, his bony knees shaking before the great man. "Yes, I think so. I enjoyed school."

"And it shows." J. P. picked up a copy of the *Herald* with Morgan's latest story about the *Titanic* in it. "You write a good story." He swatted the paper with his hand. "You had me right with you."

"I'm just glad you weren't with me."

"Yes, I know. I was almost on that ship. If I hadn't eaten some bad clams in France, I very well might have been." He cast his eyes on Call, who was still standing where Morgan had left him. "And who did you bring with you?"

Morgan stepped aside to give him a better look. "This is Call. He writes for the *Herald*."

"Ah, yes, I've read some of your material too. Quite racy, I'd say. You people at that paper tend to spin quite a yarn."

"We try to get the story right," Call said.

"And sometimes you succeed. Of course, there are other times when you only come close, close enough to meet your standards, I'm sure, but not close enough to avoid destroying the innocent." He looked at Morgan straight on. "That is why we've called you here to meet with us. You seem to be involved in a story that might be the cause of great irreparable harm."

"You mean the *Titanic*?"

J. P. picked up the paper once again and held it up. "No, not what you're writing here. But from what I understand, you're trying to tie the murder of a man into some kind of effort to conceal information about the *Titanic*. Let me assure you, there is nothing to hide. Those scoundrels we sent to Washington are making certain that every rivet on that ship is thoroughly investigated."

Call glanced over to where Connor was standing. He could see the man's face brighten. "Where did you hear about our story?" Call asked.

"I have my sources." He motioned with his hand to the men by the fireplace. "Your paper has even gone so far as to replace a woman's police protection with hired detectives. You know Commissioner Skinner, don't you?"

Skinner stepped forward. "Might I add that what you've done doesn't inspire a great deal of confidence in my men on the street or in the citizens they are sworn to protect."

Call smiled and inched toward the man. "Well, maybe, Commissioner, you can explain why we found two assassins in that hospital when we arrived with our detectives. Had we been a few minutes tardy, the women they were sworn to protect would be dead."

Skinner gulped. "This is the first I've heard of that." He turned to Connor, his chin rising slightly in the air. "Do you know anything about this, Captain?"

"Yes, sir, I'm afraid I do." Call watched as Connor's gaze went to the floor. "I was going to send the report up to you later today."

J. P. coughed out a laugh. "Now don't you two look like a couple of prized jackasses? I'd suggest you get your facts straight before you come bringing them to me." He looked at Morgan and Call. "And I would suggest the same for you two men. Get your facts straight before you write your story."

"Well, now, that's just what we'd like to do," Call answered. He glanced at Morgan. "Why don't you ask him, Morgan? You heard it the same as I did."

Morgan gulped. He straightened and faced the old man with a feeling that it was time to exchange his short pants for the long ones of a business suit. "One of the women in question overheard a conversation on the phone between a man we believe was Bruce Ismay and you, Uncle. It happened on the night the *Carpathia* pulled into the harbor. He was saying that he didn't know all those people were going to die. He said something else, too, about the *Titanic* not being the *Titanic*."

"Sheer and utter nonsense. Poppycock! I talked on the phone to no one that night. The woman was either drunk or dead on her feet. Do you really think something like that would stand up under any close scrutiny in a court of law?"

"Perhaps not," Morgan said, "but given the fact that an engineer from the *Titanic* was murdered, along with his brother that he might have talked to, it makes for an interesting set of circumstances."

"And let's not forget that someone tried to kill the woman," Call said, "twice."

"All of us who have been working on the story have been subjected to attempts on our lives," Morgan added. "Normally that might intimidate a man, but with a newspaper man, it gets his juices flowing."

J. P. folded his hands. He looked Morgan in the eye and smiled. "And now you're a newspaper man, I take it?"

"Yes, sir, I am. It's how I want to earn my way in the world."

"And I suppose you don't mind doing that without your father's trust fund then? You know I still have some power over that, don't you?"

"I know there is very little you don't have power over, Uncle," Morgan replied.

Morgan cleared his throat and then locked eyes with the financier. "Sir, that money in my trust fund is money earned by my father. It isn't mine. It never was. The only thing that is mine is my good name and a clear conscience, and I'm not about to surrender either of those for any amount of money."

Morgan heard the man grunt, but he could see his eyes sparkle with some measure of pride. It wasn't often that anyone stood up to John Pierpont Morgan, least of all someone who last was seen in short pants.

The two clergymen in robes got to their feet. The shorter of the two, the one wearing the cassock, spoke. "We understand that you are attempting to implicate the Irish cause with this story of yours."

J. P. cleared his throat. "Pardon my lack of introduction. This is Archbishop Fitzpatrick, and to his left is my own rector, Father Simeon. Father Simeon is Episcopalian, but that's close enough. Gentlemen, this is my great nephew, Morgan Fairfield."

"A number of the men we believe have been involved with the killings are men connected with the Irish cause," Morgan said. "I also have some experience with this group from my time on the *Titanic*. We know they tried to blow the ship up."

The archbishop moved closer. "Again, these are unsubstantiated claims. You must realize what harm reporting this could do to decent Irish people here in my parish. Anything at all that reflects on Ireland and the Irish as a people is looked upon as highly offensive. Such a story may cause riots and is certain to continue the discrimination they feel as a people."

"Frankly, we see these people being used by someone or some group for their own purposes," Call said. "They might not even know why."

"And what purpose could that possibly serve?" Simeon asked. The man, who seemed like the studious type, wore wire-rim glasses perched on a long nose.

Morgan shook his head. "We don't know that, but we'd like to. The closest we've been able to come is this question about the true identity of the *Titanic*."

"And what possible reason would anyone have to do that?" J. P. asked.

"In order to answer that question, I think we have to take a good look at the insurance claims from the White Star Line."

"That's right," Call added. "The figures from the *Titanic* and her sister ship the *Olympic*. From what we hear, the *Olympic*'s insurance fees were much higher, given her past mishaps, and the *Titanic* was insured far and above what might be normal for such a ship."

"And you think we would sink her, drown all those people, and subject ourselves to the greatest maritime disaster known to man, not to mention the attention in Congress and the newspapers, just for the insurance?"

"Personally, I think something went wrong," Call said. He glanced at Connor and Skinner. Connor was wringing his hands. "Maybe she was supposed to sink in a place where the people could be rescued. Maybe that bomb that your nephew says was planted was supposed to go off close to American waters. Perhaps the only man left who knew was the man killed on the night the *Carpathia* docked."

"Maybe, maybe, perhaps," J. P. spit out the words. "You have no proof, and I can assure you that if anything like that ever appears in that paper of yours, it will be my paper in short order, and you will be out on the street delivering it from house to house." He glared at Call. "With what you know about me, you must know that I don't make idle threats." He leaned forward. "I deliver on my words."

"Then show us the paperwork, the insurance claims," Morgan said. "That would be a quick way to stop this."

"You'll have to take that up with the White Star Line and Mr. Bruce Ismay. I try not to interfere with his job, and I don't want anyone else's nose in my business, especially the press."

"Then it seems we have reached an impasse," Morgan said.

"Yes, we have. You have suspicions that you dare not print without proof, and we have a business to run. You also have a responsibility to the people of this city not to divide them along the lines of their country of origin."

Call stepped closer. "That's fair enough. All we ask is that you call off your dogs." He shot a glance at Connor and Skinner, making certain they both knew he was talking about them. "If those people from the Emerald Isle don't want to be on the front page, I'd suggest that you recommend they stop shooting at us."

"Now, why would I want my own nephew gunned down?" J. P. waved his hand in Call's direction. "You, on the other hand, what happens to you is your own concern. I don't expect to be at your funeral, and I'm quite certain you will not be at mine."

Call smiled. "Oh, but I'd like to be, Mr. Morgan. I'm sure they'll lay out quite the spread for your wake, and I wouldn't want to miss that. I might even shed a tear, and that's something you wouldn't want to miss."

Morgan put his hand on Call's arm. He could see that while Call appreciated his own sense of humor, no one else in the room did. "Let me apologize for my friend," Morgan said. "He does get a little carried away at times."

"I can see that." The old man picked up his papers. "That's all the time I have for you. You had just better make sure you confirm anything that goes in that paper of yours with more than a woman who is a drunk and your own suspicions." He glanced over at the two clergymen. "I'd make certain that you don't drag the Irish into this, either."

When Morgan and Call were standing on the street a few minutes later, they found themselves staring at the house. Call let out a soft whistle. "I'd say we found out at least two things in there."

"What, pray tell?"

"We found out that we're pretty close to the truth and they don't like it. We also found out that they know much more about our business than I feel comfortable with. How do they know Gerry takes a drink? And everybody in that room knew pretty much every angle we're planning to take with our story."

"From someone who works for the paper?"

"Yes, someone working for the *Herald* who tells everything he hears to the wrong people."

CHAPTER 44

Morgan and Margaret met for lunch and then headed to the paper. She told him everything that she and Ed Leslie had heard in the pressroom the night before, and Morgan filled her in on what had been happening at the hospital and what it was like to see his Great Uncle John Pierpont Morgan.

"He sounds like some sort of king," she said.

"Bigger than that, I'd say. At least a king has a parliament to check his moves. My uncle has nobody to challenge him. He practically pulled the entire country out of a financial panic years ago, and he hasn't forgotten it."

"Could he really do what he claimed, take your trust away?"

"I don't doubt the man could do anything he claims." Morgan stared straight ahead and continued to walk by her side. For Morgan, it was more of a march to an inner drumbeat. He had always been uncomfortable around the wealthy, and now that he was one of them, it didn't ease the pull of his conscience. The fact that the trust fund wasn't money he had earned put him into a class he'd always despised, the idle wealthy. "In a way, I hope he does."

"Then you're just as bad as he is," Margaret murmured. "Perhaps the apple doesn't fall far from the tree."

"What do you mean by that?"

"You may not rise to the height of your great uncle on a financial plane, but you are already there when it comes to the matter of your righteous pride. Why can't you accept something as a gift from God without feeling the need for it to have your own monogram on it?"

Her words stung him, but only because he knew they were true. He'd always found solace in his faith and the fact that he kept the course when everyone else turned aside. "You're right, Margaret. Sometimes I can get more than a little pompous when it comes to doing the right thing. At times I'm not quite certain if I'm doing something because I love the Lord or because I love myself."

She smiled. "Well, that's easy to answer."

"It is?"

"Of course it is. A human being is prone to do things for the wrong reason. A person should never examine his motives too carefully. It's hard enough to know the right thing and do it without laboring under the need to do it for the right reason. You even whip yourself for having survived the *Titanic*. Perhaps that's the real reason you drive yourself and put yourself into danger. You feel guilty simply for being alive."

Morgan broke into a wide smile and slipped his arm around her. "You know, I must be the luckiest man in the world. I have a woman who's not only beautiful but is also about the smartest person I've ever met. Will you continue to talk to me in this way after we're both old and gray?"

Margaret returned his smile. "More, much more."

Moments later, they walked into the office. They spotted Call over by the coffeepot. "I wish I'd known about you seeing Connor here last night. It might have made for some interesting questions today in front of Uncle J. P."

"I'm glad you didn't know."

Call walked over to them, a cup of black coffee in his hand. "Nice to see you." He smiled at Margaret. "I'm glad you're here, Morgan. We have some work to do."

Morgan fished into his inside coat pocket and pulled out the article he'd been working on. "I have my next piece ready."

"You can give that to Dixon when we see him. Right now, we have bigger fish to fry."

"Like what?"

Call smiled. "You know how to catch the big fish, don't you? You catch the big fish by using the small one for bait, and at least we know where the small one swims. We also know that the man can be bought. We've seen that already. We just have to catch him red-handed and use a few choice threats to lower him into the shark tank. We're going to need help, though. The man already knows me. Pretty well, I might add."

He shifted his attention to Margaret. "Morgan tells me you've run into a Secret Service agent."

"Yes, Ed Leslie."

"Well, he might be perfect. It would be part of his job. Do you know where we can find this Ed Leslie?"

Morgan looked at Margaret. She shook her head. "I haven't seen him today, but I did leave him a message to meet me at the hotel."

"That's one of the things we wanted to talk with you about. It seems that Margaret and Leslie were here last night to see me. They came in through the pressroom and saw Connor, the man calling himself Hunter Kennedy, and the fella who runs the Irish dock workers, O'Brien. They were having a meeting there along with another man that Margaret couldn't recognize."

Call set the cup down on a desk next to him. The smile he wore was blooming into a grin. "You don't say?"

"They said something about the Francis at 11:00," Margaret added. "We weren't quite sure if that was a hotel or a restaurant."

"Well, if Kennedy's concerned, it no doubt involves a shipment of weapons. Wherever it is, there's either a delivery of guns or a payoff. It would be easy enough to find out. Might be a good story for the front page to catch them at it, don't you think?"

"I'd think so," Morgan said.

"Well, let's go to the old man's office. We'll need some hefty petty cash from him, and O'Leary's waiting for us." He smiled at Margaret. "If you'll excuse us, Miss, I'll be taking your man away from you."

Morgan turned to her. "Can I meet you later at the hotel?"

"I'll be with Gloria, no doubt. You be careful."

"I'll be very careful."

They wound their way through the desks and over to the office of Harry Dixon. The man's window shades were drawn. That in itself was a bit rare. Dixon normally had no reservation about letting anyone see him chewing out a reporter. He liked to be able to look out on the large room at any time too. He thought it kept people on their toes, and he was right.

Call looked at Morgan. "I know you aren't game for anything illegal, and I wouldn't even ask you to help if this Leslie fella was available."

"Help with what?"

"I'd like to find out just where the leak is in this newspaper. Harry Dixon is one of the few people who has known our every movement. He knew Patricia was keeping Gerry at her place, and he knows what we have in mind for our story."

"You don't think he had anything to do with this, do you?"

"Normally, I'd say not a chance, but I think there's so much money involved with this that the best of men might be tempted to take a tumble."

"What do you have in mind?"

"I've already talked this over with Fredo, so we're not exactly out on our own. I figure if the cop who has the dock beat, this O'Toole, can take a bribe and be caught, he just might tell us who's giving him his orders. The man wouldn't want to lose his job and be deported to Ireland, now would he?"

"No, I suppose not."

"Of course, you'll have to be in on it. Do you think your sensitive, all-too-Christian stomach can take something like that?"

"You want me to offer the man a bribe?"

Call smiled and put his hand on Morgan's shoulder. "No, I don't think even I would be foolish enough to make you do something like that. That's why I've got another rat to go along with us. You just have to stand there with your hands in your pockets. Do you think you can do that?"

Morgan gulped and nodded. "I think so, if I have to."

"Good, good. Then just let me do the talking. We'll go down to the docks and offer O'Toole a bribe to look away from something obviously illegal. We know he looked the other way when Fetters was murdered, and this won't be murder, not by a long shot. If he takes the bait, then Fredo's got him. If he turns away from it, we know that Dixon here's gotten word to him. Either way, it's a win-win deal for us. You following me?"

"Yes, I'm afraid I am."

"Good." Call shook him slightly. "You're about to be indoctrinated into what crime reporting is all about—dirty dealing, underhanded, shifty work. The noble press."

Call opened the door, and they stepped inside. O'Leary was standing beside the desk, looking at the copy of work Dixon was showing. Dixon had his dirty white shirt open at the collar with a tasteless red-and-yellow tie, which matched his red suspenders, dangling around his neck.

O'Leary was in a brown tweed suit that looked much too hot for the office. His vest was open, and his gold tie was pushed between the third and fourth button to hold it in place. "You busy, chief?" Call asked.

"I'm always busy," Dixon growled. A soggy cigar was bouncing in his mouth.

"Well, I'm glad. I wouldn't want to catch you sitting around here doing nothing."

Dixon leaned forward. "Well, what's this all about?"

"We're going to need your help, chief. Your help, your cover, and a hundred dollars from petty cash."

"A hundred dollars! For what?"

"For a bribe."

"Who are you going to bribe?" O'Leary asked with a grin. "The mayor?"

"No, that beat cop on the wharf, the one who arrested me. The man's name is O'Toole. A hundred bucks ought to do it. It's more than three months' salary for a man like that."

"And just what are you going to do?" Dixon asked. "Kill someone?"

"Oh, no, something pretty simple. We're going to steal one of the *Titanic*'s lifeboats."

"You looking for some kind of morbid coffee table?" O'Leary asked.

Call ignored him. "I've already got a truck, and if Morgan and O'Leary here could go down there and pull one of the boats out of the water and have O'Toole catch them, then they can offer him the hundred bucks. If he takes it, a friend of mine on the force will make the pinch. He certainly might be persuaded to change his testimony about me. Think of what that could save the paper. He also might be encouraged to tell what he knows about the Fetters murder. Either way, it's a win for us."

"And what if he just arrests Morgan and O'Leary here for attempted bribery?" Dixon asked. "What will that do to your little game?"

"That's why we're clearing this with you, chief. You know everything we're doing, and you even approved it."

"So I'm sticking my neck out with the publisher just so he can cut it off?"

Call leaned over the man's desk. "Chief, you'd just be trying to find out who's responsible for trying to have his niece murdered. I suppose if you won't do it, I can always go upstairs and ask him. Just tell me what to say to him when I tell him you refused to help."

The cigar dropped out of Dixon's mouth and onto the papers on his desk. "That's some nerve walking in here and trying to threaten me. Just who do you think you are?"

Call stood up straight. "I'm just a reporter trying to do his job and make you look good to the publisher while I'm at it. Chief, you've got to trust my instincts on this."

Dixon looked at O'Leary. "What do you think?"

"I don't like it," O'Leary said. "Too many things could go wrong, and in the end the paper could wind up on the front page of every other paper in town."

Call smiled. "Would that really be so bad? There's nothing wrong with getting your own name on other people's lips in this business. Of course, if it pans out we could have the scoop of the year here."

Dixon picked up a piece of paper and started to write. "All right, take this to the cashier and get your money." He handed the note to Call. "Just make sure this comes off without dragging us into the courts along with you."

Call took the paper and smiled. Minutes later the three men were out on the street. They passed by a flower shop just as Margaret was stepping out of it. She had a bouquet of her favorite flowers in her arm, yellow roses. When she saw them, she froze in place. There was a look of fear in her eyes, and Morgan could tell that she was more than a little afraid of what might be going on.

"Margaret," Morgan said. "I wasn't expecting to see you. We're just on our way to do some work."

Margaret took Morgan by the arm, still looking at Call and O'Leary. "I need to see you. I need to speak with you in private."

"There's no time for that," Call said, tugging on Morgan's coat. "I've got a truck waiting around the corner."

In spite of everything Morgan could see in Margaret's eyes, he patted her hand. "I'm sorry, darling, I can't talk now. We're off, I'm afraid. I'll look for you later."

With Call dragging him along, the three men walked toward the corner and the waiting truck.

CHAPTER 45

The makeshift vegetable truck had slats around the sides and a loosely tied tarp pulled over the top. The truck was painted green and had artwork on the door that depicted carrots, lettuce, apples, and tomatoes. To Morgan, the apples looked suspiciously like the tomatoes, but at least both were red. The truck also bore the name of an obviously Italian market. "I take it you got this from Fredo?" Morgan asked.

"Where else?" Call answered.

"This whole thing is nuts," O'Leary said. "What would anyone want with an old lifeboat?"

"Hey," Call replied, "people pay the highest price for anything to do with the *Titanic*. Everything off the boats has already been stolen, why not the boats themselves?"

Call climbed in behind the wheel. He started the truck and shoved it into gear. O'Leary sat with his elbow out the window, and Morgan sandwiched himself between the two men, being careful to keep his knees away from the gears.

O'Leary buttoned up his vest. "I've done a lot of stupid things in my life, Call, but anything involving you always seems to top the list." He looked over at Call. "Better give me the hundred."

Call passed over the two fifty-dollar bills. "You just need to do some good reporting and get the facts. Most of your stuff vacillates between guesswork and the obvious. By the way, I marked those bills with stars in red ink."

O'Leary looked at the bills and stuffed them into his vest pocket. "At least I don't get shot at."

Call laughed. "Why would anybody want to shoot you, other than the *Herald* for your impersonating a reporter?"

"Yeah, you just keep laughing and I'll keep working. I draw my paycheck the same as you."

"Now that's stealing," Call grunted. He looked at Morgan. "We practically raised this kid at the paper. He was selling them at eight and in the newsroom writing obituaries at fifteen."

"The streets make you grow up fast."

"Sometimes too fast. From what I can see, you plan on becoming city editor." Call stroked his chin and cracked a smile. "Might not be a bad idea for you, after all. They don't have all that much imagination. All they have to do is run a blue pencil through somebody's else's thinking."

"And bail reporters like you out of jail." O'Leary nodded his head in Morgan's direction. "I'm not sure I should take the kid here with me on this thing. He's a little young, and it might hurt his sensibilities." He snickered. "The man's an idealist. He's out to change the world with a pen, not become part of the dirty underbelly of what goes on in this town."

"Don't let him fool you, Morgan. Even though he acts like a man of the world, he probably isn't much older than you are."

Morgan wasn't quite sure how to react to O'Leary's statement. In one way, he appreciated the fact that O'Leary could recognize his morality. The idea of "letting his light shine" had always appealed to him. He certainly didn't think that a man's loss of morals should be equated with his maturity. On the other hand, there was a strong pull to be thought of as a reporter who could be called upon to do almost anything for a story. In

Morgan's mind, where to draw the line was something he wanted to be careful with.

"I already talked to Morgan about it. I want the two of you together. The idea of only one man trying to make off with one of those boats would be too hard to believe."

"Well, he doesn't have to be there when I offer the bribe, does he?" O'Leary reached over and patted Morgan's leg. "The kid's got scruples. I'm not sure he could handle that. Just one look at his pale face would tip that cop off for sure."

"Morgan will learn, and all he has to do is keep his mouth shut and smile when he needs to."

O'Leary wrinkled his pug nose in Morgan's direction, as if trying to smell fear. "I guess he's a lot like I was."

"Not that much," Call spat back. "He's much better educated and fed and obviously born with a higher sense of morals."

O'Leary grinned at Morgan. "Don't worry about me. Call here thinks he's insulting me, but he isn't. I'm not sure which of those three things would hold a man back more: overeating, being overeducated, or over-moralizing."

Morgan had always seen O'Leary as somewhat of a shallow thinker, someone who did the newspaper's dirty work without asking too many questions, but he could see that perhaps his perception had been wrong. O'Leary was more of a street dog—smart, lean, and tough. The kind of mixed breed that was too small and scrawny to stand up to a purebred English bulldog, but too smart to even try. So he'd just run along with the pack, trailing such a beast and trying to pick up the leavings.

"Call and I go back a ways. The problem is, I go by the book and Call . . ." O'Leary paused, looking over in Call's direction. "Well, he's all over the board."

"The book's a bore," Call said. "I read it once, and it was one time too many."

"Always nice to at least know what the book says, don't you think, Fairfield?"

"Yes, it helps."

"How can a man know when he doing the wrong thing unless he first finds out what's the right thing?"

"If I didn't know you better, O'Leary, I'd say you were as boring as the book." Call looked over in his direction. "But I do know you. I've lifted many a glass with you, and you're not that dull."

"Coming from you, that's a real compliment."

"I just want Fairfield here with you. If it comes down to it and we do have to go to court with this cop, we're going to need two witnesses. Your word just isn't good enough." Call chuckled. "Now that's an understatement."

O'Leary roared. "We have told us a few yarns in our day." He looked at Morgan. "Your mentor over there just keeps me around for laughs, unless there's dirty business afoot. He calls on me quick enough then. I just don't get any credit for his stories."

"And I wouldn't want any credit for yours."

The sun had started to set when they pulled up next to the park near the docks. They had stopped for a lengthy cup of coffee. Call wanted to give Dixon all the time he needed to warn O'Toole. "This is as far as I go," Call said. "I'm meeting my copper friend here, and we'll be watching you. I have some rope and a winch in the back of the truck. Do you know how to use one?"

"'Course I do," O'Leary said.

"When you pass the money to O'Toole, we'll take care of it from there. Now, Morgan, you show the man what boats look like. I wouldn't want him trying to load an old lady's flower cart by mistake."

Morgan scooted over behind the wheel and mashed the truck into gear. The grinding noise sent a chill up his back. Driving and shifting a truck was a new experience for him. They bolted out to the street, and moments later Morgan pulled to a stop beside the docks.

They got out and looked over the side of the pier at the sight of the bobbing lifeboats. Morgan was amazed that they were still there. They had become the most photographed lifeboats in history, but Morgan was sure the White Star Line would have hauled them away by now. He was almost sorry they hadn't.

"Nervous, kid?" O'Leary asked. The man had a nice smile about him. It was almost as if he cared, and that was a look Morgan didn't often see among newsmen. Most had hearts of stone. They kept their distance from real feelings for fear of getting burned in the process of reporting the news. Morgan knew enough about this business to know that a good day for a newsman was generally a day filled with tragedy for everyone else. Your father is murdered? That's a bad day for you, but a story for the newsman. Your life savings plundered? Too bad for you, but great for a reporter. It could make a man jaded long before his time.

"I'm a little nervous."

"Well, you should be. Bribing an officer of the law is serious business." He pointed down the dock. "When that policeman comes along, if you just want to take a little stroll down there so you're out of earshot, I won't breathe a word to Call. What he doesn't know won't hurt him. I know how the man can be, and, with what little I know about you, I'm sure you want to impress him. Take it from me, though, it ain't exactly worth it."

There was a glint in the man's eyes, like a laugh threatening to break out at any moment. It might be mistaken for humor, but there was a dark side to it. O'Leary could see the worst part of anything, could see it almost before it happened. Morgan imagined that the words that gave the man the most pleasure in life were the words, *I told you so*.

Morgan had seen that kind of person before, and it was never a pleasant thing to be on the receiving end of that type of wisdom.

"I'll just do what Call said and stick with you. Two witnesses are better than one."

"Suit yourself." O'Leary slapped him on the back. "You boys got yourselves quite a story going here, if it pans out for you."

"It might be even better later tonight," Morgan said.

"Oh, is that so?" The man's pudgy ears stood out from under his cap.

"Things just might break tonight."

O'Leary pushed him slightly in jest. "Well, don't keep me in the dark. What do you know? After all, I'm here taking the risk with you."

"We think there's going to be a gun shipment tonight."

"Gunrunning?"

"Yes, for the IRA."

"Where? Who?"

Morgan shook his head. "I don't think I'm at liberty to say that. Let's just say we heard it from the source."

"And you're going to be there?"

"Yes," Morgan smiled, "me and Call."

"Boy, I wouldn't be there without the cavalry. Aren't you going to bring the police?"

"I don't think so. Call doesn't think we can trust them. He thinks they'll tip the gunrunners off."

O'Leary shook his head. "Well, that's one bit of business he's not dragging me into. I plan on living to see my retirement. Sounds dangerous to me, mighty dangerous."

CHAPTER 46

Call watched Morgan and O'Leary survey the boats in the water. They were evidently trying to find one that would be easy to load onto the truck. Even then, it would take some doing for the two of them. That would be fine with Call. The clumsier they were, the better. There was nothing like thieves who couldn't steal straight to attract a cop's attention.

It saddened him to think of what he knew about thieves and crooked cops. In the years he'd spent reporting what he thought was the news, he'd seen his heart grow harder and his outlook on life become more twisted by the day. When he started as a reporter, he'd been out to change people's lives, to make them better people for having read what he wrote. Now, more and more, he saw himself as appealing to their prejudices and their prurient interest in sensational sleaze. Where he once thought of himself as a white knight in shining armor, he now truthfully thought of himself as a huckster in a carnival sideshow, beating on a poster of the two-headed woman and proudly selling tickets to a lie.

He watched Morgan walk down the dock and was almost envious. Morgan was an idealist, and Call knew full well that he had been once. At times he saw cynicism as the natural progression for an idealist. You entered a job thinking that you could make a difference and that people and events would bow before your moral influence, only to discover in time that you would bow the knee to theirs. Cynics were nothing but deeply disillusioned idealists. He wanted better for Morgan.

He didn't have long to wait before he saw Fredo walking across the park to him. There was still more than enough light for them to see the truck and the men. From what he knew of O'Toole, the man would be coming on duty any time.

"I see you're ready and waiting," Fredo said.

Call stared off at the docks in the distance. "Yes, I'm ready all right. I'm a bit troubled, though."

"Why?"

Call pointed at the two men in the distance. "Those two."

Fredo looked off at the two men who were now unloading the winch from the truck. "Fairfield and O'Leary? What about them?"

"They're both about the same age. They're both reporters, but they're as different as night and day."

"So? Everybody's different."

"Morgan's a nice kid, righteous and Christian to the core, a little naive. O'Leary's a snake, a rat who would crawl through any gutter to get a leg up. He's been raised on the streets of New York where a man has to scrounge in order to eat."

"Well, you ought to be used to that." Fredo grinned. "He sounds a lot like you."

"That's the problem. I am used to that. I'm not sure I have an unselfish bone in my body. The more I'm around Fairfield, though, the more I want to look back at the ethical side of life, the side that's willing to sacrifice for other people. I used to be like that. I must be getting soft in the head or something to even think back on it."

"Maybe just soft in the heart."

"Wherever it is that I'm soft, I'm still living and working in New York City. I can't afford to be mushy. Now this thing with Dixon. Part of me wants to see him responsible for the leaks in the paper so I can go to old man Bennett with what I know. Whoever passed on the information about Gerry and where she was staying put Patricia's life in danger and almost got her killed twice. If I tell the big man that, the least that could happen is getting the chief canned. At the worst, he could be up on charges for conspiracy to commit murder. That's the O'Leary side of me."

"Well, if it's the truth."

"At times I'm not sure if the truth matters. That part of who I am just wants to step over the bodies. The other part of me, the Morgan Fairfield side, wants to see the old man come out smelling like a rose, wants to believe the best about people and to see it all work out. Of course, then we'd all be back to square one. Not a great spot to be in."

Fredo's dark eyes sparkled, and he brushed his mustache aside with the back of his hand. "You have changed, Call. Maybe instead of you teaching the kid over there, he's been teaching you."

"It isn't so much what he says; it's what he doesn't say. The man doesn't have an unkind word to say about anyone. I know he's smart, plenty smart. I've seen him stump people who are supposed to know, but at times he just becomes silent."

"Speaking of becoming silent, I didn't have a chance to tell you about that man we captured at the hospital."

"No, you didn't. I figured if it had been important I'd have heard about it."

"The man was with another dock tough guy, a Sean James. He said they got their orders from an Irishman."

"Oh, fine. That only narrows us down to the whole East Side. I think I've heard of this Sean James."

"You should have. He beat a murder charge a year ago. Insufficient evidence—the murder weapon turned up missing in the police property room."

"The man has friends on the force, doesn't he?"

"You can be sure he does."

"I have a big job for you tonight when we finish with this," Call said. He explained what Margaret and Ed Leslie had overheard about the Francis and the rendezvous scheduled at 11:00 P.M.

"The Francis, that's a hotel downtown," Fredo added.

"Do you think they're making a final payoff for the guns there?"

"It could be. But you can't go there by yourself. You're going to need a man with a badge."

"That would be you," Call grinned.

Fredo pulled at his chin. "I guess it will have to be. I really wouldn't want to tell anyone on the force about this. It just might get back to our men in blue who took the evidence on Sean James."

"Good thinking."

Call watched as Morgan and O'Leary climbed over the dock and down into one of the boats. They were out of his sight for only a moment before Morgan climbed back on the dock and began to wave frantically. It was obvious that Morgan wanted to attract his attention. There was a desperation in the signal.

"I wonder what he wants?" Fredo asked.

"I don't know, but it looks like trouble."

"We better get over there."

Both men began a run from the park to the dock. When they got closer, O'Leary had taken a long pole with a hook on the end of it and was using it to pull one of the boats toward the wharf. They both stopped alongside a silent Morgan and watched as O'Leary drew the boat closer. There in the boat was the body of a man in a suit. He was prone, with his arms and legs flung out. Scattered around the boat were yellow flowers, as if whoever had done this laid a wreath for the dead.

Call mumbled. "Fine, they had to pick the boat with the body in it."

"Who is it?" Fredo asked.

Morgan looked at the two men, a somber look in his face. There was a personal nature to the far-off look in Morgan's eyes. "It's Ed Leslie."

"Leslie?" Call asked. "Are you sure?"

Morgan nodded. "I'm very sure."

Call and Fredo jumped down into the boat as O'Leary pulled it close to the dock. Fredo reached around the body and turned it over. Leslie's eyes were open, a look of shock and surprise frozen on his face. His mouth was partially open, showing a row of pearly teeth beneath his trimmed mustache. Fredo felt his wrist, then his fingers. Reaching out, he touched the man's cheeks. "He hasn't been dead for long. We must have just missed whoever did this."

"Better check to see if he still has his badge and gun," Call said.

Fredo patted the man down, and then reached into the man's waistband and pulled out a revolver from a holster. He opened the cylinder and checked the loads. "There's one missing." Lifting the gun to his nose, he gave it a whiff. "The gun's cold, and it hasn't been fired. I'd say the man carried an empty chamber under the hammer."

"Then whoever did this took him by surprise," Call said.

"Totally," Fredo replied. "I don't think he saw it coming until it was too late. Take a look at the entrance wound." He ran his finger down the man's shirt to a spot between the third and fourth button. A small eruption of blood had cascaded down the shirt, forming a triangle of crimson. "The man was shot right through the heart, and from close up too."

Fredo lifted Leslie's shirt slightly, showing the telltale mark of a brown burn on the otherwise sparkling white cotton. "I'd say whoever did this shoved the gun right next to his heart until he could feel the thing beat through the cold steel. Then he pulled the trigger. It was over in the blink of an eye."

"Do you think he shot him in the boat?" Call asked.

Fredo shook his head. "I don't think so. I'd say he was shot on the dock up there and then tossed into the boat. You can see that from the way the body was lying."

O'Leary began to survey the dock for a sign of blood. He took several steps and then squatted down, pointing. "Makes sense. There're spots of fresh blood up here and a shoe print."

"That would be our killer," Fredo said.

Both men looked over the boat. Fredo scratched his head. "What about these flowers?"

"Don't you recognize them?" Morgan asked. His eyes were boring into Call.

"They're roses," Call said.

"Yes," Morgan replied. "Yellow roses."

"You don't think—," Call started to answer.

"Yes, I do," Morgan responded. "Margaret was carrying a bouquet of yellow roses when we saw her coming out of the flower shop." He shook his head. "I should have listened to her this morning when we passed her. She had something important to say. I could see it in her eyes."

CHAPTER 47

Margaret dragged her heels slightly, twisting her wrist to try to free herself from the viselike grip. Her hands were tied behind her. "Where are you taking me?"

The warehouse was filled with boxes of every description. Massive shapes of wood and metal—boxes, barrels, and crates—stood up in the darkness against the peeling, tar paper roof. Margaret's heels sounded an unsteady, muffled cadence on the wet, sawdust-covered concrete floor as she was pulled along.

The warehouse reeked with odors of every description. Medical supplies seemed to bleed into leaking drums of oil. The scent of copper wire and the acrid aroma of steel cable could be detected. And there was a skin-tingling whiff of rats and their leavings.

"I said, where are you taking me?"

"Someplace where you'll be safe and out of sight, at least for now. I'm not making you any promises. You just stay where I put you."

"You'll never get away with this, you know, killing a federal agent."

"Maybe not, but it had to be done. I'll leave when the guns leave tonight. If you keep that pretty little head of yours out of sight for a while, I can go home with the guns and you can go home with that man of yours."

"You may be an actor, but you're nothing like Hunter Kennedy."

Kennedy drew her up beside a door to a shed. The brass hasp had no lock in it; instead, a small piece of sharpened wood on a string was crammed into it. He pulled it out. "Oh, is that so? I am very much like Hunter."

"Not at all. Hunter was kind and wouldn't hurt a fly. You are a cold-blooded killer. You never even knew Hunter, or you couldn't possibly say such a thing."

His crisp blue eyes worked their way past hers and into her head. They seemed to be searching her mind. She could see words inside the man that he was holding back. His thoughts and emotions, however, were flowing into her soul. Margaret almost screamed for him to say what he was thinking. And he did say it. He said it quietly.

"Hunter was my brother."

There was nothing at that moment the man could have told her that would have been more painful. She had liked Hunter from the moment she'd met him, and to have this man claim to be his brother seemed to dishonor his memory. "Your brother? That can't be." Even as Margaret said it out loud, her heart knew he was telling the truth.

"But it is. He was my little brother. My name is Fallon Kennedy. We were raised in the same home. He went on the stage. It was always his first love. I took to the stage as well, but my love has always been my country and politics."

"Then you knew he was coming to America?"

"Yes, I knew." He opened the thin wooden door and swung her around into the darkened room. There was a force to his motion, harsh and abrupt. "I knew he was coming, and I knew he was going to be in the play. What I didn't know was that he would never get here."

He took the end of the rope around Margaret's wrists and ran it under a steel bar along the wall. Margaret thought it looked like a practice bar in a ballet studio. Undoubtedly, though, it was used to tie down boxes perched on top of others. "I never knew anything about the *Titanic* going down until it was all over."

"But if you're a member of the Irish Republican Army, you had to have known."

He jerked at the rope and tied the knot fast to the bar, giving Margaret only a short length of rope to move around with. "I asked about it after you and your friend told me what had happened. You were right about one thing. Someone did pay our people to sink that ship. I still don't know who. Very few people know that."

"So your group kills for money?"

"It takes money to run a revolution."

"And it doesn't matter who gives it to you?"

Kennedy smirked. "For all I know, it was the queen herself. I don't know, and I don't care."

"And you still want to work for people who try to murder women and children—Irish women and children?"

"You English have been killing my people for centuries. Sacrifices have to be made. I just want to go home, that's all. I didn't let them kill you, did I?"

"No, you didn't, and I'm grateful for that."

"And the bomb they planted on that ship of yours didn't go off. From what I've been told, had it exploded like it was supposed to have, everyone on board would have been saved. It would have gone off much closer to the American mainland, and the ship would have taken longer to sink. We can't be blamed for the incompetence of a captain who makes twenty-two knots in an ice field, now can we?"

"Then why kill Fetters?"

Fallon shook his head. "I heard about that just today. When I did, I knew I shouldn't have mentioned the man's name to you. He was one of our men on the *Titanic*."

Kennedy shook the bar to make certain it was anchored to the wall. "From what I understand, he was a loose end. With all the hearings on the *Titanic* going on, there are many among us who don't want the name of the movement even mentioned with the disaster. Think about what that would mean."

"Less money from Americans?"

"To say the least. And we've gone to great lengths to stop the story and the investigation."

"Like murder?"

"Just what I said, great lengths."

"But you're just protecting someone else, someone who paid to use you."

"We're just finishing our job here and making sure it stays a secret. We're also protecting our supply of weapons."

"The idea of cold-blooded murder doesn't stop you, not after what I saw today."

"I didn't have any choice. I was already here at the docks when the call came in from the harbormaster. The movement has a lot of people on the payroll. When he said a Secret Service agent had been there and asked about the Francis, we knew something had to be done."

"But you didn't know it would be Ed Leslie, did you?"

"No, I didn't. Nor did I know you'd be with the man."

"I'm sorry to spoil your plans. Leslie made me wait outside while he asked about the Francis." She twisted her wrists slightly, working to keep some give in the rope. "What will you do with me now. Kill me too?"

"No, I won't do that, not me." He nodded in the direction of the window. The simple framed window looked out on an adjoining office where the lights were shining brightly. Inside, Margaret could see a large, heavyset man who was looking at his watch and a man with a black beard who was leaving. "But if you don't stay put, somebody else might. I have little control over him. I'd suggest you stay away from that window. I don't want anyone to know you're here until I get back from tonight's performance. By then, what you know won't make any difference. We'll be in international waters before you have a chance to do us any damage."

"You've got this all thought through, haven't you?" Margaret stared out the dark window. "What if he doesn't see it your way?"

Fallon opened the door and stood there, staring at her. "We'll cross that bridge when we come to it. You and your friend have made it more difficult, but fortunately for you, it's still workable. You just stay where you are and keep quiet. I told the guards we passed at the dock that I was going to take care of you, and that ought to be enough for them until I get back. If they should see you again, however, they might take care of you themselves. You wouldn't want that, would you?"

"No, I . . . I wouldn't." She stared at him. "Your father was a minister. You were raised with the love of God taught to you as a child."

"So now you're a mind reader?"

"Hunter told us about your parents. You may escape justice here, but you can never escape God. You must know that."

Fallon cocked an eyebrow. "I remember what I was taught. I just can't say for certain what I know."

Margaret watched the door close and the gloom settle over the room. She listened as Kennedy dropped the piece of wood back into position. Shadows from the windowpane formed the shape of a cross over the door and the wall around it. It put her in mind of the thing she needed to do most—pray. "Lord, please help me now," she muttered under her breath. "Help me know what to do and how to do it."

What she had seen and heard sent a frightening chill down between her shoulder blades, a tingling sensation that made her skin quiver. She had never seen a man killed in front of her eyes. The tragedy of the *Titanic* and the death of so many people had served to remind her how fragile the human condition actually was, but the suddenness of Ed Leslie's death had been terrifying. Thinking on it didn't make her cower in a corner, however; it stiffened her resolve.

Margaret looked through the window and saw Kennedy walk into the office and begin a discussion with the large man she had seen waiting there. He wasn't the least bit happy with what had happened, and from the way Kennedy was responding, she wondered if he'd be able to make good on his promise to protect her. What she knew might be too late to stop Fallon Kennedy if he left the country, but this other man was obviously staying.

She watched Kennedy wave his arms, arguing. The larger man was standing beside a desk. His arms were crossed, and he was slowly rocking back and forth, patient but seething with anger. It was obvious to her who was winning the war of words. What little she'd been able to learn from her father about business told her that the one who said the least usually held the upper hand. No matter what Kennedy had told her, if he was successful in leaving the country, that would still place her at the mercy of the other men who held her prisoner. With Kennedy gone, no one need really know what happened to her.

She moved closer to the steel rail that Kennedy had tethered her to. It was bolted into the wall, but the wall itself was old and fragile, and the bolts had been loose for some time. Kennedy obviously had no way of knowing that. He had just tied her to what he thought was stable.

She took a firm grip on the rail from behind and placed her left foot against the wall, leaning forward slowly. It gave way. She was sure it would pull away from the wall, but the last thing she needed right then was to make noise.

Backing up next to the bar, she wiggled it up and down, loosening the screws that held it in place. When she felt the first one pop free, she slid the rope down the end of the bar to the place where the screws joined to the wall. She pulled there ever so slowly, and finally it gave way.

She began to work the rope free from the end, keeping her eyes on Kennedy and the man in the office through the window. If Kennedy lost the argument, they might come for her right away. She wanted to be gone before that happened. Finally, with one tedious push, she freed the rope.

Looking around the darkened room, she spotted a box with the corner broken and splintered. She would have to use her sense of touch to get a grip on the thing from behind. Stepping over to the box, she bent down and felt for the splintered piece. Getting several fingers around the piece, she ripped it. With a tearing sound, it broke off in her hands.

Backing up against the door, she wedged the small piece of sharp wood between the door and the frame. She pushed it up, getting on her toes until she could feel the piece come into contact with the rope that held the small piece of wood into place in the hasp lock outside. She strained to lift it up, finally feeling the thing give.

Reaching behind with her fingers, she felt the crosspiece of the door and grabbed hold. She rocked it back and forth with her hips, gently but with a determined motion. Suddenly losing patience, she slammed her backside into the door, springing the hasp open.

She stared out the window at Kennedy and the other man in the office. They were continuing to talk, at least Kennedy was. Her movement and the slight noise hadn't been detected. She let out a deep sigh, a prayer of thanks, unspoken but deeply felt.

Turning her back to the room, she stepped forward into the dark warehouse. She tramped forward, through the wet sawdust, dragging the end of rope along behind her. She would have to find her way through the complex network of boxes and crates to the door.

A rat scurried across her path, darting from one box to another. It scared her slightly, but she forced a smile. Margaret understood perfectly well how the thing felt. She was like a rat in a maze too. The difference was, the rat actually knew where it was going.

She moved quickly along a row of boxes, many of which she could not see over. She focused her eyes not on the floor but on the roof overhead. The door to the warehouse was at the corner of the building, and the roof would be the only thing to tell her where that was.

Turning to her left, she followed a row of steel cables on large wooden spools. She picked up her pace slightly and then spotted what she thought was the corner. Winding her way past the cable, she turned along the side of a mountain of barrels, following them all the way to the outer wall. The sight of the wall sent a shiver of relief up her back.

Moving quickly along the wall, she soon came to the door. She turned her back to it, twisting the knob open. Having her hands tied behind her was awkward, but there was no time to stop now. Her feet could still work, and that was what she needed most.

She stepped out into the night air, the fresh smell of saltwater ripping into her nostrils. She looked back toward the door. The edge of the wall was corrugated tin with sharp edges. She backed up slowly until she could feel the rope between her wrists pressed against the edge of the wall. She rubbed the rope against the sharp metal, feeling the first strands begin to break.

Just then she heard the sound of men's voices from the warehouse. They were yelling. Her escape had obviously been discovered, and there was a search underway. There was no time to work the ropes now. That would have to wait. At the end of the dock was a tugboat, squat in the water, its engines chugging and steam rising from the small stack in the center. She ran up the dock in the opposite direction.

As she neared the crest of the ramp that led to the wharf, she stopped in her tracks. Up ahead, she could see two men smoking cigarettes, their backs against the gates that led to the warehouse and the pier below, where she was standing. Their dim figures showed their hands in their pockets; bright red glows flared at the ends of their lips.

They were relaxed, talking and smoking, obviously unaware that she had escaped. She knew that with the search going on in the warehouse, that was soon to change.

Stepping to the edge of the dock, she looked over the side. The water below was dark and no doubt deep. There would be no chance for her to swim with her hands still tied behind her.

She looked back down the dock to the warehouse and the tugboat. The boat would be the only way she could escape. No matter where it was going, it would be better than standing here. The only problem would be getting past the warehouse. She would have to move quickly. The first man to step outside the door would see her.

CHAPTER 48

Morgan curled his fists into tight balls. Anger mixed with a numbing fear raged inside him. He couldn't shake the feeling that he'd let Margaret down. The one time she'd needed him to listen, and he'd been too busy to even stop. He'd let Call drag him away when Margaret desperately wanted to tell him something.

He had to focus his mind if he was going to think. Some things were not at all clear. *Why couldn't Margaret just tell me what was on her mind when she saw me?* he wondered. *Was it something to do with our relationship?* If it had been, Morgan could understand her hesitancy to say anything in front of Call and O'Leary. But if it was about the story, something she had remembered, why the reluctance? It didn't make sense. Margaret wasn't exactly the shy and retiring type.

Morgan walked over to the edge of the dock and looked out to the bobbing lifeboats. *Why would she come here?* he wondered. He knew he hadn't told her that he was going to the waterfront with Call and O'Leary. He seldom if ever knew where Call would take him. *So why would she come here? Why would Leslie bring her to this place?*

Morgan looked the area over. The wharf was growing all too familiar to him. It was the first he'd seen of America when the *Carpathia* pulled into the harbor. He looked at the Brass Rail and the few waterfront shops and fruit stands that dotted the place. *Did Leslie want to go back there?* he wondered. Next to the docks were the waterfront offices of the White Star Line, and close by was the office of the harbormaster. The lights were on in both offices.

Call had gone to the coroner's wagon to talk with the men who were taking Leslie's body to the morgue, and Fredo and O'Leary were talking to the investigating officers and the beat cop, O'Toole. The man had finally shown up, much too late for them to spring their trap. It made Morgan wonder if Call hadn't been right about Dixon. Maybe he had gotten word to the Irish thugs who worked the docks.

After the men closed the door on Leslie's body and drove away, Call walked over to him. He put his hand on Morgan's shoulder. "You all right?"

Sweat was forming in the palms of Morgan's hands. "I know she said she'd left a note for Leslie to meet her at the hotel. I just don't know why. And why would he take her here?"

"Did you tell her we were coming here? Maybe she was just determined to tell you whatever it was that she had on her mind."

"No, I didn't exactly tell her where we were going. This place had to be her idea or Leslie's. The question is why." Morgan bowed his head and shook it. "I should have taken the time to hear her out."

"You're not blaming yourself, are you?"

"Of course I am. I was an insensitive cad."

"If it had been that important, she would have said something."

"Not if it was something about her and me. There was no way she would drag anything to do with us out into the open in front of you and O'Leary."

"You two haven't been having trouble, have you? She been having second thoughts?"

"She might have been. This job of mine isn't exactly the kind of thing that would endear a woman to a man."

"Well, I think you can dismiss that notion out of your head."

"Why?"

"Do you really think that if Margaret had something to say about the two of you that she would pick a sidewalk, in the middle of the day, surrounded by your coworkers?"

"No, I suppose not."

"Of course not! It had to be about something else."

"I guess you're right."

Call shook his shoulder. "I am right. Now we just need to find out why Leslie would bring her here and if anyone saw them. We'll get a lead somewhere, and we'll find her. Maybe she's not in any danger at all. Maybe she just left the flowers with Leslie and went to find a ladies' room. It might be just as simple as that, you know."

"Then why wouldn't she call the police when she came back here and found him? Why just disappear?"

"Women are complicated. Neither of us knows for sure what was in her head."

Fredo and O'Leary walked over to where Call and Morgan were talking. "I gave them our story," Fredo said. He looked at Call. "At least they know you were with an officer of the law when this happened. They won't be coming after you."

"Thank God for small favors."

"They are alerting the office of the Secret Service in town. I told them I thought it had something to do with a counterfeiting ring." He smiled and shrugged his shoulders. "Who knows, since that is the business of the Secret Service, they might have even believed me."

"You lie so well," Call said.

"Police training," Fredo grinned.

"Are we all done here?" O'Leary asked. He looked back at O'Toole, who was still talking to the investigating officers from homicide. "If we're not exactly going to spring this carefully laid trap of yours, then I should be getting home."

"Aren't you forgetting something?" Call asked.

"What's that?"

"We're missing one woman. It happens to be Morgan's woman."

"What can we do about that?"

"O'Leary's right," Morgan said. "You people should just go home. I'll stay and work on this. It's my fault and my business."

"Hogwash!" Call said. "It's the paper's story. Your Margaret just happened to step into it. Anything that happens to her involves all of us."

Call pointed to the offices of the White Star Line. "Why don't you and Fredo go over to White Star and see what you can find out. Ask if anyone saw Leslie and Margaret. Morgan and I will go over to the harbormaster."

O'Leary shrugged and pushed his hands down into his pockets. "Fine, we'll work it."

"Good. Then we'll meet you back here when we're done. Be wary, though. This is definitely unfriendly territory."

Morgan and Call began to walk toward the office of the harbormaster. "You think Dixon got word to the people down here that we were coming?" Morgan asked.

"I'm not sure."

"If he did, they may have had an ambush set up for us."

"And you think they got Leslie and Margaret instead?"

"I don't know what to think."

Call slipped his arm over Morgan's shoulder, giving him a pat. "We'll find out, but we have to find Margaret first. When we finish here, I'd suggest you call the hotel. She might have gotten back there and we're worrying about nothing."

"I hope you're right."

On the outside, the harbormaster's office looked to be no more than a shed. Weathered boards and shutters had been painted red years ago, and the wind and ocean air had bleached them a striated rose color. The windows were covered with dirt, some of which had handprints left by children who passed.

Morgan and Call walked up the ramp that led to the door, twisted the dented brass doorknob, and stepped inside. A small potbellied stove sat in the center of the room with chairs arranged in somewhat of a circle around it. A bucket half full of coal and a small shovel were in front of the open stove door, and a fire glowed inside. Stacks of newspapers were in the corner, hastily arranged to get them out from underfoot. The desk, piled with charts and papers, had a large map of New York harbor behind it. Pins dotted the map, and there were literally thousands of holes where pins had once stood. A black candlestick telephone stood on the desk, and a Kewpie doll beside it looked like it had been won at the state fair. On the wall were two prominently displayed photographs, President William Howard Taft and Theodore Roosevelt. Having those same two men running against each other for the Republican nomination and the fact that they were now sworn enemies made the photos ironic.

Someone was whistling a tune in the back room, but Morgan couldn't make it out. He took it to be a sea chantey.

The man came out of the back room with a second bucket of coal in his hands. He was walking with the bucket between his legs, swinging it back and forth and looking like a bowlegged duck with every step. "Just a second, gents," he said.

The man set the second bucket down behind the first one, reached for the shovel, and spaded a load of coal into the open door on the stove. He then laid the shovel into the half-empty bucket and kicked the door shut. "There, that ought to be enough for the night."

Turning around, he wiped his sooty black hands on the top of his red long underwear and then clapped them together to beat off what soot might remain. The hand cleaning did little to improve his appearance, leaving black streaks across his underwear.

Morgan thought the man looked almost comical. He wore dirty and baggy black pants on top of his long underwear. A worn and holey gray sweater vest did little to cover the top of the red underwear, and his boots were unlaced. The man's yellow suspenders were tied in place, and he had a rope fixed around his middle and tied in a knot to serve as a belt. The man's pants were safe from falling, no matter what the conditions.

Staring at Morgan and Call, he put his hands on his hips. "Now what can I do for you two gents?"

Morgan looked at the man carefully. He was still fairly young, perhaps in his thirties, even though he sounded and moved like an old man. His black beard was matted and unwashed, and his hair was pulled down across his forehead in an attempt to cover a growing bald spot. The man's brown eyes sparkled, and his large reddish nose indicated a bit of a drinking problem.

"You the harbormaster tonight?" Call asked.

"Sure am. Mulligan's the name."

"You just come on duty?"

The man reached down into his pocket and pulled out a plug of tobacco and a jackknife. "Nah. I come on at four." He opened the knife and cut a slice of tobacco off the top of the brown bar, then slipped the tobacco into his mouth with the edge of the blade. Closing the knife, he stuffed it and the remaining tobacco back into his pocket. "Be here 'til 1:00 in the morning too."

"Good," Call said, "Then you're just the man we're looking for."

The man squinted an eye in Call's direction. "Now, why would that be?"

"Did you see any strangers around here earlier?"

"Can't say as I have. Can't say as I haven't. Who wants to know?"

"We're looking for a couple of friends of ours. One's a man." Call gave a brief description of Ed Leslie. "One is a woman." He followed with a description of Margaret.

The man placed his hands back on his hips and stared passively at the ceiling, taking care not to make eye contact with either Morgan or Call. "We don't get many folks who fit that description. I sent me three pilots off to ships tonight and had me three captains who came in and paid docking fees. Apart from that, I ain't seen much in the way of people hereabouts."

He slopped back in the direction of the desk, trailing his bootlaces behind him. Sitting down in the creaky swivel chair behind it, he leaned back and landed his feet on the desk with a thud. The bottom of his boots were caked in wet sawdust.

Call noticed it right away. "You look like you've been making a tour of some of the warehouses around here."

The man gulped, almost swallowing some of his tobacco juice. He cocked his head, a scowl forming on his lips. "Why would you say that?"

"That sawdust on the bottom of your boots. Don't they lay that down on the floor of warehouses?"

Lifting up one foot, the man caught sight of the sawdust. "I reckon they do. I was out making an inspection earlier."

"So those people we described might have come by while you were gone then?"

"I guess they might have at that." He stuck his chin out. "But I never seen 'em."

Morgan stepped closer. "The man my friend described to you was murdered a short distance from here. They just took his body to the morgue."

Morgan watched the reaction on the man's face. There was no shock, something that might have been normal. You'd have thought someone had just informed him of an overdue library book.

He picked up a cup and sent a stream of brown juice into the bottom of it. He wiped his mouth with the back of his hand. "None of my business. People killed 'round here all the time. I stay out of it. Don't bother them, and they don't bother me none."

Morgan felt Call's hand on his arm, as if to hold him back or steady him. Morgan knew that he'd never been very good at hiding his feelings.

"Well, we thank you for your trouble anyway," Call said. "We'll keep looking. I'm sure the police will want to talk to you too."

"Send 'em 'round. I'll tell 'em the same thing I told you."

A few moments later Morgan and Call were walking over to where Fredo and O'Leary were waiting for them.

"Did you believe him?" Morgan asked.

"Not one word," Call said. "And that thing about inspecting the warehouses, I know enough to know that has nothing to do with that man's job. If he was there, it was for something other than his duties."

"You find out anything?" Fredo asked.

"We might have," Call said. "The man's not talking, though, and I suspect he has a very good reason."

"We got nothing from the White Star people over there. There's a new cleaning woman who knows nothing about nothing."

"Someone who took Gerry's job, I suspect," Call said. He looked at Morgan. "Maybe we should go to the Francis Hotel. If they have that meeting Margaret told you about, they might have taken her there."

Morgan turned and stared at the harbormaster's office. "Maybe. I'd sure like to stay here, though, and keep an eye on that man in there. He just might go somewhere."

"You think he's going to lead you to Margaret?" Call asked.

"All I know is that my instinct tells me that he knows where she is."

"OK." Call reached into his coat pocket and produced a revolver. He handed it handle first to Morgan. "You ever use one of these?"

"Not really. I took target practice with my uncle from time to time, but I've always favored the blade."

"We're fresh out of those," Call said. "You take this. It won't do much damage. It's a .32, but it will work. We'll go over to the Francis, and if nothing happens in the next hour or so, you can catch a cab and join us."

"Fine," Morgan said.

CHAPTER 49

Margaret ran past the warehouse and toward the waiting tugboat. She stepped around several bales of rope that were curled beside the dock and gingerly placed her foot on the gangplank. It swayed slightly with the wind that was picking up along the harbor. With her hands tied behind her back, she knew she would have to work at keeping her feet under her.

She inched out onto the swaying bridge of rope and wooden planks, doing her best to keep her weight directly over her feet. At any other time and given any other circumstance, she would have pranced across the makeshift bridge. But having her hands tied behind her and standing on the swaying gangplank in the darkness sent a bolt of terror exploding down her spine and legs to the very tips of her toes.

She stood there for a moment, looking at the dark water below. The sounds of the men searching for her in the warehouse had grown more intense. The men sounded frantic and determined. They were also getting closer to the door. If they opened it and looked in the direction of where she was teetering in despair on the gangplank, everything would be over. The boat wasn't that far away from the warehouse, and she'd be easy to spot. Her figure standing against the lights on the boat would be a dead giveaway.

She swallowed hard. For a moment she would become part of the Queen's guard. She would march without thought of the water below. She wouldn't lose her balance, because there wouldn't be time. Shaking herself slightly, she stuck her chin out and walked quickly over the lengthy gangplank. She wouldn't look down, only straight ahead.

Just as she neared the side of the boat, she heard the door to the warehouse door open. She jumped for the deck of the boat and tumbled into a heap beside the bulkhead wall of the engine compartment.

Her heart was pounding. She could hear several men yelling. They were trying to attract the attention of the men who had been guarding the gate to the docking area.

She could also hear Fallon Kennedy. He screeched, "You were right, I suppose. I never should have left her."

There was a pause while a second man mumbled his response, and then Kennedy took up the talk once again. "No, I won't go back to the play, not tonight, not ever. The play's financial backer is gone, and I'll be gone." He laughed. "They'll figure we ran off together."

"We'd better search around the other side of the warehouse," the second man said. "I doubt she'll have gotten past our guards up there."

"If we don't find her, we'll do a better search of the warehouse," Kennedy responded.

She listened as the two men began their trek around the large warehouse. It would take them some time to complete that. By then, she might find a spot on the boat to hide. She didn't know where the boat was going, and she really didn't care so long as it would take her away from here. She would have to move quickly. At any moment one of the boat's crew might discover her.

She got to her feet and ran to the aft well deck of the boat. Her blue dress blew up in the wind when she rounded the corner, and she ran directly into a stack of boxes sitting in the dark. Pain raced through her shins. She fell to the deck hard. Her dress tore with a ripping sound as she hit the deck, collapsing into a painful heap.

Margaret bit her lip hard. Not being able to cry out only added to the pain, and tears began to flow in a steady stream down her cheeks.

She rolled over against the wall of the rear cabin and slowly pulled her legs under her. Keeping her weight against the wall, she slid up, pushing with her throbbing legs. She stood there for a moment, panting and fighting the pain.

Blinking back the tears, she looked over the aft well deck. It was filled with long crates marked SPRINGFIELD RIFLES–U.S. ARMY. She had picked the one boat that was going where she didn't want to go.

Margaret edged her way along the wall of the rear cabin and rounded the corner carefully. She saw a seaman up ahead that had just come out of the lower compartment. The man had left the door open, and a faint yellow light gleamed softly out of the belly of the ship. She drew herself back around the corner, hoping the man wouldn't decide to reverse direction and come to where she stood on the aft deck.

Waiting a few moments, she peered once again around the corner. The man had gone. The door was still open, and that in itself would be a great help. Without her hands in front of her, she welcomed any open door.

She moved down the deck hurriedly. The open door hid her from the view of anyone who might decide to walk back in her direction, but that wouldn't be for long and she knew it.

Quickly she darted into the open door. To her left was a plank door that obviously led to the rear cabin. She could hear men's voices laughing. The men were obviously playing cards, and one of them had lost in a way that drew the amusement of the rest of the group.

The door to her right was open to the galley and a small dining room beyond. Margaret knew there would be no place to hide in that direction. There would be too much traffic with men coming and going at all hours. The only place left to go was below. A flight of steel stairs stood in front of her, and she walked toward them and began descending into the belly of the tugboat. From the sounds, she knew it was the engine room.

The stairs spiraled down, and she soon found herself staring at two shovels leaned against the large boiler door. A fire blazed on the other side and gleamed through the small vents. The pipes overhead were hot, and several joints spewed gassy jets of steam. The air was heavy with humidity. Sweat was beginning to slide down her back, making her very uncomfortable.

The place was empty, at least for now. No doubt the men who worked here were gambling, and Margaret wished them well. She needed the time to decide what to do next. She padded around the small room, looking for spaces behind the vents and pipes where she might hide. Several seemed to be inviting.

A large metal shield held the pile of coal on the floor in place and keep it from spilling. The shield's metal edge might offer her a chance to free her hands.

She moved over to it, stepping on and then sinking into the pile of coal. The small nodules of greasy rock crunched beneath her feet and wrapped her ankles with black, oily grime. She waded through it until she came to the edge of the shield. She turned around. The shield was smooth, but there were several notches, left there from shovels no doubt. It might be slow going, but she had to try.

She began to move her arms up and down, rubbing the rope that bound her hands over the notches. The rope ground and bumped the notch. She could feel the rope catch. She pressed back and lifted up until she felt strands begin to break. Now down again and then up, once more catching the rope with the metal tears. It was loosening. She could feel it. Bending low, she gave another push until the rope caught on the gash in the metal. She slid the rope back and forth in a sawing motion. Finally, with one last push, the rope broke.

She grabbed her wrists, massaging them to life once again. She unwound the last of the rope and stumbled through the coal and out to the floor.

Suddenly she heard voices coming from the corridor above. She would have to find a hiding place and find it fast. The engine's turbines were still, but she knew they would soon be turning. Perhaps that would be a good place to hide. With the turbines moving, few men would dare to search that area very carefully.

Several large pipes ran down the sides of the boat beside the turbine wheels. There was very little room behind them, but maybe there was enough for her. She stepped over them and lay down, stretching herself out behind the pipes. One of the pipes was cool, and a slight touch showed her the other one was hot. She would have to keep her distance from that one.

From where she lay, she could see the engine room and the pile of coal. It was then that a thought of horror hit her. She had left the rope that was used to bind her hands on the pile of coal. She could only hope and pray the men didn't see it.

Margaret waited for several minutes until she heard the sound of men coming down the metal stairs. She saw them gather in the engine room. One was evidently the captain of the tug. She could clearly see Fallon Kennedy with his bright red hair.

"She wouldn't have come down here," Fallon said. "It's too dirty."

"You think not?" the captain asked. "I don't have much time for a search. We have to unload this cargo of yours on the *Francis* before the tide."

"I'd say just get underway when you're ready, Captain. Even if the woman is here, she can't do us much harm."

Then Margaret saw the large man come down the stairs. From this distance she could recognize him. It was one of the men that she and Leslie had seen that night in the pressroom, the man Leslie had identified as O'Brien. Leslie had said the man controlled the mob on the coast, and he acted the part. He got to the bottom of the stairs, a smug expression on his face.

"Your man here doesn't think the woman would come down here," the captain said. "Guess he thinks it's too dirty for a lady."

"Oh, is that right?"

"She might not even be on board," Kennedy said.

"She's here all right. I found this."

Margaret had to stifle a gasp when she saw what the man held out in his hand. It was the piece of her dress that she had torn on the crate.

CHAPTER 50

Fredo knew right where to look for the Francis Hotel. It was located in one of the seedier locations in town, near the waterfront and the rundown tenements of the lower East Side. It hardly looked like a hotel, with shutters drawn and a faint light in the lobby that peeked out around the painting on the smoky glass of the front door.

The three men bounded up the concrete steps, and Fredo jerked open the front door. They spotted a man behind the desk, hunched over a newspaper and using a pencil to make notes. The man was thin with a liquid, pasty complexion broken up only by the dark circles around his eyes. He was bald except for three separate bunches of hair that he had plastered with grease to the top of his otherwise smooth head.

Call pulled Fredo aside. "I think you'd better talk to the man since you're the only badge we have."

"Yeah, sure. A woman involved, and you do the talking. A bald man, and you give the job to me."

Call grinned. "That's about the idea." He sauntered up to the counter. "Do you have a phone I can use?"

The man looked up at him, cocking his head. "Phones cost money."

Call reached into his pocket and pulled out a dollar bill. He laid it on the desk. "Will that work?"

"OK by me," the man replied. He hooked his thumb in the direction of the back office. "We got us a telephone in there. Is it a local call?"

"Of course," Call said. "Won't take more than a minute or so."

The man reached across the desk and picked up the greenback. "You aren't expecting change are you?"

"From you?" Call said. "Not on your life."

"Then go ahead. Take as much time as you need."

Call swung the waist-high door open and stepped behind the counter. He walked into the back office and closed the door behind him.

The man looked up at Fredo.

"How can I help you?"

"I'm supposed to be at a meeting here tonight. You seen any men come in looking for a room?"

"Lots of men look for rooms."

Fredo smiled. "This one is a rather large man. He has red hair, or at least what's left of it is red. He would be well dressed in a suit and tie."

The man scratched his chin, blinking his eyes rapidly as he thought over Fredo's description. "I can't see as I've seen anyone like that. I'd have remembered it, too, if I did."

"Well, we'll just wait around for him. Maybe he'll show."

"Fine." The man pointed to a threadbare red sofa and chair with a pile of papers strewn over a rickety coffee table set in front of them. "Just have yourself a seat and wait all you want."

Fredo stepped back and motioned for O'Leary to join him. The two men took a seat.

"Now who would Call be on the phone to?" O'Leary asked.

"Beats me," Fredo shrugged. "He's got no wife and kids."

"Who would have him?"

"That's probably a good question for any of us. Young Fairfield's the only man among us who looks like the settling-down kind. I think this thing tonight hit him rather hard."

"In his frame of mind, do you think it's a good idea for him to have a gun?"

"Normally, I'd say no. But he doesn't strike me as the kind of man to go off half-cocked. Now you, on the other hand, O'Leary, I don't know if I'd put a loaded weapon in your hand."

O'Leary laughed and slapped the left side of his chest. "Well, I carry one anyway. I ain't about to go spooking about in this town in the middle of the night without one." He leaned in Fredo's direction. "You really think Dixon had anything to do with this?"

"All I know is somebody is getting information to the Tommy-knockers who run the shipping trade around here. It ain't me, it ain't Call, and it ain't you. They have a powerful reason to keep our noses out of the Fetters murder too. I suspect it's to try to stop us from finding out about their gun shipment."

"So you don't believe this business about this being connected in some way to the *Titanic*?"

"I haven't heard anything about that. You must know a lot more than I do."

O'Leary rolled his head. "I hear stories."

"A fine thing when the newspapers know more about what's going on in this town than the police."

"Stories like that have legs."

"Well, what's the story?"

"Something about the Irish planting a bomb on the *Titanic*. I guess things didn't work out quite right, though. The blamed thing sunk before it was supposed to."

"Why would they do a thing like that?"

O'Leary scooted closer to him. "Somebody paid them, somebody who had a personal reason to do it."

Fredo smiled. "That does sound like nonsense. I don't think anybody would believe it, even if it were true."

"Oh, I'm not saying it's true. I'm just saying it's a story."

It took about ten minutes longer for Call to emerge from the back office. His face was hard. He barely said a word of thanks to the man at the desk before he marched over to where Fredo and O'Leary were seated. "Let's go," he said. "We're on a wild-goose chase here."

Fredo and O'Leary got to their feet and followed Call out the door and down the stairs. "How do you know that?" Fredo asked.

"Because the *Francis* we're looking for is a ship, not a hotel."

"How'd you find that out?" O'Leary asked.

"I called the harbormaster and pretended to be the Navy. I asked if the pilot for the *Francis* had showed up yet." He shrugged. "Just on a bluff."

"Remind me not to play poker with you," Fredo said.

"The man said the pilot was due in any minute, so we don't have any time to waste. We've got to get to the Brooklyn navy yard." Call put up his hand and signaled for a taxi.

"Why the navy yard?" O'Leary asked.

"That was the second call I made, to Senator William Alden Smith in Washington, D.C. The man owes me a favor."

"Wasn't exactly a local call," Fredo smirked.

"No, I guess not. I told Smith about what we suspect and the fact that it might be tied in with the *Titanic*. I also told him a Secret Service agent was killed tonight. He's calling the navy yard and having a launch and a boarding party stand by for us. If we don't get there when the guns are on board, we'll just wait for them to show up. Ought to be quite a fireworks display."

"What about Fairfield?" Fredo asked.

"We don't have time to go by and get him, I'm afraid. Besides, I'd kind of like to keep the boy out of harm's way."

CHAPTER 51

Morgan stood near the edge of the dock for some time and then began to pace back and forth. He felt like a fool for playing a hunch and not staying with Call. It was so unlike him. Morgan had always believed in doing the thing that was clear and right in front of his eyes, not in obeying some hidden impulse that he couldn't see or put his finger on. But here he was, doing just what he'd told himself he'd never do.

The Brass Rail nearby was doing its usual business. Morgan could tell by the small amount of smoky noise pouring out the door that there wasn't a big crowd. The lights were on, however, and a pair of women who looked to be drumming up business for the night straightened their skirts and marched inside as if they owned the place. Minutes later one of the women came out with her arm draped around a sailor. The man was barely able to stand, but he did laugh. She joined him in the merriment, and arm in arm they staggered into the darkness down the street.

The harbormaster's office was just as they had left it, and he'd been wrong about the man inside leaving the place to go somewhere he could follow. With each minute that ticked by, he felt more and more foolish. *Suppose Margaret was at the Francis Hotel?* he wondered. *She'd be there needing him and he'd be taking a walk near the dock. How would he be able to explain it to her?*

It comforted him to think of Margaret as still alive, still in the present tense. If she was alive, he wouldn't care what it took to explain his actions. He'd be so overjoyed at seeing her that he'd gladly take the next fifty years to make amends.

He watched as a taxicab rounded the square next to the waterfront, wondering if Call and the others were coming back for him. He hoped so. He felt foolish enough as it was.

He stepped away from the streetlamp and watched as the cab pulled up alongside the harbormaster's office. A man dressed in a blue peacoat and a cap pulled low over his eyes got out and paid the driver. The man turned abruptly, marched up the ramp to the office door, and walked in.

When the taxi started to pull away, Morgan stepped out in front of it, signaling it to stop.

The driver slammed on his brakes. Morgan saw the panicked look on the man's face at being brought to so sudden a stop. The driver stuck his head out the window. "You need a ride?"

Morgan walked around to where the man sat. "Not right now. I'd just like to know who you dropped off at the harbormaster's."

"Just a pilot," the man said. "I take them fellas here all the time in the middle of the night."

"Fine. Thank you." Morgan stepped away from the vehicle.

"You sure you won't be needing a ride?"

"Not yet. Maybe in an hour or so if you swing back by here."

"All right. If I can, I will."

With that, the man stepped on the gas and sent the car chugging around the circle and back out to the main thoroughfare. Morgan watched the taillights disappear.

He walked over to the front of the office and stood next to the rail that led up the stairs. He could hear the two men talking inside, but he couldn't make out what was being said. He waited several minutes and then walked off into the darkness to wait further.

It didn't take long before the pilot came out the door and down the stairs. Morgan watched as the man walked quickly away, moving down the row of gates that led to the docks below. Morgan fell into place, working at keeping up while staying out of sight.

It wasn't long before the man heard Morgan's footsteps behind him. He came to a sudden stop and turned around. "Hey, who goes there?"

Morgan sheepishly stepped out of the shadows. "I'm sorry. I didn't mean to frighten you. I was out for a walk and thought I'd stick close to you for a ways. This doesn't seem to be a very safe place."

The man looked Morgan up and down and, seeing his suit and boyish face, smiled. "No, I guess it's not at that. You're welcome to walk with me for a ways, but I'm not going much farther. I have a job to do tonight."

"Is that so? And what is your job?"

The two of them walked along the street.

"I'm a pilot. I take the ships out of the harbor and make sure they get to a safe place before I come back."

"You must know this place pretty well then."

"Yes, I do."

"Do you know any warehouses around here that use sawdust on the floor?"

The man stopped and stared at him. "You must be new." He pointed to the numerous warehouses that dotted the water below. "I'd say they all do. They think it makes it easier to slide the crates and boxes into place."

This was a job the man had obviously done for some time, Morgan decided. The man was just over six feet. His build was average, filled out at the chest. The beard he sported was trimmed in a square shape at the jaw line. Morgan placed the man in his forties.

They began their walk once again.

"And which ship will you be piloting tonight?"

"The *Francis*. I'm picking her up here on the Hudson and taking her down just past Governors Island."

Morgan's mind raced. If the *Francis* wasn't a hotel but a ship, then that was what Ed Leslie had found out. That was why he'd been in the office of the harbormaster. And it stood to reason that if the men who kidnapped Margaret had taken her anywhere, it would have been to that ship. He tried to sound calm, but his heart was racing. "And how will you get out to the *Francis?*"

The man stopped and pointed to a gate, not more than a hundred yards away. "See that gate?"

"Yes."

"I have me a tug waiting to take me on board down there. So you see, I don't have much farther to walk with you. You'll be on your own."

"And do they know it's you that's coming?"

The man grinned. "I do know most of the tug captains. They might not know it's me, but they'll be waiting on somebody."

Morgan reached into his pocket and pulled out the handgun. He pointed it directly at the man. "Then it will be me they're waiting on, not you."

The man's mouth fell open. "What are you trying to do, rob me? I don't carry much money and, from the looks of you, you don't appear to need any."

"No, I just want your coat and hat and your silence."

"What for?"

"Someone's life is at stake." He waggled the gun. "Now take your coat off."

The man took off his coat and dropped it at Morgan's feet and then threw his hat on top of it. "This is silly. I don't understand."

Morgan reached into his pocket with his left hand and pulled out a ten-dollar bill. He handed it over to the man. "That ought to cover the cost of the coat and hat."

The man looked at the fresh bill. "By twice. I just don't understand why. You won't be able to pilot that ship."

"I won't have to. I just need to get on board."

Morgan took his own suit coat off and handed it over to the man. "Here, you can wear this." He shrugged on the man's coat and then felt in the pockets. There was a pipe and a pouch of tobacco, some matches, a length of cord, and a pocketknife. He pulled out the cord. "This ought to do. Now turn around."

The man slowly turned, and Morgan tied his hands together. There were a good two or three yards left of the cord when he finished. He pulled the man over to a lamppost and secured him there, tugging the knots tight. "Good, that ought to hold you for a while. The police will find you in an hour or so, and then you can tell them your story."

"They won't believe me. A man pays me for my coat and hat and then ties me up. Now would you believe that?"

Morgan walked around to face him. "No, I suppose not. You try anyway. Do you carry any identification with you?"

The man nodded. "In my inside pocket."

Morgan felt for the papers and pulled them out. He held them under the streetlamp. They were certificates and a license. "Good." He turned to walk away but then stopped and looked back. "I'm sorry. I didn't get your name."

"Mannix, Jeff Mannix. And I didn't get your name either, mister."

"Fairfield, Morgan Fairfield."

"I just don't understand why you're doing this, Fairfield."

"Well, if everything goes all right, you can read about it tomorrow on the front page of the *New York Herald*. If it doesn't go so well, you can read my name in the obituaries."

CHAPTER 52

Morgan stuck his hands in his pockets and tried his best to whistle as he walked to the gate the man had pointed out to him. He knew he had to do everything possible to maintain a look of boredom about him, to notice very little and to react to nothing. Only if he blended into the surroundings could he possibly hope to discover Margaret's whereabouts. He had gotten her into this mess, and if it cost him his life he was going to make certain that he got her out of it.

It was only a hunch that Margaret was actually on the tugboat. Leslie might have discovered the *Francis* was a ship, not a hotel. Whoever killed him and took Margaret would no doubt be taking her to the *Francis*. At least he hoped so.

When he got to the gate he could see men running on the dock below him. They were frantically looking for something or someone. If he could board the tugboat and have it make its rendezvous with the

Francis, then perhaps he could leave her here in the safety of whatever hiding place she had already found. The idea gave him hope, but it made him nervous too.

One of the guards spotted him as he walked down the docking area toward the warehouse. The man shook another man next to him and pointed at Morgan. They both turned and walked in Morgan's direction.

When they got closer, Morgan could sense the toughness of the men in the way they scowled at him. "Who are you and what do you think you're doing here?" one of them asked.

Morgan forced a smile. "I'm the pilot, Jerry Man . . . freid." He almost made the mistake of using Mannix's name, but then at the last moment changed it. It might sound similar enough to shake any suspicion if anyone had heard of the man. Of course, there was the possibility that he'd be questioned closer. He pushed that idea out of his head.

The guards exchanged glances and then looked at the tug below. "All right," the man who had questioned him said, "you better get down there then. They're probably expecting you."

"I'm sure they are." He sauntered between the two guards and made his way down the dock and past the warehouse. He could hear activity inside, along with shouting.

When he got to the gangplank, he walked across it and toward the stern. The men were in the area of the aft well deck spreading tarps over a collection of large boxes. Morgan tried to look away when they spotted him. He had managed to see that one of the boxes was marked U.S. ARMY, and he did his best to give the men the impression that he hadn't seen a thing. "I'm the pilot," he said. "I'm looking for your captain."

One of the sailors stood erect and pointed forward. "He's up in the wheelhouse." The man looked at him carefully. "Where's Mannix?"

Morgan started walking forward. "He came down with the flu so they sent me." He didn't stop to endure further questioning, He only hoped the captain wouldn't be so inquisitive. Morgan knew that he would seem to be quite young to be a pilot. Maintaining a degree of silence would help him. It had always been his experience that the young and inexperienced people talked the most. Silence spoke of maturity, and he was going to do his best to give that impression.

He passed an open door that no doubt led down to the engine room and the galley area. He could hear men talking loudly and the noise of boxes and gear being moved. He climbed the stairs that led to the wheelhouse and opened the door, stepping inside.

Three men stood talking by the gauges and the ship's wheel. One seemed to be the captain. He had a cap and a white beard, along with a look of salty authority. The man beside him was a sailor, and the third man was dressed in a suit, a large man with balding red hair.

The captain looked up in Morgan's direction. "Who are you?"

"I'm Jerry Manfreid, the pilot for the *Francis*," Morgan said.

The man cocked his head at Morgan and blinked his eyes. "Where's Mannix?"

"He came down sick with the flu, so they sent me."

The captain shook his head. "I don't know about that."

Morgan once again forced a laugh. He did his best to make it sound as low as possible. "Why? Pilots may be godlike, but we do get sick."

The remark brought a smile to the captain's face and a temporary sense of relief to Morgan.

"You have your papers?" The Captain asked.

"Of course I do." Morgan reached into his inside pocket and pulled out the folded pilot's certificate and license. He shook them and stuck them back down into his pocket.

The captain held his hand out. "Well, let me see them."

Morgan reached into his coat pocket and, pulling out Mannix's pipe, stuck it in his mouth. He figured it would give him that same sense of authority it no doubt gave its owner. "Why should I? I'm not piloting your tug here. That's your job. Mine's the *Francis*. I'll show my papers to the captain there."

"The man's got gall," the sailor said. "He sounds like a pilot."

The captain looked at the large man in the suit. The man returned his glance with a wave of the hand, almost dismissing the entire event.

Fixing his gaze on Morgan, the captain stroked his beard. "All right, I'll let you be his problem."

"I won't be his problem, captain. I'll be his solution. You think I've got nothing better to do than come out on a night like this for a boat ride?"

The captain stuck his hands in his pockets and rocked back and forth on the balls of his feet. "You seem a little young to me, that's all." He looked Morgan over carefully. "That looks like Mannix's pipe."

"Jeff got me started on it," Morgan said. The fact that he had used the man's first name seemed to make some difference in the captain's demeanor. He appeared to relax a little.

"The man's a bloody chimney."

"That he is," Morgan said. "But it does keep the hands warm on a cold night."

Morgan fished around in his coat pocket and pulled out the tin of pipe tobacco that Mannix carried. He pried open the lid and began to fill the bowl of the pipe. The sound of the door opening brought him to attention. The man who'd been calling himself Hunter Kennedy stepped onto the bridge area. His red hair was tousled, and his eyes blazed.

"We found this in the coal pile," he said. He held out the piece of rope Margaret had cut from her wrists. Kennedy spotted Morgan.

Morgan pushed the back of his cap up, lowering the bill over his eyes. Kennedy would be the only man who could recognize him, and that would be disastrous. If that happened, he not only wouldn't be able to help Margaret, someone would have to help him.

"That's the pilot we're taking out to the *Francis*," the captain said.

Morgan nodded his head in Kennedy's direction and poked his hand into his coat pocket. He groped for a match and, turning his back to the group, struck it against the bulkhead.

He raked the flame over the brown substance, moving it back and forth and sucking gently. The bowl of the pipe came alive with glowing embers. Puffing the thing to life, he bit his tongue. He had hoped the smoke might help disguise his looks, but it was making him queasy instead. He was still glad he had thought of masquerading himself with Mannix's habit. Anyone who had ever met him would never place him with the use of tobacco.

Kennedy ignored him. "We best get underway, Captain, if everything's ready." He glanced at Morgan. "I really don't think we need to worry about our problem."

The large man in the suit nodded at the captain, and he reached over and slid open a window. Looking down at a deckhand below, he bellowed, "Cast off." He then pulled a plug from a brass tube on the bulkhead. Leaning over, he shouted into it. "All ahead slow."

They could hear the engine turning and the blades chopping at the black water. Easing its way from the dock, the tugboat churned into the middle of the river.

Morgan turned and stepped to the door. He needed to get as far away from Kennedy as possible. The darkness on the bridge area helped him to conceal his identity, but that might not last. He started to open the door.

"Where are you going?" the captain asked.

"Down to the galley for some coffee," Morgan said. He forced the words out in a semigrowl, maintaining the attitude that people seemed to associate with pilots.

When he opened the door, Margaret was standing there, held by a sailor who had his hand on her arm. The man had been reaching around her for the door to the bridge, but Morgan had opened it first.

She looked him in the eye and knew at once who he was. There was no way to fool Margaret, and he could see the panic in her face. She almost screamed.

Morgan quickly stepped back into the wheelhouse. He looked at the captain. "You seem to have a passenger." He spoke nonchalantly, just as if it was the business of the tug to take people out to waiting ships. Morgan didn't want to let on that he knew something was amiss. He also wanted to communicate some words of comfort to Margaret, something that said he had a plan, even if he didn't.

The man marched Margaret onto the bridge; Morgan's eyes riveted on her. She made eye contact with him but didn't linger long with her gaze. The woman was smart. She would do anything to keep him free.

"Well, I'll go get my coffee." Morgan turned to face the captain. "I'll let you tend to your passenger. Call me when we get close to the *Francis*."

He closed the door behind him and started down the stairs. His heart was beating faster now. Margaret had been captured. A thought flashed through his mind. *That might not be so bad. Without them looking for her, I just might have the ship to myself.*

CHAPTER 53

Morgan climbed down the stairs, pain lancing his heart at the thought of leaving Margaret up there with the men still holding her. He would have to think of something that would occupy them so that he could get her away, but what?

He moved along the side of the tug to a door that was not closed securely. It opened when the tug bounced over the water and then closed with a bang, only to creak open once again. Grabbing the door, he pushed it ajar and stepped inside. He turned and fastened it securely.

The stairs in front of him led down to the engine room. He could hear the chugging of the engines and a growling whine from the turbines. The galley was to his right, and he trudged inside, bracing himself against the door. It might take some time for him to get his sea legs, especially on a boat this small.

A sailor was downing a last cup of coffee when he walked in. The man looked up at him from the table. He was caked in coal dust, and Morgan imagined that he might have been one of the men who had found Margaret. The man was thin, with beady black eyes set in a weathered face, sunken and old before its time. His face was covered with scruffy black hair, too thin to be called a beard.

"I'm the pilot. Just looking for a cup of coffee."

The man motioned with his head to a pot that sat on the small gas stove. It was secured in place by a thin brass rod, and the flame was so low that it was barely a flicker. Morgan picked up a dirty white cup with an oversized base from a rack on the counter. It was marked by red letters that spelled out the name of the tugboat, THE GLORY B. He unhinged the coffeepot and poured a cup, then secured the pot back into position.

Turning, he faced the man. "Looks like we have a little chop tonight." He knew the observation might sound lame coming from a pilot, but it was the best he could do.

The man set down his cup and pulled a cigarette from behind his ear. "I suppose. It's worse most nights." He got to his feet and took the knit cap from his head. He picked up the globe that surrounded an oil lamp. The thing was swinging above the table in a brass cradle that was secured to the bulkhead. Bending his head into the flame, he puffed the cigarette to life and gently pressed the glass cover back into place around the flame.

Morgan noticed several of these lamps suspended in the galley. They were all set in the wall and had flames burning brightly, their wicks sapping up the oil from the clear glass reservoirs. He held his cup of black, tarlike coffee up to his lips. "How long you figure before we get out there?"

The man cocked an eyebrow at him. "You ought to know that." He felt the table to pick up the vibrations of the engine. "Skipper's got her up to half speed, that'll put us out there in thirty minutes, or maybe a little better."

"I thought so," Morgan lied. "Just wanted to see what you thought."

The man took off his black peacoat and hung it on one of the wooden pegs behind him. He wiped the top of his forehead with the back of his hand, producing a black smear. "I best get back at it." Grinning, he jerked his thumb back in the direction of the coat. "I don't need that much where I come from, only when I come up here." With that the man left the room and climbed down the stairs to the engine room. Morgan walked over to the table and took a seat.

There was a slight chill in the place, but the heat coming up the stairs from the engine room made it far more comfortable near the door. He could only imagine what working on a tug must be like in winter, when most of the men would probably prefer the duties down in the engine room.

He sloshed the coffee around in his cup, watching it as it coated the sides with an oily brown residue. Drinking it would be out of the question, but it felt good in his hands. His mind raced as he thought what to do next. There was little time to form a plan, but somehow he knew he had to find a way to get everyone's attention away from Margaret and away from him.

Where could Call be? he wondered. *No doubt he's waiting at the Francis Hotel. Or else he's looking for me.*

Morgan paced, occasionally looking down the hall at the engine room and then out the small porthole at the lights of the city. The sight of a police boat would have been welcome, as would anything else that might have meant some change in the smugglers' plans. As it was, there seemed to be nothing he could do, nothing but wait until they had made contact with the *Francis*. Morgan still had Call's revolver. He would use that then.

It was more than twenty minutes later before the sailor who had been on the bridge with the captain opened the door and tramped into the galley. He walked over to the rack and picked up a cup, then unfastened the pot and poured.

The man turned and held the cup to his lips. "Captain wants me to tell you that we got the *Francis* in sight. You'll be wanted on the bridge now."

Morgan pulled the pipe out of his coat pocket. It still had the tobacco he'd let go out stuffed inside, crammed down into a mass of charcoal cinder. "You go ahead. I'll just relight my pipe and be up with you in a minute."

"Suit yourself." The man set down his cup with the remains of his coffee and walked past Morgan and out the door.

This is it, Morgan thought. *If I ever had an idea, it has to come now.* Having to think was enough to drive the last vestige of creativity out of him. But thinking was a reporter's job, and he knew it. A man with a deadline couldn't wait on a muse. The muse had to come in a busy room full of people and noise while the reporter hunched over a typewriter and begged for his brain to function.

His eyes fell on the lamp swinging overhead. Jumping to his feet, he looked around for something to lift it out of its cradle. He grabbed for a towel that had been used to wipe off the leavings of the evening's meal. The towel was caked with something orange, probably chili. He lifted the hot lamp slowly from its carriage.

He moved out into the hall, bracing the flaming lamp as he opened the door. There was no time for mistakes. If anyone saw him, all would be lost. He only hoped the men would all be forward to watch the *Glory B* as it nestled itself into position beside the *Francis*.

He stepped out onto the bobbing deck and made his way along the passageway to the rear of the tug. Stopping at the corner, he craned his neck to see if any of the men he had seen when he came on board where still there. They were gone. The tarp that covered the boxes had been secured.

He walked over to the boxes and set the glowing lamp down beside the covered cargo. Morgan tore back the corner of the tarp and unscrewed the small lid on the top of the glass reservoir. He picked up the lamp and began to shake some of the oil over the corner of the first box. Then kicking at the tarp to free it, he continued to spread the liquid over the first row of the deadly cargo.

Morgan wondered if there might be ammunition mixed in with the shipment. He knew that would provide more than a simple fire; it would produce an explosive inferno. It no doubt would also keep the men who might try to put the fire out at a safe distance.

He stepped back to put some room between him and the boxes. He was standing beside a fire bucket that hung on the bulkhead. *Just what they're going to need*, he thought. He held the lamp up. Just as he started to throw it, a sailor stepped around the corner. "Hey, what ya doing back here?"

Morgan held up the lamp like he was trying to see. "I . . . I . . . was trying to look over your cargo."

The sailor frowned. "You ain't got no business here. We better go see the captain."

Morgan smiled. "I guess we'd better." He held the lamp out away from him and stared at the flame. "I think I should do something with this first."

He flung the lamp into the first row of boxes. It erupted into flame, spreading along the row as it lapped up the oil Morgan had poured.

The sailor's eyes widened. He yelled. "What are you doing?" He gazed back down at the spreading flame, frozen in terror.

Morgan grabbed the fire bucket off the wall and came down hard with it on the back of the man's head. The bucket broke, pieces of it flying in all directions.

The man moaned, dropped to his knees, and fell forward. Morgan was on him in a flash. He grabbed his head and sent it crashing to the deck with a loud thump. The man was motionless but still breathing. Morgan got to his feet. Grabbing the sailor by the ankles, he dragged him around the corner and away from the spreading fire. Looking back, he could see the flames licking the large wooden boxes. There wasn't much time.

Morgan straightened his jacket. Taking his cap off, he ran his fingers through his hair. It was hard for him to imagine doing such a thing, and under any other circumstance he knew it never would have happened. This night was different, though. Margaret was being held prisoner because of him. The whole idea sent a river of rage through him. He dropped his hands to his side, his fingers shaking.

Taking a deep breath, he marched toward the stairs that led to the bridge. He raced up the stairs and opened the door, stepping inside and forcing a smile. He lowered his voice. "You got the *Francis* in sight?"

The mate who had been sent to get him pointed out the window. "Can't miss her now."

Morgan glanced in the direction of the far wall. Kennedy blocked Margaret's face from his view. He was talking in muted tones, and from the way she was standing with her arms crossed, Morgan was certain the man's words, whatever they were, were drifting over her without effect.

He looked out the window at the *Francis*. He could see the outline of a ship in the darkness. Lights were twinkling from a number of the portholes. They formed the illusion of a bridge suspended over deep black water.

The captain shouted into the pipe on the wall, "All ahead slow."

Morgan heard the engines below chug and sputter. The *Glory B* was gliding now, right in the direction of the ship. The dark outline grew larger in the black sky. Stars were disappearing as the monolith swallowed them up.

The mate pointed in the direction of the big ship. "They have a ladder over the side and a docking station. We can off-load our cargo there."

The big man in the suit stepped out of the darkness and toward the window. The prospect of off-loading the cargo obviously interested him.

The captain blew down the pipe once again and yelled into it. "All stop." He then slid the side window open and shouted to the men below. "Make ready your lines. Get us secure to the landing dock." He looked back at the mate at the wheel. "Edge her into the loading dock."

With every moment that passed, Morgan was growing more restless. He could feel the *Glory B* gliding to the big ship. He stuck his hand in his pocket and felt for the revolver. For once the feel of cold steel was comforting. He had done so many things that were out of character—stealing a man's clothes at gunpoint and bashing another over the head with a bucket—that he wasn't about to stop with Margaret still in jeopardy.

The *Glory B* hit the loading dock with a jolt, the blow being absorbed by the coiled-rope cushion and rubber mats that lined the bow of the tug. Morgan reached out to take hold of the bulkhead.

He stepped forward and glanced in Margaret's direction. Her eyes were on him. They drew the attention of Kennedy, who turned around.

Just at that moment, everyone on the bridge heard the first alarm of fire. From down below the initial warning was followed by the sound of fast-running feet and yelling men. The captain stuck his head out the window and looked back. Morgan was certain the man could see the light from the flames. It was then that the first of the ammunition began to explode, bursts of loud charges that erupted into a deafening series of thunderclaps.

CHAPTER 54

The explosions on the aft deck sent everyone on the bridge of the *Glory B* into a panic, everyone, that is, except Morgan and Margaret. They both stood still while the others ran to the windows, opened them, and craned their necks for a look.

The captain continued to shout orders to the men below. "Break out the water buckets. Tie her up to the loading dock. Move, men, and fast."

He turned back to the bridge and tried to act calm, but Morgan could tell the man was in a panic. He was shaking as he spoke. "You're all going to have to get off and now. You, too, Mr. O'Brien." He spoke to the big man in the suit. "Go below and get on the *Francis*' loading dock. They have a ladder you can use. This boat can't stay tied up here for long, not with a fire on board."

The big man in the suit cursed. "I'm not going anywhere. None of us are, not with that cargo of mine going up in flames."

Kennedy stepped forward, holding Margaret by the elbow. "What about the woman here? We've got to get her off."

"Do what you want with her. You brought her."

Morgan waited until Margaret and Kennedy had gone down the stairs and then followed them. Several sailors were waving their arms, motioning for them to move quickly.

One by one, the group sided up to a spot on the bow where they could jump. A sailor had already gotten into position on the loading dock, and he caught them as they landed. Morgan followed Margaret and Kennedy and landed on all fours as new eruptions sounded from the aft deck of the *Glory B*.

The sailor untied the lines to the dock and threw them back onto the tug. "You're on your own now." With that he leaped back on board the tugboat and ran to fight the fire.

Morgan pointed to the ladder and once again lowered his voice. "We better get up there as quickly as we can. We don't know just when that thing is going to blow."

Morgan thought the *Glory B* made quite a picture. The blaze was in full bloom on the aft deck. Several crewmen were lowering their fire buckets into the ocean and then drawing them back up. They handed them off to others who ran and tried to douse the flames. Fresh explosions drove them back to cover.

"After you," Kennedy said to Margaret.

Margaret started up, followed immediately by Kennedy. He was several rungs behind her. The ladder, with small flat boards held in place by knots in the rope, was better than Morgan might have expected. Morgan knew it would be best to wait until both Margaret and Kennedy were safely on board before he started his climb. Having Margaret out of his sight, though even for a moment, grated on him.

He watched as Margaret lost her footing several times and grabbed the rope. His heart skipped a beat when he saw Margaret lose a shoe, the thing tumbling down the side of the ship and landing beside him on the loading dock with a thud.

Morgan bent down to pick it up, stuffing it into his pocket. As he pushed the shoe into his pocket, the revolver he'd been carrying slipped out. He tried to grab it, but it tumbled free and made a banging sound all the way down the side of the ship, finally hitting the water with a splash.

He breathed a sigh. The thing had made him uncomfortable, but it was something he might need. Looking up, he was relieved when he saw Margaret clear the side of the *Francis* with Kennedy behind her.

What happened next was up to him, and he knew it. He climbed the ladder quickly, all the while hoping Kennedy wouldn't decide to release it and send him tumbling to the deck below. There would be one less witness, even if he was the pilot. With each step he took on the ladder, his heart raced all the more. The higher he got, the more deadly the fall.

When he got to the top, he grabbed hold, swinging his leg over the side. Just as he went over the top of the rail, a gust of wind tore his cap off. Morgan looked down and watched it tumble into the darkness below. He hit the deck with a muffled thud.

Even from where he was on his hands and knees, it was plain to see that Kennedy recognized him. The man's eyes blazed. He was holding a gun on Margaret. "You! It was you, then."

Morgan got to his feet. "Yes, it was me."

"You started the fire."

There was another explosion on the *Glory B*. It rattled the windows on the tug. They all turned around to watch the eruption of flame.

"Yes, it was me, I'm afraid." He took Margaret's shoe from his pocket and handed it to her. She took it, and Morgan could tell that she wanted to kiss him for it.

Kennedy and Margaret stepped to the rail to watch the fire. It seemed to be gaining strength with each blast. They could, however, still make out the dark shapes of men trying to put the thing out. "You don't know what you've done." There was a sadness in his voice. "You must realize men could die there because of what you've done," Hunter said, "innocent men."

The thought was a sobering one for Morgan. It dropped a heavy curtain over his innocence, which was something he prized above everything. He had no desire to become the type of jaded man he'd seen at the newspaper, the kind of person who had no lines drawn around the perimeter of his soul. He knew there had been a desperation to his actions that had seemed to erase the lines. "I had to do something." He glanced at Margaret and then studied Kennedy. "Sometimes a man has to do what he wouldn't otherwise think about doing. You of all people should understand that."

"I've been doing things against my own desires for years. My father would call it a searing of the conscience."

"This is Fallon Kennedy," Margaret said. "Hunter was his brother."

"You're Hunter's brother?"

"That I am. I don't think he'd claim me, though, not at this point."

Morgan bowed his head slightly and shook it. "The man was quite a rogue." He looked up. "But he wasn't a murderer."

Once again the blaze on the *Glory B* roared. They all turned to look.

"And now we no doubt both are, for our own set of reasons, of course. Amazing, isn't it, how men in extraordinary circumstances manage to do extraordinary things?"

"I'm just trying to save the woman I love."

Fallon smiled. "And I am trying to save the country I love. Which is more commendable?"

"So now what are you going to do?" Morgan pointed at Kennedy's grip on Margaret. "You might as well let her go. She can't be of any further use to you."

It was then that they heard the sound of a megaphone from the water below. "Ahoy, the *Francis*. This is the Navy. We're coming on board."

Kennedy kept his hands on Margaret and pulled her over to the side. Morgan followed along. They looked down to see the small launch bobbing in the water beside the *Francis*. There were a number of armed sailors, and one officer was starting his climb up the ladder.

Morgan looked up and could see who he supposed to be the captain of the *Francis*. The man had stepped out on a catwalk that surrounded the bridge. He had his hands in his pockets and obviously appeared troubled.

Kennedy pointed his revolver at Margaret and then in the direction of the bow. "Let's go over there."

Morgan stepped toward him. "Let her go. Surely you can see now that all this is useless. She can't possibly help you."

Fallon looked over the side of the ship, staring at the water. "She just might be able to help me a great deal."

"Can't you see how hopeless your situation is?"

"Listen to me, schoolboy. I'm going to hold my gun behind her back and the three of us are going to stand here like we've been waiting for those swabbies all along, all grins and smiles. Then you're going to send them to find that captain up there. If you're a good boy, nothing will happen to her. Do you understand?"

Morgan nodded. "Perfectly."

It was only a matter of minutes before a dozen sailors carrying rifles and revolvers assembled on deck. They separated into two groups, the first going to the rear of the ship and the second, with the officer in the lead, stepping over to where the three of them were standing. "And who are you people?"

"I'm Morgan Fairfield from the *Herald*."

The man smiled and put his revolver back in his holster. "We have a couple more of your people in our launch." He smiled. "They ought to be up here in a minute or two, if they can work up the nerve to climb that ladder. Are you all right?"

Morgan glanced at Margaret and Fallon. "Yes, officer. We're fine."

The man looked back at the ladder area, and Morgan could see Call scrambling over the side. "There they are now. I'll leave you to them." He tipped his hat at Margaret. "Ma'am."

As the officer led the group of men away, Morgan turned to Kennedy. "Let me ask you something to satisfy my own morbid curiosity. Did your organization have anything to do with the attempt to plant a bomb on the *Titanic*?"

Fallon let a smile spread across his face. "Some of them did. They were paid and paid well. O'Brien, the man you left on the tug"—he paused to make certain the man's name connected with Morgan—"was quite insistent on making sure it never got out. Personally, I thought it would be good publicity."

"And that is why he had Fetters, the engineer from the *Titanic*, murdered?"

"Yes, his orders. I had nothing to do with it. My only interest were those guns you torched."

"And what about your contact on the paper?"

Call walked up just as Morgan asked the question. He stepped over to Morgan and put his hand on Morgan's shoulder. "If it was you that started that fire, I think you've been seriously underestimated. I also think you're being way underpaid." He looked at Margaret and smiled. "And, Miss Hastings, we're glad to see you. You've worried us considerably."

Fredo and O'Leary stepped up behind Call. It was plain to see that Fredo hadn't cared for the climb up the ladder. He was holding his arm and bending his elbow, and then he dropped both arms to his side and shook them. "That's why I joined the police force and not the fire department, a fear of heights and rickety ladders."

O'Leary was a good deal more chipper. He slapped Fredo's back and grinned. "I was right behind you, old man. I wouldn't have caught you, but I would have watched you fall. Would have made a nice story."

"Fine—my death, your story."

Morgan cleared his throat. "Gentlemen, this is Mr. Kennedy, the actor."

Fredo immediately sensed that something was wrong. He unbuttoned his coat and dropped his hands to his side.

"Nice to meet you, Kennedy," O'Leary said.

Margaret had been standing in silence. The gun behind her seemed to freeze her into place. She reached out for Morgan and grabbed his coat, pulling him closer. "That man. That's what I tried to tell you at the flower shop today."

Morgan looked back at O'Leary, along with Call. "Jake O'Leary?"

Margaret's words, and more importantly her stare, brought O'Leary to attention. His smile disappeared.

"He's one of the men Leslie and I saw talking that night in the pressroom. He discussed the plans about the *Francis* with the police captain and Fallon here."

"The mick!" Call hissed. He looked over at Morgan. "So Jake's the one who gave the orders for the men at the hospital. He's the reason the note we found wadded up in Fetters' brother's hand had the *Herald*'s phone number on it." Call moved toward O'Leary. "You little rat! You just couldn't wait, could you? It's not enough to have the power of the press. You have to manipulate the news and feel the power."

"What of it?" O'Leary took a step back. "I got in with those guys so I could learn more."

"So you could learn to collect their money and cover their tracks you mean. You're the one who told them where Gerry was staying. You put Patricia's life in danger and almost got her killed."

Call reached out and grabbed the man by the lapels of his coat. He shook him hard and then slapped him across the face, sending him to the deck.

O'Leary got to his knees, rubbing his cheek. "You'll be sorry about that." He reached into his coat and pulled out his revolver, pointing it at Fredo. "Take the copper's gun, Kennedy."

Fallon stepped from Margaret's side, revealing the gun in his hand. He stepped over and, opening Fredo's coat, pulled out the man's revolver. "You better get over there with them," he said.

"Just where do you two think you're going?" Fredo asked.

"We're not going anywhere," O'Leary responded. "We're staying right here. Of course we will have to shoot the four of you." He looked at Call. "It's simple. We'll put the gun in the madman's hand here. He's already been arrested for murder. He can even be the plant at the paper. Now he tries to kill us and shoots the woman by mistake. We wrestled with him and killed him before he could kill us all."

"Who would believe that?" Morgan asked.

"People don't have to believe it. We'll just tell it to our good friend Captain Casey. Homicide is his territory. The report will go down just as we say." He grinned. "It'll be a great story."

He shook the gun in Fredo's direction. "Move over there with those other two." He smiled. "We want a nice grouping."

Morgan pushed Margaret behind him. They were next to the rail. There was nowhere else to go. He could only hope the sailors who were conducting their search of the *Francis* would move quickly. One word from any of them would stop this in its tracks. He looked at Margaret and then at Fallon. "Hunter's brother, huh? Quite the hero."

"Shut up," O'Leary bellowed. "I'll get to you." He stepped closer to the small group. He lifted the gun and pointed it in Call's direction. "But first I'm going to deal with our ace reporter here. To be frank with you, Call, I've wanted to write your obit for years."

Fallon grabbed the man's arm. "I can't let you do that."

O'Leary seemed stunned. "Just stand back. You got as much riding on this as I do."

"Give me that." Fallon grabbed for the gun, but O'Leary fired. Fallon fell to his knees on the deck.

Both Fredo and Call pounced on the man in a flash. They grabbed for his arm and the gun but were greeted for their efforts by several more shots. Morgan had pushed Margaret back. Gunfire flashed while they wrestled with the man. Then O'Leary slowly slid to the deck. His eyes were wide open. His mouth was trying to form words that wouldn't come out.

Both Morgan and Margaret stepped over to Fallon.

He was clutching his upper shoulder, and blood oozed between his fingers. "Never mind me. I'll be all right."

The two of them then stepped over to where Call and Fredo were standing over O'Leary. "It's bad," Fredo said. "He won't make it off this ship."

Margaret looked back to where Fallon had been kneeling. The man was on his feet and had hobbled over to the railing. He was taking off his jacket.

"What do you think you're doing?" Morgan asked. Both he and Margaret moved closer, trailed by Fredo and Call.

Kennedy pointed his revolver at the group. "Just stay right where you are. Don't come any closer."

"That was a brave thing you did back there," Margaret said.

"And a cowardly thing to bring you into this. I should have known better." He looked past them. "But you'll do fine; those sailors of yours heard the shooting."

Morgan looked around and saw a group of the Navy men rounding the superstructure on the far side of the ship.

"But I won't be around to be arrested." He looked down at the dark water of the harbor. His red hair was flying in the breeze. "This is where I get off this cruise."

"You'll never make it," Morgan said, "not with that wound of yours. Stay here and we'll get you to a hospital."

Fallon smiled. "So you can patch me up to hang? No, thank you. I am only glad I won't have you people hanging over my head when I go to the God of my father."

"He is your God too," Margaret said.

The group could hear the sound of the sailors running along the deck behind them.

"He may not have been my God in times past, but I fear He soon will be."

Once again he looked down at the dark water below, then back up at Morgan with a smile on his face. "By the way, speaking of God's judgment. I had our poor little rich girl taken care of."

"Who are you talking about?"

"I figured you'd never be able to bring her to justice, not the way you work. It seemed to be up to me, with a little help from my friends."

"Are you talking about Kitty Webb?" Margaret asked.

"She did murder my brother. You know it and so do I. It's all the judge and jury I needed." The smile on his face widened. "Now she sleeps with the fish."

He looked at the group and then stepped over the rail. "Free Ireland." With that he stepped off the bow of the ship and plunged into the deep water far below.

The four stepped to the rail as the sailors ran up behind them. Fredo and Call took the men over to O'Leary and began to explain what had happened.

"Do you see him?" Margaret asked, still standing at the rail.

Morgan shook his head.

"Do you think that what a man does in the end can ever make up for what's gone before?" she asked.

"Forgiveness belongs to God."

"And to us. We can forgive."

"When it comes to Fallon Kennedy, forgiveness is something I find rather hard to deal with just now."

Margaret put her arm around him. "Perhaps you should just begin with forgiving yourself, Morgan."

"Perhaps I should."

APRIL 1913

EPILOGUE

The elegant mausoleums of Woodlawn Cemetery were more than enough for any industrial giant or even king to guarantee remembrance and a high degree of awe. Many of those buried there simply sought the respect in death that they hadn't been allowed to enjoy in life. While money had brought homage and deference to many of them, it had seldom earned them a kind word when their backs were turned. Those were the words reserved for funerals, words carefully searched out and prepared, perhaps even rehearsed. After all, many of the people who gave the speeches also left the funeral for the reading of the will.

The lawns were carefully manicured, and the sloping hills and tall shady trees gave it a sense of peace. The blue sky overhead made it a beautiful spring day for New York City, even if it was the day for a funeral. It had been almost a year since the *Titanic* disaster and six months of marriage for Mr. and Mrs. Morgan Fairfield.

Morgan and Margaret got out of their car, which was one of a long line of black limousines. Call and Gloria stepped out behind them. The four of them followed the small crowd past an ostentatious mausoleum that depicted the sphinx of ancient Egypt, complete with stone lions and baldheaded guards frozen in granite. The nine-foot giants had their arms folded and their eyes trained straight ahead.

"Quite impressive," Gloria said.

Call chuckled. "Most of these people are far more impressive as the subject of a tomb than they ever were in life. They built little of real importance, but they knew how to dig their graves."

"That is sad," Margaret said.

"I think it can be said," Call went on, "these people really know how to die."

"The truth is found in how we're looked upon by God," Margaret said, "not how our graves are viewed by the ones we leave behind."

Call smiled. "It's their last chance to spend what belongs to someone else now. If you ask me the poor are much happier."

"Speaking of the poor," Margaret said, "How is that woman Morgan told me about, the one who was shot at Patricia Bennett's house?"

"Gerry?" Call grinned.

"I think that was her name."

Call chuckled. "She's walking with a limp and cleaning the halls at the paper now. Of course she's walked funny since I've known her. Most of the time it's the booze. Now she has a real reason. She has her own place and a dog, a surly thing that's meaner than she is."

They walked over the gentle hill to the place where the Morgans had always been interred. The massive, angel-laden structure was made of polished white marble. Row upon row of chairs were set out on the surrounding lawn, and off to the side a string quartet was softly playing a piece from Mozart.

As the four of them took their seats, Morgan surveyed the crowd. His eyes roamed over the guests before coming to rest on the face of one old woman. He nudged Margaret, pointing the woman out with a subtle gesture. "Do you see whom I see?"

"The Saunders woman." She was seated in the second row, along with her servant Mortimer. "Why in the world would she be here?"

"This is a funeral she wouldn't want to miss. She's even wearing something besides that bridal gown of hers, even if it is a black mourning dress."

"It's amazing to see her here."

"She hasn't been outside that house of hers for forty-six years."

"She even has her hair done."

"Yes, every strand in place."

When the service was complete, the family stood in a reception line, with Morgan and Margaret at the end. Morgan kept his eye on Irene Saunders. The woman bypassed the rest of the family.

"Don't look now," Morgan said to Margaret in a low voice, "but she's coming in our direction."

The woman took short steps, an ivory-handled cane by her side. It was something she carried but didn't need. Mortimer walked along behind her. No matter how fragile she might appear, Morgan could tell that she was strong for her age. On this day, above all days, she seemed even stronger. Her face was still a pasty white, but she had a blush brushed into her cheeks for color.

Morgan nodded at her as she approached them. He reached out and took her hand. "How nice to see you, Miss Saunders. It is a lovely day, and I am glad you were able to come."

She smiled. "Yes, it's a beautiful day, and I wouldn't have missed it for the world." She took Margaret's hand. "And I am glad to see you, my dear."

Margaret bowed slightly. "Thank you, Miss Saunders. And thank you for the lovely silver tea service you sent as a wedding gift. I am only sorry you were unable to attend."

"I never go to weddings."

"Well, I do think Uncle J. P. would have been happy that you came here today."

The woman smiled. "I don't think so. In fact, I think the thought might upset him very much, which is exactly why I did come."

She looked at Margaret, squeezing her hand slightly. "My dear, might I borrow your young man for a few minutes?"

"Of course," Margaret said.

Taking Morgan's arm, Irene Saunders excused herself from her servant, and the two of them walked off to a spot under the shade of a large oak tree.

"I suppose this must be a happy day for you then, Miss Saunders. Wasn't it you who told us how sweet bitterness could be?"

"Yes, it was. I said it and I meant it." She looked around, over the cemetery and the markers as she watched the crowd begin to leave. "But it surprisingly doesn't feel nearly as good as I'd hoped."

"You've wasted a lot of years waiting for this day, Miss Saunders. I must say, my heart goes out to you."

"Don't you feel sorry for me, young man. If anything, you should hate me."

"Why would I do that?"

"Because, had it not been for that iceberg, I would have been the one responsible for the sinking of that ship and the terrible loss of your friends. The fact that I wasn't had nothing to do with any lack of effort on my part."

"Why would you do such a thing?"

"Your great uncle was scheduled to be on that ship." She bowed her head. "I suppose this was a day I had grown tired of waiting for."

"I read about what happened to you, Miss Saunders. I know it must have been exceedingly painful. But wouldn't it have been better to have forgiven the man and gone on with your life?"

She lifted her head, her ice-blue eyes boring into Morgan. "You don't understand. I loved your uncle. To forgive him would have meant letting go, and I've never wanted to let go of the man."

"I see."

"There's another matter in this forgiveness thing you speak of. It implies that I am better than he is, more virtuous, more righteous. I'm not, you know. I never was. He had very good reasons for leaving me at the church the way he did."

"I would suppose, then, that you're the one who needs the forgiveness, Miss Saunders."

"Yes, I do. That is why I came to you."

"But why me?"

"Because you are a very good man. I've seen that. I did have your life spared once during this investigation of yours." She smiled slightly. "I do have my ways among some of the rougher elements of this city. Frankly, I was more than a little afraid that you would find out about my involvement with this *Titanic* thing. At the same time, I was also hoping you would put the blame at your uncle's doorstep. You did neither."

"I didn't want to run with a story that I was only half sure of."

"You see, again your conscience protects you."

Morgan looked her in the eye. "For what it means, Miss Saunders, I forgive you. I'm sure that I'm speaking for my uncle, too, when I say that."

She hunched her shoulders, breathing a heavy sigh. "Good, I know that means a lot to you. I may have to think about it, though. You see, I have spent much of my life in bitterness, waiting for the man to die. Perhaps in time."

"We did pass a little chapel on our way into the cemetery. If it's forgiveness and peace you seek, I might suggest you go there. God's forgiveness is offered. It cost Him His Son, but it's yours for free."

"I pay for everything I get, young man."

"And you have been paying for years. Don't you think it's time you received something?"

She nodded, ever so slightly. "Perhaps you are right."

He squeezed her hand. "I know I am."

The two of them walked back to the group. Morgan looked up and caught sight of a man with windblown red hair, standing on a hill, looking down on them. It probably was no more than his imagination, or some bystander who happened to be passing by. He shook Margaret's arm. "Look, darling."

Margaret turned around and stared at him. "Look at what?"

He pointed up the hill, and Margaret turned to see. There was nothing there. The man was gone.

AUTHOR'S NOTES

The history of the *Titanic* disaster is the story of fascinating people and has shaped many of their lives forever. The motion picture *Titanic* unfortunately only made passing reference to many of these characters. I say *unfortunately* because I find the lives of these historical characters far more interesting than the fictional characters depicted by the movie.

It always amazes me how God uses circumstances in our lives to shape us as people. Of course, it is accurate to say that the events of life do not make our character, that they only serve to reveal what has been there all along. Life becomes the anvil where a man's and woman's contribution and destiny are pounded out and shaped. We, however, bring the metal into the process. It is a picture of God's sovereignty. What follows is an accurate history of some of the major players in the drama of life that represents the *Titanic* disaster.

Madeleine Astor. Mrs. Astor was left millions in her husband's will. She married an elderly stockbroker in 1919 and became Mrs. William Dick. After Dick's death she took a third husband, a professional boxer named Enzo Fiermonte. After two marriages to older men, her union with the young athlete became a source of depression. Mrs. Astor committed suicide in 1937.

Joseph Boxhall. Boxhall was the *Titanic*'s fourth officer. He continued his employment with the White Star Line, serving as the chief officer aboard the *Ausonia.* He served with the Royal Navy before retiring in 1940. He was the technical advisor for the *Titanic* film *A Night to Remember.* Boxhall died in 1967, and his ashes were scattered over the site of the *Titanic*'s sinking.

Harold Bride. Bride was the surviving member of the wireless crew for the *Titanic.* He worked in the same capacity for the steamer *Mona's Isle* during World War I. After the war he worked as a salesman, and he died in 1956.

Molly Brown. Molly was a colorful character who finally managed to become a member of polite society after the *Titanic* disaster. She considered a run for Congress in 1914 and died of a stroke in 1932. After her death, she was immortalized by the successful Broadway musical and film, *The Unsinkable Molly Brown.*

The Californian. The *Californian* was torpedoed and sunk during World War I.

The Carpathia. The *Carpathia* was torpedoed by a German submarine. It sank on July 17, 1918.

Billy Carter. Billy Carter and his wife were prime examples of how the disaster would forever affect people's lives. In January 1914, Mrs. Carter sued her husband for divorce on the grounds of "cruel and barbarous treatments and indignities to the person." Her charges stemmed from the night the *Titanic* went down. After placing his wife and children safely on lifeboat No. 4, Billy Carter made a dash for Collapsible C. Due to the chaos of the night, Carter's collapsible departed the *Titanic* some fifteen to twenty minutes before lifeboat No. 4. Mrs. Carter took this to be a breach of their marriage vows and a sign that their relationship was over. A judge agreed and granted her the divorce.

Frederick Fleet. Fleet was the lookout aboard the *Titanic* who spotted the iceberg. He continued to work for the White Star Line at sea until turning to the shipyards of Harland and Wolff. After World War II, Fleet sold newspapers and worked as a night watchman. After suffering financial despair and the loss of his wife, Fleet committed suicide in 1965.

Lady Lucy Duff Gordon. Lady Gordon was a successful designer of women's lingerie. Her company, and indeed her entire financial world, collapsed in 1934, and she died broke in April 1935.

Sir Cosmo Duff Gordon. Gordon was accused of paying the crew members of the lifeboat he was in five pounds each not to return to the ship to pick up survivors. He spent the rest of his life denying the charges, and he died in 1931.

Colonel Archibald Gracie. Colonel Gracie wrote the first historical account of the *Titanic*'s last voyage, *The Truth About the Titanic*. He died on December 12, 1912, and the book was published after his death.

Bruce Ismay. Mr. Ismay had every intention of staying on as the chairman of the White Star Line, but the news reports of his action in connection with the disaster played havoc with his ambition. He was constantly subjected to the whispers of those around him, and on June 30, 1913, he retired as chairman. He retired to his estate in Northern Ireland and died of a stroke in London on October 17, 1937.

The Lifeboats of the Titanic. The *Carpathia* docked in New York harbor with thirteen of the *Titanic*'s lifeboats on board. The boats' numbers and nameplates were removed, by looters it was supposed. They were later returned to the White Star Line and served its other vessels.

Charles Lightoller. Lightoller was the second officer aboard the *Titanic*. He returned to the White Star Line and became chief officer aboard the *Celtic*. On his retirement, he wrote newspaper columns and raised chickens. He also designed and built his own yacht, the *Sundowner*. In 1940 he sailed the *Sundowner* into the battle raging at Dunkirk and rescued 131 British soldiers.

Captain Stanley Lord. Captain Lord lost his command after the hearing on the *Titanic*. His failure to bring the *Californian* to rescue the floundering ship was and still is widely believed. After the success of the book and motion picture *A Night to Remember*, Lord appealed for authorities to reopen the investigation and explore his contention that another ship, a third vessel, had come between his ship and the *Titanic*. Lord died in 1962, having never been granted his request.

Edmund and Michael Navratil. These were the famous orphans of the *Titanic* traveling under the assumed name of Hoffman. Their father was taking them away from their mother, and for months their pictures were circulated until recognized by their mother in France. Edmund served in the French army in World War II. He was a prisoner of war but managed to escape. He died at age forty-three. Michael became a psychology professor and still lives in Paris, France.

The Olympic. The *Olympic* was the sister ship of the *Titanic*. It was rebuilt and refitted after the *Titanic* disaster. In 1918 the *Olympic* collided with and sank a German submarine. Subsequently, the *Olympic* was given the nickname of "Old Reliable."

Captain Edward J. Smith. In some respects Captain Smith's fate may be the most mysterious of all. There were reports of his being picked up by a lifeboat and still other accounts of his rescuing a small child and then swimming away to die. He was not among the recorded survivors aboard the *Carpathia*. On July 19, 1912, Captain Peter Pryal gave an account of seeing Captain Smith on a street in Baltimore, Maryland. "There is no possibility of my being mistaken," the captain is reported to have said. "I have known Captain Smith too long. I would know him even without his beard. I firmly believe that he was saved and, in some mysterious manner, has been brought to this country. I am willing to swear to my statement." Most, if not all, historians would disagree with Captain Pryal.

The White Star Line. On paper, the White Star Line was actually owned by the American industrialist J. P. Morgan. It merged with the Cunard Line, the owner of the *Carpathia*, in 1934.